THE CARVER

The Carver

This book is a work of fiction. Names, characters, places, and incidents are the product of the author's imagination or are used fictitiously. Any resemblance to actual events, locales, or persons, living or dead, is coincidental.

ISBN print: 978-1-7324984-0-2
ISBN ebook: 978-1-7324984-1-9

http://authorjakedevlin.com/

Cover Art by Kim G Design
https://www.kimg-design.com/

Library of Congress Control Number: 2017946110

Blaze Publishing, LLC
64 Melvin Drive
Fredericksburg, VA 22406
Visit us at www.blazepub.com

Second Edition: August 2018

Dedicated in memory of
Rachel Barthel, the truest believer.

Each of us is carving a stone, erecting a column,
or cutting a piece of stained glass in the construction of
something much bigger than ourselves.

—Adrienne Clarkson

CHAPTER ONE

TODAY—THE NEW WORLD: JUST OUTSIDE RICHMOND, VA

The Carver's joints ached as he nurtured a piece of oak with his old paring knife. The ivory handle, cool to the touch, was always a treat for Pino's fingers. Soon, he would get to coat his figurine with a palette of beige, scarlet, and splashes of azure.

He sometimes carved with his eyes closed, letting the memory of Enzo's laughter wash over him. Those joyful snickers and loud appreciative chuckles had once been music to his ears. The Carver wanted nothing more than to bring his son's joy back. After the boy lost his mother and his best friend, it seemed he was only capable of anger.

"Another toy, Dad?" There it was again. Enzo's constant irritation. He didn't bother to look up from his phone anymore. "How many of those stupid things are you gonna give me before you realize I don't want any more? I'm not four."

Pino hoisted himself out of his chair, his knees crackling and the bones rattling in his back. He set his piece of oak down and rubbed out a crick in his neck. He knew quite well: *My son is not four years old.* He laid his hands on Enzo's shoulders and kissed him on the forehead. Without looking up, Enzo wiped his face with his sleeve.

"You grew up too fast, my boy. But you're still *my* son. And these are very special figurines. You'd do well to take care of them."

Enzo's fingers flew across the screen of his phone. "Yeah, whatever. They're toys."

"You used to like toys, you know. You'd spend hours and hours playing with your figurines and building Lego houses for them. You're only fifteen, son. You're allowed to have some fun! Who says you have to grow up?"

"The world says grow up, Dad." For the first time, Enzo looked up, and Pino's heart sank. There used to be a warm light in Enzo's eyes. A firefly, Carla used to call it. Since Carla disappeared, the light changed. It was still there, but it had lost some radiance. "And the world stopped being fun once Mom disappeared."

Pino sighed and slumped down on the couch next to his son. He could feel, almost hear, the crick-crack-click in his bones as he settled. *Darn joints.* "You still don't believe she'll be back?"

Enzo clicked off his phone. "No! I don't think she'll be back! And you do after all this time? After almost three years?"

"I've told you, something tells me we haven't seen the last of your mother. She's a strong woman if I ever knew one. She's got a whale of a heart."

"That's stupid. I'm sorry, but it's true. Unless you have hard evidence that she's still alive, you're being an idiot. Every day that you sit there and make your toys, thinking Mom's just gonna walk in with an armful of groceries or something, you're setting us up for disappointment."

Pino shook his head. "You think you know so much about this world—"

"I know about disappointment, and I know this world sucks. And I know that anybody who can say this world is fun has never lost anything before. Did you even care about Mom?"

Pino looked down. "My son. For you to think I don't care . . . What have I done to make you think this way?"

"What have you done? Nothing!" Enzo bounded off the couch and snatched a three-inch figurine off the coffee table. "You sit there every day since she disappeared, and you make these stupid toys! Come on, Dad. You're so sure Mom's okay; do something productive! Go get her back! Write her a letter! Or, I don't know, tell *me* where to find her! But stop wasting your life sitting there carving wood, and stop giving me things meant for babies."

Pino crossed his arms defiantly. "A baby would swallow these things whole. I wouldn't dream of trusting an infant with my figures." He picked up his half-formed project. "And anyway, this one isn't for you. It's for Peter next door."

"You mean *Pietro?* Why would he want any of your toys? He's a grown man."

Pino cracked his neck. "I don't know how to explain that, Son. You'll understand when you're older."

Enzo groaned. "I hate that excuse! And you wonder why I don't like to talk to you."

"So then tell me how to talk to you! You won't talk about your mom, you won't talk about your figures, you never want to talk about school . . . I give up. How do I have a relationship with my son?"

"That's the easiest thing ever," Enzo said. "You don't. Just leave me alone."

⌘⌘⌘

Two weeks later, Pino put the finishing touches on his oak figurine. The whole process took him about six weeks: sketching, carving, smoothing the edges, detailing, and finally applying the paint. When he was done, he drank a glass of wine, put on a red baseball cap, and shuffled out the door with his small heroine in his palm. He whistled a jolly tune as he hobbled down the sidewalk and into his neighbor's yard.

Pietro used to keep his lawn fresh and green, but about a year ago, he surrendered it to a tangle of weeds and pond scum. Even the big stone fairy looked morose, cobwebbed, and muddy.

Pino coughed into his sleeve, tipped his cap to the fairy statue, and stepped onto Pietro's porch. The ground thumped with every step, each hollow knock of heel against wood bringing back a memory of his childhood.

He rang the doorbell, and a minute later, Pietro appeared in his pajamas.

Pino grinned. "Good morning, my friend!"

Pietro yawned, stretched his lanky arms over his head, and rubbed his face. "Mornin', neighbor. Come on in."

"Thanks. Did I wake you?" Pino stepped inside and removed his hat.

"Naw, you know I barely sleep anymore. Coffee?"

"Sure." Pino looked around his friend's house. *Poor Pietro.* Dirty dishes piled up in various corners. Neckties, wrinkled button downs, dark socks, and several pairs of khakis and slacks lay draped over the TV, mashed between couch cushions, and trampled into the floor. A black suit jacket collected dust on the coffee table. "Have you been, uh, going to work, Pietro?"

Pietro ran his fingers through his sandy-colored hair. The Keurig machine sputtered and steamed. "Oh, yeah! Well, kinda. I work from home now. I talked to my supervisors, and they figured out a way for me to do most of my work over the phone, you know, email. I only have to show up in person on Tuesdays."

"Good for you, good for you," Pino said. "And still no sign of Zack or Wendy?"

Pietro shook his head, shoved a pair of black Nikes off a wicker chair, and gestured for Pino to sit down. "Not a clue. Nothing from Carla?"

"Not yet. Poor Enzo's lost all hope. I almost want to tell him the truth about everything . . . about Zack and Wendy. About us."

"We can't. This is the new world, buddy. We wanted it. We got it. We still gotta follow the *rules*." Pietro made a face, like the word tasted sour on his tongue.

A longing sigh fluttered Pino's lips. "Still, it doesn't stop me from wishing things could've been different for my boy. Probably the worst heartache in the world is having to hide secrets from your kid."

"Well, try losing a kid." Pietro poured two cups of coffee and handed one to Pino. "Then we can compare notes."

Pino stared apologetically into his coffee. "I'm sorry, Pietro. I didn't mean—"

"Don't worry about it." Pietro waved an arm. "Anyway, you have a plan, yeah?"

"I do. And you already know it." Pino held the wooden girl over Pietro's lap. "But you're going to have to trust me and take some time off work."

Pietro palmed the carving and studied it with childlike wonder. She looked so real, with the individual strands of her straight, dark hair, the subtle creases in her jeans, the wrinkles in her red hoodie, and the resolve in her green eyes.

Pietro took a deep sip of coffee. "You still think this is the answer?"

Pino nodded.

After setting down the figurine, Pietro stood, picked up a pair of jeans, and shook them in the air. A tiny storm of lint trickled in the light. "You get why I can't do this, right?"

"No. Why can't you do this?"

"Well, I can't exactly abandon my job to go looking for toy models. We're adults now."

"Remember what Violet said. You know these aren't just toys. Isn't it worth taking some time off work if it means you have the chance to save Wendy and Zack?"

"Dude, I can't afford to take time off anymore. You should know better than anyone how much I despise working, but if I take a vacation to follow a hunch from you . . ." Pietro sighed and tossed his jeans on the couch. "I just need to try to be more responsible. You get that, right?"

Fighting back a laugh, Pino gestured around the room. "Is this responsibility? Look at this mess! I think a lot of people would beg to differ."

Pietro stared at his bare feet. "Rude."

"You know me these days." Pino chuckled. "Brutally honest."

"That's for sure. Man, being an adult sucks even worse than I always said it would. You fall in love, have kids, you think you're happy, and then you lose everything."

Pino clutched Pietro's shoulder. "That's why I'm giving you a chance to save everything! These carvings are the key to putting everything back to normal. But my son's right: They're useless. They're useless unless someone goes out and finds these people."

"Someone like me." Comfortable silence hovered between the men, and Pietro chewed on his cheek.

Pino sipped his coffee patiently.

"You really think if I go find this girl you carved, I can bring Wendy and Zack back home?"

"And Carla. And anybody else who might've disappeared since that night."

"Pinocchio, I wish I still knew how to tell if you were lying."

Pino shrugged.

Pietro held the figurine up and ran a finger along its smooth edges. "So, where would you expect me to find her?"

"Not here."

"Not helpful." Pietro sighed.

"It'll do you some good to get out of the house," Pino said. "Take Enzo. He doesn't wanna be around me anyway, and he has fierce intuition. He got that from Carla, I think."

A rivulet of coffee trickled from Pietro's lip as he failed to suppress a laugh. "Too bad he got your nose! Poor dude."

Pino scowled over his mug, then let his mouth curve into a smile. The old Pietro was coming back to the surface. "Anyway, you'll go? Look for my wife and your family?"

With a sigh, Pietro rubbed his face so hard his eyelids drooped. "Would you come with me?"

Pino wiggled his thumb: *click, click, click, click*. "Do you not hear my joints crackling?"

"Still?" Pietro rested his elbows on his knees. "What's happening to you?"

Pino lowered his voice. "My guess is there's some real dark stuff goin' on back home. After all, we're not supposed to be here, and I was once a . . . Well, you know. I'm afraid I won't get very far out the door, if I can even move anymore in a week."

Pietro drummed on his lap, shooting air through his teeth as he contemplated. "Fine. I'll go. But I have a question. When do we tell Enzo who we really are?"

"I trust you'll figure it out, Peter." Pino winked. "After all, you were the boy who learned how to *fly*."

CHAPTER TWO

THREE YEARS AGO—THE OLD WORLD: THE WOODLANDS

Nine people sat at the table, eight men and one woman. They dug into apple pie, tart and steaming warm, while they drank frosty-cold milk.

"So, what do you think?" the woman asked. "Tell me what you're feeling."

The man at the foot of the table, also the tallest by far at five foot ten, stroked his rough chin. "Look, your Majesty . . . ."

The woman smiled, and her lips parted to reveal a mouthful of brilliant teeth.

She's gorgeous, the man thought. *Too bad she's taken now. Just a little too late.*

"Oh, please, Hansel," she said, "there's no need for that level of formality with me. You know that."

Hansel nodded. *And still so humble to boot.* "Okay. Look, Snow, you'll understand if I have some reservations about moving into houses in the woods. They don't exactly evoke the sweetest memories for me."

Snow patted Hansel's hand, rippling his body with warmth. "Of course I understand. That whole experience, everything you and your sister went through, couldn't have been easy on you."

Finn, a dwarf who always smelled strongly of soap—unlike his brother Jinn—brushed a miniscule pie crumb off his sleeve and stood to wash his hands for the third time since eating. "But we've only fond memories in this house. No witches here, Mister Hansel! Life has been orderly and safe here."

Wayde, perpetually red-faced and sweaty, took his thumbnail from his mouth. "Yes, I think I agree. Oh! Except the time Zid brought home the baby dragon."

Zid groaned. "Aw, can't you live a little? Draco wasn't gonna hurt nobody."

"That's what you say about all your dragons." Chann clutched his stomach, an audible rumble gurgling under his vest. "And yet one of us always has to ask Lord Bellamy for time off at the mine a few days later. Healing time. Hey, Snow, is there more pie?"

Snow rose and started preparing a new pie, not pointing out that it would be Chann's third. "Really, life in this house has been wonderful. Even with Zid's dragons. Will you accept it, Hansel?"

Hansel stroked his chin. It *was* a beautiful house in the quietest part of the Woodlands, cozy and sturdily constructed with smooth stones from the crystalline brook nearby, and the air always smelled vaguely of cinnamon. Perhaps that was Snow's scent. Really, who in his right mind would deny a request from the fairest in the land?

"Here's the part I don't understand," Hansel said. "Why leave?"

"Lord Bellamy's closing the mine," Garon, the eldest dwarf, chimed in. "We can't afford this place anymore."

Hansel's ears perked up. *The mine*. The gears in his head whirred to life. "Why is the mine closing? And where will you go?"

"Well, we're going with Snow, of course," Jinn said, pie filling trickling down his dirty chin. "Prince Liam was generous enough to invite us into their castle."

Hansel forced a smile. The prince's name was a dagger to his ears. *Liam*. "I'm sure you must be thrilled."

Zid shrugged. "Dreading it. His Majesty said no dragons. No

blunderbusses. No fun."

"But think of all the room we'll have for swordfights!" Bo said, flexing his arms. "Archery! Sport and game!"

Garon sighed, fluttering his bushy, ashen beard. "If we're to be honest, it's hard to leave home. We wish not to impose on Snow and Prince Liam, but this is our only option. We want this house to go to somebody we can trust. Snow picked you."

Hansel frowned. "Well, what if there's one more option?"

Snow wrinkled her eyebrows. "What do you mean?"

"I'll buy the mine."

"You'll *what*?" Finn said.

"I'm serious. I'll buy the mine and then it won't have to close. If the mine stays open, you can still afford your home. You could keep your jobs. You'd just work for me."

Snow's jaw dropped. "Hansel, there is no need to—"

"Hurray!" The dwarves leapt to their feet, joined hands, and formed a circle, wheeling around in song. "*We can keep our jobs. We can keep our house. Hansel is the greatest!*"

Snow leaned in close to Hansel, her voice low, "You're doing this for your sister, aren't you? Buying the mine?"

Hansel's gaze fell to his lap. She knew him too well.

"Are you really sure this is the best thing? I mean, what if . . . ?"

"Let me worry about the best thing," Hansel said. "If you're implying that my sister's probably dead, you're wrong. When somebody that close to you dies, you can feel it. She's still alive somewhere."

Snow glanced at the rowdy dwarves and took Hansel's shoulder. "The boys have been excavating that mine for years. They've never seen her or any evidence that she ever went down there."

"It's the one place I haven't looked. I know there's a very small chance, but I need to feel like I'm doing something productive. Twenty-three years without a sister is too long."

Snow chewed her lip and studied him. "Then maybe this is meant to be. For you and for these boys."

"Meant to be," Hansel repeated. "Perhaps I'll even take the house too. If . . . if they wouldn't mind having me as a roommate, that is."

Only then did the dwarves stop chanting.

"Roommate? Really?" Zid tugged on his beard. Finally, his face lit up. "That's *awesome*!"

Chann pounded the table gleefully. "Let's have a pint!"

"Hurray!" The circle came back together.

⌘⌘⌘

Hansel dressed in his finest the next morning and then set off to talk to Lord Bellamy.

Lord Bellamy was the proprietor of several provinces in the Old World, including the Woodlands. Following his marriage to Queen Avoria of Florindale many years ago, he was technically the king of over half the realm, but this was a mere formality. The queen continued to oversee all the realm's affairs, but Lord Bellamy's primary interest was always in the Woodlands, and he only seemed to care for the mine and his daughter. This was especially true when a few years after the royal marriage, the queen was said to have gone insane. The lord disappeared for several years. Shortly thereafter, Avoria went silent.

When Hansel was too young to care about the monarchy, Lord Bellamy quietly returned to the realm and moved into a humble house in the Woodlands, resuming his role as a landlord and acting as though he had never been king. People started whispering that the queen was gone forever, right around the same time that Gretel vanished.

Hansel grew up in a strange time. His life hanging in a state of pain without his sister, while the people tried to pull together without a true ruler. The role of protecting the realm unofficially seemed to fall to Princess Violet, the fairy daughter of Lord Bellamy. Nobody proposed a new rule, and nobody pestered the mysterious lord. After all, it seemed that the darkest days were behind the Old World, and Violet would do a fine job on her own.

At least, this was the story as Hansel had heard it.

Hansel rapped three times on the door, going over the offer in his head.

Lord Bellamy appeared a minute later, tall, hook-nosed, and red-eyed.

"Good day, Mr. Bellamy! My name is—"

"Hansel," the lord growled, "I know who you are. Come in."

"Thank you, sir." Hansel entered the house and analyzed his surroundings. Clean. Orderly. Simple. But it was *dull*. Nothing shined. Nothing held a reflection. Dark curtains had been cast over what Hansel assumed was a mirror. "How are you this morning?"

"Spare me the small talk." Lord Bellamy gestured to a leather chair, and Hansel took a seat. "What brings you to my door?"

"It's your mine, sir. I understand you're closing it."

Lord Bellamy made a sour face and poured some dark wine into a pair of goblets, offering one to Hansel. "Ah, yes. I should've known that would bring you here."

"It's the only one that hasn't been investigated," Hansel said. "I have a feeling my sister's down there. We used to play there, you know."

Lord Bellamy sipped his wine, his eyes hovering over the goblet and drilling through Hansel's soul. "Garon and his company have been down there nearly every day since Gretel disappeared, boy. And you say it hasn't been investigated?"

"Well, it's more like it hasn't been fully investigated. It's enormous! How long have people been mining it?"

Lord Bellamy's mouth twisted in thought. "Mmm. Two hundred years, give or take."

"Exactly!" Hansel raised his arms. "Yet you still haven't excavated half of it. I bet nobody's seen the whole thing."

Lord Bellamy leaned in, his voice barely above a whisper. "Be assured, if Gretel went down there, she would have been seen by now."

Hansel folded his arms, refusing to break eye contact. "I can't accept that answer."

The old man stood and stalked to the window, tracing a bony finger over the wooden panes. "You'll have to. I'm closing the mine for good."

"Why?" Hansel rose, followed Lord Bellamy to the window, and stood behind him. "How is closing it in anybody's best interest? You're putting Garon and his friends out of a job, and they think they have to give up their house. You're also giving up everything that's still down there. Natural resources, precious gems, gold . . . Not to mention, you're slamming the door on my last hope of finding Gretel. Give me one good reason why you should close the mine."

Lord Bellamy took a sip and kept it in his mouth for a minute. In the silence, Hansel began tapping his thumbs together behind his back. He couldn't decide if the old man was trying to choose his words carefully for the sake of diplomacy, or if he was simply analyzing the wine's acidity. Either way, Lord Bellamy was stalling, and it made Hansel nervous. Hansel had the right to some fast, hard answers. He gave the back of Lord Bellamy's head a nudging gaze. *Well?*

"Because there's evil down there. Darkness."

The iron words hung in the air. They seemed so final, so cold and harsh, and yet Hansel had no idea what they meant. What kind of evil was the old man talking about? What did it mean for Gretel? What did it mean for the world? Was Lord Bellamy even telling the truth?

"Explain," Hansel demanded, clenching his fists at his sides.

"About a month ago, Wayde made a discovery that I cannot choose to ignore." Lord Bellamy stared out the window, fixing his gaze on the brook.

Hansel took a few steps forward, trying to get around the old man. Stepping between Lord Bellamy and the window, Hansel narrowed his eyes. "Go on."

Lord Bellamy turned his back to Hansel again and walked a bit briskly to his chair. "Their discoveries pertain not to your sister, and certainly not to you."

Hansel followed, cutting Lord Bellamy off before he could sit back down. *Stop running away and help me, old man. Can't you see I'm desperate, here?* "Sir, if what you found is really so bad, why would you send the boys back there and expose them to it?"

"I was giving them time to sort out their affairs. The seven dwarves are professionally minded. I worry not of their exposure to the dark temptations in that mine. They will resist." Lord Bellamy sighed. "That being said, it's only a matter of time before the wrong person goes down there and puts everyone in danger. There was no sign of Gretel, boy. I'll swear on my life."

Hansel sucked in his cheeks, choosing his next words carefully. *If this next move doesn't work . . .* A thin film of sweat surfaced in his palms. "I'll buy the mine from you, my lord."

Lord Bellamy lowered his voice again, making each word slow and clear, "It's not for sale."

"But, sir—"

"You'd best be on your way."

Hansel thrust his arms out to his sides. "Just tell me how much gold you want."

"I've no desire for your gold. You can't *buy* a mine. I want it sealed. Destroyed."

Hansel sighed and put his hands on his hips, his sweaty thumb jittering below the pocket of his vest. "I thought you might respond this way, Lord Bellamy. You have a reputation, you know."

"Oh, I do?"

"Yep. They say you're a man of your convictions. You care a great deal for the Woodlands and never go back on what you believe. You live up to your reputation, sir. I'm really disappointed, but I respect you."

Lord Bellamy took a seat, sipping from his goblet. "Mmm. Thank you, boy."

Hansel nodded and took slow steps toward Lord Bellamy. "*However*, you should know that I'm the same. You see, I'd do anything for my sister. When she disappeared, I promised I'd get her back. Nothing will stop me. Not you, not your reputation, and not your mine."

Quick as a wink, Hansel produced a long black dart from his vest and plunged it into the side of Lord Bellamy's neck. The old man went down without a sound, and then he simply vanished.

CHAPTER THREE

TODAY—THE NEW WORLD: PINO'S HOME

Enzo rambled around his bedroom with an open duffel bag and the volume cranked up on his earbuds. Lately he'd been binging on 80's music, like his mother always did. As he packed his duffel, he lip-synched with such enthusiasm that he didn't notice his father chuckling in the doorway.

Pino rapped on the wall, and Enzo ripped his earbuds out.

"Yeah?"

"Bra-vo, my boy!" Pino clapped his hands. "Have you ever considered auditioning for that idol show everyone watches these days? What's that new one called?"

"Ha. Funny, Dad." Enzo reached in his bag and removed a pair of heavily pocked drumsticks and a wooden yoyo his father had made him. "What do you want?"

Pino sat on the bed half-made and fixed in black bedsheets. "Just wanted to ask you how packing is going, that's all."

Enzo tossed the bag next to his dad, opened his drawer, and then pulled out some socks. "It's good. Getting to the little things now." He paused and peered at his dad. "Listen, are you sure this is cool? Going away for a whole week?"

"Why not? It's summer, you're bored, Pietro's lonely . . . ."

"But are you sure he's cool with me going with him?"

"Of course!" Pino traced a thread on Enzo's comforter. "I could not be happier to know that you and Peter are taking this trip together."

"Why do you keep calling him Peter?"

"Pardon me. *Pietro* needs company. He's been through so much pain, losing his wife and his son. It brings me such joy that he's finally decided to get up and take a little vacation. You've been hurting, too, son. You and Pietro can use this time to lean on each other a bit."

"I don't need to lean on anyone. I'm fine."

Pino shrugged. "Then enjoy the opportunity to get out of the house. When's the last time you went on a trip?"

Enzo thought for a minute. "It was"—he caught a glimpse of a photo he kept on his drawer—"when we went to New York with Mom."

"Maybe you and Pietro can go to New York while you're traveling," Pino said. "Go see some things that remind you of your mother."

Enzo nodded. That didn't seem like such a bad idea. "So Pietro doesn't even know where he wants to go?"

"We're improvising that part."

"We? You're coming too?"

"No, no. I could barely get out of bed this morning. A trip across the country would give me a heart attack." Pino attempted to stand up, but Enzo heard a crack in the knees, and his dad winced. "Help me up?"

Enzo took his father's hand, firm and rough, and pulled him up. "Why aren't your joints healing up? Shouldn't I stay and help out if it's been hurting you to walk?"

"No, no. I'll be fine."

"Really? I'm, uh, actually kinda worried about you." Enzo chewed his lip. He almost couldn't believe the words came out of his mouth.

Pino smiled. "No need to worry. But do one thing for me, please? Pack the most recent figurines I made you. Keep them safe."

"My toys, Dad?" Enzo's eyebrows shot up.

"Please. Put them in your bag while I'm standing here."

Enzo rolled his eyes and opened the bottom drawer. "Why?"

"Maybe as reminders of how much I love you."

Enzo winced. "Too sappy."

"Deal with it."

Enzo took a knee and pulled a handful of oak figurines out of his drawer. Each was no taller than three inches and no heavier than a nickel, but they were all rendered in stunning detail. He laid each figure in a line from tallest to shortest on his bed.

First was the old man with the red eyes and the hooked nose. He gave Enzo the creeps and *never* came out of the drawer. Enzo imagined he was modeled after the world's strictest high school principal or the husband of a miserable lunch lady.

Then there was the woman with the purple gloves and the long dark hair. Her beauty was so striking Enzo imagined that she would do movies if she were real. Even so, she looked kinder than the standard actress. Her face was warm and schoolteacher-friendly, reminding him a little bit of his mother.

After the woman, there was the dark-haired man, who looked like he stepped out of a Robin Hood play. In a certain way, he looked regal. His gaze was skyward, eyes blue and resolute, and his fingers curled near a long black dagger tucked into his belt.

Next was the Chinese woman, stoic and important-looking. She wore a charcoal business suit, and her hair hung halfway down her back. A tiny Bluetooth snuggled in her ear. If she could talk, she'd be shushing Enzo and telling him she had an important call.

Finally, there was a burly, bearded man with an orange baseball cap. The other figurines seemed to look right back at Enzo when he picked them up. This one deliberately cast his gaze aside, red-cheeked and tight-fisted.

What a weird bunch, Enzo thought. Still, he couldn't deny his father's talent.

"How do you come up with these?"

Pino waved the question away. "Who knows? How did Bartholdi come up with Lady Liberty? Oh, and speaking of"—Pino snapped his fingers, dug into his pockets, and produced a perfect miniature of the Empire State Building—"let's say this one's for good memories."

Enzo palmed the miniature. "For good memories."

"And maybe good fortune." Pino laid his hands on Enzo's shoulders. "I never wanted to put strings on you, Son, but I want you to be careful. It would be too much for me if you didn't come back. And sometimes you never know what's out there."

NEW YORK CITY

Rosana hated the subway, but she spent every day there, looking for signs. It still hurt to see the face on the missing posters: *Have you seen Alicia Trujillo?* Her mother didn't really look like an Alicia Trujillo, with her buttercup hair and ocean eyes. Rosana didn't even feel like much of a Trujillo. Then again, she didn't know what a Trujillo felt like because she never knew her father. She didn't care where he was. She only cared about the poster.

Where are *you, Mom?*

She disappeared about six months ago, the same day they had gone to the Statue of Liberty together.

"Most people who live in New York don't appreciate what this statue means because they see it every day," her mom had said. "But every time you look at it, sweetie, think about all the great things you love about this country. I love living here. It's simply beautiful."

After lunch at a local pizzeria, Rosana and her mother descended into the subway station and prepared to go back to Harlem, but Rosana noticed that something—or rather someone—in the distance had caught her mother's eye. Her mom kept craning her neck and concentrating on a newspaper stand. There, a thick man in an orange baseball cap sat against a wall painted with tiny gold stars, his nose hovering above a magazine.

"What is it, Mom? Do you know him?"

Her mom pulled her purse closer to her chest. "Gosh, there is something familiar about him."

The man lowered the magazine, met Rosana's gaze, and then quickly looked away.

"He looked at me. Where do you know him from?"

Rosana's mom hesitated before she answered, "I think he's from, uh, an old job that I used to have with your father. In, uh, France."

"You never told me you lived in France!"

The man stood up, turned his head in Rosana's direction, and without making eye contact, made a very clear gesture: *come here*. His hands dropped to his belly, and he wrung them profusely, beads of sweat dotting his forehead.

"I should go talk to him," Rosana's mom said. "Come with me, Rose. I'll introduce you."

Rosana studied the man as they approached him. His nose was crimson and bulbous, his ears thick. He had a neat salt-and-pepper goatee, and his eyes were a warm shade of brown, but he wouldn't hold her gaze long enough for Rosana to decide if she liked him. Her mom, however, seemed thrilled to see somebody she knew.

"Oh my gosh!" She met the man in a tight hug and rocked him back and forth until his face turned red. "I remember you! It was a very brief encounter, but I'll always remember how you saved our lives." A pause hovered between the two and Rosana mentally filled it with a million questions. *Saved our lives? What?* "What are you doing here in the Big Apple?"

The man fidgeted with his jacket zipper. "It's good to see you too, uh—"

"Alicia," Rosana's mom replied. "It's Alicia Trujillo now. Oh, and this is my daughter, Rosana. Rosana, this is Wa . . . ." She snapped her fingers and tapped her temples as if trying to bring a memory to the surface.

"Wayland," the man finished.

Rosana shook the man's hand, his sweaty palm turned slightly skyward.

Wayland flashed a tight-lipped, awkward smile. "She looks just like you."

"Thank you. That's sweet," Alicia said. "They say the apple doesn't fall far from the tree."

Wayland's eyes brightened. "You've reminded me!" He reached into his jacket pocket and produced a shiny red apple. "I'm trying to do the whole apple-a-day thing. Would you want a bite?"

Alicia rubbed her belly. "Rose and I actually just had pizza. Have you had Petrelli's yet? Best in Manhattan!"

Wayland shook his head and offered Rosana the apple. "Want some?"

"I'll have a small bite. Thanks!" Rosana wasn't hungry, but the apple looked so plump and perfect that her mouth watered without invitation. She had nearly closed her fingers around the apple before it rolled off Wayland's palm and onto the ground.

Wayland kicked the ground. "Shucks, I'm so clumsy sometimes! You don't have to eat it off the ground."

"No, no. It's fine!" Rosana bent down to retrieve the apple. However, it didn't stop rolling when it hit the ground. It continued past the newspaper stand and into a crowd of tourists. Rosana broke into a jog to catch up with it. For a small piece of fruit, it carried tremendous momentum, seemingly gaining speed as it moved. It rolled uncontrollably until it curved and plummeted into the subway tracks.

Rosana turned to make her way back to her mom, but she was gone, and so was Wayland.

It took less than a minute for them to disappear, along with every boundary of the world Rosana knew and every definition of the word *normal.* She knew Wayland had something to do with her mother's disappearance. She'd consider every explanation, no matter how impossible, and go as far as she needed to learn the truth.

But what did Wayland do? There was no way he and Rosana's

mother simply walked away together, but that's what the officers assumed when Rosana went to the police. They refused to believe it was abduction.

"What you're telling us is impossible," the officer told her. "The subway is filled with people day in and day out. No matter the time of day, you can be damn sure somebody would've seen a fat man in an orange hat grab her and leave."

Rosana balled her hands into fists and shoved them in the pockets of her red jacket. "Well, can't you at least fingerprint the apple that rolled down into the subway? Do some forensics! I wanna know who that man was."

"Well, we looked for your 'runaway apple.' Wasn't there. Must've been the rats."

Rosana couldn't take it. She jerked her hands out of her pockets and punched a wall.

"Hey!" the officer barked, causing several heads to turn in alarm. "Take it easy! I didn't say we aren't going to look for her. We'll put up posters with your ma's picture. We'll have you meet with a sketch artist and try to find out about this 'Wayland' guy. We'll do whatever it takes to try and put your mind at ease. Now, is there any other information you can tell us about your ma?"

Rosana steadied her breathing and tried to compose her thoughts.

"Any nicknames, maybe?"

Her mother kept quiet about her past, but there was one thing Rosana remembered. "She went by a different name once. Before she came to New York."

"That's a start. Keep going. What did she go by?"

The new name felt foreign on Rosana's tongue, but somehow it made more sense to her than Alicia Trujillo. She closed her eyes and breathed her mother's name: "Alice."

PIETRO'S HOUSE

Pietro was afraid.

His journey would begin at dawn. Now that his bag was packed, it was real. He sat on his bed, sipping chocolate milk from a coffee mug.

Why would Pinocchio trust me with so much? The idea weighed on his head.

After all, it was probably the weight of the world. *Two* worlds.

If that wasn't enough, Pino invoked his son and made Pietro responsible for another human being. Pietro had grown used to caring for other people since he grew up, but since Zack and Wendy disappeared, he was sure he hadn't done a good job in the responsibility department. Sure, he had provided for them. He put food on the table, he gave Wendy his undying love, and he made sure Zack had grown to be happy and healthy. There was nothing Pietro wouldn't do for them. But it didn't matter if he couldn't keep them safe. He came home from work one day and they were gone.

It's all my fault, he told himself. *I should've watched them more closely.*

He couldn't help wondering if Pino was right to trust him with his son.

So many things could go wrong. He could disappoint the kid, or worse, he could lose him.

Sooner or later, Enzo would have to know that Pietro was taking him to go find his mother. And if what Pino had said was true, they were going to have to start by finding a needle in a haystack.

Pietro picked up his friend's wooden figurine and twirled it in his palm. There was something maddeningly familiar about her. Pietro was positive he'd never met her before, but there were features in her face that he'd seen before. The shape of her eyes. The bow-shaped lips. She almost looked like . . . No, she couldn't be related to Alice?

Gosh, what a mess. If everything was really heading in the direction

Pietro thought it was, he could fracture the kid's mind completely.

It was one of the New World's conditions: *We can't let on who we really are unless it's absolutely necessary.*

Pietro feared that soon after he set off with Enzo in the morning, it would become necessary. Eventually, he'd have to tell the kid who he really was. How? *By the way, you're the son of Pinocchio, kid. And I'm Peter Pan. Wanna stop for some McDonalds?*

Pietro put his head in his hands.

The New World was supposed to be simple. If things weren't even simple in the New World, allegedly bound by some rudimentary magic called *physics* or something, then what on earth had gone wrong back home?

CHAPTER FOUR

THREE YEARS AGO—THE OLD WORLD: THE WOODLANDS

Eight men sat at the table. There was beer, bread, and pumpkin soup, and much to celebrate. Garon and his friends could keep their home after all. They had a new housemate. And best of all, Hansel brought good tidings. Lord Bellamy willingly accepted his offer and signed over the mine. They could keep their jobs.

Zid took a swig of ale. "So you're both our roommate and our boss now?"

"Aww, c'mon, boys. No need for labels. We're all chums here. Just be sure to work hard and report anything interesting you may find down there." Hansel winked, hoping this would cue the men to tell him about whatever they had shown Lord Bellamy.

"Gosh, this is great!" Finn wiped a puddle of beer off Jinn's part of the table. "We have to go say thank you to Lord Bellamy for letting you keep the mine!"

Hansel's heart picked up speed. "Oh, no! That won't be necessary."

Chann crammed a hunk of bread into his mouth and spoke with full cheeks, "And why the hell not?"

Think fast, Hansel. "Well, you see, Lord Bellamy had actually been looking at some property by the sea for a while. He heard all these fascinating stories about mermaids and pirates and, I don't know, *fairy tale stuff*. Anyway, when I offered to buy the mine, he took the opportunity to move on and buy some new property. He's far, far away now."

"Really?" Wayde said. "Shucks, he didn't even say g'bye to us!"

Hansel frowned, a tinge of guilt pulling at his heartstrings. "Don't worry. I thanked him for you. He knows you appreciated him. He expresses his deepest regrets for leaving in such a hurry, and he thanks you for all your years of hard work."

The dwarves sat in silence for a while, and Hansel took the opportunity to refill their goblets.

"Anyway, seeing as how I own the mine now, I'm gonna need to know all the ins and outs of it. Do you think you can maybe draw me a map of all the parts you've seen?"

Jinn tipped his cap, and a cloud of dust soared out of his hair, causing Finn to erupt in a fit of coughing while his brother went on.

"We'd be glad to, Mister Hansel. Wouldn't we, gentlemen?" Jinn said, giving Finn the side eye.

"Allow me." Garon cleared his throat and produced a yellowing scroll from his vest. He unfurled the scroll across the short end of the table and gestured for Hansel to look. "I've been updating this map on a regular basis. When we make new discoveries or find new parts of the mine, I draw them."

Hansel stood over Garon's shoulder and studied the intricate map, sipping from his goblet. This was the last clue Hansel needed to find his sister.

Garon moved a thick finger across the parchment. "Here, by the entrance, you have your basic metals: iron, copper, you know. Then come the gemstones: rubies, emeralds, sapphires, but not diamonds. Those are a little farther in, past your more precious metals. Gold. Silver. Platinum. The diamonds go on forever. If people knew how many diamonds we have down there, they'd be worth nothing anymore."

Hansel lowered his goblet and leaned in. "Go on."

"Well, more gemstones, another pocket of gold and silver, diamonds, diamonds, diamonds, and then we come to a crossroad. Here's what you need to know about that."

The other men averted their gazes. Hansel leaned in, determined not to miss a detail.

"If you turn right, you'll find more metals. Straight ahead, every element known to man, and probably about a thousand elements people *don't* know about. But if you turn *left* . . . ." Garon's voice acquired a gruff edge, and he raised an eyebrow.

Wayde hiccupped.

"If you turn left and you follow the path a little ways, there's something peculiar down there that we don't really understand. A sort of chamber. The trail stops there. Lord Bellamy seemed convinced it was evil. He swore us to secrecy when we told him about the chamber, but now that the mine is yours, you've a right to know."

Hansel steadied his jittering ankle, thinking his heart might shoot out of his chest. "Great work. All of you. Why don't we toast to our new partnership? And if you don't mind, Garon, I'd like to borrow that map tomorrow. You all can have the day off."

"Gosh, are you sure?" Wayde asked. "Lord Bellamy never gave us the day off."

Bo raised a triumphant fist. "Huzzah! I'm going running!"

"Don't you worry." Hansel raised his goblet. "To friendship, and prosperity, and the fruitful discoveries this new partnership shall yield. Cheers!"

"Cheers!"

Hansel swigged his wine and pocketed Garon's map. There was always the chance that it would lead him nowhere . . . that his sister was gone forever. However, what he'd done to Lord Bellamy had set Hansel on an irreversible course, and like the map, he was determined to follow that course to the end.

⌘⌘⌘

Hansel turned left.

Through most of his journey, the mine captured the light of Hansel's lantern in the most enchanting way. Splashes of scarlet, peacock, chartreuse, and butterscotch danced on the walls. Gold and silver threw stars in his eyes.

But when he turned left, the gems lost color.

The rubies, emeralds, and topazes darkened with every step. Rose turned to crimson, and crimson gave way to dried blood. Cerulean sunk to the bottom of the ocean until it wasn't blue anymore. And the hue of a crisp green apple rolled along until it was lost in the deep shadows of pine. Then, there wasn't even pine, blood, or ocean floor anymore. There were only dark gems, starless midnight skies imprisoned in rock.

Then he spied a hole in the wall, just tall enough for a man of Hansel's stature.

Hansel took a deep breath, pushed through the hole, and lowered his lantern. The air dampened and smelled of old wood. His legs ached like he'd been walking for hours. Or maybe it was days? He had come to the trail's end, a round cavern at least a few hundred feet in diameter. Dark stones lined the walls, filled the ceilings, and coated the ground. Stranger still was that when Hansel stepped on them, they were spongy to the touch. He poked at one with his toe, watching the gem collapse on itself. When he removed his toe, the gem expanded again, ballooning to its original shape like a tiny black lung.

Strangest of all were the seven enormous rubies, each translucent and at least twice as big as Hansel, protruding from the cavern walls. While their magnitude and color were interesting enough, the most curious feature was their symmetrical arrangement. Two of them jutted from the wall to Hansel's left. To his right, two more bulged out. Each gem seemed to have a "window," a tall flat surface carved into the facets. Straight ahead, three more red gems stuck out in a line. The one in the center was the largest, commanding his attention.

Somebody made *this cavern like this,* Hansel decided. Nature had its jokes and fun little designs, but when it came to the symmetry of this cavern and its giant rubies . . . No. Nature wasn't that perfect.

Even if nature *did* build this cavern, it certainly didn't go untouched. Somebody else had been here before, and Hansel was sure of that. The biggest clue was at the cavern's center. An ivory pedestal, smooth and shiny, rose from the sea of dark gems. Etched in scarlet letters were the words: PROPERTY OF THE IVORY QUEEN.

Hansel cringed. There was a name he hadn't heard in years, the nickname of the lost Queen Avoria. Could she have been down here the whole time? *What really happened between her and Lord Bellamy?*

On top of the pedestal, a wooden chest gathered dust.

Hansel's heart accelerated.

"Hansel," a woman spoke, the light, feminine timbre familiar to Hansel's ears.

Hansel turned and beheld a tall woman with glistening indigo wings. It was Violet, the purple fairy who had unofficially taken charge of the realm after Queen Avoria mysteriously went silent. While many people loved Violet, Hansel harbored mixed feelings toward her. After all, she delivered him the news that his sister had vanished.

"Violet . . . What brings you here?"

Violet wove her hands together, scrunching her mouth to the side as if she were thinking really hard. "I followed you, Hansel. Forgive me for spying."

Hansel scowled. She was going to ruin everything. "Why? Are you going to tell me that I should seal the mine, like Lord Bellamy did?"

Violet rubbed her forehead. "I'm afraid my father was right. You've stumbled on a dangerous secret, one that can put everyone in mortal danger. Not only in our world."

"What makes this cavern so awful? Does it have anything to do with Gretel's disappearance?"

"My dear, some secrets are too dangerous to be explained. I can only ask that you listen to your heart. Something's telling you there's evil here."

"But my heart led me here, didn't it?"

"What does it tell you now? Aren't you afraid?"

Hansel touched his chest, his heart tapping his fingers like a woodpecker. "I think I'm *excited.* There are answers here! I'm so close!" Hansel gazed at the pedestal again, where the chest's keyhole stared back at him. "Violet, what's in that chest?"

Violet waved the question away. "Come with me. We'll seal up the mine. We'll make sure the dwarves live happily ever after and keep their house."

"You've avoided my question."

Violet averted her gaze. "It's been hidden away for a reason. Hansel, by coming down here, you've started something terrible, but you don't have to let it continue. I have watched you grow since boyhood, and I know you have the strength to resist the darkness."

Hansel clenched his fists. "Stop talking in riddles! Give me some answers!"

"Something horrible is going to appear right now. I cannot be here to help you, but you must fight it. Should you prevail, you will have a choice: leave this mine and never come back, or continue down this path. I must believe you'll do the right thing."

Hansel's tongue turned to cotton. "What's coming? You're leaving me here?"

"I must." Violet chewed her plump lower lip. "But to aid you in your upcoming battle, I offer you this power. Please use it for good."

Hansel shook his head in disbelief. A second later, his forearms grew heavy, and he closed his fingers around the cold handle of a bronze sword that had appeared in midair. Chinese characters adorned the blade.

"A sword?" Hansel breathed. "But I've no training with blades!"

"Listen to your heart, Hansel. May the light be with you."

Violet vanished with a pop, and Hansel was alone again. It occurred to him that he hadn't been entirely honest with the fairy; he *was* afraid, burdened by a heavy blade and a crippling sense of incapability. What if he didn't have the skill to defeat what was coming for him?

Hansel closed his eyes and lowered his head. *Deep, cold breaths . . . in . . . out.* A thin film of mucus coated the inside of his nose, and he shivered.

When he heard his sister's voice, he grew even colder.

"*Hansel! Get me out of here! Help me!*"

Her scream curdled his blood.

"*Hansel!*"

Hansel opened his eyes. The chest convulsed on the ivory pedestal, shaking dust into the damp air.

"I'm coming, Gretel! Hold on!"

Hansel tightened his grip on the sword and broke into a run for the center of the chamber, the dark gems squelching under his boots. The chest bounced and shook more violently, while Gretel's screams grew louder.

"I'm coming!"

Hansel was an armspan away from the chest when a bone-white hand burst from the ground and stopped him cold, freezing his joints. He recognized that hand. In fact, he had never forgotten it.

"I wake."

The icy voice echoed through the cavern, masking Gretel's pleas as a veiny arm clawed its way through the dark gems. First the hand rose slowly and the fingers stretched like a snake uncoiling its body, and then a pale woman shot out from the surface all at once. She rocketed twenty feet in the air with a sword of her own, showering the cavern with dark stones.

Hansel didn't have time to process his fear. As the woman

plummeted back to the ground with a sneer, she raised her sword high above her head and prepared to cleave Hansel in two.

On reflex, Hansel hoisted his own blade in the air. "No!"

Ssshing! Clang!

The blades met perpendicularly in a deafening ring of metal on metal as the woman's bare feet connected with the ground again. There, Hansel held his position and looked her in the eyes, milky with cataracts and nearly hidden by her mess of stringy, white hair.

"You roasted me, dear."

She didn't move her lips, yet her voice was everywhere.

Hansel's breath grew heavy. "H-how . . . How are you here right now?"

The witch snarled. "*Why, you brought me here, my sweet. This is the Cavern of Ombra. It shows you the things you're most afraid of . . . the things that bring you closest to death. I am most flattered that I made such an impression on you. Am I really so frightening, handsome?*"

Hansel closed his eyes, holding his blade against the witch's. *She's not really here,* he repeated to himself.

"Oh, but I am, dearie, but I am."

Hansel's eyes snapped open, the cold air stinging his corneas. He blinked until the blur cleared from his vision and the witch's knowing grin contorted into focus. Could she really have been listening to his thoughts?

"I don't have to read your mind, boy. The fear is written in your heart. Your spirit trembles with it. Open your heart to darkness, and let it vanquish your fears. Embrace your hidden potential, and reclaim your sister!"

"*Where's Gretel?*"

"Release my spirit from this cavern, and I will help you find her."

For a terrible minute, Hansel considered the witch's newest offer. What if she was telling the truth? Maybe she had something to do with Gretel's disappearance. Perhaps she wanted to return to the land of the living, and Gretel somehow became her bargaining chip. Would that really be so bad of a trade, the witch's freedom for Gretel's? After all, it was Hansel's own fault that he and his sister got in trouble with the witch in the first place. She hadn't aggressively gone after them, or any other children for that matter. He found her candy house, gave in to temptation, and she took advantage of his stupidity. Sometimes Hansel would lay awake at night and think about it. If she'd cooked him that night, he would've had it coming. Maybe if he let her spirit free, she would be more peaceful.

"That's right, my sweet. Set me free."

On second thought, if she did have anything to do with Gretel's disappearance, there was no way he was going to reward the witch.

Hansel gritted his teeth, drew his sword, and lunged forward with two quick cleaves, missing the wicked woman by only a hair. "Not on your life, hag!"

The witch threw her head back and cackled. Hansel took the opportunity to swipe at her again. This time, he should've landed a blow. He watched the blade cut straight through the witch's shoulder, but to his horror, the woman exploded into vapor and rematerialized on the far side of the cavern.

"Sorry, handsome. You'll have to do better."

Hansel's nostrils flared. What was the point of Violet giving him a sword if he couldn't use it on the witch?

The chest shook again. "*Hansel! Brother! Let me out of here!*"

"*Release me first,*" the witch demanded. "*It's simpler than stew.*"

"Never!"

"Then you'll die in the Cavern of Ombra!"

The witch rematerialized in front of Hansel and swung her sword, leaving a long gash across Hansel's left cheek.

The pain was blinding. Hansel ran his arm across his face, soaking his sleeve in warm blood. "You'll pay for that one! Watch me roast you again!"

Hansel threw his sword down and reached into his belt for one of his special darts, just like the one he used to put Lord Bellamy down. It was a long shot, but if this worked . . . .

He returned the dart to his pocket. There was no way he could send this witch to the other realm.

"You poor, simple fool," the witch droned. *"You don't have the strength to vanquish me. You don't have the heart to save your sister. You're just a hungry little peasant!"*

Hansel retrieved his sword, dodged a blow from the witch, and approached the chest.With one mighty swing, he carved the iron lock in two.

"Enough games," the witch said. *"You roasted me in my own home. Now I'll roast* you *in the fires of hell!"*

The witch raised her blade, and a column of flames erupted throughout the Cavern of Ombra. In their glow, the witch looked nastier than ever. Her grin spread from ear to ear, revealing a dry mouthful of crooked teeth. The dark gem on the ground seemed to fuel the fire, churning the flames into a hefty shade of raven. Hansel's lungs turned to iron. He clutched his chest and sank to one knee, watching helplessly as the chest on the ivory pedestal rattled again.

"Help me! Let me out!"

"Gretel . . ." Hansel toppled onto his side, cushioned by the gems. The fire's heat closed in on him. "My sister. I'm so sorry."

CHAPTER FIVE

TODAY—THE NEW WORLD: PINO'S HOUSE

Enzo awoke to a strange new sound: silence.

Usually his father was up before dawn, and Enzo would awake to a symphony of sounds. A coffee pot sputtering. Wood peeling under a knife. A fresh newspaper snapping open.

There was a time when the house was alive with potatoes shredding, bacon and warm butter popping in hot pans, the swish of a page turning in a book while the washing machine whirred through its cycle, the appreciative laughter of a middle-aged woman, the soft pucker of a kiss on the forehead. *"Good morning, my dear. It's time to get up for school."*

Three years ago, all of these sounds stopped.

His father had pulled him out of school one day, and he was crying. "She's gone, Crescenzo. I think somebody took her."

And that made Enzo mad at his father, because how could he claim that somebody took her if he didn't even see her leave? What could he have been doing that distracted him so much that he couldn't save his own wife?

He was probably carving another stupid figurine.

In what he thought would be the lowest point of his life, Enzo was lucky that his best friend was also his neighbor. Zack Volo was like a brother, just as their fathers were like brothers in their own way.

Ever since they were five years old, Zack and Enzo took turns spending the night at each other's house. Enzo's father carved them wooden swords, and the boys would sit in front of the TV with them, playing video games, watching cartoons, drinking Capri Suns, and eating grilled cheese sandwiches. When the sun went down, Pietro would take the boys outside and teach them to spar. Zack was always a little better, quicker on his feet, but Enzo was a little smarter, quick-witted, and used his intellect to think up new maneuvers and blocks. It was a friendship for the ages.

So when Enzo found out about his mom when he was twelve years old, he drew strength from Zack and his family. It sometimes made Enzo cry to talk about his mother, but Zack never judged. It seemed to be the same with his father and his close friendship with Pietro and Wendy, who never hesitated to come over with dinner or invite the boys out for a movie.

A year later, Zack and Wendy vanished too, and Enzo had never felt more alone. His father went on carving figures out of the oak trees in the backyard, and Enzo hardly ever saw Pietro again.

Maybe Dad's right, Enzo thought. *Getting out there again and hanging out with Pietro might actually be good for us.*

Enzo rolled out of bed before his alarm, showered, threw on some jeans and a Muse t-shirt, and then ran a comb through his dark hair. He threw the rest of his essentials into his duffel bag, and after lacing up his Converse, he knocked on his father's bedroom door. It was strange that he wasn't already awake, carving away or sipping his coffee, but perhaps he decided to take a day to sleep in.

"Dad?"

Silence.

Knock, knock, knock. "Dad?"

"Uhnh . . . ."

Enzo's stomach dropped. That was definitely a moan. Not the tired kind. The suffering kind. He opened the door and found his father on his bed. His eyes were wide open, but the poor man lay stiff as a tree stump. "*Dad*!"

"Son . . . ." Pino breathed. But it came out the way Enzo heard it from behind the door: uhnh. His father couldn't even move his lips.

Enzo rushed to his father's side, heart jittering with worry. "Dad, what's happened to you? Can you stand? You can't move, can you?"

"Uhnh."

Seeing his father lying in such pain and to have no idea the cause was a new kind of hurt Enzo had never experienced. It brought on a sort of responsibility. *What can I do?* But he was lost. He always called his father an old man, but he hadn't even approached forty yet. His hair was still shiny-dark, and Enzo was sure he only wore glasses for show. It wasn't until three years ago that his dad started complaining about his joints. Arthritis, maybe? Enzo was no medical expert, but he wondered: How does a man go from standing at the door watching his son pack, to bedridden and stiff the next day?

Enzo grabbed his father's hand, stiff, but still warm. "Can you feel my grip, Dad?"

"Uhn . . . leaf . . . ."

"Leaf?" Enzo squeezed his dad's hand and leaned in. He knew he wasn't going to get very far. He needed to get his father to the hospital. A wave of nerves boomed in Enzo's mind. What if he dialed 911, panicked, and couldn't even recite his name or home address? What if they expected him to pay for an ambulance? What if there was one person his father trusted above anybody else—someone who could drive faster than anyone Enzo knew?

"I'm going to get Pietro, Dad. We'll take you to the hospital."

Enzo sprang up, but a quick, subtle squeeze from his father's hand made him freeze.

"Uhn . . . I . . . luf . . . you . . . ."

Enzo's heart bled. *Don't start talking like that, Dad.* "Yeah, Dad, I know. Don't strain yourself. Don't try to move. We need Pietro."

He bolted out of the house and ran so fast that he nearly knocked over a muscular, jocky sort of figure who sauntered to Enzo's doorstep with a basket of apples. The figure wore a green jacket and kept his hood up, even though the weather was anything but cool. In Enzo's rush, he bumped the stranger's shoulder and the basket of apples tumbled onto the sidewalk, shining red orbs scattering the lawn like billiards.

"Dude, watch it!" Enzo snapped. He left the stranger at the door and bounded off the porch. The figure remained silent, but his gaze haunted Enzo all the way to Pietro's house, past the hedges and the stone fairy. *Creepy.* Enzo pounded on Pietro's door.

"Come in!"

He opened the door and found Pietro with one foot on the coffee table, lacing up his Nikes. "Mornin', Enzo! You almost ready to head out?"

"Pietro . . . no time." The words came out in forced breaths. "We gotta . . . we gotta get my dad to the hospital."

Pietro froze. "What happened?"

Enzo grasped the doorframe for support, drawing shallow breaths. "He can't move. He's just lying there. I think he's paralyzed or something."

Pietro drummed on his knees and looked around the room, as if something on his coffee table could save Enzo's father. "Shoot. Okay. Try to keep calm, kid. Try giving him some water or something, and I'll be right over. We'll take him to the hospital."

Without answering, Enzo sprinted back home. Though he didn't see the guy with the green hood again, the basket of apples sat fully replenished by the wide open door. Enzo couldn't remember if he closed it on the way out.

When Enzo reentered his father's room, he was surprised to find a strange new man standing at his bedside. Tall, lean, and broad-shouldered, the man stood with his back to Enzo, gazing upon his father, who lay perfectly still. He wasn't even moaning anymore.

"Hey, you, who are you? What are you doing in my house?"

The man turned, and Enzo felt that there was something off about him. His eyes were cold, and his stubble wasn't quite dark enough to conceal the long scar across his left cheek. And the way the man was dressed entirely in thin black cloth and brown leather? Clearly not with the times.

"Ah, you must be The Carver's son," the stranger spoke, his voice deep and edgy.

Enzo almost averted his gaze, slightly unsettled, but he held his ground. "I asked you what you're doing here."

"I've come to pay your father a visit." When the man smirked, his scar looked rougher and shinier.

Enzo narrowed his eyes. "Do you know what's happening to him?"

"Your father doesn't belong here. This world must not agree with his . . . wooden nature. But I'm afraid I've no time to dawdle." Before Enzo could process the words, the man shoved a gloved hand into his vest and produced two long black darts.

Enzo winced. He hated needles. "What are you doing with those? Who *are* you?"

"Don't trouble yourself. Neither is for you. They're for me and your old man." The intruder took a knee and rolled Pino onto his side. "Sorry, Carver. You've gotta come with me."

Enzo's blood boiled. "No! Leave my father alone!"

The stranger raised an eyebrow. "You'll see him again. I imagine I'll be back for you and The Flying Man any day now."

Enzo's mind swam. *Flying man? What?* But one thing clicked in his mind. "You took my mom away."

"Bravo, kid." The man raised the darts above his head. "No time to dawdle. I've much to accomplish. Auf Wiedersehen!"

With a feral scream, Enzo lunged forward and tackled the stranger, sinking his knees into the man's back. A second later, his legs hit the ground with a hollow thud.

His father and the stranger were gone.

Enzo blinked, rubbed his eyes, and shook his head as if to clear his vision. *No. That did not just happen.* Where did they go? Were they even there before? The world had rules, and Enzo was sure of at least one thing: people did not just vanish into thin air, not even at a magic show. *Am I going crazy?* Enzo pulled himself to his feet and looked around the room.

"Dad? Where are you?"

The resounding silence put a bubble in Enzo's stomach. He was pretty sure he was going to be sick. *Or maybe I already am. Food poisoning? Schizophrenia?*

No. Enzo knew his mind was sound. He hadn't imagined a stranger in the bedroom driving a dart into his father's neck and disappearing without so much as a puff of smoke. They were both there, clear as day, and then they weren't.

"No!" Enzo yelled. "That doesn't *happen!*" He flung his father's closet door open, tore the sheets off the bed, and ransacked the room for a logical explanation. Every few seconds, Enzo would pinch his arm, beat his forehead with the sides of his hands, and try to will himself out of a bad dream. *It's a prank. It's a nightmare. It's not real. The stranger was a Martian. The truth is anything other than what I just saw.*

After opening the closet door for the sixth time, an iron weight descended on Enzo's mind. Whatever had really happened, the cold, hard fact was that his father was gone. Pain started somewhere in Enzo's gut, and it rose through him like a geyser. It put a knot in his throat and burned his eyes, intensified by confusion.

"Dad!" *I didn't even say I love you too.*

The sounds of swift footsteps in the living room cut through Enzo's thoughts. "*Enzo!* Kid, we've gotta go!"

Enzo pulled himself up and called out to his neighbor, "Pietro! My dad is . . . he's . . . gone!"

He shuffled out of his father's room and beheld another strange sight. *I* am *going crazy*.

Pietro was in the living room with hooded person—the guy with the apples. The figure strafed around the room, pelting Pietro with a seemingly infinite supply of fruit. Pietro knocked them away like baseballs with a wooden sword: Zack's wooden sword.

Enzo dodged an apple and heard shattering glass. "Pietro!"

"Enzo, grab your things! *Now*! We gotta get out of here!"

CHAPTER SIX

THREE YEARS AGO—THE OLD WORLD: THE WOODLANDS

When Hansel came to, he was in his own bed. Not what he expected.

Also unexpected: everything hurt. His face burned white-hot, especially his left cheek. His calves screamed. His wrists were stiff, and his shoulders were heavy. His eyes stung and his vision was funny, like looking through fog.

Worst of all, his soul was crushed. *I couldn't save Gretel. I heard her screaming, and I couldn't save her.*

Hansel squinted and saw that somebody had covered him in thick wool blankets. His bandaged feet popped out of the other side.

Another thought crossed his mind. *How am I alive? How am I back here?*

"Good to see you're still breathing."

A beautiful woman with raven hair approached his bed, holding a bowl of pumpkin soup.

His heart fluttered. "Snow!"

Snow White sat down to Hansel's left. He noticed the tall man in navy-blue royal garb sitting to his right and shifted uneasily. "Oh, Prince Liam. Always a pleasure."

If you can call it that.

"Sir Hansel." Prince Liam removed his cap and shook Hansel's hand, palm perfectly vertical and his grip firm. "The pleasure is mine. How are you feeling, my friend?"

Don't fake it, you glorified knave. You've never even slain a dragon.

"I've seen better days. What the devil happened to me?"

Snow tipped a spoonful of soup into Hansel's mouth. The pumpkin and fresh herbs went down easier than ale, warm, smooth, and sweet to the palate. "Something happened to you in the mines."

Hansel tried to sit up, but Prince Liam applied a gloved hand to his chest. "Don't strain yourself. You need to recover."

Don't touch me, you jerk.

Hansel grimaced. "I remember the witch was there. God, she was awful. She's back."

Snow and Prince Liam exchanged looks, and there was a subtle upturn in the corner of Liam's lip that looked an awful lot like disbelief.

"Who pulled me out?" Hansel continued.

Snow tucked a silky lock of hair behind her ear. "Your housemates carried you home. They asked if I would take care of you while they worked today. You will be able to thank them later."

"They followed me?"

"I believe it was Violet who sent them after you." The corners of Snow's eyes creased in concern. "Hansel, they said nothing about a witch. They found you somewhere deep in the mine. You've been unconscious for three days."

Hansel's mind spun with questions, concern, but mostly anger. Anger at himself for failing Gretel. Anger at Prince Liam for sitting by his bed and flaunting Snow White in his face. Anger at Violet for trying to stop him from rescuing his sister. For sending the dwarves into the chamber. No, he couldn't be angry for that. After all, he was alive because of them.

"She was there, Snow." *But was she? The sword went right*

through her, and she said something about the chamber showing you your fears. Was *she there?* "I saw her myself. She cut my face with her sword and set part of the mine on fire."

"So that explains the wound on your face." Prince Liam stroked his prickly spade of a chin. "Still, it's curious. I imagine it must've been difficult seeing her."

No, you think?

Snow wrung her hands, pausing only to shovel more soup into Hansel's mouth.

"The dwarves," Hansel said. "Did they say anything about Gretel? I heard her voice. She was calling out to me, screaming. I have to go back down there."

"Not until you fully recover. They didn't mention Gretel. They only found you and a big wooden chest."

Hansel's heart jumped into his throat. "That's right! The chest! That's where I heard her voice coming from! I have to go back for it."

Prince Liam stood and stretched before he began pacing back and forth. "You don't have to go back for the chest, lad. Garon and his friends carried it back with you."

"The chest is here? I must open it!" Hansel sat straight up, knocking his bowl to the floor. The cracks in the wood filled with thickening orange soup.

Snow flittered from the room, presumably to grab a rag.

"You need to take it easy," Liam said. "The chest is at the foot of the bed. Nobody touched it since you got here."

"Give it here."

"As you wish."

Prince Liam took a knee and hoisted the dusty wooden crate onto his stool. The iron lock was still split where Hansel remembered cleaving it with his sword, but the chest didn't make a sound. No rattling. No voices.

Hansel pushed himself along his bed, his body screaming the whole time. Snow returned with a clean rag, which Prince Liam promptly took from her and used to soak the pumpkin soup from the ground.

Snow put her hands on her hips and tapped her foot. "I really wish you wouldn't try to stand right now. I want you to rest for at least another day."

"I'm only going to see what's in this box."

Hansel shifted to the bed's edge and reached for the iron lock, his hands trembling and his heart being faster with every inch. The broken lock was rough and cool to the touch, and all Hansel needed to do was give the lid a gentle push.

The hinges creaked. Dust trickled out, dancing in the air before settling like fresh snow. Hansel peered inside the box.

Well. This isn't what I expected.

"What is it?" Liam asked.

Hansel reached both arms into the box and produced a single item with a flat oval surface. Its edges were made of polished ivory. It was about as long as Hansel's torso and quite heavy, yet no thicker than his thumb. Hansel blew away a thin film of dust, and his reflection appeared. He was the same man, save for the large gash on his face, yet he hardly recognized himself. When he tilted the surface, Snow and Prince Liam appeared behind him, arm in arm.

Hansel shook his head and sighed. "It's nothing. It's only an old mirror."

TODAY—THE OLD WORLD: CAVERN OF OMBRA

Alicia Trujillo awoke standing in a strange new place.

Small. Hollow. Translucent. Deeply unsettling.

Where am I?

Alicia pressed her fingers to the surface in front of her. It looked almost like the window of a cathedral and cast an eerie red glow onto Alicia's fair skin.

She made a tight fist and banged on the sturdy red window and quickly realized that it wasn't made of glass. Alicia was inside something more like a diamond. Her fist didn't make a sound. Most terrifying of all was the realization that this strange substance was protruding from a cavernous wall, at least fifty feet in the air. *I'm in a cage!*

Panic seared Alicia's veins, and she pounded even harder.

She pressed her face to the gem's surface and was horrified to see an ivory pedestal at the cavern's center, surrounded by dark gems. While everything she saw held a red tint, the gems frightened her. She'd seen both the pedestal and the gems before.

When Alicia looked straight ahead, her eyes met another large gem. There were six others in the cavern. Three of them were empty, but each of the others, including the one across from her, contained another person. He was a tall boy, lean and handsome, probably no older than sixteen. He stood straight up, clad in Nikes, jeans, and a thick hoodie. His head drooped at a slight angle, but the rest of his body remained straight as a board. And he was asleep.

To the boy's left, a woman slept in this same strange position. She appeared to be about forty years old, and the subtle lines under her eyes barely aged her. Light, wavy hair fell to her shoulders, and her full eyebrows and perfectly symmetrical nose mirrored the boy's beside her. Neatly tucked into her skirt was a plaid, short-sleeved blouse.

The woman in the gem to Alicia's left seemed the oldest, but not by much. She wore sandals and a simple dress, and her hair was dark and wound into a neat bun.

The thought hit Alicia in the gut. *Rosana.*

Where is my daughter?

The last thing Alicia remembered was descending into the subway with her. They'd just enjoyed a delicious lunch together at Petrelli's Pizza and were heading back home in Harlem after visiting the Statue of Liberty.

She pounded on the walls of her cell again. *"Hellooo! Can anybody hear me?"*

No use. She was a prisoner.

A familiar voice cut Alicia's thoughts short. It was amazing how crystal clear that lazy drawl was, even though its source did not come from within the gem.

"Well this is interesting! Look who's awake!" Alicia looked down and beheld a short stocky man leaning against the ivory podium. When she made eye contact with him, the man tipped his cap and bit into a greasy turkey leg.

"You," Alicia breathed. "I remember you. You're one of the seven dwarves."

The man swallowed hard and rubbed his belly. "We prefer the term *miners.*"

"Chann," Alicia recalled. She pounded on her ruby prison again. "You brought me here?"

"Oh, no, that wasn't me. That was Wayde. He said you recognized him in the subway station. Then again, that was a little over"—he glanced at his pocket watch—"six months ago."

"I've been sleeping in this thing for *six months*?"

"Mhm. Don't feel bad, princess." Chann jerked his thumb behind him, indicating the gem on the other side of the cavern. "See that handsome fella over there? He and his ma have been sleeping for two years. *Two years!* Oh, and the lady right next to you? She's been snoozin' for three. Her husband, The Carver, will be joining us shortly. Right in time for lunch again." Chann smiled and crossed his arms behind his head.

Alicia bit her lips. "Where's my daughter?"

"That is a very good question." Chann scratched his head through his dusty cap. "I dunno. I'm just the watch dog."

"Look," Alicia said, "there must be some mistake here."

"Don't think so, Alice. You do remember that's your real name, right?"

Alicia sighed. "I left that all behind! This is absolutely impossible!"

"Wasn't it you who, and I quote, *believed as many as six impossible things before breakfast*?"

Alicia had never exactly forgotten her trips to Wonderland, but she made a conscious effort not to think about them ever again. She was tired of people treating her like she was crazy.

Maybe I've finally gone mad, she thought. Waking up in a jewel in the middle of a cave? This was stranger than any trip down the rabbit hole.

"So why am I here? At least tell me that much."

Chann shrugged. "The mirror asked for you."

Suddenly overcome by a dizzy spell, Alicia drifted back to sleep.

CHAPTER SEVEN

TODAY—THE NEW WORLD: JUST OUTSIDE RICHMOND, VA

Pietro slung his duffel bag behind the driver seat and jammed the key in the ignition.

Enzo followed Pietro's lead and slammed the door, sealing his home outside.

"Put on your seatbelt," Pietro said.

"You're not wearing yours."

"Buckle."

Instead, the boy spun around and stared out the back window. As Pietro hit the gas and drove away from his house, he sympathized with the kid. He should have a chance to wave goodbye to his home. Who knew if he would ever return? Even if they did, how different would their lives be?

Pietro supposed the same went for him. His spirits wilted as his cozy neighborhood shrank in the rearview mirror. What if he never came back?

No more mortgage, I guess. No more responsibilities.

No. Pietro loved this life. He hated being an office broker. He hated bills, house repairs, and truck maintenance. He hated stupid things like taxes and pretending to care about politics every four years, but he loved this life.

Silence hung in the air as Pietro drove on thinking of all the great things he loved about the New World. He loved his beautiful Wendy. He loved Zack. Pepperoni pizza and video games and Nike shoes. Starbucks. Oh, the great fun Neverland would have with a Starbucks.

Pietro tapped Enzo on the shoulder, breaking him out of an almost catatonic gaze. "Hey. Wanna stop at Starbucks?"

Enzo jerked his head in Pietro's direction and snapped his hand away. "What do *you* think? Do you wanna know what I just saw? What happened to my father? To your best friend? I don't need a latte, Pietro. I need to find out what happened to my dad!" The boy's voice shook with a quality Pietro recognized all too well. He was trying to sound angry, but that quaver was induced by fear. "Where are we even going?"

Without looking back at Enzo, Pietro decelerated and put on his blinker. "I don't know, kid. Away. We're not safe at home right now." He sighed. *Please don't make me say too much, yet.* "You hungry at all? You like Chipotle?"

"I'm not hungry." Enzo scowled. "What do you mean we're not safe? Pietro, what happened to my dad?"

"Why don't you tell *me* what happened?" Pietro stole a side glance at Enzo and added, "Dude, I really, really wish you'd buckle up. You're making me nervous."

"You first." Enzo pointed to a sign on the side of the road. "Click it or ticket."

Pietro snapped on his seatbelt, and Enzo followed suit. "There," Pietro said. "Now tell me what happened, unless you want the radio on. I don't do well with silence. You like country music? Or maybe you're more of a metal guy. I have some Muse cds! You like old Muse or new Muse?"

"Pietro, am I crazy? Like, is all of this actually happening right now?"

"Crazy? Why would you think that? Am I driving crazy? Do I have something crazy on my face?" Sticking his tongue out the side of his mouth, Pietro crossed his eyes.

"*Watch the road!*"

"Relax, dude! I don't mean to toot my own horn, but when it comes to this driving thing"—Pietro swatted the car horn with the heel of his palm—"I've got this. Easier than flyin'. Anyway, you were saying? Why would you think you're crazy?"

"Because my dad just disappeared right in front of me."

Pietro said nothing.

"Great." Enzo made a face out the window. "Now you think I'm crazy too."

"No, kid, no," Pietro said quickly. "I think this conversation deserves our full attention." He put on the blinker. "We need to discuss this over some food."

A few minutes later, they sat down at a McDonalds, and Pietro ordered two Happy Meals with chocolate shakes. Enzo picked at his food, swirling fries around a blob of ketchup.

"So," Pietro said, wiping some mayo off his face with the back of his arm, "tell me how your dad disappeared."

"I don't *know* how he disappeared! I still don't understand it, Pietro. One minute he was there, all stiff and weird, and the next minute, after I ran to get you"—Enzo ran his hand through his inky-dark hair—"some other guy was sticking a dart in his neck and . . . *poof*."

"Poof?" Pietro set his burger down and crinkled his nose.

"I swear!" Enzo said. "And you know what the worst part is? Before I came to get you, his eyes were open, but it looked like he was hurting, and he kept trying to say 'son,' but it came out all funny because he couldn't move his lips, and then I think he tried to tell me to leave, but I couldn't understand him." Enzo drew a strobe-like breath that caught in his throat as his eyes filled with tears. "And then he was like 'Son, I love you,' and I just stood there and told him to stop trying to talk because he was gonna strain himself. I didn't even tell him I loved him back, and I'm such a *dumbass*!"

The boy put his head in his arms and convulsed with silent sobs, a sight that broke Pietro's heart. He grabbed Enzo's arm. "Hey, hey, hey, kid, no. I don't want you to talk about yourself that way. You're not a dumbass, even though you really shouldn't use that language anyway, but whatever; you're a teenager, I guess. Anyway, your dad loves you *so* much, dude. Like, *so* much. It's unreal how much the man loves you, but I understand it because that's how I feel about my son. And I mean"—Pietro leaned back—"you and Zack have been best buddies since you were in diapers. And your dad and I? We've been best friends for, like, I don't even know *how* many years. That makes us like family almost."

Enzo looked up and wiped his face, avoiding eye contact.

Pietro sipped his chocolate shake, rich and thick. "And do you know, if there's one thing family understands, it's love, kid. I know how much your dad loves you, and I know how much you love your dad. You know why? Because I love Zack to pieces, and I know he feels the same about his mom and me. He didn't have to say it every day. He didn't have to really say it *ever*. In fact, there were days when 'I hate you' was the kid's favorite thing to say. But I always knew the truth."

Enzo hiccupped.

"Because you see, love between family members, or friends, or lifelong sweethearts? It's more than words. If there's one thing I can tell you for *damn* sure"—Pietro pounded the table to drive his point—"your father knows you love him too."

There it was. Enzo finally smiled, a subtle flicker on one side of his mouth, but Pietro saw it. It was a smile. *I should win an award for that speech,* Pietro thought.

"Thanks," Enzo muttered. "So, wait, do you believe me about the whole *poof* thing? You don't think I'm crazy?"

Pietro threw his head back in a roar of laughter. "*Crazy*. Hilarious, dude! Did you not see me get attacked by a hooded freak throwing apples in your living room? I *know* you saw that because I had to pull you off of him to get you out of the house! I don't know what he wanted, but I'd say *he* was the crazy one."

"I think it's the other guy we should be worried about," Enzo said. "The one that took my dad."

Pietro leaned in, arms folded across his chest. "So tell me more about the other guy."

"Well, the first thing I noticed about him was how he was dressed. Pretty sure he doesn't shop at Fashion Square. He got his clothes from, like, a Renaissance festival or something."

That could be anybody *from home,* Pietro thought. "Okay, what else? Did he have a hook for a hand, by chance?"

"Nah, he didn't look like a pirate. More like, I don't know, a peasant. If we're sticking to the whole Renaissance theme."

"Mmm." Pietro stroked his chin. "Was he old?"

Enzo scrunched up his face. "I'm guessing mid-twenties, maybe? Younger than you. Dark blond hair, almost brown. Average height, I guess. Not as tall as you. Oh, and he had a scar across his left cheek."

Pietro didn't remember anyone with a cheek scar back home. So far this was going nowhere. "And what did he say? What did he do?"

Enzo leaned in. "He said he'd be back for me and the 'flying man,' and then he took out these black dart things and stuck one in his neck and one in my dad's neck, and they disappeared. On my honor. I tackled the guy myself, and that's when—"

"*Poof,*" Pietro finished, eliciting a wide-eyed nod from Enzo.

Pietro concentrated. He didn't understand any of these details. Black darts that made someone vanish into thin air? He didn't question their existence, but they weren't something he'd ever seen in the Old World. Most disturbing of all was the detail about the "flying man." *Obviously this jerk knows me, and he's gonna come for me and the kid. Who is it?* Pietro drained the rest of his milkshake. *I really hope I can protect this boy.*

Enzo sighed. "You never told me whether you believe me."

"I believe we need to hit the road." Pietro blew a raspberry and rubbed his face. “Where do you wanna go?”

“Well, where were you planning to go before?” Enzo stared at his lap. “I feel like I ruined your vacation.”

“Kid, you and I were *never* going on vacation. You and I were gonna pack up this morning, and we were gonna go look for your mom and my family. No more sitting around. Nothing has changed except that now we’re looking for your dad, too.” Pietro saw the scowl dying to surface on Enzo’s face. For him, *everything* had changed. “I don’t think this is all coincidence, Enzo. I think it’s all connected.”

“Do you think Zack and Wendy went *poof*, too? And my mom?”

“I think they’re out there somewhere, and we owe it to them to do everything we can to bring them home. I just wish I knew where to start. Anywhere but here.”

Enzo pulled a small, white object from his pocket and spun it between two fingers. “Well, I was thinking about one place. My dad and I were talking about it last night because it kind of reminds us of my mom. Maybe we can go there, and while I’m thinking about my parents we’ll come up with something else that will help us find one of them.”

When he finished talking, Enzo set a carving of the Empire State Building on the table.

Pietro’s heart jumped. Pinocchio made that. He remembered his old friend’s words: *These people I’ve been carving? I* know *they’re the key to putting everything back to normal.* Places counted too, right? It had to be a start. Pietro leapt out of his chair and hugged Enzo from behind.

“Kid, you’re freaking brilliant, you know that? You’re not a dumbass; you’re a *badass*!” Pietro drummed on Enzo’s back and grabbed the car keys. “Come on. Take your food with you, and let’s hit the road. We’re going to New York City.”

CHAPTER EIGHT

TWENTY-FIVE YEARS AGO—THE OLD WORLD

Pinocchio was disappointed.

Being a real boy should've been fun and full of adventure, but there he was, stuck cleaning his room again while his best friends were out exploring the mines.

"I told you, Son," his father, Geppetto, said, "if you would put your blocks away when you were done playing with them and learn how to fold up your clothes, your room wouldn't get so messy like this."

I hate folding clothes, Pinocchio thought. *Life was so much easier when they were painted on my body.* "But, Pop! Peter's with Alice and Hansel and Gretel, and they're all playing in the mines together! And I wanted to go with them." Pinocchio hung his head. "I'm bored."

"Then why don't you make a little game out of cleaning your room? Pretend this is the mine, and if you clean up really nicely, you might find a treasure under all this junk. Besides, I don't approve of you playing in the mines. It's very dangerous, you know. Frankly, I wouldn't be surprised if that little girl falls down another hole and gets herself lost again. Mines are not for kids."

Pinocchio crossed his arms. "Then how come my friends' parents let them play in the mine and you don't?"

His father sighed, creasing his face with wrinkle lines. "Oh, I don't know, Son. I suppose you'll understand when you're older."

"I *hate* when you tell me that," Pinocchio said.

His father shook his finger. "Don't ever use that word again, Pinocchio! Hate is ugly."

"But you always say I'll understand things when I'm older, and I hate it. I wanna be older now so I can understand things and go play in the mines with Peter Pan and my friends any time I want!"

"Oh, that's what you want?" his father challenged.

"Yes." Pinocchio looked up with defiance in his eyes, his knuckles locked on his hips.

His father tapped his foot and chewed his lip. "Well, that's too bad. I can't do anything about that. Now pick up your blocks!"

⁂⁂⁂

Peter Pan was morose. He'd been having so much fun until Hansel had to go and ask, "How come Wendy isn't here?"

Peter plopped down onto a large diamond and put his chin in his hands. "Wendy doesn't wanna play with me anymore."

Gretel gasped. "Why *not*?"

Peter lowered his head. "Her dad won't let her. He told Wendy, 'I don't want you spending any more time with that scruffian. He's bad in fluents.'"

"Oh, how awful!" Alice said. "I don't even know what that means, but it sounds so mean!"

"That's what I said! I told her not to listen to her dad and that he was just being a big stupid. And then Wendy told me that I really was a scruffian and that I was never gonna grow up. And then she told me that she didn't wanna play with me anymore because she wasn't gonna get to grow up."

Gretel toddled over to Peter and sat by him on the diamond. "Sorry, friend. I don't think you're bad in fluents."

"But she does. And now she's not my friend anymore, and I'm sad."

"Don't be sad. My brother and I are still your friends. And Pinocchio. And Alice. We don't think you're scruffians."

Alice nodded in agreement.

"Thanks. But I'm still sad. When I think about Wendy, I feel her in here." Peter pounded his chest. "It's kind of like my heart starts crying."

"You were in love!" Hansel sang. A big smile spread across his face. "You fancied her. And guess what? The pretty girl who always picks flowers by the meadow? I think she fancies *me*."

When Peter's posture wilted, Gretel punched her brother in the shoulder, and his smile quickly receded.

"I mean, I'm sorry, Peter. Someday we'll find girls who feel us in their hearts, too. I know it."

"I agree!" Alice said. "We'll all find someone real special one day."

"But when?" Peter asked. "Tomorrow?"

Alice shrugged. "I don't know. I suppose most people find it when they're grown-ups."

ONE WEEK LATER

"I'm telling you all the *truth!* Why doesn't anybody ever believe me?" Alice stamped her feet and scrunched her face into a pointed glare. "It's so mean!"

"Because what you're saying is stupid," Peter said. "You can't just get sucked into a mirror and battle evil queens on the other side and stuff. You know what? I bet you didn't even fall down a rabbit hole, either. You just like to lie."

"*Ugh!*" Alice put her hands on her hips. "Nobody ever takes you seriously unless you're a grown-up. Gretel, do you believe me?"

"Mmm, I guess so. It *is* kind of silly. But was it fun?"

"No, it wasn't fun! Are you kidding me? I had an evil queen after me. Again! Now I come back and nobody believes me. I should've let her have my head. I hate it here." Alice plopped down, a deep pout on her face.

Peter dashed onto a tall, skull-shaped rock and crossed his arms. "Me, *too*. So let's do something about it! Let's go somewhere we can live like grown-ups."

Gretel looked at Peter like she didn't recognize him. "Um. Really?"

"Yeah! I'm being cereal right now."

"You mean serious?" Alice said.

"Yeah, that, too. Let's go find a way to grow up! What do you say?"

Gretel took a handful of her dress and wrapped it tightly around her finger. "I don't know."

"Whattaya mean you don't know?" Peter hopped off the rock and leaned into Gretel's face. "Did your parents believe you and your brother about the candy house?"

"No."

"So there," Peter said triumphantly. "Being a kid is stupid. We don't get love, and we don't get taken cereally."

"Seriously," Alice corrected.

"Yeah, that." Peter returned to his rock and made a fist. "Alice, are you with me?"

"I suppose, but what do we do?"

Peter folded his legs under him and rubbed his chin. "Hmm. Hey, how did Pinocchio turn into a boy?"

"Why, he had help from that nice fairy lady! Violet."

"That's right! Let's go see if Pinocchio will take us to the Violet lady. If she turned Pinocchio into a boy, maybe she could turn us into grown-ups!"

Alice climbed onto the rock and kissed Peter on the cheek.

Peter grimaced and wiped the moist, warm lip prints away with the back of his hand.

"That's brilliant, Peter!" Alice exclaimed. "Gretel, do you want to come meet Violet? And would Hansel want to come, too?"

"Hansel's trying to talk to the girl in the meadow. I'll come with you, but I have to be home by sundown."

"Not if the fairy turns you into a grown-up!" Peter said. "You can be home whenever you want when you're a grown-up. C'mon. Let's go get Pinocchio."

VIOLET'S DEN

When Pinocchio arrived with his friends, he was awestruck by the fairy's dwelling. On the highest part of a towering boulder on the shore, carved out of a rock, was Violet's cozy den. On one side, ocean water slapped against the jagged surface below. On the other, Violet could see far beyond, beholding forests, rivers, mountains, and a dark castle to the east. The inside was just as impressive. One of her walls featured a detailed mural depicting six circular panels, five faces revolving around a shining bell in the center. Fixed on another wall was an ornate mirror, tall and pristine and encased in an ivory frame. Violet, the fairy guardian of the realm, sat on an enormous red cushion with her knees bent beneath her.

"My dear children, I'm so glad you came to see me. However, I'm afraid growing up isn't simple. Time is funny in our world. Some age naturally as a tree grows big and strong. Some peak at a young age such as yours. If you insist on growing up so fast, you may need to go elsewhere."

Pinocchio clapped his hands excitedly. "You mean it's possible?"

Violet smiled. "Yes. Other worlds aren't bound by our magic and rules. Few can know of their existence, but in these other worlds, you can grow and live the happy lives you dream of."

Peter tilted his head to the side. "But how?"

"Listen carefully. I am in possession of something very special." Violet gestured to the wall behind her, where the ivory mirror captured their youthful reflections. "I'm rather fond of this mirror, children. It shows you the things you need to see. It tells you what you need to hear. Just as we all have a reflection, the mirror also has a twin. If you bring me the twin, I can help you get what you desire."

"Where's the other mirror?" Alice asked.

"It's in the dark castle to the east"—Violet gestured to the horizon—"where the Ivory Queen resides."

Gretel gulped. "The Ivory Queen? Who is she?"

"Queen Avoria of Florindale," Violet said. "My wicked stepmother."

"Wicked?"

Violet nodded. "She was once a wonderful ruler, always acting in the realm's best interest. She repaired the bells of Florindale when they cracked, she fixed the rivers when they turned to mucus, reversed our famine when all the fruits started spilling sand, and stopped the venomous spiders from raining from the sky. She loved her people, until the Giant Wars."

Pinocchio gasped. "My dad told me about those! The giants!"

"Oh, they were horrible! They came down from the clouds and destroyed so much. You cannot possibly fathom how dark those days were. There were secret armies fighting them every day. Imagine leprechauns forging weapons of gold, fairies cutting and dying magical fabrics for the armies, mermen searching the seas for resources. We thought we had it all, mages, warriors, marksmen, but we just kept losing. Queen Avoria was entrusted to win the war."

Alice's mouth rounded in curiosity. "And what did she do?"

"She turned to her scientist, Dr. Victor Frankenstein, and he gave her a weapon: a serpent named Kaa. But he wasn't just any old snake, kids; he was a dead snake. Dr. Frankenstein brought the snake back from the dead."

Peter flinched. "I don't like snakes."

It was the first time Pinocchio had ever seen his friend express fear.

"Neither did the giants. Dr. Frankenstein manipulated the serpent to hypnotize them and inflict its venom on them. Kaa attacked them all, one by one, fervently aiding the military of Florindale. With a single bite, each giant fell, collapsing into a dark gem no bigger than your palm. It appeared, children, that he took their souls away."

Pinocchio gulped. "That's a good thing, right? He stopped the giants."

"'Twas a wonderful thing," Violet confirmed, "but Dr. Frankenstein forgot to account for the serpent's appetite. With every bite, Kaa got bigger and bigger until he was thicker than a tree and longer than a field, and after the giants fell, he was still hungry. You can guess what happened next."

Alice covered her mouth.

"Kaa started to attack the people. He was out of control, biting everyone in sight, rampant and angry, and nobody could kill it. The people accused Queen Avoria of allowing her weapon to harm them. They said she planned it, that she wanted to control the population. They turned on her out of fear."

"And then?" Gretel whispered.

"She got angry. Depressed. She was losing her followers, her sense of duty. When she couldn't have their loyalty, she wanted power. So one day, she made a spectacle of marching into Florindale Square, and she made a grand speech about how the people would be hers again, but in the middle of her speech, Kaa bit her on the ankle."

"And she became a gem?" Peter guessed.

"No. She became Kaa's equal, just as she intended. Kaa's powers of soul reaping transferred directly to her, and she grew hungry for both souls and power. She took many souls away, gaining strange abilities, youth, and terrible strength. She then decided that she wanted to acquire the other provinces by force. Determined to stop her, my father made the first stand."

Pinocchio gasped. "Did she eat your father's soul?"

"No." Violet turned and studied her reflection. "She found an enchanted mirror, just like the one you see before you, and she put my father inside of it."

"That's awful!" Alice exclaimed.

"There's so much more I could tell you, about the Battle of the

Thousand and the Order of the Bell, but I believe the matter at hand is to retrieve the mirror from my stepmother's castle."

"That sounds dangerous!" Pinocchio said. "What if she takes our souls?"

"You've nothing to fear. After I learned what happened to my father, I enchanted the rosebushes outside of her castle. The enchantment put her straight to sleep."

"The queen is sleeping? Will she ever wake up?" Peter scrunched his face and suppressed a gag. "Eww, does somebody have to kiss her?"

Violet giggled for the first time that night. "No, no, Peter. She sleeps forever, that is, until the mirror leaves her chamber. That was the price of my magic. To sedate the queen, I gave up my chance at taking the mirror back. I must confess: Many times I've tried to return to the castle, so I could retrieve it myself and free my father, but the castle boundaries have been enchanted to keep me out. I cannot move past the rosebushes."

"It sounds awful dangerous to wake her up," Alice said. "We don't have to grow up, Miss Violet. We can stay here!"

Gretel looked up hopefully, while Peter and Pinocchio looked down.

Violet lay a gentle hand on Alice's shoulder, her wings shimmering in the moonlight. "I would only do this for you, children. I want to grant your wishes more than anything. If I can help you while also setting my father free, I am confident that I can put an end to Queen Avoria's terror as well. Best of all, once you leave this realm, she will not be your concern. You will be free to grow up and do as you please in a world where she cannot touch your soul."

Peter leapt to his feet and hoisted a wooden dagger in the air. "I'm not afraid! I'm not afraid of anything! Miss Violet, I'll go get your mirror back tonight."

Pinocchio chewed a fingernail, but he followed suit and threw his arm around Peter's shoulder. "I'm coming with you, friend! I won't let you go alone!"

Violet smiled and pressed her fingers together. "Bless you, boys. You've the bravest of hearts."

"Ahem." Alice crossed her arms. "Not just the boys. Right, Gretel?"

Gretel lowered her head and sniffled. She did that thing with her dress again, winding it around her finger in tight circles. "I don't know. I'm afraid."

Peter took a knee and plucked a moonflower out of the ground, creamy white and star-shaped. He sniffed it, smiled, and offered it to Gretel. "Hey! Don't worry, Gretel! You don't have to be afraid. As long as we're all together, we'll be okay, right?"

Gretel didn't look up or accept the flower.

Alice sat down again and hugged her friend. "He's right, you know. We'll all have each other to look out for!"

Pinocchio nodded.

Gretel sniffled again.

Violet took a knee. "It's okay, Gretel," she said. "You needn't accompany them."

A tear rolled down Gretel's cheek and dripped onto the ground. Another moonflower sprung up in its place. "B-but they're gonna think I'm a scaredy-pants!"

"Nuh-uh!" Pinocchio said. "You and your brother killed a witch once."

"I would never call you a scaredy-pants," Alice added. "You're brave! Right, Peter?"

Peter didn't say anything. He twirled the moonflower between his thumb and forefinger, staring at the petals. Then he tossed it over his shoulder and stuck his chin in the air. "I don't care. I guess we'll go on our own, just the three of us. We'll have our own adventure."

Gretel wiped another tear from her face.

"Come here, my dear." Violet extended her arms and intercepted Gretel in a warm hug, folding her wings over the small girl. "You can stay here with me while Alice and the boys go to the castle. Nobody's judging you. You've already fought one too many witches in your life. You needn't fight anymore."

Peter cleared his throat and hoisted his dagger. "So, uh, what else should we know? Dark castle. Magic mirror. We just try not to wake up the sleeping lady and come back with the mirror?"

"That is correct," Violet said. "When you make it to the castle, hurry to the eastern turret. There, you will find the Ivory Queen sleeping in her bedroom. Take the mirror off her wall and leave. You mustn't dawdle."

"Got it." Peter grabbed Alice and Pinocchio by the shoulders. "It's time for an epic adventure! Let's go take the mirror from that scruffian!"

Pinocchio gulped. "Yep."

Alice narrowed her eyes and nodded confidently. "Let's go."

"To aid you in your quest," Violet added, "I offer you these powers. Peter Pan, the young at heart, may your spirit forever maintain its levity. I offer you the gift of the hummingbird. You don't need to be in Neverland to fly anymore. You can fly wherever you want. So can your shadow."

She waved her wand in front of her, and Peter's shadow stepped away from his body and jittered independently.

"Not again!" he cried.

"Peter, do not be angry when your shadow eludes you. After all, shadows are born from the light."

Peter's shadow spread its arms and soared around the room in wide circles. Then Peter himself hovered off the ground, staring down at his feet. "Cool."

"Alice the brave, your adventures have attracted quite a bit of attention in this realm, and a young girl like you needs space to grow up. May you always find your escape when you need it. I offer you the gift of the unseen."

Violet waved her wand again, and a red cloak appeared in front of Alice, hovering like a wraith. "The girl who used to wear this hood has grown up, and it no longer fits her. Since her last adventure, her cloak has acquired the curious ability to render its wearer invisible, so long as she thinks the right thoughts. Guard it well, my dear."

Alice took the cloak and threw it over her shoulders.

A puff of air escaped Pinocchio and he turned his head, eyes wide with concern. "Where'd she go?"

Alice's voice sounded in Pinocchio's ear. "I'm right here, silly!"

"Weird!"

Violet smiled. "And for you, Pinocchio, the real boy. You've learned a great deal of lessons in your life and mastered the craft of honesty. May the world always be honest with you in return. I offer you the gift of The Carver."

A knife with an ivory handle appeared in Pinocchio's hand, smooth and cool to the touch. "A knife? Miss Violet, I'm just a kid. My dad would never let me hold something like this."

"That's more than a knife, dear. Being a Carver is a grand responsibility. It is not often my place to bestow this gift on another, but there is no boy I would trust more. Someday you may find yourself feeling alone, and you won't know where to turn. But if you follow your heart, you will hold the answers in your hands. Carve away, my dear, and your legacy may shape the future."

Pinocchio stuck the knife in his belt loop and joined his friends. Alice reappeared next to Peter's side with the cloak slung over her shoulder, and Peter's shadow retreated somewhere in the darkness of a nearby corner. As for Gretel, she watched her friends from behind Violet's wings, rubbing her eyes until they were red. Pinocchio wondered if maybe she was sad because Violet didn't give her a present.

"Be on your way," Violet called, "and please, do be safe. I should warn you that Kaa is still alive, and I would never forgive myself if something happened to any of you."

CHAPTER NINE

THREE YEARS AGO—THE OLD WORLD: DWARVES' COTTAGE

"Who is that handsome gentleman? I must know."

"Why, it's still you, Master. You, Hansel, the bravest, ablest, and most handsome lad in the land."

"Sir, how you flatter me with your words. If only you were a real person."

"I am very real, Master, real as the sun in the sky. You can free me from my prison."

"How I long to set you free . . . Tell me how to liberate you from your ivory prison, other Hansel."

Hansel stood less than a foot away from the mirror, waiting for his reflection to say more, but the other Hansel went silent.

This had been going on for nearly a week. Hansel would wake up in the morning, send the dwarves off to work, and wander to the mirror on the wall. He couldn't explain the strange pull the object began to exert over him shortly after he recovered from his injuries and Snow White and Prince Liam returned to their castle. The mirror's gravity pulled Hansel out of bed, away from the dinner table, and right back into his bedroom every time he tried to leave. He soon forgave the fact that it didn't contain a strong lead on Gretel's whereabouts, and the mirror became important in its own right.

Hansel talked to the mirror every day. Most times, it talked back. His reflection took on a life of its own, complimenting him and telling him what a wonderful human he was. But every time his reflection went silent, Hansel experienced a pang of loneliness and put his hand up to the cool glass. "Won't you speak to me? I wish to set you free."

One day, Hansel grew impatient with the mirror's silence.

"You answer me this instant, and you tell me how to free you from the looking glass!"

Silence.

"*I order you this instant*!"

Silence.

Hansel couldn't take anymore. He picked up a stone goblet, its rim dyed blood-red from wine, and he raised it high over his head. Baring his teeth, he wound his arm back and jammed the goblet into the mirror.

CRACK!

The goblet bounced off the glass, a thunderous vibration jolting his elbow. Hansel looked down, his breathing heavy and forced, and beheld scattered fragments of stone on the ground. The mirror, however, remained unscathed, and that's when he knew that it was cursed.

"You're the devil. You torment me with your poetic words and your flattering comments, and you don't tell me how to set you free. I cannot be rid of you, and yet I must be rid of you. I shall remove you from my wall and return you to your infernal cavern in the mines." Hansel gripped the mirror's smooth ivory edges, met his own brown eyes, and scowled. "You won't woo me with your gaze."

Hansel rocked back onto his heels and pulled on the mirror with all his force.

A thousand curses, wretched looking glass! Move!

Hansel pulled until his fingers screamed and his arms threatened to fall off. The mirror simply wouldn't move. It stuck to his wall like his shadow stuck to his toes, his reflection defiant.

Angry and exhausted, Hansel stood upright again and pressed his forehead to the mirror, his eyes tightly shut and his fingertips digging into his palms.

What have I done? Think, Hansel, think.

Then he had one more idea.

I'll cover it up with a drape, so I can never see my reflection again.

Hansel strode confidently into the dining room and swept a thick black cloth from the table, shaking out a collection of breadcrumbs he assumed Jinn or Chann had left behind. Hansel returned to his room, fluffed the cloth in front of him, and he sealed his reflection away forever.

"Good riddance," he hissed.

That's when it happened.

Hansel's joints locked as he watched the cloth take a brand new shape. First it was just a small bulge in the center, protruding outward as if being pulled away from the wall. Then five bulges, evenly fanned out and reaching for his face. *Fingertips.* His heart skipped a beat, and he prepared to turn around and run. But when the fingertips receded, the imprint of a slender face leapt forth. The cloth fluttered and rippled as the face began to shriek, and Hansel thought he might keel over with insanity. He knew the voice behind the cloth.

"Hansel, help me! Get me out of this mirror!"

CHAPTER TEN

TODAY—THE NEW WORLD: JUST OUTSIDE THE EMPIRE STATE BUILDING

Rosana was losing hope.

She was pretty sure the police gave up. She called from a payphone every day, asking about her mother or any leads on the mysterious "Wayland." She always got the same answers. "Nothing, kid. Chin up and go home."

She'd jump on the subway. She'd ride it forward and back, and then she'd take another one. And another. She'd cover every inch of the underground tunnels, paying special attention when she caught a glimpse of an orange cap, a newspaper stand, or an apple on the ground. She kept her earbuds in and her guard up. Sometimes, after a fruitless day of searching, she'd grow tired and stare at the gold stars on the wall, letting them lull her to sleep.

Finally, she decided to find another perspective. All this time, she'd been underground, on the streets, too close to the problem. She wanted another angle.

So she put on her earbuds and stood in line outside the Empire State Building.

Maybe a bird's-eye view is what I need, she thought. *Yeah, right. As if I'll spot my mom from eighty-six stories off the ground.*

In the line, the burden of loneliness weighed on her heart. If she didn't get any new ideas, she didn't know what she'd do next. All she knew is she couldn't do this alone anymore. She needed help. She needed to get to a place she had once shared with her mother, if only just to feel close to her again.

Maybe somewhere out there, somebody else felt just as helpless as she did. Maybe they were out there at the same time, needing her, too.

⌘⌘⌘

Enzo was finally hungry.

Pietro pulled over several times during the long drive to New York City, refilling his truck with gas and dodging into Circle K's for Cheetos and Pepsi. Enzo wondered how in the world Pietro maintained his lanky form with one hand on the wheel and the other in a bag of Cheetos. "You sure you don't want any, Enzo?"

"Yup. Not hungry."

"Okay, suit yourself!"

By the time they got to New York, Enzo's stomach was doing flips.

"Don't act like I'm starving you," Pietro said. "I offered you all my Cheetos."

"Yeah, but I need *real* food."

"What do you mean real food? It's not like Cheetos are made of plastic."

Enzo and Pietro sat down at Petrelli's, a cozy pizzeria lit by cheese-grater lamps, and ordered a meat lover pizza pie. That's when Pietro started talking funny.

"Hey, wouldn't it be cool if we were walking around the city and we randomly saw somebody who looks like *this*?" Pietro dug into his pocket and pulled out—Enzo couldn't believe it—a wooden figurine, no taller than three inches. This one was a beautiful girl, probably about his age, with straight, dark hair, green eyes, and a red hooded jacket. Pietro made her do a little jig on the Parmesan shaker.

"Pietro, you're weird." Enzo took a napkin and absorbed the grease off his pizza. "Why are you walking around with one of my dad's carvings in your pocket?"

"Because why not? You are, too. I'm just saying it'd be fun if we found someone who looked like her."

"Um, fat chance, dude. That's like trying to find the guy on the oatmeal box. You can't, because he's not real. Even if he were, why would you wanna meet him?"

Pietro showered a load of peppers onto his pizza and took a huge bite. With his mouth full, he answered, "There you go with your 'it's not real' thing again. Cheetos aren't real. The guy on the oatmeal box isn't real. This girl isn't real. Who cares about real? The oatmeal box would be boring without that goofy Quaker's face on it. And life would be less fun without your dad's carvings. Live a little. We're in the Big Apple, and there are probably millions of other people here with us. I'm only saying it would be a fun coincidence if we found her." He pushed the carving closer to Enzo. "Plus, she's kinda cute, isn't she?"

Enzo rubbed the back of his neck. "Well, yeah, but . . ." He shook his head. "C'mon, Pietro. I'm more concerned about finding my parents right now. Didn't you just tell me that was our main concern this morning?"

Pietro sighed and balled up a napkin. "You're right. Forgive me for trying to lighten the mood. It's not like I'm not worried about them, Enzo."

"Then let's do something! I don't wanna sit here and eat pizza and watch you play around with those stupid toys." Enzo regretted the words as soon as they came out of his mouth. If he never saw his father again, those *stupid toys* would be one of the only things he'd have to remember him by. He thought about all the times he'd snapped at his dad, and his heart wilted. "Look, can we just go somewhere else now? Anywhere else?"

"I know where you really wanna go!" Pietro slid back in his chair and hopped up. "Let's take the subway!"

⌘⌘⌘

Before they boarded the subway, a poster caught Pietro's eye near the turnstiles:

Now Showing at the Gershwin Theater: Peter Pan on Broadway! Starring Angela Queen.

"This is ridiculous. You see that, Enzo?"

"See what?"

"That Peter Pan poster on the wall. I don't like it. Look who's playing Peter Pan."

"So? A chick always plays Peter Pan in live shows. Pretty sure Tinker Bell in Disneyland is a guy, too."

Pietro cringed. That was the weirdest thing to think about. "Okay, but look at the color of her hair! In what world does Peter Pan have black hair?"

"It's Angela Queen. She can do what she wants."

"Hmph."

When they boarded the subway, Enzo spent most of his time staring out the window. Pietro stood with one hand on the rail, scanning the passengers. He studied every individual he could see in three-hundred-and-sixty degrees, pausing when he spotted anyone with long dark hair and wearing a simple hoodie. His efforts were fruitless. Nobody on the subway looked remotely like the girl his friend carved for him.

Pino, you suck. This is gonna be a wild-goose chase.

They got off on 34th Street and ascended to street level, where Pietro grumbled over another advertisement for *Peter Pan on Broadway*. Day turned to twilight, and the sun met the horizon. A sea of people made up the line to get into the Empire State Building, wrapping all the way around the corner and stretching past one of the many Starbucks.

Pietro elbowed Enzo as they fell in line. "Should be quite a sight, huh? NYC all lit up at night?"

Enzo pulled out his figurine and held it up to the horizon. "Yeah, for sure."

⌘⌘⌘

"Well, Enzo, here we are. Sure is a beautiful thing, isn't it?"

"Yeah. It's pretty cool, I guess."

"Bit nippy though, huh? Did you pack a jacket in your duffel bag?"

"I think so."

"Good."

They didn't say anything for a long time. Enzo took pictures with his phone, and Pietro mostly stared up rather than out. In the distance, a star flew across the sky and trailed off somewhere over the Brooklyn Bridge.

"There!" Pietro said, pointing into the horizon. "You gonna make a wish?"

"You can have it. I don't believe in that stuff."

"I see. Well, whenever you're ready." Pietro shoved his hands in his pockets. "I think we should probably head back down soon. I don't remember where we left the truck, and we need to find a hotel."

"Sounds good."

"But hey, why don't we ask someone to take a picture of us? We can start a little photo journal and show your dad all the cool places we visited when we find him. Cool?"

"Cool."

"Who should we ask?" Pietro's gaze flittered around the crowd. His eyes froze on a single point. "Wait a minute! Enzo! Doesn't she kind of look like . . . ?"

Enzo saw it, too. Pietro was gesturing to a girl who had been staring out toward the Statue of Liberty. Even with her back turned, it wasn't hard to see what he was excited about. Her dark hair. Her red hood. When she turned around, Enzo's heart nearly stopped. It was like watching a wax figure come to life. The stark green eyes. The slight tan. She literally *was* the carving Pietro had shown him at the pizza place. *No way.*

Pietro smirked. "Wanna start looking for that oatmeal guy now?"

Just then, something equally strange happened. On the other side of the tower, Enzo saw a guy he recognized. His stomach lurched when he realized the young man he was looking at was the same guy who pelted Pietro with apples back at home. Enzo blinked a few times, certain his eyes were playing tricks on him, but when he glanced again, there he was, with his hood and basket of fruit. *How'd he get* those *through security?* But this time, another person accompanied him, a short, chunky man with a graying beard and a thick maroon coat that said *I Heart Dragons*. The two walked side by side, making a deliberate beeline for the red-hooded girl.

"What did I tell you, Enzo? This is insane!" Pietro held his figurine between his face and the girl. "She looks just like her. We should get her over here! Ask her to take our picture!"

"Sure but um, Pietro?" Enzo nodded in the apple guy's direction. "Look who else is here."

Pietro's mouth fell open in sheer terror. He ducked behind Enzo and stared vigilantly at the strange men. "Oh, no, I can't take another apple beating!"

Enzo fixed his gaze on the girl. "Who do you think she is?"

Then he thought about what had happened at his home, and he had another thought. *She's probably in danger.*

⌘⌘⌘

Most people who live in New York don't appreciate what this statue means because they see it every day.

As Rosana stared out at the Statue of Liberty, she heard her mother's soft voice and wondered if the same was true about everything else in life. When Rosana saw her mother every day, she was pretty sure she didn't say I love you enough. She didn't give her enough hugs. She didn't carry enough of a conversation. Maybe she didn't appreciate what it meant to have a mother.

If you were here now, though, I would never let you go again.

Rosana sighed and watched a shooting star blaze through the sky. *I just wish you'd come home.* She turned around and decided it was time to head back to the subway. As she made her way through the crowd, a scrawny guy a little taller than her, clad in jeans and a Muse t-shirt, sped toward her. He half-walked-half-jogged in front of a tall, lanky man with sandy-colored hair, who looked like a walking Nike advertisement. She wanted to assume they were father and son, but they didn't look related at all. The younger stranger stopped in front of her, his forehead coated in a thin film of sweat.

"Excuse me. Um, I know you don't know me and this is random, but will you walk with me for a sec?" He glanced nervously over his shoulder, took Rosana's sleeve, and pulled her around the corner.

Rosana jerked her arm away. "Yes, excuse you! What's your problem? Do you always start conversations with girls this way?"

"No! It's not like that! I mean . . ." The boy peeked around the corner, and his eyes widened in alarm. "Look, I'm sorry. That was rude, but there are two shady dudes up here, and one of them broke into my house this morning. A few minutes later, my dad disappeared, and now those guys are here and they were totally checking you out right now. Please walk with me?"

The taller man put one hand on the boy's back and used another to seize Rosana's hood and pull it over her head. "Come on, let's do a lap," he said briskly. "Keep your hood up and keep walking."

Rosana's nervous system whirred into action. *This guy's dad disappeared. Red flag!* "First of all, don't touch me again, either of you. Second of all, who *are* you people? And who was checking me out?"

"I'm gonna confront them," the boy said to his friend. "I want them to give me answers."

"Don't you do it, Enzo! Don't walk away from me! Hey, you, I told you not to take your hood down. Come over here and stay out of their sight!" The tall man took out his phone. "Let's act like we're taking a selfie."

"How is that gonna help, Pietro?"

The man named Pietro hooked his fingers into the neck of Enzo's shirt while Enzo tried to squirm away. With the other hand, Pietro pulled up the camera on his phone.

Rosana found it hard not to stare at the two, her gaze darting between them like they were two acts in a three-ring circus. *What is going on?*

Then, the third act began. Something shiny and red soared into view and popped Pietro in the side of the head. "*Ow!*" Pietro cried. "That *hurt!*"

"There they are!" a deep voice bellowed from behind Rosana. "That's The Carver's son and The Flying Man! And *her*! Get 'em, Bo!"

Rosana turned and faced a short man in a maroon coat. *I Heart Dragons*. There was something disturbingly familiar about him. He reminded her of Wayland, the man who probably took her mother away. Next to him, an athletic-looking, hooded guy started launching apples at Pietro. Rosana's heart accelerated, and she opened her mouth to tell the guy to stop, but her thoughts were interrupted when the bearded man seized her wrist.

"You're coming with me, princess."

"Hey!" Rosana dug her nails into the man's hand. "Let me go!"

"*Ow! Ow! Ow!* Cut that out, ya jerk!" Pietro had his arms up in front of him, trying to block the constant barrage of fruit coming at his face. Enzo broke into a run, seemingly ready to tackle the men.

"Help me!" Rosana cried. "He's trying to abduct me! Abduction, abduction!"

A crowd of bystanders turned their heads, and a fuss began.

A man in a cowboy hat pointed to Rosana. "Hey! That man is trying to leave with that little girl! Somebody stop him!"

Rosana cringed to hear herself be called a little girl, but she was grateful to hear somebody trying to defend her. The man in the cowboy hat raised a fist at the bearded man but promptly went down and landed on his back when the hooded guy pelted him in the forehead with an apple.

More people tried to come to Rosana's rescue: security guards, women with heavy purses, men who knew karate, teenagers with cell phones, but the apples got every last one of them before they could touch Rosana or the bearded captor. His arm moved with lightning speed, and his basket of apples didn't seem to have a bottom. Soon, people were slipping on fruit and tripping over unconscious bodies, and the only people left standing on the Empire State Building were Rosana, Enzo and his lanky friend, and the two strange figures who had come to abduct her. Pietro and the boy stood with their fists clenched, ready to dodge any apples the hooded guy might try to throw at them.

"Now, now, princess, let that be a lesson to you," the bearded man said. "When you open your mouth and start screaming, people get hurt. Look at all these people my friend just knocked out. Highly unnecessary, and not at all what we had planned."

"Let her go!" the boy shouted. "She's done nothing to you!"

"Not in the mood to argue." The bearded man snapped his fingers. "Bo, take him down. The Flying Man, too. No more playing around."

Rosana watched in horror as the hooded guy produced one more apple and chucked it at the boy's face. He tried to dodge it, but the apple flew too fast. It clocked him in his temple, and the boy went down without a sound.

But strangest of all was what happened to Pietro, something Rosana wasn't sure if she saw correctly. First, his shadow stretched out along the ground and seemed to dance away from his body until it was independent from his toes. Then the shadow peeled itself off the ground, hovering in the air with arms spread like eagle wings, and it darted around the top of the tower with dizzying agility. The strange hooded guy watched it fly and tried to pelt it with apples, but the shadow was too fast.

Rosana looked back to Pietro. *Whoa.* His Nikes hovered about a foot off the ground, and he was holding his unconscious, younger friend over his shoulders. "Wow, it *does* work here! Wicked!" He nodded at

Rosana. "Don't be afraid, kid. Whatever you do, hold on tight."

Rosana gasped as Pietro floated ten more feet off the ground, stuck his tongue out at Bo, and at almost supersonic speed, he and his friend soared over the railing and into the New York night.

The bearded man growled. "Curses, I told you we should've brought a dragon! Let's get the girl out of here!"

Rosana heard a thunderous *slap* and the bearded man winced in pain, releasing his grip on Rosana's wrist. In his place, someone else took her hand. Or some*thing*. It was Pietro's shadow, dark and slender, and much warmer than Rosana would've expected. *What the . . . ?*

"Bo, don't let her escape, you idiot!" The bearded man reached for Rosana's other wrist. He was too late. The shadow lifted Rosana high into the air, her heart racing like a hummingbird. It hovered for a while, taunting Bo and his friend, and then it flew Rosana away from them at a terrifying speed.

CHAPTER ELEVEN

THREE YEARS AGO—THE WOODLANDS

Hansel had uncovered the mirror again.

He wasn't concerned with talking to himself anymore. His reflection still spoke to him sometimes and assured him of his strength and handsomeness, but Hansel was much more interested in the other things the looking glass began to show him.

Sometimes the mirror seemed to be more of a window. Sometimes Hansel saw his face, scarring over before his eyes. Other days, he approached the glass and beheld a vision of a distant part of the realm.

The strangest one was the vision of the tall edifices reaching for the stars, almost entirely surrounded by dark water. The image panned across a vast expanse of land Hansel had never seen before, and he wondered what sort of black magic powered the structures. There must have been a thousand buildings, including a statue of a pale green woman in the water, clutching a book and raising a torch to the night sky. Not a single structure was made of materials Hansel was used to seeing. Straw. Wood. Clay. Polished rock. Instead, it appeared to be a city of glass, concrete, and artificial lights brighter than any lantern. And how beautiful it was!

"Mirror, where is this?"

The mirror didn't reply. Instead, a blur like running water cleared the city away, and a new place appeared. This one looked slightly more familiar, but only marginally. Trees. Mud. Men and women donned in royal garb. In the distance, a small castle rose from the mud. The image froze on the castle before a deep voice boomed through the scene, "*Lords and ladies of the wood, there will be death on our fields this day!*" The castle portcullis opened, and two cavaliers on horseback burst forth with lances. The two armored men battled each other, their steeds charging in circles, while a familiar figure watched the action from the sidelines. He looked like nothing more than a mere peasant, an image at which Hansel had to smirk and marvel. Where was his royal attire?

It couldn't be.

"Is that Prince Liam?" Hansel inquired. "Where's Snow? What are you showing me?"

The image faded again, and the other Hansel returned. "Master, I show you what is yet to come. I reveal your glorious destiny."

"I don't understand any of this. What's my destiny?"

The other Hansel stepped away, and his sister took his place. Hansel's heart leapt to his throat, and he reached for Gretel's image. She hadn't aged a day since he last saw her. Her eyes were big and blue, and her hair was still in a tight braid. She wore a long white gown decorated with pink bows. She was still the innocent little girl that used to journey through the woods with him.

"Gretel! It's really you?"

Hansel thought he might cry when Gretel reciprocated his eye contact. "Brother, it's me. You have to get me out. You must set me free."

"My God. You're really in the mirror! I heard you calling my name from the cavern! I knew you were down there! Everyone kept telling me you were lost forever, but I knew! I knew it in my heart!"

Hansel placed a gentle hand on the mirror, half expecting to feel the texture of his sister's hair, but his fingers only met cool, smooth glass.

Gretel nodded. "It's really me. I've been here all along. It's dark and scary in here. Please let me out!"

Hansel fought back a sob. His emotions congealed in a lump, tightening his throat.

"Tell me how to release you. Please, tell me how to free you!"

Gretel's lips curved into a frown. "Do you promise to help me?"

"I promise! With all of my being, I'll do whatever it takes to rescue you and bring you home safe."

"Okay . . . ."

Then Gretel's face faded to ash and billowed away, leaving only darkness in the mirror.

A sharp tug yanked on Hansel's stomach, and he sank to his knees. "No! Where are you going? Gretel! Come back!"

It was getting to be too much. Over the years, he'd repeatedly gone through every wave of emotion. Denial. Anger. Bargaining. Depression. Brief periods of acceptance followed by haunting phases of guilt.

The day he learned about her disappearance, he had been in the meadows with Snow White, talking and looking up at the clouds. Hansel and Snow named all the colors in the sky as the sun melted away, signaling the beginning of a shimmering spectacle of constellations.

Then Violet appeared.

Her eyes were ridden with worry, and her wings wilted like old rose petals. She took a knee, grasped Hansel's hand, and calmly told him that his sister had vanished in "an unfortunate accident." The rest of her words may as well have been made of sand, as Hansel's memory washed them away with time. He only remembered insisting that it wasn't true, then demanding to know where Pinocchio and his friends were, and, finally, crying until he thought his eyes would bleed.

Hansel found comfort in Snow White during the following years, but never enough to keep him from wondering what could've been. Snow asked him to continue meeting her in the meadow every day so she would know that he was okay. Most days, he did, but there were intervals where Hansel's grief was too strong, anchoring him to his bed or pulling him into other parts of the realm to seek answers. He didn't know if these periods lasted days, weeks, or years. He only knew that one was long enough for Snow White to find love, and that none were long enough to find Gretel.

I couldn't save her, he kept thinking. *She saved me from that witch, and I couldn't save her from whatever took her away.*

That's what Hansel was thinking again when he watched Gretel's image fade away from the mirror. She had come back and taunted him, insisting that she was still alive and that Hansel could have a chance to bring her back, and then she turned to dust and left him in ruins again. It was the last straw. Hansel curled into a tight ball, hugged his knees tight against his chest, and lay on his side, crying for what seemed like an eternity.

I wish I'd done things differently.

I wish I'd never let my sister out of my sight.

I wish I were dead.

"Get up."

The voice that cut his thoughts short was rough, harsh, and icy, just like the witch's in the Cavern of Ombra.

"Off the ground. Face me."

Wiping away the last of his tears, Hansel pulled himself back to his feet and looked into the mirror once more. It didn't show his reflection, his sister, or the city of lights he found so mesmerizing. It showed him the chamber at the end of the mineshaft, dark, circular, and adorned with large red crystals. It was the Cavern of Ombra.

"So you'd do anything to save your sister?"

"Yes. I'd do anything. Just tell me what I have to do."

"You shall be my huntsman. You shall gather seven souls of my choosing and bring them to the Cavern of Ombra, one at a time and only when I ask for them."

"Huntsman? Seven? What do you mean? Who are you?"

"I am Queen Avoria, your only hope of finding your sister."

The image on the mirror changed, and a woman appeared in a padded chair, reading a novel and drinking a fizzing beverage. She appeared to be about forty years old, her mousy hair with flecks of silver gathered into a neat bun. "This is The Carver's wife," the alleged queen explained. "You will start with her. Bring her to me, and you will be one step closer to freeing your sister."

CHAPTER TWELVE

TODAY—THE NEW WORLD: SOMEWHERE IN NEW YORK CITY

Pietro couldn't believe it.

He actually flew! He'd wanted to do that again for ages. He'd never tried in the new world, but man, how he missed it! The feeling of weightlessness and freedom and becoming his own navigator in three dimensions . . . There was nothing like it. Doing it here added a new element of fun. He felt like, what was that guy's name? *Iron Man!* What's more, his shadow flew, too. He wouldn't have known what to do if that hadn't worked.

They came back to the ground somewhere near the edge of Manhattan, in a quiet, dark alley where presumably nobody would see a flying man and his shadow descend from the stars. His shadow lowered the panicked red-hooded girl gently to the ground and then returned dutifully to Pietro's heel.

"Good shadow." Pietro shifted the unconscious Enzo to his other shoulder, worked out a kink in his back, and made eye contact with the girl. *Poor thing*. The sheer terror in her eyes. Pietro rubbed the back of his neck and smiled nervously. And that's when the girl opened her mouth to scream.

"Ah—"

"No, no, no. Don't scream!" Pietro pleaded. "Please! Let me explain! I'm one of the good guys. I promise."

The girl narrowed her eyes. "You'd better start talking or I'm gonna call someone. I have NYPD on speed dial."

"Don't we all? Anyway, I really need you to stick around and keep calm, but this isn't the best place to talk. We need to find a room, somewhere this little guy can rest his head and I can tell you everything. At least give me time for that, please."

The girl put her hands on her hips and tapped her foot, clearly unimpressed with Pietro's offer.

"Aw, c'mon! I did save you from those creepy dudes on top of the Empire State Building. You have to give me that much."

The girl aimed her chin at the air. "I had it under control. I could've saved myself, thank you very much."

Pietro didn't budge. Finally, the girl sighed.

"Okay, fine. I'll come with you. But if you do that weird shadow thing again without asking, or if I feel like you're lying to me, I'm going to the police and telling them you kidnapped me. Got it?"

Pietro's eyes lit up. "Yup. Now we need to get to my truck, and then we need to check into the nearest hotel. If I don't set this guy down soon, I'm gonna drop like a codfish."

⌘⌘⌘

Rosana knew she wasn't stupid. Any other day, she would've run away before she would enter a hotel room with two male strangers, but today was far from normal. How could *anything* be normal when a shadow had just peeled itself away from a grown man's body, lifted Rosana into the air, and carried her far away from two men who allegedly wanted to abduct her? While she didn't entirely trust The Flying Man, her adrenaline beckoned her to follow him. She needed to know his story, and she knew that, somehow, they were supposed to meet. Her mind had barely had time to come back to the ground when The Flying Man tossed her a pair of duffel bags from his truck and carried the unconscious boy down the street.

They walked into a hotel and got some suspicious looks from the staff, but the man was able to reserve a room for three, where he set the boy down on one of the beds and tucked a pillow underneath his head.

Rosana cornered Pietro and folded her arms. "Start talking. Who are you?"

"My name is Pietro Volo. A friend sent me to find you."

"Keep going. Who sent you, and why?"

Pietro fished a wooden carving out of his pocket and tossed it to Rosana. "His name is Pino DiLegno. He's my best friend. He's a woodcarver, and a pretty good one as you can see."

Rosana caught the figurine and studied it, eyes full of awe. "This is me!"

"Yup. Pretty cool, huh? He carved a whole bunch of those things in his free time. Men, women, children, animals, buildings, everything. Before he was abducted, that is."

Rosana shifted her gaze between Pietro and the figurine. "Abducted?"

"Yup. This sleeping prince on the bed here? That's Enzo, his son. The poor kid watched his dad get taken from his home just this morning."

Rosana felt a wave of pity for the sleeping boy. She knew how he must've been feeling. "That's terrible, but I don't understand. Why would this Pino guy make a tiny wooden statue of me?"

"I'm still trying to figure that out, but his instructions were clear. He told me to take the kid and find *you*, and here we are all together now. Also, those freaky dudes who attacked us up on the Empire State Building? One of them attacked us this morning, too, just outside Richmond. My guess is this wasn't a coincidence."

Rosana sat on the bed and rubbed her face. "I think I need coffee."

Pietro grinned. "Sweet! You should hang out with this kid more. He needs more coffee in his life. What's your name?"

"Rosana."

"Rosana, can you think of a reason why that man and his freaky apple guy might've been after you today?"

Rosana chewed on one of her fingernails. "I don't know. But six months ago, somebody took my mom away. He looked a little bit like the guy who grabbed me tonight."

Pietro's expression wilted. "I'm sorry to hear that. Your mom, what was she like?"

"Kind of a mystery sometimes. She had this raging thirst for adventure. Always traveling to different countries and states. I'm pretty sure she's been everywhere, but she never talked about any of the places she'd go to."

"She sounds cool," Pietro said. "I kinda knew a girl like that when I was growing up. And you have no idea why she was taken away?"

"Nope, but I know I'm getting her back."

The boy opened his eyes and jolted up on the bed, startling Rosana. "No more apples!"

"Whoa, easy, kid!" Pietro said. "How ya feelin'?"

The boy rubbed his forehead and frowned. "I have a headache. Hey, you're that girl!"

"Enzo, meet Rosana."

"Hi." Rosana tucked a lock of hair behind her ear and reached out to shake Enzo's hand. When she touched his hand, a spark of electricity cracked between their fingers.

"*Ow!* Um, hey. I'm Crescenzo DiLegno. Enzo for short."

The way his full name rolled off his tongue. It was distractingly beautiful. "Wow, that's a cool name. Does it mean anything?"

"Um, I think it has something to do with being made of wood or whatever. It's kinda stupid."

"I love it." Rosana's gaze lingered over Enzo's face for a minute. *Don't stare too hard. Think of something else to talk about.* "So, I have a question that's been bugging me, Pietro. How come you can fly?"

Pietro aimed his back at the teenagers. "I don't know what you're talking about."

"The part where you carried Enzo off the roof and basically dive-bombed back to the ground? You flew! And you did this weird shadow thing that made me fly, too."

Enzo's eyes widened. "Pietro did what?"

Great, now he thinks I'm insane.

Pietro's face flattened. "She's talking in riddles, kid. We took the elevator down together like normal people, and we pretended we were flying."

"Come on!" Rosana groaned.

"Pietro, what's she talking about?"

"Really don't know. Crazy talk. Who wants food?"

Rosana marched up to Pietro and stuck a finger in his face. "I'm not talking crazy. You know what I'm talking about. I'm fed up with people telling me that I'm talking crazy! Why am I with you, anyway? What's the point?"

Pietro held up a hand. "Chill, kid. We can help you look for your mom."

"Wait a minute," Enzo said. "Your mother's missing?"

"Yes, taken. Sorry about your parents, by the way."

"Thanks. Wait. Your mom, and my mom and dad, and Pietro's family?" Enzo scooted off the bed and stood next to Rosana. "Pietro, what's really going on here? Give us answers!"

"Can I have some time to think already? I don't know what's going on, okay? That's what I'm trying to figure out, but I can't think with all this teen angst in the room!" Pietro sighed through his nostrils. "Look, Rosana, I know nothing makes sense to you right now, but please come with us? I think we're supposed to help each other. My family's missing, too. I have a wife and a kid out there somewhere, and I need them, just like you need your mom and Enzo needs his parents. Let's just stick together, okay? Agreed?"

"Not until you admit that you flew." *But it's not like I have anywhere else to go.*

Pietro scowled. "Rude. Whatever, we flew. Happy now?"

"Good enough."

"Wait a minute," Enzo said. "I'm not happy! I'm, like, really confused, actually."

"Good," Pietro said. "Now let's think for a minute. Where do we go from here?"

Enzo rubbed his temple. "I don't even know anymore. My head still hurts. I'm gonna take a shower and go to bed. It's uh, nice to meet you, Rosana."

"You, too, Enzo." *Don't blush.* When Enzo was out of earshot, Rosana socked Pietro's shoulder. "What the hell was that all about? You trying to make me look insane? We flew off a building, and you totally just denied it in front of your friend!"

Pietro massaged his shoulder. "Look, I'm sorry if the flying shadow thing freaked you out, but I don't wanna tell Enzo the truth yet. We'll try to stick to the ground from now on, okay?" Pietro leaned back in the desk chair and propped his feet on the phonebook. "I'm going to sleep too."

"And then tomorrow?"

"Tomorrow, take me to wherever you were when your mom disappeared. G'nite."

Rosana removed her hoodie and threw her head back on the pillow. This was by far the weirdest day she'd ever had, and she had a feeling things were only about to get weirder.

CHAPTER THIRTEEN

THREE YEARS AGO—THE OLD WORLD: DWARF COTTAGE

Seven men sat at the table.

"Gentlemen"—Garon sat at the end with his hands weaved together—"we gather this morning to decide the fate of our housemate, Mister Hansel."

The words hung in the air. Nobody made eye contact. Nobody drank beer or ate pumpkin soup.

"Who would like to begin?"

Conversation exploded.

"He's gone mad!"

"He's our boss!"

"He's off his rocker!"

"He's providing for us!"

"He's only out for himself!"

The words clashed in a chaotic jumble until Garon seized a stone goblet and brought it down on the table with thunderous force. "Silence!"

Nobody dared defy the eldest dwarf.

"One at a time, please."

Jinn raised a greasy hand, prompting Wayde to duck under the table and hold his nose. Garon signaled Jinn to make his case. "I don't think it's fair for us to be so critical of Hansel after two weeks of living with him. We've barely given him a chance, and look to whom we compare him, the fairest in the land! If we compare anybody to Snow, we're bound to find flaws. The fact is this: We shall never have another housemate like her."

Zid pounded the table. "Nobody means to criticize Mister Hansel for not being Snow. That is not why Garon called this meeting. We are civil men. Our complaints have little to do with his lower standards of cleanliness and his subpar cooking, or the fact that his dreadful singing scares the birds away."

There was a general murmur of agreement before Zid continued, "My complaint in particular has to do with Hansel's increasing disregard for a civil tongue and his abominably short temper."

Nobody argued.

Garon stroked his beard, a troubled gleam burning in his eyes. "Does anyone wish to specify an occasion in which Hansel has not been civil with you?"

"Yesterday." Wayde twiddled his thumbs and averted his gaze from the rest of the party. "I went to speak with Mister Hansel, and I found him gazing into his mirror on the wall."

Bo let out a long, fastidious groan. "He's *always* in front of that mirror now! That's what it is. That's the source of our problems. Hansel has become so obsessed with his appearance that he cannot bear to part with his own reflection."

"One has to wonder why," Jinn said. "The man's no Prince Liam, especially with that new gash on his cheek."

"Hmph. You're no treasure yourself."

"You button your lips, Finn!"

"Silence!" Attention returned to Garon. "We've lost focus again. Wayde, please continue."

"He was staring into his mirror, and I asked him if he would like someone else to prepare supper tonight. He wouldn't acknowledge my presence. I confess, I got a bit frustrated, and I tried to pull him away from his reflection. And you know what he did?"

"Kissed himself goodbye?" Bo guessed.

"No."

"What did he do?"

"He struck me across the face!" Wayde wailed.

"I don't believe you!" Chann said. "Hansel would do no such thing."

Wayde looked down.

Garon raised an eyebrow and tugged on his beard. "Wayde, this is a grave accusation. Why raise it only now?"

"I was nervous to say anything. If we confront Mister Hansel, what will he do?"

Silence passed as the miners considered Wayde's words.

Garon broke the silence. "Are there additional complaints of this nature?"

"I think we should give Mister Hansel the benefit of the doubt," Jinn said. "We know not what troubles his mind. He could be thinking of his sister, he could be stressed about the move, and we know not what happened in that cavern! Snow and Prince Liam say he woke up mumbling about the old witch he and his sister torched in her own oven."

"That is to be considered," Garon said. "Perhaps we should trace the problem to its source."

"It's that damned looking glass," Zid said. "I know it in my bones! When we brought Hansel and that chest back up from the mines, we brought something else back with us, and we must do something about it. We must save Mister Hansel and banish his demons back to hell! That cursed mirror has got to go."

CHAPTER FOURTEEN

TWENTY-FIVE YEARS AGO—THE OLD WORLD: EN ROUTE TO DARK CASTLE

It hadn't been so long ago that Pinocchio was made of wood.

His joints creaked, his fingers were stiff, and he didn't have a heartbeat. That was one of the strangest things to get used to after Violet had turned him into a real boy, that vital sign of life pulsing within his chest and the way its movements depended on his emotions. When he was sad, it jumped into his throat and made him cry. When he relaxed, so did his heart, pumping blood only a little faster than his father's pocket watch ticked. Then there was the way it acted on the road to the Dark Castle.

Pinocchio paused in the middle of the serpentine trail and stared at the castle ahead, eyes wide with wonder and fear. It was just the kind of place his father would forbid him from going into. Like the mines.

Peter and Alice turned around and gazed at their friend. "What is it, Pin? Are you alright?"

Pinocchio put his right hand over his chest and concentrated. His heart seemed to be tapping a secret code into his fingers. "My heart. It's dancing, but it's not like a happy dance. It's beating like a scared hummingbird."

"Don't be frightened, Pinocchio," Alice said. "Violet gave us protection."

That's right, Pinocchio thought. He traced the smooth handle tucked into his belt. *A knife, a red cloak, and a runaway shadow.*

"Plus," Peter said, "as long as we stay together, nothing can get us."

Pinocchio fixed his eyes on the structure looming ahead. It was made up of a dull material so black and empty that it looked like somebody had taken his knife and carved a jagged, asymmetrical hole out of the horizon. It was more shadow than substance and more darkness than light. Its turrets reminded Pinocchio of stalactites, or of crooked wolf teeth.

"Can we hold hands on our way in?"

Peter sighed. "Pinocchio, you wanna be a grown-up, don't you? You want people to take you cereally?"

"Yeah."

"Being grown up means you're not allowed to be afraid of stuff."

"Oh, Peter, don't be mean. We're still children. We're allowed to be a *little* afraid. Pinocchio, take my hand."

"You two are such scruffians! We'll never get anything done if you two are gonna be stupid chickens. We have to be fearless."

"If you're so fearless, Peter Pan, you go ahead of us. By yourself."

"Fine, then."

"Fine!"

"Fine." Peter hovered a few inches off the ground and prepared to fly away.

"No," Pinocchio said. "We shouldn't split up. Stay with us. Please?"

"Just let him go, Pinocchio. He'll come right back to us, crying."

"No, I won't. Just wait and see. I'll be in and out before you even make it to the castle. I'll bring the mirror back without you two!"

"Fine!"

"*Fine*!" Peter hovered far above his friends' heads, stuck his tongue out, and sped away toward the gloomy shadows ahead, spidery tree branches threatening to grasp his feet.

Pinocchio swallowed a lump in his throat and took Alice's hand, cold and sweaty. Together, they continued down the winding and narrowing path to the castle. Alice sang and hummed songs she said she learned in a place called Wonderland, quelling Pinocchio's fears. As Alice sang louder and the trail grew smaller, he grew braver.

But then, something cut Alice's song short in the middle of a word, and Pinocchio felt a tight squeeze on his palm.

"Pinocchio, have I gone mad, or is this road moving?"

Pinocchio squinted and tried to adjust his eyes. It was tough to see the path with all the shadows washing the world with darkness. Once he found his focus on a point not so far away, he understood what his companion meant. "I think so. It looks like it's making an 'S'. And it's dancing."

Alice looked at her toes. "But the road under our feet isn't dancing, is it?"

"I don't think so."

Pinocchio watched in horror as the dancing road made a small hump and inched forward. He was becoming more and more certain that the road ahead wasn't made of cobblestones, dull and cracked. They looked a bit more like scales, icy rainbows bouncing off shimmering ridges.

Alice turned ghost-white. "Pin, that isn't the road."

Pinocchio gulped, and a long portion of the path ahead slithered toward him and his friend at a frightening velocity. He wished more than ever that Peter hadn't left them. Alice was right. They weren't looking at the road anymore.

They were looking at a hundred-foot snake.

CHAPTER FIFTEEN

TWENTY-FIVE YEARS AGO—
EN ROUTE TO DARK CASTLE

Peter always said the worst part about having a shadow was that sometimes it got away from him and it didn't always go where he wanted it to go. He remembered one time when he chased it all the way into the bathtub, and then he had no choice but to take a bath. That really made him mad.

Luckily, even when Peter couldn't see where his shadow was going, he always had a pretty good idea where to find it again. Most peoples' shadows were hardwired to stick to their bodies. Peter felt hardwired to stick to his shadow.

And so it happened that shortly after Peter separated from Alice and Pinocchio on the way to the Ivory Queen's castle, his shadow separated from him, too. The sun had already gone down and he hadn't been able to see his shadow for a while, but he had that gut feeling. Whenever it slipped away, it felt *wrong*, the way it did when he lost his first tooth.

Peter floated in the air for a while and concentrated as hard as he could, scrunching up his face and sniffing around. He wasn't sure if the sniffing helped, but it seemed like something he should do. *Where could it have gone this time?*

When he sensed it, he tumbled to the ground.

The good news was that his shadow hadn't gone too far. He could reunite with it without straying too far from his quest for the mirror. But the location also brought him a feeling of sorrow—the kind Peter had trouble explaining to his friends. He didn't want to chase his shadow anymore. He would've preferred to continue along the dark trail and venture into that nasty, old castle by himself. He would've even preferred to take a bath.

But that wasn't an option. Peter needed his shadow.

Alright, I'll go see her. Just this one last time.

When he arrived at Wendy Darling's house, he flew up to the second floor, where his freckled friend with honey-brown hair knelt in front of an open window. She stared up at the sky, arms crossed over the windowsill.

Peter hovered by the window and waved at Wendy.

Wendy's eyes brightened, and she reached for Peter's hand. "Peter! You've come back! I was so worried I'd never see you again!"

Instead of taking Wendy's hand, Peter crossed his arms and stuck his nose in the air. "I thought you didn't want to see me again. I only came back because my shadow flew away, and I think it's in your room."

Wendy sighed heavily and put her slender chin on her fists. "Oh. I see."

"Well? Have you seen it?"

Wendy hesitated. "Yes, Peter. Your shadow is here. Before I give it back to you, I must tell you something."

Peter lowered his chin and gazed into Wendy's eyes. "What is it, Wendy?"

Wendy spun and faced her door, evidently embarrassed. "I'm sorry for what I said. I don't really think you're a ruffian. Or a bad influence. And I really do want to be your friend."

Peter drifted to the windowsill and sat down, his heart twittering with glee. "You really mean that?"

Wendy paced around her room, tracing her fingers over worn

leather book spines and ceramic music boxes. "I really do. My dad is such a brute sometimes. He tells me to act like an adult, but he treats me like a child. He never lets me do anything for myself, and he's always bossing me around! *Wendy, you can't wear that to school tomorrow; let your mum pick out your clothes for you. Wendy, go fix your hair; it's dreadful. Wendy, pick up your room this instant or we'll send you to bed without supper*. Ugh! The only time I ever have fun is with you, Peter Pan. My life would be so dull without you."

Peter said nothing. His heart was crying because it was happy, like it had just found something it previously lost. Something vital that couldn't be seen, like the air he breathed.

"Peter?"

"You made me really sad. I was gonna go away so I wouldn't have to see you and be sad ever again."

Wendy stopped pacing, and her shoulders wilted. "Peter . . . ."

Peter finally uncrossed his arms and smiled. "But now I'm really happy!"

"Really? Does that mean you're not going away anymore?"

"I don't know. I have to help Alice and Pinocchio with something very important. We're on a mission from Violet, and Violet says if we help her, we'll grow up." Peter thought for a minute, rubbed his chin, and squinted his eyes. "Hey, you can come with us! Then you and me, we can grow up together and always be happy!"

Peter expected Wendy to smile, laugh, or hug him. Instead, she wrung her hands.

"How do we grow up?"

"We have to get two mirrors and make a wish! But not any two mirrors. They're *special* mirrors. Violet has one, and her stepmother, the queen, has the other. We have to steal the one from the queen and bring it to Violet, and she'll send us to a place where we can grow up!"

"We have to steal from the queen? I don't know, Peter, that sounds dangerous."

"But the queen put a man inside her mirror! We can be heroes and set him free, Wendy. And then we can be free. No more grown-ups telling us what to do, no more not getting taken seriously, no more spankings! Come on, what do you say? At least come to the castle with me. If you change your mind, I'll have time to say goodbye to you."

Wendy thought about it for a moment, and Peter could almost see the gears turning in her brain.

"I really want you to come with me, Wendy," Peter pleaded. "If not, my heart will be sad again."

"Hmm. Okay, Peter. I'll come with you. Just let me write a note for my family."

Peter couldn't stop himself. He scooted off the windowsill and wrapped Wendy in a tight hug. "I think my heart is dancing right now. It's happy."

Wendy kissed Peter on the cheek. "Mine, too, Peter Pan. Mine, too."

"Can I have my shadow back, then?"

Wendy turned red. "Oh, why yes, of course. It flew in through my window after I brushed my teeth, and I trapped it in my toy chest."

"Rude," Peter said. "You can't put my shadow in the toy box. It's not a toy."

"I know, Peter. It was silly. I just missed you and didn't want to let it go."

When Wendy opened her toy chest, Peter's shadow leapt out and glided around the floral-printed walls.

"There you are, you scruffian! Come back here!"

Peter dove for his shadow's ankle, but the silhouette zipped around the room and taunted him. It tap danced, made chicken wings, and Peter knew it would've been sticking its tongue out at him if it had one. Wendy covered her mouth and tried not to laugh.

And then in one swift motion, the shadow rocketed out the window and into the night sky. Peter already knew where it was headed. He wasn't so mad this time. He could go a few more minutes without a shadow, but he couldn't spend another without Wendy Darling.

CHAPTER SIXTEEN

TODAY—THE NEW WORLD: NEW YORK CITY SUBWAY

Pietro sat on a bench with Enzo and Rosana, drinking a caramel macchiato and trying to process what Rosana had just told them.

"So," he said, staring at the missing poster Rosana showed him, "you really come down here every single day no matter what?"

"Every single day, no matter what. Why wouldn't I?" Rosana sat in the middle with a bag of Cheetos, licking orange dust off her fingers.

"I just feel like I would get really frustrated coming here every day," Enzo said. "It's way too crowded. Plus, there's still no sign of your mom after all this time. How can you be so patient?"

"Wouldn't you do anything to find your family? Haven't you been looking every single day like me? The police aren't really helping me, so I'm doing everything myself."

Pietro thought for a minute. He *had* been doing everything he could, right? He was fairly certain that Zack and Wendy were both taken from home on a Saturday afternoon. It was a workday for him. He came home at six with Panda Express, and there was nobody there. Wendy's SUV was still in the driveway, but there was no clacking from her sewing machine, no blipping and blooping from Zack's PlayStation, no pattering of fingers on a laptop.

They weren't at Pino's, they weren't in the backyard, and nobody was doing laundry. Pietro called everyone he knew: Zack's school counselors—*"No, Mr. Volo, I'm afraid there was no field trip today"*—Wendy's coworkers—*"I'm sorry, dear, she had the day off"*—nothing from Zack's youth group, or Wendy's book club. After a few drives around the neighborhood, Pietro stayed up until four in the morning watching both his phone and the front door.

"I'm going to the police," he had told Pino. "I'm putting up missing posters and offering a reward and everything."

"You need to face the truth, my friend. Something from home got them."

"No, Pin, we left that home behind, remember? This is home now."

Pino's silence always hurt the worst.

A subway roar brought Pietro back to the present. It was surreal to be spending time with Rosana, a girl with so much in common with both he and Enzo.

"Rosana," Pietro said, "where's your home?"

Rosana put a drawstring from her hoodie into her mouth and chewed on the end. "New York."

"I mean your *home, home?* Where do you sleep?"

Enzo and Pietro watched Rosana cram more of her drawstring into her mouth and lower her gaze.

For a while, Rosana said nothing. She just chewed on her string and watched the trains go by. Then, without looking at either of the boys, she raised a hand and jerked a thumb behind her. "Right there."

Pietro wanted to hug the girl, but Enzo hugged her first, making Rosana turn red.

Pietro spun around and looked in the direction she had pointed her thumb. "Rosana . . . you sleep in the subway?"

"Yep. Have a bunch of clothes stashed behind that newspaper stand. I sneak back there when I'm ready to go to bed and I sleep. You'd be surprised how easy it is to be homeless in New York City. I was pretty scared, but hey, six months later, I'm still alive."

"And people leave you alone? What about food and showers and stuff?"

"Oh, they leave me alone. I can't really explain why. And it's not hard to find a place to shower. As for food, I basically live off the kindness of strangers, on a good day. People waste like it's their job. When it's not a good day, well . . ." Rosana shrugged. "I borrow things without asking and then I usually don't give them back."

Enzo's eyes widened. "A.K.A. stealing."

"I was trying not to use that word, but thanks."

Only then did Pietro realize his jeans felt lighter. He stood up and dug through his back pocket. His wallet wasn't there.

Rosana sheepishly produced a tattered, brown wallet from her jacket pocket. "Here. Sorry . . . I kinda borrowed your credit card for the Cheetos. I won't do it again."

You little thief. Pietro's blood pressure rose, but the guilt in Rosana's eyes brought it back down. She was just a young girl doing whatever she needed to do in order to survive. He used to be the same way. Maybe he still was.

Pietro pocketed his wallet and grasped Rosana's shoulders. "*Please,* don't do it again. I have to be able to trust you if we're going to help each other. If you need food, Rosana, just ask, okay? You don't have to steal anymore. We're all in this together until we find our families."

Rosana kept her drawstring in her mouth and avoided eye contact, nodding silently.

"So, uh, did you take anything else from me? Be honest. I know a guy who used to get in serious trouble every time he lied."

Rosana sighed and reached into her pocket again. Her fingers closed around something, and she hesitated before she pulled it out. She started tossing Enzo a series of small wooden figurines. Enzo caught them one at a time, his expression growing flatter with every figure he caught.

Pietro leaned forward and stared at the small items in Enzo's hands. "Enzo, where did you get those? More from your dad?"

"Yeah, he made these. He was dead set on making sure I took them with me."

"I'm sorry," Rosana said. "I saw them fall out of your bag before we left the hotel, and I picked them up. I was gonna give them back to you right away, but one of them reminded me of someone I know, and I wanted to hold onto it. I just think they're really interesting, that's all. I didn't know they were your dad's."

"No, it's okay," Enzo said. "Honestly, I only care about them now that he's missing. I used to hate these things."

"Can I see them, please?" Pietro aimed a palm to the ceiling.

"Sure." Enzo passed the figures.

"The short guy with the orange hat?" Rosana said. "He looks *exactly* like the guy who took my mom. It's creepy. Your dad really made all of these, Enzo? They're amazing."

Pietro studied the figurines, one by one, his mind reeling. The guy in the orange cap also looked like the man who tried to abduct Rosana yesterday, but his face was structured differently. Then there was the old man with the hooked nose and the red eyes. Truly the stuff of nightmares. The Chinese woman. The guy with the green tunic and the knife in his belt. And finally there was *her*, the woman with the purple gloves. Pietro lingered over her, fraught with disbelief. *What on earth could she be doing in the New World?*

"Pietro?" Enzo said. "You alright?"

"Yeah, yeah, I'm fine. Catch, kid."

Pietro tossed the figurines. The old man, the cap guy, and the gloved woman landed neatly in Enzo's hands. But at the same moment, something long, slender, and transparently dark scurried out from underneath the bench and snatched the other two figurines away.

Pietro's shadow had run away with the Chinese woman and the man with the knife. In a split second, it made its way out of the subway station and through the streets of New York.

Here we go again.

Enzo sprang to his feet, and his jaw dropped. “What the hell was that? Where did my figurines go?”

Pietro stood as well and helped Rosana to her feet. “Don’t worry, Enzo, we’ll get ‘em back. We gotta get out of New York. Rosana, are you in?”

“I’m in.”

“Pietro, I’m serious! What *was* that?” Enzo’s breath came in short puffs, and he started sweating. Rosana also looked a little freaked out, but she had already seen Pietro’s shadow in action. She would be fine. The other tourists in the subway didn’t seem to notice. *Whew, thank goodness for that.*

Still, he wasn’t going to be able to fool Enzo much longer. Pietro took a deep breath and half-sarcastically answered, “It was my shadow, what do you think?”

“Your shadow? Yeah, right! And just where is your shadow going with my stuff?”

Pietro closed his eyes, listened, and concentrated. Trees began to whisper in his ears, and a phantom scent greeted his nose. *Turkey legs.*

“Pietro! Answer me!”

Pietro smirked. “Maryland.”

CHAPTER SEVENTEEN

THREE YEARS AGO—THE OLD WORLD: VIOLET'S DEN

"I'm glad you've come to me, my dears. What you tell me about Hansel's recent behavior is disturbing. You've been right to be concerned."

Violet sat on her giant velvet cushion and kept her legs crossed beneath her. Garon and the dwarves formed an arc in front of her, keeping their hands behind their backs and their expressions flat. Garon did most of the talking.

"We're sorry, Miss Violet. We didn't know where else to turn. All seven of us tried to remove that wretched mirror from the wall, but the damn thing's a curse. The more time Hansel spends with it, the more hostile he becomes. We think he means to do somebody harm."

"You're certain the mirror is the source?"

"We're sure it's the mirror. He cannot take himself away from it except to venture into the mines. What could it mean?"

Violet stood and fluttered her wings, pacing back and forth. "I'm almost afraid to say it, but I believe it means a great evil is rising, and it resides in the looking glass. It's using the power of darkness and Hansel's love for his sister to control him through the mirror. You're right, my loves. He is no longer the Hansel we know."

Wayde wrung his hands and looked nervously around the room.

"Well, gosh, isn't there anything we can do? Can we ever get the old Hansel back?"

"I'm afraid I don't know the answer to that, but we can try. We *must* try. If this is the evil I suspect, we will need all the help we can get." Violet clasped her hands together and gazed over the water below her den. "Have you spoken with anyone else about this matter?"

"I've enlisted Prince Liam," Garon said. "Tonight, we're going to wait for Hansel to go back into the mines, and he's going to help us try to destroy the mirror."

"This is good," Violet affirmed. "But I fear it may not be enough. Tell me, have you ever heard Hansel speaking to the mirror?"

"Why, just this morning! I overheard him saying something new."

"And what did he say?"

"He said, 'I'll collect her tomorrow.' What could he have been talking about?"

Violet's eyebrows shot up. "Oh, dear."

"Miss Violet?"

"Hurry, my dears. Find the prince, and lift Hansel's curse. Destroy the mirror *tonight*."

"And if we fail?"

"Then we must assemble an army. The Ivory Queen means to return."

⌘⌘⌘

Hansel was ready to go. The cavern made sure of it.

It was the witch's form that stood before him again, wispy-haired and graying, but Hansel wasn't afraid anymore. She was just a shell, a medium for the cavern's voice to convey itself, as the mirror did when Hansel was at home.

"Remember, my hunter, you will bring me The Carver's wife only. She should be alone in her filthy New World house right now; it is the opportune moment. Bring her straight back to the Cavern of Ombra. She shall be the first of seven."

"Understood."

"Good dear. Take care to leave the woman unharmed. And you would also do well to remain unseen. Be on your way, and please—"

A loud crash echoed through the cavern, and the witch started trembling. No, she was *vibrating*. She covered her ears and doubled over. Her image was blurred and scattered, like Hansel was looking at her through drops of water or a diamond.

Meanwhile, the ground rumbled beneath Hansel's feet, which was a strange sensation because it was made up of spongy gems.

The most unsettling part was the sound. In addition to the witch's shrieking, a hollow and metallic *humm* reverberated off the cavern walls.

Crash! Hummm.

Crash! Hummmmm.

"I'll be on my way now!" Hansel called. "I'll be back with the woman tonight!"

"No, you fool! Forget the woman! Go to the mirror! Somebody means to destroy it!"

Hansel broke into a run as the fourth *Crack*! sounded, and the witch waved her gnarled hands in front of her.

"Don't be dense. You don't need your legs to get around anymore. Concentrate and will yourself to where you need to be. Open your heart to the darkness I have offered you, Hansel. If that mirror breaks, you will *not* have your sister back."

For a second, Hansel ran faster, and his heart rate sped up to match his pace. But the witch closed her fists, and Hansel stopped. It was like his knees were rusted stiff.

"Focus, hunter. Listen to my voice, and let me guide you. Let me liberate you."

Hansel shut his eyes, and the cold whisper of the witch's voice sank into his veins.

"Let me unlock your potential. What do you desire, huntsman?"

"I want my sister."

"More than that, dear?"

"I want . . ." Hansel gasped for air as a wave of darkness washed over him. He felt all the light fading from his life, all the warmth fading from his body, all the humanity fading from his soul. "I want the *power* to save my sister."

"You shall have that power. I'm giving it to you now. What do you want right now?"

"I want . . ." Hansel opened his eyes, blinked, and rolled his neck. He felt more powerful already. Lighter. More agile. Stronger. "I want to protect my mirror." His voice came out differently. Deeper.

"Then concentrate, huntsman. Focus on the mirror, and protect it with your life. When you have done what you deem necessary, you may go and collect The Carver's wife."

"Yes, Master."

"Good."

The voice echoed in the cavern, and Hansel felt himself fade away.

This darkness.

This power.

This feels good. This feels right.

And then Hansel found himself standing in his room, staring at the back of eight men's heads.

Crash!

Prince Liam and Hansel's housemates were heaving a large jagged boulder, bigger than Hansel himself, at the ivory mirror, knocking several photographs and paintings off the walls.

Hansel gritted his teeth, and his blood boiled. His hands shook with rage. *That's* my *mirror.*

Prince Liam released his share of the boulder, and it promptly fell to the floor, raising a cloud of dust. The seven dwarves turned around with him.

"What are you doing here?" Hansel asked.

Prince Liam mopped a thick film of sweat and dirt from his forehead. "My chum, we can talk about this."

"We've nothing to discuss, knave. Leave my house."

Garon stepped in front of Prince Liam. "We've been worried about you, Mister Hansel. You haven't been yourself, and it's all because of this mirror on your wall. Let us destroy it for you. It's for your own good."

"You know nothing of what's good for me. Step aside, Garon."

Garon narrowed his eyes and spread his arms wide, blocking the mirror. "Never."

"You would defy the man who spared your jobs? Your home?"

"You're not that man. You're something else. I shall not answer to you!"

Wayde whimpered. "Garon, don't argue with him! I don't like this!"

Prince Liam took Garon's shoulder and gently brushed him aside. "See here, Hansel, and have reason. We've come together to destroy this mirror because we have reason to believe that there are dark forces at work inside of it. I know that you're a good man, and you would not willingly submit to darkness if you had the choice. Help us destroy it."

"Spare me the patronization. You've no right to meddle in my affairs."

"Respectfully, old friend, your affairs are not the sole focus here. This is for the greater good."

"Don't pretend to be so noble and brave. You've never even slain a dragon before! You're a passive prince, no better than a peasant. What have you done for the greater good?"

Prince Liam frowned and shook his head. "Well, I—"

"When Snow was asleep. When her stepmother poisoned her, I did everything in my power to hunt her down and bring her to justice. What did you do?"

Pain crossed Liam's face. "Let's not make this about Snow. We have an important matter at hand. I'm asking you as a friend: Help me destroy the mirror. Please."

With a long stride forward and a roll of his neck, Hansel whispered, "Leave my house."

"I'm going to offer you one more chance, Hansel. Come to your senses and help me, or I shall have to use force."

Hansel threw his head back and released a deep guttural laugh his housemates had never heard before. "Force. Liam, I would love to see you try."

Then Hansel swung his fist with lightning speed, narrowly missing Prince Liam's face.

The agile prince dodged the blow and his hand flew to his side, where he withdrew a black metal dagger from his belt. "Garon! *Go!*"

The dwarves dropped to the ground and attempted to scramble under Hansel's bed, but there simply wasn't enough space for the seven of them. Their feet stuck out and the bedframe bulged at least a foot in the air, supported by the thick men's backs. Bo hiccupped, and Wayde covered his eyes.

"Get off me, you smelly oaf!" Finn growled to Jinn.

It wasn't a surprise that Prince Liam was extremely gifted with blades. After all, his tutor was Hua Mulan, the great woman warrior, and Liam was almost as quick as Hansel imagined Mulan to be from all the stories he'd heard. With one hand balled into a fist and the other clutching the handle of his blade, Liam swiped and slashed with stunning agility, but he had one major flaw: he was entirely on the defense. He took several steps backward, and though he managed to block every one of Hansel's blows, he refused to retaliate. There were whispers that Liam was a resistant student, one of Mulan's toughest. Hansel finally understood why.

Hansel dodged and skidded across the room, taunting his rival and laughing from deep within his gut. When Prince Liam stumbled over one of the dwarves' feet and went to steady his balance, Hansel saw his opportunity. He reached into his vest, whipped out a single black dart, and plunged it into Prince Liam's shoulder.

"There's no Snow where you're going, *old friend*. Don't worry. I'll take great care of your wife."

Prince Liam opened his mouth, his eyes wilted with pain and defeat, and then he vanished without a sound.

"Good riddance."

That left one more order of business to take care of before he could start rounding up the seven. He had to do something about the *other* seven.

"Up, you fools."

The bed shook and toppled onto its side, and the seven dwarves stood up. Only Garon and Zid looked him in the eyes, defiant expressions burnt onto their faces.

"I suppose I should thank you all for setting me along this course. You retrieved the mirror for me. What wonderful servants you'll be!"

"I'll never serve you!" Garon spat.

"You're despicable!" Zid said. "Prince Liam was a good man! What have you done?"

"The same thing I'm going to do to you if you don't do exactly as I say from this day forward. An old man once told me that he thought you incorruptible. I'd like to test that theory. Now, listen to the sound of my voice."

The dwarves' eyes drooped, and Hansel's irises darkened as he made his commands.

"Listen carefully. You all do my bidding now. We are going to make some changes in this realm, one sacrifice at a time. We have much work to do, and it shall not happen quickly, but you will do everything I tell you. You are not to speak to Princess Violet. You are not to speak to Snow White or anyone associated with her. The only contact you may maintain is with Master Hansel and his mirror. Is this understood?"

The seven dwarves, eyes glazed over, responded in unison. "Yes, Master."

"Good. Because if you break the rules, you will suffer until your last breath, and so will those you love. Now, let me explain the game. We are going to start a collection . . . ."

CHAPTER EIGHTEEN

TODAY—THE NEW WORLD: SOMEWHERE IN MARYLAND

Enzo wasn't excited about spending four more hours on the road, especially when Pietro was acting so weird, but he had to admit that having a girl along made the ride a little more tolerable.

Rosana was cute; Enzo couldn't deny that. She was confident, smart, and endearingly moody without being a nightmare. She was mysterious, but not impossible. She sat in the middle when Pietro ushered them into his truck and set course for Maryland. As the three drove on, Enzo was hyperaware of Rosana's arm brushing against his, first tentatively, and then more boldly.

Of course Pietro made routine stops for food, coffee, and gas, and their time on the road wasn't so bad. Conversation started flowing naturally, with hardly any need for the radio. The only thing Enzo felt like he was lacking was *answers*, especially when their lush green destination came into view after 2:00 p.m.

"Annnd we're here," Pietro announced. "I'm excited."

Enzo slid out of the truck, offered to help Rosana down, and then stretched his arms behind his head. Ahead of him, a tall cobblestone wall blocked a forest of white oaks and magnolias. Above the wall's grand archway, a long wooden sign with royal-blue letters spread from end to end.

"Pietro, can you explain to us why we're at *Ye Old Renaissance Faire* now?"

"C'mon, Enzo! That's not the first question you should ask. You should be like, 'Wowww, Pietro, we're at *Ye Old Renaissance Faire!* What should we do first?' Let me answer that for you. They have these huge greasy turkey legs and fried macaroni and cheese on a stick and chocolate-covered—"

"Fried mac and cheese on a stick?" Rosana interrupted. "How does that work?"

"I don't even know. It's magic. That's about the easiest way to explain it."

Pietro bought three tickets to the fair, and then Enzo and his friends stepped into a beautiful reconstruction of a village that reminded him of *Monty Python and the Holy Grail.* Enzo couldn't tell who was a guest and who was an actor. Three out of four people sauntered about in capes, cloaks, chainmail, armor, crowns, feathered felt hats, and thick leather boots. Only a few people came dressed more like Enzo, Rosana, and Pietro.

Enzo marveled at all the little cobblestone shops. There was a woodworker who made Enzo think of his dad. In another little shop, a young man sold wooden swords, which made Enzo think of Zack and their backyard duels. Rosana glanced at a leather mug shop, and Pietro already had his eyes on the turkey legs, their smoky scent dominating the air.

Not five minutes later, they were eating fried macaroni and cheese on a stick, thin rods skewered with creamy gold triangles.

"This is all really neat and everything, Pietro, but uh, why are we here?" Enzo asked.

Pietro shrugged. "I'm kinda wondering the same thing. We'll have to walk around a little more."

Enzo shook his head and snapped his macaroni stick in half. "Such bullshit."

Rosana and Pietro froze.

"You said what now?"

"I said this is bullshit! I'm tired of you talking in riddles, being stupid, not taking any of this seriously. I thought we had an agreement here. You're supposed to help me find my dad, and what have you done so far? Ran out of the subway, babbling some nonsense about your shadow, and now look where we are! We're at a stupid Renaissance festival."

Narrowing his eyes, Pietro took Enzo by the shoulders. "Dude, I've about had it with your moods. I'm just doing what I know how to do. If you and I really have an agreement, it's a two-way street. Wanna find your dad? Then you've gotta trust me. It doesn't seem so hard for Rosana here; she got in a truck with us and let us drive her four hours away from home! She's happy with her mac and cheese! Why are *you* still grumbling?"

Enzo leaned about a foot away from Pietro's face. "Because! Because you're not telling me everything! There's some really weird stuff going on, and I don't understand any of it, but you're casually walking around acting like my dad didn't vanish into thin air, like we weren't harassed by some apple-chucking weirdo twice in one day, and like your shadow didn't run off this morning with the carvings that my dad was so obsessed with!"

"You forgot the fact that one of those carvings looks like me," Rosana added.

"Thank you, Rosana!" Enzo nudged her. "See? She gets it!"

Pietro groaned and rubbed his face and pulled down so hard that his eyelids sagged. "Alright, kid, you want the truth?"

"Yes, I want the truth. Spill it now or I'm leaving."

"You have nowhere to go."

"So?"

Pietro sighed. "Fine. Sit down, and I'll tell you the truth. Both of you."

"I'll stand," Enzo insisted.

Rosana jammed her hands in her pockets and chewed on her lip.

Pietro took a deep breath. "Okay, Enzo. What do you know about your father's childhood? Where did he grow up? Where did he come from?"

"Same place you did. You two grew up together."

"Okay, so where did I grow up?"

Enzo shrugged. "Arizona?"

"No, we didn't grow up in Arizona. We came from somewhere else."

Enzo whistled long and low. "Wow, way to be specific."

"We came from another world, Enzo."

Enzo stared blankly for a minute, smiled, and threw his head back and laughed. "Haaa! That's a good one."

Pietro scowled. "Alright, let's try you, Rosana. Where's your mom from?"

Rosana nibbled a macaroni triangle. "I don't really know. She's been all over the place. Just before she went missing she told me she worked in France for a while. That was news to me."

"Did she ever talk about her childhood?"

"Nope."

"Well, she came from the same place I did. I used to know a girl where I grew up, and I kept thinking you look so much like her. Her hair was a lot lighter, she wasn't quite as tan, but she had the same face. Then I saw that missing poster in the subways. You're Alice's daughter."

Rosana took a step back. "How did you know her real name?"

"Because we were best friends in the Old World. Me, your mom, and Enzo's dad."

Enzo rolled his eyes. "Pietro, what are you *talking* about? Old World? You think you're in a fairy tale or something? And Rosana's mom is supposed to be who, rabbit hole Alice?"

Pietro nodded.

Rosana shuffled over to a wooden bench and sat down.

"Wait," Enzo continued, "so I'm right? You actually think this is all a big fable?"

"Call it what you will, but you'd better start believing in it. What you saw running through the subway today? That really was my shadow. It carried Rosana off the Empire State Building last night, like I carried you. We didn't take the elevators. We flew."

I am traveling with a crazy man. "We flew off the Empire State Building? With your shadow? That's cute, Pietro. So who do you think you are? Peter Pan or something?"

A hollow ding sounded behind the turkey legs. Apparently, a dark man in a pirate costume had succeeded in hitting the bell at the *Test Thy Strength* tower.

Pietro smirked. "The one and only."

"Ha. Ha, ha, ha. I'll play along with this, I guess," Enzo said. "You think you're Peter Pan and Rosana's mom is Alice. Who's my dad then? Or my mom? Are we the Brady Bunch?"

"Nope. Your ma grew up in Kansas. Your dad didn't live too far from me in the Old World. We used to play in a mine with Alice and two kids about our age, Hansel and Gretel. Your dad always got in a lot of trouble for coming with us. It was usually my idea." Pietro winked. "Parents hated me."

Enzo never heard stories about his grandfather. His dad never talked about him or a grandmother. Ever.

"Wanna know what your grandfather's name was, kid?"

Enzo giggled. "Sure, whatever. Wait, let me guess. Jack Frost? Muffin Man? Oh, wait, I've got it. King Triton!"

"Nope. Your grandpa was a Carver like your dad. He made your father with his bare hands. His name was Geppetto."

Enzo had enough. He shook his head, scoffed, and kicked the trashcan nearby. "You're just like my father. You have all these problems in front of you and you just run away from them. What did you do when Zack disappeared? Or Wendy? Hmm? You sat there in your house and didn't do a damn thing."

Pietro crossed his arms. "I'm *trying* to help them *now!*"

"By making up stories? By pretending that you came from another world and that we flew off the Empire State Building? And somehow your shadow ran away with my father's carvings, which is why it was so important that we come to the stupid Renaissance festival. How does making up stories help them *or* my parents?"

"Look, you asked for the truth, and I wasn't supposed to tell you, but I did anyway so you would stop sniveling. Take it or leave it, but deep down, you know it makes sense to you."

"It makes no sense, Pietro. It's crazy."

"Is it crazier than watching a man vanish in thin air with your father yesterday? Because you saw that happen. You think I'm lying about my shadow? Where is it, then? I don't see it on the ground anywhere."

Pietro was right about that part. The sun was high up in the air, throwing long silhouettes all over the faux village, for everyone but Pietro.

Enzo's head spun a bit, blurring the trees. "Oh man. I'm going crazy."

"No, you're not," Pietro said impatiently. "Try and stay with me here. I'm being one hundred percent honest with you right now. Your dad is Pinocchio. I'm Peter Pan, and I'll bet my PlayStation that Rosana's mom is *the* Alice. I don't know why we're all disappearing, but it has something to do with that man you saw in your house and those freaks we met in New York last night. They're gonna come back for us if we're not on guard. It's either we find them, or he finds us. So what are you gonna do?"

Enzo aimed his back at Pietro. "I'm going for a walk. Grow up, Pietro. Fairy tales aren't real."

"Whatever. Take a hike. Just don't go too far and meet me back here in an hour. And keep an eye out for my shadow, will ya? In case you haven't noticed, those figurines are what we're really looking for."

"Whatever, crazy man. You coming with me, Rosana?"

Enzo turned to the bench where Rosana had been sitting, expecting to catch a glimpse of her bright red sweater, but she wasn't there. He did a slow, full turn, scanning as far as his eyes could see. Pietro did the same.

But she wasn't there.

Rosana was gone.

CHAPTER NINETEEN

THREE YEARS AGO—THE WOODLANDS

Violet was known to be one of the most powerful beings in the Old World, unrivaled in her knowledge and skill of white magic. She could trace the source of almost any curse, and while she couldn't always break it, she could usually find some way to work around it. For instance, there was the problem of Pinocchio's wooden nose. She would never be able to stop it from growing when he told a lie, but she could give him a redeeming quest and set him a path that would make him human.

The way the people of the realm came to see it, Violet wasn't powerful because of her powers; she was powerful because of the way she used them. She was generous to a fault. She was righteous, determined, and altruistic. The way she saw it, her powers gave her a calling. She felt responsible for the people of her world—every one of them.

But she was cursed with the most emotionally draining of powers: empathy.

Violet cared so much about the realm that when somebody was hurt, she felt it. When she was young, it was almost too much to bear. She couldn't come into contact with anybody without absorbing their hidden pains and taking on their heaviest burdens. It took years to internalize the pain and learn to draw strength from humanity's brightest emotions, joy, amusement, relaxation, triumph . . . .

Her empathetic link to the realm had one particularly interesting effect: She could sense almost anybody's presence in the Old World. It was quite jarring when she sensed their absence.

When Prince Liam disappeared from the Old World, Violet felt it. She felt it as sharply as she felt the disappearance of her father, Lord Bellamy. It was the strangest sensation when they left, like straying too far and realizing she left her wand at home. She felt it somewhere in her stomach, but her heart reacted, too.

One day, she felt Hansel leave.

It wasn't long before he came back, but she sensed another presence among them: a woman who wasn't from their world.

That's when Violet knew she had to go to the bell tower.

She hated going to the Clocher de Pierre. It was one of the tallest structures in the realm, having doubled in size during its reconstruction after the Giant Wars. Violet was thankful that it was also clear on the other side of the land, the farthest possible point from her den. A place where all its pain could barely touch her.

Violet had only gone to the tower on one other occasion, the day after Peter Pan, Alice, and Pinocchio left the Old World. She had a good reason to speak with the man at the top then. Now that Hansel had brought in a woman from the outside world, she would have to speak with him again.

She flew because if she teleported, she wasn't sure she could handle the pain coming from the tower. She had to close the distance slowly, like building a tolerance for misery. Her wings buzzed as she sailed through the Woodlands, over Mount Colossi and the Lakes of Balen, past New Oz and the red sands of the Coyote Desert, and into the City of Florindale, where the bell tower stood.

The happy people of Florindale buffered the pain pulsing from Clocher de Pierre, but it wasn't enough to stop Violet from flying a little slower. Ultimately, she descended into Florindale Square and watched the people dance in colorful masks and bright dresses and handsome suits. *Focus on their jubilance.* She took in the sound of the street orchestra, which plucked and bowed a jovial melody she knew all the words to. It was an even happier place before the Battle of the Thousand, but Florindale celebrated every day since the Ivory Queen disappeared.

Violet smiled and greeted the townspeople as she made her way through the square and approached the enormous stone tower along the city's edge. As she walked, her heart grew heavier and her light spirits wilted. By the time she approached the tower, her smile had faded completely.

Violet took a deep breath, raised the brass knocker on the door, and brought it down three times.

As she suspected, it was Holmes who answered.

Jacob Isaac Holmes was at least six heads taller than Violet—and probably three times as wide. He had the head of a lion, though his eyes were red and somber and he had three horns positioned symmetrically about his forehead. His body was humanoid, and he stood on two legs, but he was scaly like a snake and had cloven feet. Despite his menacing form, Violet learned not to fear him. The fact that he answered the door in jeans made it easier to remember that he was only a man. At least, he used to be.

Jacob studied her for a moment before he spoke in a deep, ashy sort of voice, "Violet. If you're here, then that means . . . ."

Violet nodded solemnly. "Yes. I need to see the bell ringer. Is he up there?"

"You already know."

Quasimodo never left Cloche de Pierre.

Jacob motioned for Violet to enter, and she stepped inside. The air was musty, and only the lights of torches illuminated the spiral staircase. Jacob shut the door behind her and approached an archway under the stairs, just tall enough for him to pass through without ducking. With his scaly hand on the doorknob, he turned to Violet and asked, “How soon will you need me?”

“How soon can you be ready?”

“Understood.” Jacob nodded and turned away, sealing the brass door behind him.

Violet began her ascent. The steps were short enough that she could easily have taken them two at a time, but she took them one by one and walked with her eyes straight ahead.

As she ascended, her mood darkened with the weight of the bell ringer’s misery. The Beast had lived with a lot of pain as well, but no man lived with grief like Quasimodo.

Quasimodo’s upbringing and figure left him too ashamed to leave the tower. His back curved so far forward that it was almost impossible for him to lift his head up. His mouth was crooked, his eyes asymmetrical, and one of his ears was distinctly pointier than the other. But Violet would readily admit that he was one of the gentlest and most genuine souls she had ever met. And it showed in every human interaction he’d ever had. By the time Violet reached him at the top of Clocher de Pierre, she was ready to burst into tears. She found him smiling and nurturing an injured butterfly that had flown into the tower. His breathing was heavy as he tried to sooth the butterfly.

Violet folded her wings and spoke softly. “Quasimodo.”

Quasimodo hugged the fairy, his embrace firm and warm. “Miss Violet, is it time?”

“It’s time, my dear. We must assemble the Order.”

Quasimodo was silent as he looked over Florindale. He had a bird’s-eye view of the town every day. Violet had to wonder about the things he saw and how the world must’ve looked to him. How had it evolved over the years? What changes did Quasimodo see that nobody else could perceive? Looking into the horizon, Violet was sure that the sky was a shade darker than normal. Did the bell ringer notice that, too?

Quasimodo hung his head and spoke slowly. “Has she returned?”

"Not yet, but she means to. She's using Hansel as a vessel to do her work, and I believe it has already begun. He's banished Prince Liam, and today he kidnapped a woman from another world and brought her back here." Violet's fingers twitched at her sides. "I believe he's preparing for a ritual of some sort."

"And he's already begun?"

"Yes. That's why we need to assemble them tonight and stop him from doing any more. Will you do your duty?"

"Yes, Miss Violet." Quasimodo lowered the butterfly onto a ledge. "Are you ready?"

"We're all going to have to be. Sound the bell."

With no further discussion, Quasimodo reached up and jerked on the enormous rope with intense force.

Claaang! Claaang! Claang!

Violet closed her eyes and waved her hands, and when she opened her eyes, she was back in her den. She could still hear the bells clear across the realm: low-pitched and hollow with a long reverberation.

Claaang!

If Violet could hear the bells from her den, surely her warriors would hear them too. The only question was whether they were all in shape to answer her call. She looked to her mural, six circles in a flower-like formation. Five large disks centered on a smaller one depicting the bell of Florindale. Each external circle bore the face of one of her warriors from the Order of the Bell, the five she had enlisted to defend the realm if a great threat should arise.

In a circle at the top, there was Jacob, of course. The man who lost too much. He would risk his life in a heartbeat because he felt that there was nothing left to lose.

Opposite The Beast in the bottom circle was a young Chinese woman, Hua Mulan. The woman warrior tutored Prince Liam and risked her life to save her father, just to see him killed in the Battle of the Thousand.

In the circle to the left, there was an old woman. Her name was Augustine, and she was the best cook in the entire realm. After her granddaughter moved out, everyone became Augustine's grandkid. She was also impossibly skilled with a blunderbuss. Violet knew this because she saw the old woman take down a rogue giant who descended from the clouds one day, sometime after the Giant Wars. She defeated him all by herself. Her only complaint was that she'd left her pie in the oven for too long.

Opposite Augustine were the two most mysterious individuals: Merlin, a gifted but reclusive mage, and Hook.

James Hook.

Hook had the nasty reputation of being a liar, a swindler, and a cheat, and he also had a rocky history with young Peter Pan, but the pirate was one of the bravest men Violet knew. He gave his right hand to save the realm from a shape-shifting dragon, or so he claimed. Surely, he would rise to occasion of using his crafty swordsmanship and natural cunning to defend his realm from danger once again.

Violet traced the circles on her wall, closed her eyes, and hoped. *Please, help me keep the Ivory Queen at bay. Please, make your stand.*

CHAPTER TWENTY

TWENTY-FIVE YEARS AGO—EN ROUTE TO DARK CASTLE

Alice had encountered some curious creatures in Wonderland. She never forgot the Cheshire Cat. The Caterpillar. The Jabberwockies. The horrible bugs. But nothing in Wonderland ever terrified her as much as Kaa.

When she saw that hideous serpent, charcoal black and thick like the trunk of an oak tree, wriggling and slithering toward her and Pinocchio on the road to the Dark Castle, her blood froze. She knew it was Kaa.

"A-A-Alice," Pinocchio stammered. "I'm scared."

Alice did her best to sound braver than she felt, still having to force the words out of her mouth. "Don't move, Pin."

Through heavy breaths and with his whole body shaking, Pinocchio fretted. "Why aren't we running away?"

Alice wanted to tell Pinocchio that they shouldn't run because the snake would smell their fear, become even hungrier and thus faster, and he would devour them before they could take ten steps in the other direction. But the fear subsided, and an image of a jungle filled her mind.

A beautiful jungle.

The moon vanished and the sun thrust the world back into daylight, casting hefty shadows across Alice's skin. The ground tingled with warmth, and the air sizzled with the sounds of bugs, steam, and cackling birds.

She was alone. Her eyes were fixed on the gorgeous creature that slowly descended from the trees. The way he writhed and contorted, muscles contracting and expanding in every inch of his body, Alice couldn't look away. She thought of a flame twisting and dancing in the wind.

When he flicked his tongue, Alice understood the words the serpent meant to say.

"I was summoned here to dance for you, Alice. You, who are always so keen to observe the natural beauties of your world. You, whose imagination brings the impossible to life. Shall you join me in a dance, dear princess?"

As if her chin were on strings, Alice nodded involuntarily. "Yes."

What was it about him? His voice? His movements? It was probably his eyes. With every second she gazed into them, something washed away her colossal fear of snakes and the voice of reason she carried with her in the most impossible places. She knew in her mind that she should never approach a venomous animal, but her heart told her she *had* to.

Without any conscious effort of her own, Alice put one foot in front of the other, drawing closer to Kaa as he inched toward her. They were at eye level with each other, Kaa's eyes like bulbous cherries, his tongue continuing to flicker.

"Trust in me. Dance with me."

"I trust in you. I'll dance with you." Alice's voice sounded foreign in her head, a dull and distorted drone as if through water.

Her other foot moved.

"Trust in me. Have faith in me."

"I trust in you. I have faith in you."

Somewhere in the background, a boy was trying to shout, "*Stop*!" But the voice was fuzzy and far away, like the boy spoke through cotton. "*Alice, stop*!"

Alice? Who's Alice?

Another step forward. She was inches away from the beautiful creature, whose mouth had opened to reveal a set of brilliant teeth. They were long enough to cleave a watermelon in two with a single cut, and how clean they were! They were like shining ivory daggers that almost seemed to glow, and Alice made out the ghostly image of a young girl's face staring back at her in wonder. Blonde hair, blue eyes wide with curiosity, the girl reached toward her.

She didn't even feel her own hand moving, her fingers inching closer . . . closer . . . .

⌘⌘⌘

Don't look at his eyes. Don't look at his eyes. Look anywhere but his eyes.

Pinocchio was about to lose his voice. Desperation burned his throat and singed his nerves as he screamed at his friend to back away, "*Alice, stop*!"

It was creepy. He saw the fear in her face at first, but then the fear melted away and Alice sunk into a catatonic state, lolling toward the infernal serpent like one of the undead. Pinocchio didn't believe in zombies, but Alice was starting to look like one. She even sounded like one, the way she spoke to the reptile. Pinocchio's blood ran cold, to the point that he could barely move. His fear locked his joints in place, and he felt wooden and awkward.

"*Alice, stop*!"

Pinocchio's skin prickled up on the back of his neck when he watched Kaa open his mouth, his cavernous throat running deep and wide, a starless night filled with rib-like protrusions and razor sharp fangs.

What do I do? Pinocchio pleaded. He wished Violet were around to save him, and he hoped adulthood wasn't going to be nearly as scary as this night had been. What other surprises could possibly be waiting before he got to the real world?

He needed to be brave, but he didn't know how. In fact, he didn't know how to move. How could he stop Alice from getting closer?

Whoosh!

Pinocchio blinked.

Did he just imagine something round and orange soaring past his face? Something bigger than the dinner table, coming at him from the side?

Whoosh! Whoosh!

Two more flying objects went by, these narrowly dodging the serpent's scaly belly. One of them burst as soon as it connected with the ground, spraying a fleshy-colored pulp and tiny bits of orange confetti everywhere. It took Pinocchio a while to realize that it was a fruit. Somebody was lobbing massive pumpkins at Kaa.

And then a booming voice like talking thunder commanded, "Aim for the eyes, Bo!"

Another voice, this one a bit gravellier, argued, "I'm *trying*, Chann! Don't distract me! And stop eating the pumpkins!"

Whoosh!

Splat!

Pumpkin guts everywhere.

The snake reared its ugly head and whipped its gaze in the direction from which the pumpkins soared, and Pinocchio made out the figures of seven stocky men convened in the darkness. Three men stood out in a field, yanking colossal pumpkins from the ground and rolling them to a fourth man, who wound them over his shoulders and launched them in Kaa's direction. Two other men hid in a tree with their fists clenched, seemingly offering moral support, while the tallest—but not by much—waved a torch at the snake.

To Pinocchio's relief, Alice blinked. Once. Twice. Three, four, five. And then she covered her mouth and took a step back.

"Alice, come over here!" Pinocchio swallowed a pool of bile before it could reach his throat, and he waved his hand at his friend. He didn't know who the seven men were, but it sure didn't look like they were friends of Kaa's. Alice scurried over and clutched Pinocchio's elbow, her hands cold and clammy.

"Over here, you beastly rodent!" The man with the torch made a swirl in the air, drawing Kaa closer to him and eliciting an icy hiss. Through the orange glow, Pinocchio could make out the man's graying beard and wiry frames.

Whoosh! Whoosh! Splat!

"Garon, I don't think that's a part of the rodent family," another said. "Just saying."

Garon scowled at one of the men in the tree. "Technicalities matter not, Jinn. All dark things are born of the same womb, in the absence of light."

With a gust of wind, the torch went out.

"You *had* to provoke Lady Fortune."

"For the love of all cobbler, just keep the pumpkins coming!"

Alice buried her face in Pinocchio's shoulder, her hair falling in a cascade by her side. "I'm so frightened!"

"Your hood!" Pinocchio said. "Get under your hood!"

Alice untied her cloak and then wrapped it around both her and Pinocchio. Short, moist breaths escaped her lips as she mouthed the exact words Pinocchio was thinking: *Please don't see us. Please don't see us. Let us disappear*. From underneath the cloak, he had no idea if it was actually working until one of the men spoke up.

"Where did those children go off to?"

"One would hope someplace safe."

Whoosh, whoosh, whoosh!

Splat, splat, splat!

Hisss!

Like a phantom dancing in a void, the snake writhed and dodged, lurched and struck at the seven men, and hollow shapes continued to sail past him and burst along the ground, coating the earth in sticky pumpkin goo.

"We have to help them," Alice said.

"Are you crazy?" Pinocchio snapped. "We can't let the snake see us again! We should get out of here."

Alice jerked her head and Pinocchio found himself staring into her eyes, narrowed with anger and defense. "*Don't* call me crazy ever again, Pin. Understood?"

Pinocchio gulped down another wave of fear and closed his eyes. *Alice sure is scary when she's mad.*

Whoosh!

Whoosh!

Whoosh!

Gak!

Deafening silence.

Gak, gak!

"I told you to aim for the eyes, Bo!"

"Can't you stop your groveling and be proud the damn thing's choking?"

Pinocchio's peeled his eyes open. Kaa was bone still, a great portion of his body reared upward and facing the seven men. A massive bulbous protrusion swelled from his neck, stretching his belly and turning his skin a milky shade of purple. He twitched. *Gak!* He twitched again. *Gak!* The twitching became a series of violent convulsions. Kaa contorted into a crooked-L shape, and then an S, hacking and writhing.

"He's choking on a pumpkin," Pinocchio whispered. "I didn't know snakes could choke."

"They can't," Alice recalled. "This one's something else."

Kaa's cherry-red eyes faded, and the seven men watched in anticipation as the snake tried to force the fruit down its pipe. Pinocchio thought he could make out an extra stretch in his throat, where he supposed the pumpkin's stem probably was.

He had to admit, he felt sort of sorry for Kaa, watching him suffocate like that. He knew in his heart that this was a creature born of evil, but should it really be left to suffer as it was? To have its life forces cut off by a pumpkin in its windpipe? It seemed inhumane. Cruel, even.

But with one final wretch, the fruit shot out of Kaa's mouth like a bullet from a gun and sailed far away, high over the trees and into the darkness. The snake was free, and he was livid.

With the speed of lightning, Kaa lunged for the seven men who had provoked him.

"More pumpkins!" the man called Garon bellowed.

"There are no more pumpkins!"

"Plan B, gentlemen?"

"*Run*!"

The two men in the tree pushed off their branches and tumbled down on top of two of their companions, while the others tripped over them in their rush to escape. They became a dog pile and resorted to punching and kicking in desperate attempts to stand up.

"Jinn, this is all your fault! You didn't even shower today; you had to go jumping out of the tree—"

"Will you shut up and stop squirming so I can stand up?"

"Chann, curse you, *get off me*!"

Hisss!

"Ahhh!"

Seeing the snake come close to suffocating to death was one experience for Pinocchio. Watching these seven men come close to death was another. It was almost too much for his poor heart to handle—and a scene he couldn't stand to watch from under the cover of Alice's cloak.

Without another thought, Pinocchio sprinted for the snake. His legs carried him faster than ever before. His lungs felt like they were made of lead.

A whirlwind of sounds filled the night air. The deep, guttural screams from the seven men, ranging from the highest pitch of terror, to the lowest pitch of certainty.

Kaa's menacing hiss filled Pinocchio's ears, almost blocking out Alice's desperate pleas, "Pinocchio, what are you doing? Come back here! Please!"

But the boy only focused on a voice repeating on a loop in his mind. *"I give you the gift of The Carver."*

Pinocchio dug his hand out of his pocket with the pads of his fingers closed around something smooth and cool to the touch. He approached Kaa from behind.

Without a sound, Pinocchio slashed.

The blade went through Kaa like dust, and when Pinocchio retracted his arm, he couldn't believe his own actions. He looked at his palm, and Violet's knife looked back at him. Expecting to see blood, Pinocchio was surprised to see only clean metal casting his reflection . . . a weary-eyed youth with dark hair matted and clumped with sweat.

The snake let out a terrible shriek–and one long, final hiss. Then the reptile fell and disintegrated in a smoky haze, fading and diffusing into the bone-cold silence of the night.

Nobody moved.

Nobody breathed.

Nobody made a sound, save for the rumbling of a dwarven belly.

"Why, I think that little boy vanquished the serpent king!"

"No, you think? Of *course* he did, Finn. The snake's gone!"

"A big cheer for the small lad!"

"*Huzzah!*"

"Now, how about we finally stand up?"

"*Huzzah!*"

The men straightened themselves up and dusted blades of grass and moist dirt off their clothes. Meanwhile, Alice emerged from underneath her hood, her eyes wide with shock and mouth rounded into a tiny 'O.'

The man with the torch approached Pinocchio and extended a pudgy hand. "You have our eternal gratitude, young lad. What's your name?"

Pinocchio reciprocated the handshake. The man's hands were rough and callused. "I'm Pinocchio. And she's Alice."

Alice curtseyed. "How do you do?"

"Young Pinocchio and Alice, the slayers of the serpent king! Have you any idea what danger you put yourselves in tonight? You must take caution along this road! Tell me, where is your destination?"

Pinocchio opened his mouth to speak, but Alice cut him off, "Oh, my cousin and I, we were just out for a walk since the weather's been so wonderful. We're on our way back home now." She stepped forward and looked the men up and down. "Who are you folk, anyway?"

The tallest man spoke first. "We're the Seven Miners of the Woodlands. I am called Garon, and this is—"

"Finn."

"Chann."

"Zid."

"Jinn."

A moment passed and Finn thumped the man next to him, who was staring at his feet instead of at the children. "Oh, why, I-I'm Wayde. And that's Bo over there, the champ who got the pumpkin stuck in the serpent's throat."

The youngest miner, veiny armed and bulky, winked.

"Lovely to meet you all."

Finn raised a bushy eyebrow. Pinocchio decided he was the cleanest of the bunch, his boots somehow managing a shine after the battle with Kaa. "Likewise. Listen up, 'f you need anything, you don't do anything *stupid* again, got it? You call for us straight away, and you let us handle the problem."

Pinocchio gulped. "Yes, mister. Sorry."

"Sorry?" Finn repeated. One of his companions doubled over in laughter. "You've eliminated a threat of the Ivory Queen. One hears rumors, you know. *She's not really dead. She's just sleeping. She's looking for servants to reap souls for her.* Blah, blah, blah. All I know is that demon serpent used to be one of her pets. There are whispers that she had a scientist working for her and he brought this heathen back from the dead. But whatever made Kaa possible, you unmade. 'Twas a moronic move, lad, but a terrific one, understood? You're stupid, but a hero."

Pinocchio wasn't sure whether to be offended or grateful. Most of his mind was still processing what the man had told him about the queen. All he could manage to say was, "Yes, sir."

Garon beamed. He reminded Pinocchio somewhat of Santa Claus. "Should you ever need some helping hands, beat a simple rhythm, like so." He doubled over and drummed a not-so-simple signal on his knees. *Tap, tuh-tap tap, tuh-tack tack!* Twenty taps total. "Now you try."

Pinocchio repeated the beat, having to start over twice before he got it right.

"Good enough. Same for you, young lady. Can you remember our signal?"

Alice repeated the rhythm, mastering the beat with ease.

"Attagirl! We'll be off now. You keep that pocketknife safe, boy. That's some magic of the purest kind. Some people rely on magic to control the world. We can't ever rely on magic, lad, but we *can* rely on the heroes who wield it for good. Do you understand?"

"I understand."

"Good boy. You, too, Alice the Brave. Carry on, younglings! And go home. It's not safe to be on this road at night." Garon raised his empty torch and saluted the children. The other miners followed suit. "Gentlemen! Onward!"

Alice wrapped her cloak around her waist and scooted close to Pinocchio. Pinocchio grabbed her elbow. Garon and his friends shuffled away in the opposite direction. The companions didn't say another word. They didn't move again until the miners faded out of sight. Then, they turned and faced the infinite path ahead of them, where the Dark Castle loomed far along the broken horizon.

CHAPTER TWENTY-ONE

TODAY—THE NEW WORLD: YE OLD RENAISSANCE FAIRE

Rosana stopped paying attention when Pietro started talking about fairy tales, mostly because she believed him.

It all makes sense.

In a way, none of it made sense, but Rosana was willing to accept any explanation for her mother's disappearance. Or why she hid so much about her past. Or the reason she changed her name. How the apple vanished from the subway right along with Rosana's mother. How Pietro was able to fly and make his shadow do the same.

She knew she wasn't crazy. There was only one thing Rosana didn't believe in, and that was the word *crazy*. She'd known people who she'd call foolish, naïve even, or maybe clinically insane, but she was none of those things. Not in the least bit.

As far as she could tell—despite having known him for less than a full day—Pietro Volo wasn't crazy either. He was goofy, odd, and perhaps a little childish, but Rosana was certain he meant well, and she didn't want to believe he would lie about knowing her mom. After all, he knew her real name. Nobody knew her real name. At least, that's what Rosana had always thought. She still wasn't sure how much that Wayland guy knew and how he was connected to her mom, but when she thought about it, she was certain Pietro was connected to her, too.

Then there was Pietro's theory about who her mother really was. *The* Alice, who fell down a rabbit hole and spent who-knows-how-long in a magical, terrifying place called Wonderland. Rosana wasn't quite sure how she felt about that one. It wasn't crazy. Farfetched, maybe. Downright whimsical. But not crazy, especially because it made all the sense in the world that Pietro was really Peter Pan. Well, except for the part about him being an adult.

Rosana sat on a wooden bench, silently nibbling her fried mac-and-cheese on a stick and processing what Pietro had just said. She tuned out the rest of the conversation and ruminated over the Alice part, trying to decide if she believed it. If she did, what that would mean for Rosana? More importantly, what would it mean for her mother? If her mother really were Alice, looking for her would be harder than Rosana thought.

So-called normal people *vanish every day*, Rosana thought, *and they can turn up anywhere. Hopefully alive.*

But where would a person like *The Alice* turn up? Someone like her mother?

Rosana scratched her head and stared at the muddy ground, thinking to herself, *If I were to suddenly disappear, where would I go? Where does a disappearing woman end up?*

When she looked up again, Pietro and Enzo were spinning around and looking lost.

"Great, where did she go?" Pietro asked.

"She probably ran away because you were talking crazy!" Enzo retorted. "I don't know why I haven't run away from you yet."

Are they looking for me? Rosana thought. *Um, guys, I'm right here!*

"Enzo, now is not the time to be blaming each other. Look, we'll split up and we'll meet back here in an hour, okay? If you find her, call me."

"Fine."

"Fine."

"Fine!"

"Ummm, hello?" Rosana said. *Is this a joke?*

But Pietro and Enzo stormed away from each other, with Pietro going to Rosana's right and Enzo going to the left.

Against her better judgment, she stood up and broke into a power walk in Enzo's direction. She couldn't wait to ask Pietro more about her mom, but she figured she'd have quite a bit of time for that in the near future. She had to process everything first.

There was something about Enzo and his little mood swing, though. She found it sort of endearing. With his hands jammed into his pockets and his face pulled into a grimace, he worked his way through the crowd of peasants, jesters, and nobles. Rosana found herself growing annoyed too, as people bumped into her and walked into her shoulder.

When she had almost closed the distance, she called out, "Enzo! Enzo!"

"Rosana?" Enzo whirled around on his heel. He craned his neck and did another full turn.

Rosana was barely three feet away from him now. "Enzo, I'm right here."

He spun around again, and Rosana waved. *Earth to Enzo?* At one point, she thought she had made eye contact with him, but he seemed to be looking through her instead of at her.

"Enzo, give it up."

Enzo furrowed his eyebrows. "How are you doing this? Where are you?"

"Right here, space case. Joke's over now." Rosana sighed, threw her hands up, and then grabbed Enzo's sleeve.

Wide-eyed, heavy-jawed confusion crossed his face.

"Okay, this is trippy. Honest to everything, I can't see you right now. I feel you pulling on my sleeve, but . . . ."

Fine, I'll play along. Rosana took her chances. She puckered her lips and made a kissy face at Enzo. She balled her hand into a fist and swung within an inch of his face. She poked his arm a few times. She could see herself, but Enzo didn't process any of it.

"You didn't see *any* of that?"

"No! Stop freaking me out like this!"

A man in a court jester hat slammed into Rosana's back, looked around in bewilderment, and then kept going without apologizing.

Rosana's heart sank. *Oh, no, I'm turning into the Invisible Woman! Maybe this is what happened to my mom.*

The thought alone had sweat trickling down the back of her neck. She brushed her sleeve across her forehead and took her hoodie off.

Once it was over her head, Enzo finally locked eyes with her. "There you are!"

Rosana froze. "You can see me now?"

"How did you do that?"

"I have no idea." She tied her jacket around her waist like a belt and scratched her head.

Enzo brought his hands up to his temples and rubbed his forehead. "This is getting weirder and weirder. I'm going crazy."

Rosana grabbed Enzo's arm. "Enzo, chill, okay? I'm a little freaked out, too, but ease up on the C-word."

"You were *invisible.*"

Rosana didn't know how to answer. She smiled half-heartedly and shrugged. "Trick of the light?"

"Is the light from another planet or something? Because I swear, one minute you weren't there and then you just appeared out of nowhere."

"I have no idea. For all we know, it could be some other world. We should go catch up with Pietro."

Enzo shook his head. "I need to get away from Pietro for a little bit."

"That's fair, I guess." Rosana walked beside Enzo at a slow pace, soaking in the light breeze whispering through Maryland's trees. "Although to be fair, I think you were kinda hard on him."

"Great, so you're siding with him? You're gonna go along with the whole other world fairy tale thing he made up?"

"Hey, I'm not going along with anything. My first priority is to find my mom, and right now I feel like you guys are my best chance to do that. I don't know either of you that well, but I feel like Pietro means well. He seems to believe this story he's telling. If you don't believe it, just let him have some fun with it."

"Yeah, well, there's fun and then there's stupidity."

Rosana raised an eyebrow. "Interesting dichotomy. So then, what's fun to you? If I may be so bold."

"Literally anything else. Anything that involves not being stupid."

"Oh, come on, that's such a boring answer. There's gotta be more to you than that. How old are you, like eighteen?"

"Fifteen," Enzo muttered.

Rosana's heart skipped a beat. She never would've guessed they were the same age. "Okay, so exactly. You're young! I wanna know what you do for fun. When you have no responsibilities, no chores, no homework, what do you do?"

Enzo's mouth curved, and he thought for a minute. "Well, I like to play the drums. Sometimes I draw. Used to be kind of a beast with a yo-yo at one point."

Rosana beamed. "Wow! I was afraid you were gonna say something like, I don't know, chess."

"Hey! What's wrong with chess?"

Whoops. "The point is: Apparently you're not *entirely* two-dimensional. And Pietro? What's his thing? What does he do?"

Enzo rolled his eyes. "He's your standard twelve-year-old in a thirty-something's body. Video games, fencing, comic books, skateboarding, corny magic tricks."

"That's kind of awesome," Rosana said. "What's wrong with that? At least he has a job, right?"

"Yeah, he works. Pretty sure he's just been bumming around

at home since Wendy and Zack disappeared, though. That's what infuriates me. This little trip we're on? It's the first time he's done anything proactive."

"Good for him. Good for both of you. I'm sure if we stick together, we'll figure out what's going on."

Enzo scoffed. "Sure hope so."

Rosana tugged on Enzo's sleeve again. "Know what I think is really fun?"

"What?"

She pointed to a purple tent decorated with silver and gold stars. The banner across the top read, *Madame Esme's Foolproof Fortunes: Discover Your Destiny!* "Magic! Wanna get your fortune told with me?"

"A.K.A. wanna get scammed? Not especially."

"Oh, come *on*. We can laugh about how ridiculous it is afterward. Let's just pop in and see what she has to say, and then we'll go tell Pietro we're still alive."

"Alright, fine."

They crossed through the mud together, dodging people with turkey legs and leather mugs, and Rosana peeled back the curtain to find Madame Esme, a young dark woman with rich, wavy hair sitting in a wicker chair with her iPhone.

Madame Esme scrolled and tapped her screen until Enzo lightly cleared his throat. She eyed them, stood, and spread her arms in a welcoming gesture. "Oh, why *hello*, my dears! Madame Esme can't believe it's really true! She predicted your arrival, but she didn't believe Lady Fortune would treat her so kindly. If it isn't the Daughter of Alice and The Carver's son, live in the flesh! Please, take a seat!"

Rosana and Enzo exchanged incredulous looks, and the two sat in wicker chairs at a round table.

She knows us, Rosana thought.

"I'm guessing Pietro's already been here," Enzo muttered.

"I'm guessing you're Madame Esme?" Rosana said.

Madame Esme clapped her hands and returned to her seat. "You are correct, bright one. Do you also have the gift, then?" She chuckled at her own joke and folded her hands. "Now, I gather that you two have come to see Madame Esme to gaze into the future. Am I correct, Son of Pinocchio?"

Enzo gripped the arms of his chair and looked at his nose. "Um."

"Don't you worry! Madame Esme asked you a rhetorical question. *All* of her questions are rhetorical, because she's always correct! Now, what can Madame Esme do for you? Would you like a peek into the future?"

"Um—"

"We'd love one," Rosana said.

"Shhh, shh, shh, shh, my children. Madame Esme already *knew* that. Let me take care of everything." She clicked her iPhone on and set it on the table.

Rosana caught a glimpse of the screen. *Future 101*. "Um, a smart phone app?"

"Oh, you know. Madame Esme likes to keep up with the times. She used to read bones, but that always made her feel a little . . . *icky*." Madame Esme flicked imaginary cooties off her sleeves. "She used stones for a while, but oh, child, stones are so heavy! She's used cards, crystal balls, tealeaves, magic 8-balls, but these new iPhone apps are Madame Esme's *favorite*. Okay, hons, I'm gonna need you to type in your names."

Rosana picked up Madame Esme's phone. The screen showed a crystal ball in front of a purple, cloudy background, and in Comic Sans font, the ball read *Name?* Just to see what would happen, Rosana typed, *L-i-n-d*, but before she got to the 's', Madame Esme snatched the phone out of her hands. "Madame Esme should've known you'd try that. I'll do it."

Enzo smiled for the first time since he sat down. "Whose name were you putting?"

"Lindsey Lohan." Rosana's lips parted in an impish grin.

Enzo laughed. Rosana loved it when he laughed.

Madame Esme narrated as she typed into her phone. "Let's see. We have the bold and beautiful Rosana Trujillo, and the dashing and gallant Enzo DiLegno. There we go."

"How do you know our names?" Enzo quizzed.

"No more asking how." Madame Esme set the phone down and peered at Enzo over her half-moon glasses, shaking a finger. "The powers of the mystic are for Madame Esme to understand and you to marvel upon. Now, hons, let us join hands and begin." She reached across the table and clasped Rosana and Enzo's hands.

This is so tacky, Rosana thought to herself. She tried to convey her thoughts to Enzo, and he seemed to understand. He gave her a look like, *Can you believe this lady?*

"Ahem. Hold hands, you two. She won't bite you, Son of Pinocchio."

Rosana and Enzo exchanged an uncomfortable glance, but they followed the woman's directions and grabbed hands. Madame Esme giggled through her nose when they touched. Rosana had to look away out of fear that she might have turned red. She was pleasantly surprised by Enzo's firm grip. His hands were warm and smooth, and she hoped she wasn't about to get them all sweaty.

"Very good. Now that we are a circle, let us gaze at the circle of life. Let us study the cosmos and understand our places."

Madame Esme's phone flickered, and then Rosana's jaw dropped when a bright light shot out of the tiny camera lens, expanded, and filled the tent with purple and silver holographic clouds. The clouds hovered above their heads, swirling like a second hand circles a clock.

"Whoa," Enzo breathed. "My phone definitely doesn't do that."

"Shhh," Madame Esme cooed.

The clouds gathered in the center of the tent and changed form. Rosana was reminded of watercolor paints running together on paper and becoming something entirely new. In this case, the purples and silvers and grays became a group of rubies floating in a half circle. Rosana counted seven.

The image didn't bother Rosana until she noticed that five people were sleeping inside the rubies. There was a boy no older than Enzo, a man, and three women, including–

"*Mom!*"

Enzo tightened his grip on Rosana's hand. "Those are my parents! And Zack and Wendy!"

The image broke Rosana's heart. Her mom stood perfectly straight, her hands cupped at her sides and her head slightly bowed, but there was no doubt that she was asleep. Asleep in a giant gem.

"What are you showing us?" Rosana demanded.

"This is not the future, little ones. This is occurring as we speak. Fear not, children. Take comfort in knowing that your parents are alive, and the two empty gems indicate that there is still time."

Rosana swallowed hard. "Time for what?"

"For their rescue. For the realms' salvation."

"Their rescue from *what*?" Enzo said.

The gems and the sleeping people disappeared, gathering in the tent's center like watercolor paints again, and Rosana wanted to cry. She wanted to make Madame Esme bring her mother back.

The image changed again, and suddenly Rosana was looking at herself. She, Enzo, and Pietro became life-sized holograms, walking side by side on top of Madame Esme's table. It was the strangest thing to watch, carbon copies of herself and her friends walking as if on a treadmill. And then a fourth figure appeared behind them, a man in dark cloth and brown leather with a scar across his cheek. He followed them, silent and smug, carrying a long, black dart in his hand.

"Madame Esme knows you three are on a quest, you two and Mr. Peter Pan here. Aw, how handsome he's grown to be."

Enzo cleared his throat. "I've seen that man before. He took my dad. Who is he?"

"Why, if I'm not mistaken, that is young Hansel of the Woodlands, but he doesn't seem to be himself here. He's a shell. A puppet, if you will. Now Madame Esme understands why the Cavern of Ombra is active today. Hansel is hunting for sacrifices."

"Wait, wait, wait. Hansel as in, Hansel and Gretel? Bread crumbs and candy?"

"Correct, Daughter of Alice!" Madame Esme's voice went up an octave. "You really do possess the gift! Unfortunately, I fear for your lives right now, my dears."

"Back up," Enzo said. "The Cavern of what? Is that where my dad is?"

"Ombra, Son of Pinocchio."

"How do I get there? What state is it in?"

"'Tis in the Woodlands, my dear, in a world apart! But you cannot go there without help. You must gather those who have the power to help you, as Hansel is gathering his own people to bring back the wicked Queen Avoria. You must succeed before he does, and I fear you're already so far behind."

Rosana sighed. This was too much to process in one short time. "Who are we gathering?"

"You must follow The Carver's signs," Madame Esme said. "As for Hansel, he does the bidding of the Ivory Queen. He will gather whomever she requests so that he may open the portal to set her free. You mustn't let this happen, loves. Heed my words, Queen Avoria must never return. If she does—"

"Who's Queen Avoria?"

Madame Esme shushed Enzo and turned her attention back to the holograms on the table, where the scar-faced man began throwing darts at Pietro, Rosana, and Enzo. One by one, they disappeared, and finally, Hansel himself vanished. The hologram turned into purple clouds again.

"Oh, my. That was not good. Oh, dear. Oh, dear!"

"What is it? Tell us everything you know!" Enzo demanded.

Madame Esme sighed deeply. "What you've witnessed means that you are likely destined to fail. One of you three will not finish the quest.

Hansel and his henchmen hunt you as we speak. Some of them are at this very faire today. He will collect one of you, and you will be one of his seven sacrifices."

Enzo jerked his hands away from Rosana and Madame Esme, and the clouds vanished. He pounded the table and rose. "Whatever! I don't believe any of this. I don't know how you got footage of my family, but if I ever find out how, I'll tell everyone what a phony you are. This is a load of fairy tale crap."

Rosana stood up as well. "Enzo, please!"

"No. We're done here, Rosana. Let's just go find Pietro and leave."

It was Madame Esme's turn to stand. "So you will not save the realms?"

"I don't believe anything you're saying right now. I've had a crazy past couple of days, and no, I can't explain a lot of it, but I'm pretty sure there's a better explanation than fairy tales."

"Just you wait, then, Enzo DiLegno. Just you wait."

The tent curtain peeled open again, and a man clothed entirely in green burst inside. He was a slender figure who looked to be in his early to mid-twenties, and he was easily the best-looking man Rosana had ever seen. In fact, she was pretty sure she had seen him before.

Before anyone could react, the man gripped Enzo's shoulder. "There you are! Stars, I have been looking *all over* for you! You, and *you*"—the man pointed to Rosana—"must come with me."

CHAPTER TWENTY-TWO

TODAY—THE NEW WORLD: MARYLAND RENAISSANCE FAIR

Pietro had no idea how it happened.

His argument with Enzo took away his appetite. Pietro tossed his unfinished mac-and-cheese stick in a trashcan. He shuffled past sizzling bratwurst stands without pause, ignored the smell of melted cheese drifting out of Round Table Pizza, and he skimmed past the sugary funnel cakes without looking twice. When he passed a small open tavern where three large men were playing some Lady Gaga song on the bagpipes, he quickened his steps.

I shouldn't have told the kid.

Violet warned him a long time ago. *In the New World, you have to live in secret.* He knew he'd have to break that rule with Enzo eventually, but was it too soon? The kid hated him now. He thought Pietro was nothing but an overgrown man-child playing games to keep him from suspecting the worst.

Worse still, Rosana vanished from right under his nose. *After I promised to keep these kids safe and get them back to their parents.* If he was failing them, he most certainly wasn't doing right by Pino, and that meant he *definitely* wasn't doing his family any good.

How long will it take Zack to think I've given up on him?

As he walked, his mind wandered to the times when he would spar with his son and Enzo in the backyard. Or sit down with Zack and play a few rounds of Mario Kart after dinner. Or help him build a giant Lego tower. Those last few weeks before Zack and Wendy disappeared, he was having some trouble getting along with Zack, who didn't care much for sparring or Lego towers anymore. It was all about girls, cologne, and most of all, privacy. That was hard for Pietro.

Pietro ruminated over his situation for a while, and after he passed by the mini museum of torture, something caught his eye.

His shadow lay perfectly still by the frozen lemonade stand, still enough that Pietro almost missed it. Then his foot hovered over a tiny wooden figurine.

The man in green with the knife in his belt.

Before his foot made contact, his shadow raced the figure away again. It was interesting how nobody seemed to pay attention to the silhouette carrying the tiny figurines and darting through the faux village. Pietro figured they must've been too deep in their mugs full of ale, or dazzled by the village's colorful sights, jubilant sounds, and smoky smells. Still, he didn't want to draw too much attention to himself, so he continued walking casually, keeping his eyes on the shadow all the while. It didn't stray far this time, but the "where" was still problematic.

Pietro watched it soar past a wax-hand booth, a Dunk the Wench tank, and ultimately under a curtain that read, 'Cast Members Only.'

Annnd that's a problem.

There was no way he could get back there in Nikes and jeans.

But he couldn't finish his quest without his shadow. He was going to get it back one way or another—Pino's figures, too—and this time, it was going to stick firmly to his toes and never escape again.

If I just pop in and out . . . .

Pietro inched the door open, poked his head inside, and caught a whiff of hairspray. He glimpsed his silhouette taunting him under a rack full of leather and velvet on the other side of the room.

"You little jerk, get back here! We're wasting time!" Pietro mouthed.

But his shadow remained firmly planted under a scarlet cape.

Pietro glowered, pushed the door open, and sauntered in as casually as he could, chin high and arms at his sides. He made eye contact with nobody, not the queen in the make-up chair, not the knight who had his back turned to him, and not the man in the green tunic with the knife in his belt.

Wait a minute! That's him!

As soon as Pietro made the connection, the man spun around and dashed to him. "Stars, you guys are both running so late today! If you don't give them a good show, the king's gonna take your head off!"

Before Pietro could open his mouth, the man pushed him behind a red curtain and started chucking pieces of shining knight armor into Pietro's arms. Grieves, gauntlets, a helmet, a chest plate. "Get dressed. Make it fast."

"Wait a minute," Pietro said. "I'm not actually a—I mean, I just came to grab something really quick. Can I just?"

The man's hand flew to his dagger, though his expression looked nervous. "Get dressed. I have not the time to argue with you."

"But—"

"Now!"

The man in green walked away, and ten minutes later, after much struggling and a couple of falls, Pietro confronted himself in the mirror. He felt heavy, awkward, and a little violated, but he had to admit, he looked awesome. Noble and heroic, even.

Now if he could just grab his shadow . . . .

He peeled back the curtain and made a laughable attempt to tiptoe out of his makeshift dressing room. *Clink! Clank! Clink!* When he realized there was no way to tiptoe in a suit of armor, he picked up the pace. His chest weighed him down and his legs felt like marble, but at least he managed to stay upright.

The queen, red-haired and young, spun around in her make-up chair. Pietro's field of vision had decreased by about ten percent on each side, but the queen's fierce gaze pierced his armor. "Sir Gallivant, couldst there be a buffoon more raucous than thee?"

Pietro figured the queen was talking to the other knight, posing in front of his own mirror, but when he didn't answer, she cleared her throat. "Well?"

Uh-oh, does she think I'm Sir Gallivant?

"Um, apologies for the racket, lady. There canst notteth be a lad more louder than me."

"Ahem! Whilest we are in character, thou shalt address me as 'Your Majesty', though I do believe I was addressing Sir Gallivant, not *you*, Sir Diffident. Thou art always bumbling, and Sir Gallivant is astonishingly quiet today. Her Majesty was merely being sarcastic."

"Oh. Gotcha."

"Well, Sir Gallivant?"

The other knight stumbled as he tried to turn around in his armor, nearly tripping over his feet. "Your Majesty, thou art magnificent. I humbly offer my apologies for my distractions this day."

Pietro took his opportunity to inch closer to his shadow, still dormant under the long velvet robe, and then, in the blink of an eye, it flickered and promptly returned to his body. He felt the figurines appear somewhere in his jean pocket under his grieves.

Finally! Now I can make a run for it and find Enzo and Rosana!

Pietro made a wild turn, stumbling over his own toes and clinking and clanking like the Tin Man, and he made a beeline toward the door. *Yes!* But the dreadful man in the green outfit entered before Pietro could touch the doorknob, and he stopped Pietro in his tracks.

"Oh, no, Sir Diffident, where do you think you're going? It's time for the show! You, too, Sir Gallivant! Out you go! Are you ready, Queen Radiant?"

"Oh, please, Willahelm, we're always ready for a great show!"

The next thing Pietro knew, the man in green forced him out the door and strapped him onto a white horse facing a black portcullis. "I should warn you, Sir Diffident. Tinker Bell here hasn't been on her best behavior this day. If you're not careful, she'll throw you on your spine and kick you in the grandkids."

"Thanks for the warning." Pietro gulped. It was a good thing he'd had a bit of experience with horses before. He took Zack, Wendy, and Enzo out a few times and learned to become a pretty good rider. There was one thing he'd never tried, though, and it only occurred to him when the man in green produced a long metal pole and offered it to Pietro.

"Your lance. Good luck to you, Sir Diffident. Remember, make it a good show or King Competent will send you to the prison."

Great. Or, you know, I could die.

The man in green turned around and helped the other knight mount a black steed, darker than midnight. "And you, Sir Gallivant, take caution. Maid Marian has a rather violent jerk in her gait today. Don't let her be the one to throw you off. Good day to you, my friends."

Pietro gripped the reins and turned to face the other knight. So he was supposed to be knocking this guy off his horse with a pole, apparently. The other guy faced him, and they shared a brief nod. "Uh, may Lady Fortune guide us!"

"I don't believe in luck."

"Then may the best man win?" Pietro smiled to himself. The acoustics of the helmet added a foreign buzz to his voice, and he couldn't help but feel amused, even if he was probably about to get himself killed.

"Yep."

A male voice sounded through a megaphone on the other side of the portcullis. "Lords and ladies of the wood, there will be death on our fields this day!"

Thunderous applause erupted. Claps, screams, whistles, and some hearty "*Huzzahs* rang through Pietro's helmet, although it was difficult to focus on them over the sound of his own pulse jackhammering through his body. *Yeah, you bet there's gonna be death. I'm gonna have a heart attack right here.*

The portcullis creaked open, and Pietro faced an open field surrounded by people.

The amplified voice sounded once again. "This day, the noble Sir Gallivant and his steed, Maid Marian, have challenged Sir Diffident and his pony, Tinker Bell!"

"Tinker Bell?" Pietro whispered to the horse. "You better not let me down, here."

"Today, our knights shall compete to win the heart of the lovely Lady Elegant! The winner shall have her hand in marriage; the loser shall die!"

Explosive applause.

Oh my god, oh my god, oh my god.

"And without further ado, let us see our knights ride into battle! *Charge*!"

CHAPTER TWENTY-THREE

THREE YEARS AGO—THE WOODLANDS

Hansel couldn't sleep. He lay in bed with his eyes wide open and his arms at his sides, staring at the ceiling.

He knew it was wrong, but he did it anyway. He banished Prince Liam to the other world, to a place from which he could never return.

Truth be told, it didn't seem like such a big deal to Hansel until he had visited the New World himself earlier that day.

What a vile, repulsive place!

He would almost be doing The Carver's wife a favor by snatching her away from that hellhole. The dirty white squares people walked on. The mechanized monsters that people used to travel from place to place. Is that really what magic looks like in some places? Oh, and what about those houses that were smashed together, stacked on top of each other, and looked exactly the same? Or the strange way people dressed?

Walking around that strange new place, Hansel actually experienced remorse for Prince Liam.

I've damned him. I've confined him to an eternal nightmare.

But Hansel did have a job to do, and it came together almost flawlessly.

Carla DiLegno, The Carver's wife.

Hansel found her in her own home, reading a book in a cozy rocking chair and sipping a fizzy drink with a straw. He saw her through the screen door, guessing that she must've left the main door open on account of the realm's pleasant weather. A few fluffy clouds. A gentle sun. A light breeze.

Hansel knocked, of course. He didn't want to raise suspicions from her or perhaps any neighbors. Besides, there was no way she'd ever see the dart coming.

He rapped on the door.

"Be there in *one* second." Carla's voice was soothing and warm. She sounded like a woman who would teach the young or care for the sick. The woman tucked a shiny bookmark into her novel and lowered it on a round wooden table. She took a quick sip of her drink and approached the door, a brisk edge to her walk.

Carla opened the door and smiled warmly, but there was a playful glint in her eye as she looked Hansel up and down with her arms folded. Hansel understood immediately. People in this world didn't dress like the people back home. He could've kicked himself for not knowing this. His leather boots and thick belt and linen trousers were going to draw too much attention. He'd need to bring the dwarfs with him as distractions from that point on.

"Can I help you, sir?"

Hansel flashed his most gentlemanly smile and did his best to speak naturally. "Good day, Madam. I was having a walk through the land and I wondered if I could trouble you for a glass of water? I'm rather fatigued."

Carla covered her mouth, concealing a chortle. "A leisurely stroll through the kingdom today? How lovely."

"Uh, well yes. Quite lovely indeed."

Carla winked. "I'm sure. Stay right here, and I'll be back with some water for you, sir."

Hansel found himself squinting and studying the house through the screen as Carla walked away. *A tidy little place*. There was a rectangular table big enough for four to sit and eat at, decorated with white candles and a crystal vase filled with sunflowers. Hardcover books snuggled together on a bookshelf nearby, where a goldfish sat on top and jetted around a bowl of clean water. Next to that bowl, a thin blade with a polished white handle gleamed in the light, casting a blurred spot of light upon a hunk of wood.

And behind this hunk of wood, the DiLegno family smiled back at Hansel through a photo in a silver frame, Carla, her son, and Pinocchio. They all had the same signature dark hair and radiant smile. Hansel scowled. *So Pinocchio's The Carver.*

Carla's footsteps clicked back toward Hansel, and she reappeared in the screen with a bottle of water and a plate wrapped in tin foil.

"Here you go, sir. A bottle of water, and I also wrapped you some of my famous cherry cobbler. One bite of this, and you'll feel all your energy come right back to you." She opened the door and held her offering out to Hansel. "I do hope you enjoy it."

For a short moment, Hansel hesitated. He looked at the water and cobbler, his heart growing sore. That picture of the DiLegno family would remain fixed in his mind. He couldn't help but feel like he was about to erase those smiles for good. This woman was so pure and generous, so much like Snow.

"Sir?" Carla nodded and extended her arms out further, concern washing over her face.

Hansel blinked. "Oh, um, why, thank you, Madam. This is really quite a wonderful treat. I hardly expected such kindness from a stranger."

Carla tilted her head. "You must not be from around here. From Richmond all the way down to Charlottesville, you'll hardly find a soul who won't open up the door to serve someone in need. What's your name?"

Finally accepting the bottle and the dessert, Hansel improvised. "Um, I am called Ansel."

"Ansel. That's not a very common name. It's unique, I must say, and somehow quite fitting. Where are you from, Ansel? Let me guess: You're from far, far away!" Carla's voice acquired a light, dreamy touch to it, like she was telling a story to a group of young kids.

Hansel nodded subtly. “Quite.”

“Well, Mr. Ansel, if there’s anything more I can do for you, don’t hesitate to come back and knock on our door. I make enough dessert to feed an army.”

“That’s quite generous. Thank you, Madam.”

“It’s my pleasure. Pleasant travels to you.” Carla smiled and reached out for a handshake.

Accepting the handshake, Hansel smiled back. “Thank you.”

“You’re very welc—”

She didn’t see it coming, and in retrospect, Hansel almost didn’t see it either. He was already growing so fond of the woman and her maternal kindness toward him. He had to pull out the dart before he could give her any more chances to grow on him. He almost didn’t do it, but another look at that photograph changed his mind. Pinocchio. Pinocchio didn’t get to enjoy a happy ending while Gretel was still missing.

How very morose Carla’s family would be without her.

When he appeared back in the Cavern of Ombra with her, she was asleep with her head on his shoulder, and he felt the burden in more ways than one.

He hated that icy voice when it spoke again. *“So you have succeeded, my hunter. You have brought me The Carver’s wife.”*

Hansel’s nostrils flared. “Yes.”

“Then you are one step closer to freeing your sister. Rest, my huntsman. Your work shall continue later.”

Carla vanished from Hansel’s side. He watched her appear upright in one of the seven large gemstones protruding from the walls.

Hansel went to bed with a heavy heart that night, unable to take his eyes off the ceiling. He also covered the mirror again. *What have I started? What have I done? Somebody, help me undo this mess.*

A hollow knock sounded at the door.

Who could that be at such an hour? Hansel felt that he had been lying awake for so long the sun was probably due to rise at any moment.

Another knock.

"Coming! Wait a second!"

Hansel rolled out of bed, dressed in his day clothes, and shuffled to the door.

When he opened it, he was surprised to have Snow White collapse into his arms, convulsing with sobs.

"Oh, Hansel! Something awful is going on around here! You have to help me! It's Liam. He's gone missing, and I don't know what to do!"

"Start from the beginning, Snow. What happened?"

"He left the castle in a rush yesterday, and I didn't bother asking him where he was going. I assumed he was training with Mulan or off to market or doing some everyday Liam task. Oh, how I love him, but he can be such a mystery. He promised he would be back by sundown, but I haven't seen him since."

Hansel listened attentively while Snow poured her heart out to him, doing his best to appear understanding and supportive. However, pretending that he knew nothing was the hardest part. An assault of thoughts nibbled at the back of his mind, growing louder. *What would Snow do if she knew her search efforts were in vain?*

"I'm sure he'll turn up."

"Can you help me look?"

Hansel grabbed a lantern and they walked together for hours, searching high and low for the missing prince. Or pretending to, at least. With every step they took, Hansel could see the toll it took on Snow, and it only compounded that heavy feeling he had carried to bed. Her eyes were red with dark circles beneath them, and it seemed her face would be perpetually damp with all the tears she cried. Every now and then, she would stop and manage to make conversation or pull a glimmer of hope, only to break down once again.

At one point, Snow sat on the ground and slumped her shoulders, shaking her head at the moon. "If somebody did something to him . . . If somebody hurt him, I swear . . . ."

Her words were cold against Hansel's ears. She spoke daggers. He sat by her and placed a tentative hand on her shoulder. "Come now. You don't truly mean such hostile thoughts. You're good. Surely you wouldn't hurt anybody?"

Snow sighed and brushed a tear from her eye. "I don't know, Hansel. This hurts more than anything. It hurts because I have the very distinct feeling that we're looking for *nothing*. Liam wouldn't abandon me. We love each other. Madly and deeply. Do you remember when my stepmother poisoned me?"

Hansel frowned. He remembered it all too well. Her lifeless body. Her still, cold features. "How could I ever forget?"

"When I ran the comb through my hair and fell into that sleep, Liam said he knew. He felt that something had happened to me. I have that exact feeling right now. Somebody has done something to my husband." She was shaking, her hands balled up into fists and her lips quivering with anger. "I feel it, and I'm going to find out what happened. I'm going to find out who and why, and I'm going to hurt them. I'm going to make them regret it if it's the *last* thing I do!"

Hansel brushed her arm. "This isn't you talking right now. You don't mean this."

"Wouldn't you do anything for someone you love? I know you would. The way you've always talked about getting your sister back, you would do anything, even if it means losing a part of yourself, and now I finally understand that." Snow nodded. "I really do."

Hansel suppressed a shudder. He didn't like hearing Snow talk this way, especially because he understood her sentiments so clearly. He couldn't bear to think about the day she would find out what happened. How would she treat him? *She must never find out.* He had to distract her.

He squeezed Snow's shoulder. "Come, stand up. Let's keep walking."

He led her down a winding cobblestone path, where crickets sang and frogs croaked. The breeze rustled a droopy tree, causing the leaves to sway back and forth in an entrancing lullaby. Hansel approached the tree and separated the branches, gesturing for Snow to walk through the opening he'd created. He followed closely behind her and took in the sight of fireflies fading in and out of the night, dotting the hills and burning serpentine patterns into his vision. Above him, stars splattered the sky, some of them rocketing toward the moon and fading away.

Hansel spoke in a gentle whisper. "Look where we are."

For the first time that night, she managed a radiant, full-faced Snow smile. "The meadow."

"Yes, the meadow." Hansel blew out his lantern and lowered it to the ground.

Snow waded through the grass with her head down to the earth, her arms swinging casually by her sides. She looked so cute, Hansel thought, studying the ground the way she had when she was a little girl. "There used to be flowers here, remember?"

"I do. I remember it all like it was yesterday."

Snow spread her arms out and let herself fall back into a bed of grass, her hair sprawled out behind her as she stared up at the moon. "Nothing's the same anymore. It's not even the way it was yesterday. No flowers. No birds. How long has the moon been out tonight? We've been out here for hours. The sun should've come up long ago."

Hansel took slow strides through the meadow with his arms folded. It was true. Things weren't the same, and he knew it must've been because of him. He'd changed things. He banished another man from the kingdom and brought in a woman who didn't belong, a prisoner. All for an evil queen who could take the form of the witch his sister burned years ago.

He collapsed on the ground next to Snow and laced his arms behind his head. "I know. Nothing's the same. I don't know what to do."

"Why should it fall on you? You've lost as much as the rest of us. You're a wonderful man, Hansel, but it doesn't fall on you to save everything. Just be a part of it with us."

"What part of it do I have? Who am I?"

"You're the Hansel I grew up with. The Hansel I met here in this very meadow."

Hansel closed his eyes. "You remember that day?"

"Of course."

Before he could stop himself, Hansel rolled onto his elbow and took Snow's hand. Her skin was warm, soft, and velvety. Pure. Even in her sadness, she was the most beautiful thing he had ever seen. He leaned forward and brushed his lips against her cheek.

Snow turned her head away and retreated her arm. "Hansel. Please don't."

Hansel felt a small pang of hurt in his chest. He closed his hand and stared dumbly at the woman in the grass. "I was just trying to help. I can see how you're hurting right now."

"Yes, but I'm hurting for my husband. Wherever he is, whatever's happened, Liam is still my husband. He always will be, until the day I die."

Hansel flopped onto his back again, feeling stupid and dejected. "So why did you come to me?"

"I needed my friend right now, Hansel. That's all I needed."

Hansel sighed. "You know, there was a time when we would come here every day and lay here like this, holding hands and enjoying each other's company. We would do that every day. I was so sure you liked me the way I liked you. You looked at me the same. You shared your innermost secrets with me. Tell me this, Snow, did that ever mean anything more to you?"

Snow sniffed and rubbed her face with both hands. Hansel wasn't looking at her anymore, but he heard her begin to cry again. "Did it *mean* something to me? Of course it did! It was *you* who stopped showing up for so long. You stopped coming, and you were so cold and distant when you were here. I didn't know how to talk to you anymore. Every day that I waited here, you left me wondering why. What were you doing all that time? What happened?"

Hansel's own eyes flooded with hot emotion and his fingers touched the stem of one of his black darts, the ones he'd received from his old employer. "I was collecting bounty for a man named Robin Hood.

He promised to help, to hunt whoever took Gretel away from me. A million gold for every job. Every witch, creature, and monster I killed, everyone I banished to the other world, it was supposed to bring me closer to my sister. But it only took me further from you."

"Bounty hunting." Snow White wiped another tear from her eye. "I've hardly known you all this time. Now I hardly know myself, because I know I would do the same thing to get Liam back. And now I know you understand what I'm saying. I will do *anything* to bring him back to me. I feel very sorry for anyone who stands in my way."

Hansel swallowed a lump in his throat. "As do I, my old friend."

My hunter, I require your presence.

The voice chilled Hansel to the bone. He'd never heard it so far from the Cavern of Ombra or away from the mirror before, but there it was in his head again, clear as the stars above and icy like a winter night.

Not only that, Hansel felt a sort of danger he couldn't understand. There was something new in the mines. Or some*one*. Five someones, all of whom were a threat to his mission, a threat to his sister. He sensed it as easily as he could smell a rising loaf of bread.

In an instant, Hansel jumped to his feet. He needed to get to the Cavern of Ombra.

Snow White sat up and brushed blades of grass out of her hair. "Are you leaving, then? You don't have to leave. You do understand that I will always have a special place in my heart for you. We will always be friends, Hansel."

Hansel smiled through his tears. "Indeed we will, Snow, but for now I need to be alone. I'm terribly sorry for what's happened to Liam. Truly."

He broke into a sprint, his boots swishing through dying grass and growing weeds, leaving Snow White alone in the meadow. *How many steps will it take me to forget you?*

Make haste, my hunter.

He waited until he was out of sight, beyond the drooping trees that surrounded the meadow. He closed his eyes, caught his breath, and let himself disappear.

CHAPTER TWENTY-FOUR

TODAY—THE NEW WORLD: MARYLAND

The horse rocketed forward and Pietro nearly toppled off, not that he was steady on the beast to begin with. Between the suit of armor weighing him down, the lance, and the fact that he hadn't been on a horse in years, he felt like a china set trying to balance on straws. Not that the strange dude in the green had given him much of a choice.

Pietro was going to gallop to his doom on a dark horse, all at the pleasure of an audience. He tried to think of everything he taught his son about horses when he used to go riding with his family.

"Eyes forward. Look where you wanna go and not down at your feet, okay? Most importantly, keep your hands on the reins, dude," he would say. "No selfies. You need both your hands."

Pietro felt pretty good about remembering his rules, and then that dude came back and put a lance in his hand. What was he supposed to do? One time he'd driven a car with his elbows because he was trying to talk on the phone and drink a coffee at the same time. He supposed jousting was probably the same thing.

When the announcer yelled, "Charge!" Pietro was off, bouncing on his horse like a rodeo cowboy, and suddenly he forgot his other rule: Look where you wanna go.

Jeebus, this arena is filled with people!

Pietro's field of vision was narrow, but everywhere he turned his head, people chanted and jeered and gnawed on turkey legs, and he was riding dangerously close to the crowd straight ahead. He drew his lance further back out of fear that he might poke someone's eye out, but that didn't ease his fear of trampling them to death.

Oooh no! Pietro squeezed his eyes shut and prepared for impact, imagining himself tumbling off the horse and skewering a leg.

Luckily, Tinker Bell seemed to know where to go. The horse must have been around the arena millions of times. She made a smooth turn along the arena walls without his guidance. Pietro opened his eyes, tried to steady his hammering pulse, and refocused. The horse was following the curves.

The sound of galloping hooves doubled as the other horse approached from the left, seemingly appearing out of nowhere. Sir Gallivant sat firmly planted with his lance pointed in front of him.

Pietro closed his eyes again and silently screamed, *This is really going to hurt!*

But nothing touched him, and the sound of Maid Marian's footsteps receded. The two knights had crossed paths without impact.

Wait a minute. Why didn't he knock me off my horse? Pietro basically gave Sir Gallivant a free shot at winning the joust, yet he was still rooted to the horse and gradually finding a sense of balance. He was grateful that Sir Gallivant hadn't knocked him to the ground. The crowd, however, was not so pleased.

"Booo! Booo! Disgraces!"

The amplified voice sounded again, and Pietro looked up and realized it was coming from the king. The king stood on the balcony of a makeshift castle, and the horrible queen lady stood at his right.

"This is a fight to the death, gentlemen! Think of Lady Elegant! Are you really worthy of having her hand in marriage?"

Pietro's eyes flickered to the girl at the king's left, clad in a pink dress and a pointy veiled cap—Lady Elegant, he supposed—and he realized in horror that Lady Elegant was actually Rosana. She stood still with her hands behind her back and her mouth shut, but her eyes seemed to be pleading with Pietro under her veil.

Renaissance fairs were supposed to be fun. So far, Pietro really hated this one.

The horses rounded the corner and crossed paths again, and still, nothing came close to knocking Pietro off his horse.

"Where be the tomatoes when they are of need?" the king said. "These fine lords and ladies came to be entreated to a *fight*, not a pony show! Fight, you miscreants!"

The crowd roared with laughter and continued to jeer. Something dull clanked against Pietro's arm, and he was pretty sure somebody had thrown a turkey leg at him. He narrowed his eyes, exhaled deeply through his nose, and rolled his shoulders as best as he could under his heavy metal plates.

"I don't want to be here!" he growled.

He adjusted his balance and steadied his grip on the lance, waiting for the horse to make its rounds again. When Sir Gallivant came into view, Pietro took aim.

Clank!

Pietro's lance scraped Sir Gallivant's breastplate, but it wasn't quite enough to throw him off his horse. The horses thundered on.

Pietro's heart accelerated. *I might actually have a shot at winning this thing!*

When the next thing happened, Pietro's wasn't sure if he heard it or felt it first, but he definitely didn't see it. There was a deafening crash, a series of clanks, and then he was on his back instead of on a horse. He heard Tinker Bell gallop out of the arena, and when he pried his eyes open, his lance lay uselessly at his side. Everything hurt, from the back of his head to his shoulders. His ankle screamed, pulsed, throbbed, and stung all at once.

"That's the warrior's spirit, gentlemen! Sir Diffident takes a tumble!"

Boisterous applause blanketed the crowd, and another turkey leg landed on Pietro's chest plate as a set of white horse legs thumped past his head.

Oh, no, you don't!

Pietro hoisted up his jousting stick. He rolled onto his elbow with some difficulty and hurled the lance like a javelin, aiming for Sir Gallivant.

Crash! Sir Gallivant toppled off his horse, and Maid Marian galloped away.

Now the crowd was *really* happy. Pietro tuned out the sound of their cheering and pulled himself up to his feet, electric pain shooting through his ankle.

"Preposterous!" the king roared. "Sir Diffident has broken the knight's code of old!"

And probably my ankle. So what? That guy knocked me on my ass!

Pietro looked up at the balcony where the obnoxious king pointed at him, and Rosana remained silent and still.

"Shame on the code-breaker! You bring shame unto your kingdom, unto your mother, and unto Lady Princess Elegant! Be gone!"

"Rosana!" Pietro yelled. "Let's get out of here!"

And where the hell is Enzo?

Pietro started hobbling out from the arena's center. Sir Gallivant stood up with his lance.

That guy knocked me off my horse! Jerk! Pietro removed his helmet, and the air rushed back to his sweaty face. He narrowed his eyes, flared his nostrils, and channeled his remaining energy. Despite the weight of his armor and the fatigue in his muscles, Pietro could make himself feel as light as a feather when he really wanted to. He looked down at his feet and smiled. He was hovering slightly above the mud.

"Take this, you codfish!" he yelled as he propelled his body toward the other knight. He didn't give Gallivant enough time to react.

Clang!

Pietro and Sir Gallivant collided in a heap of momentum. They rolled around the mud until they crashed into the arena wall with another ring of metal on metal. The crowd applauded the whole time.

"Mommy, how did he fly off the ground like that?" a small child asked.

"It's special effects, sweetie! You can't see them, but there are wires everywhere."

"Man! I thought he was magic!"

Pietro stopped to catch his breath when a familiar voice reverberated from Sir Gallivant's armor. "Pietro! Pietro, get off of me!"

Gallivant removed his helmet.

Pietro gripped his hair, eyes round with alarm. "*Enzo*? Why are you here?"

"I don't even know anymore. Some jerk in green. Did you . . . did you just fly?"

On the castle balcony, Rosana remained stone still, and Pietro was becoming increasingly certain that her hands had been tied behind her back and that her mouth was taped shut. And the king's face brimmed with horror.

"What is this sorcery? Sir Diffident's a witch and a cheater, and Sir Gallivant is but a young boy! Doom upon these wretched souls!"

Pietro's blood boiled as scraps of food rained down on him.

"Seize them! Throw them in jail! Let them be punished!"

The first to appear was the green jerk with the knife in his belt. He marched through the portcullis with a team of five other men, and before Pietro knew it, they seized him and Enzo.

"Put me down! Put me down, stupids!"

One of them held Pietro by his sore ankle, sending streams of pain up his leg. The green man held him under his arm. The man's knife bounced in his belt, not three inches away from Pietro's face, and that's when Pietro thought about the figurines in his pocket.

"I don't know who you really are, dude," Pietro said, "but you're a horrible human being. I told you there was a mistake."

"There's no mistake here, chum. I always knew who you really are. You're no jouster. You're Peter Pan, the man-child Madame Esme told me to look for. You, your buddy, and your princess on the balcony are going just where I need you to go."

"And where is that, exactly?"

"Jail, my friend."

"Jail? Okay, but it's just for show, right? How long will we be stuck there?"

Green Man shrugged. "Your call. We can leave when you're ready. See, it's not you or your chums who are stuck anywhere. 'Tis I, stuck in this dingy world to which I don't belong."

"You're from the other place!" Pietro reasoned. "Dude, who *are* you?"

"I was once known as Prince Liam. A troubled man doomed me to live in this realm as a knife thrower not so long ago. But I've a lovely wife to return to, and you three are the ones who are going to take me back to her."

CHAPTER TWENTY-FIVE

THREE YEARS AGO—CAVERN OF OMBRA

Hansel expected something bone-chilling in the mines, like a line of warriors pointing steel in his face, a crazy man with an army of apes, or an old, bearded man in a sparkly robe and a pointed hat. Instead, when Hansel arrived at the Cavern of Ombra, he was greeted by five black-robed people having a tea party at a round table.

If you could've called them all *people*, that is. The first to speak looked more like a horned lion, his voice deep and ashy with an elegant ring.

"Good evening, Hansel." The man, or whatever he was, aimed a scaly paw at the empty seat to his right. "Please, join us."

Hansel studied the feral man's strange company. On the other side of the empty seat sat a bald man with a graying goatee and a gold earring. He possessed a distinct air of sophistication, sitting straight in his chair and sipping from a china cup.

Next to the bald man, a taller man poured more tea with his good hand. Where his other hand should've been, a long iron hook protruded from his sleeve and scratched something into the table. While the other four wore robes of black linen, the hooked man wore leather.

Then there were two women. Hansel had heard stories about the old woman, stern-faced and feather-haired, and her rug made out of wolf fur. People also said she took down a giant *by herself* before Hansel was born.

Then came Hua Mulan, Prince Liam's tutor and allegedly the only survivor of the Battle of the Thousand that took place long ago, claiming the lives of her father, a group of princesses, the baker of Drury, and hundreds of others who had defied Queen Avoria. Hansel had only seen Mulan once, and though they'd never had any interaction, one look from her made his bones go cold. It wasn't a glare, a sneer, or any real threatening expression. It was more of a non-expression. She was too still, too calm. Hansel wondered what might've been bubbling under the surface.

"We aren't going to bite you, Hansel," the beast continued. "I know we may look intimidating, but we only wish to engage in civil discourse with you."

Hansel nodded and edged to the stone table. With every step he took, the terrible dark gemstones squished and contorted beneath his feet. He took his seat between the lion man and the bald man. "Thank you, Hansel. Allow me to introduce myself. My name is Jacob Isaac Holmes. I reside in Clocher de Pierre in Florindale. The man on the other side of you is Sir Merlin of Camelot. To his right, Captain James Hook, Ms. Augustine Rose, and Ms. Hua Mulan." As Jacob spoke everyone's names, each member of the table nodded and raised a porcelain mug. Except for Mulan, stone still. "Now, Ms. Rose has graciously brewed a very special blend of tea for us this evening. Please help yourself to as much as you'd like."

Augustine, the old woman, shoved a cupful of tea across the table with surprising momentum. Hansel caught it by the handle and a small drop of liquid sloshed over the brim, transparently dark and soothingly warm. "I do hope you like Darjeeling, dear."

That was Hansel's favorite.

Captain Hook winked at Hansel and flashed a mouthful of gold. "Drink up, lad!"

Hansel stared into the cup, wondering if these people intended to poison him. "I'm not so thirsty, actually."

"Pity." Jacob took a slow sip of his own drink and wove his hands together on the table. "Now, I would imagine you wonder why we've gathered here today, so we might as well get right to the point."

Even though his palms were sweating, Hansel leaned back and crossed his arms behind his head. He'd come too far to let these court jesters think they could break him. He swallowed, feeling his Adam's apple rise and fall again before he took a deep breath. "Yes. Let's."

"Hansel, my boy!" Merlin's voice carried a jolly ring, loud and deep, and Hansel watched his peppered goatee bounce up and down as he spoke. "We were summoned here by Miss Violet to speak with you this evening. I believe you two are acquainted?"

"Well, yes. Who doesn't know Violet?"

"Who indeed? And yet, we sense that there must be somebody in the Old World who is not acquainted with Miss Violet, because trouble is on the horizon. And one would have to be a fish's tail to invoke trouble with Miss Violet or her realm."

"It's not technically *her* realm."

"But she cares for it as if it were her own," Jacob asserted, "and that's why she's most interested in knowing why there's a prisoner from the outside world being held captive here. Right here inside this very mine, in fact."

Hansel's shoulders tensed, and a bead of sweat bubbled on his forehead. *So they know*. Of course. Each robed figure remained silent, eyes fixed so intently on Hansel that he felt like they were drilling into his soul . . . analyzing it, dissecting it, and peeling it like a vegetable. Hook raised an eyebrow. Mulan's expression didn't change. *She hasn't said anything this whole time. What is she thinking?* Only Merlin seemed to wear a hint of a smile.

Hansel decided to play dumb. "Really? A prisoner from another world? That is most curious indeed. Who is she?"

"I never told you the prisoner was female, my boy," Merlin said. "What might *you* know about her?"

Curses. "Lucky guess. I wouldn't know anything at all."

"That is most convenient, isn't it? Especially because we can all see her imprisoned in that gemstone in the wall." Jacob turned and flicked his paw to indicate an enormous ruby protruding from the cavern walls, in which Carla DiLegno remained upright and dormant, facing Hansel with closed eyes. "Who is she? How did she get here?"

"I surely have no idea."

Without taking his eyes off Hansel, the pirate breathed onto his hook and polished it with a leather sleeve. "You don't want to be lyin' to us, lad. That would be unwise."

Hansel smirked. This man was actually threatening him with a hook hand?

"James doesn't mean to threaten you, Hansel. None of us do. We simply wish to come to a peaceful agreement," Jacob said. "Now, you say you've no idea where the woman came from. Would you swear that on your life?"

"Certainly."

"Would you swear it on Gretel?" Mulan spoke for the first time, and Hansel's head snapped in her direction. Her tone was low, cool, and collected.

Hansel sprang up from his seat. "How dare you invoke my sister in this conversation?"

Mulan sipped her tea.

Merlin put a firm hand on Hansel's elbow. "Calm down, my boy. Please sit down and compose your temper."

"I will *not* sit down. She hasn't the right to—"

"Are you aware that approximately one month ago, Lord Bellamy of the Woodlands vanished from his home?" Apparently unfazed by the outburst, Mulan continued, "And more recently, a student of mine? I must tell you that I care for my pupils like I would care for a son or a daughter. When one of them goes missing, I take it personally. So I ask you this: Where is Prince Liam?"

"You wicked woman! You sit there this whole time with that smug look on your face and you don't say a word, and when you open your mouth you defile my sister's name and vomit your filthy accusations upon me!"

"*Where* is Prince Liam?"

"You're as wretched as he is! Prince Liam is a spineless codfish and the son of a—"

Pop!

As blaring as the sound was, Hansel was the only one to jump. He looked across the table, ears ringing and heart pounding. Augustine had fired a blunderbuss into the air. It remained upright in her hands, oozing thin wisps of smoke, and the woman's eyes drilled a hole into Hansel's heart. Hansel didn't know she was carrying the gun on her. "I'm sorry, dear, did that hurt your ears? Tame your anger and *sit down,* or you'll feel the next one in your knee."

Hansel swallowed and eased back into his chair. "Who the devil are you people, anyway?"

"We're the Order of the Bell, Hansel," Jacob said. "We've been sworn to protect the realm from any threat, at any cost, and we are *very* proficient at what we do. We played a major role in gathering forces to win the Giant War before Queen Avoria intervened. We slayed the chameleon wolf that ate young Tommaso Buggia. Together, we've slayed many a dragon before the people of the realm even knew they were in danger."

"And you, lad, have been deemed a threat to the realm," Hook said.

"Have you anything to say in your defense?" Merlin asked.

Hansel narrowed his eyes. "Only that my actions are perfectly logical and I've had a very clear motive from the beginning. As Hua Mulan has made so clear, you already know that I lost my sister when she and I were children. You say you all protect this realm from danger, at any cost? That's what I'm doing for Gretel. I found her; I need only to set her free, and I will do so at any cost."

Mulan folded her arms. It was the most dramatic movement she'd made the whole time. "Was Liam a necessary cost?"

"Yes, because he went too far in his meddling. He, Lord Bellamy, and anybody else who should choose to stand in my way shall pay the price."

"So where is he?"

"I sent him to a place where he can't meddle. He's in an entirely different realm now, and I feel no shame."

Mulan nodded. "Would this be the same realm from which you took that woman?"

"That is correct."

"Why did you take her?" Jacob asked.

"Because the mirror asked me to. If I gather seven people, my sister goes free."

"So you intend to imprison more?"

"Precisely."

"There *must* be another way," Augustine said.

"There is no other way."

Hook raised an eyebrow again. "Are you aware that you are also doing the Ivory Queen's bidding? If you continue down this path, lad, you may get your sister back, but you will also be responsible for single-handedly bringing about the greatest threat our realm will ever see. And that woman and anybody else you stick in those prisons will most likely die. We cannot allow that to happen."

"So you would stand in my way?"

"We would formally request that you cease this operation, my boy," Merlin said. "Return the woman to her proper home, and destroy this mine. Leave us to deal with the mirror."

"Let us help you, dear," Augustine added. "These sorts of things are our specialty, you know."

Hansel looked into her eyes and knew that she was telling the truth. Augustine genuinely wanted to help, and she truly believed that she could, as well. There was something about the old woman that resonated with him. He really wanted to like her, and he was sure he would have if circumstances had been different. The same went for most of the other people sitting at the table with them. Jacob Isaac Holmes—beneath that freakish exterior, there was kindness and strength of heart that Hansel suspected was born out of pain. Clearly Jacob was a man who knew what it was like to lose something important. A home? A family member? Perhaps a lover? There were men who lost their possessions and cast their will aside with them, but not Jacob. Whatever he'd lost remained within and gave him something to fight for.

Hansel didn't know how he felt about Hook. He sat there polishing his gruesome appendage while flashing looks of distrust that negated any sense of hope Jacob and Augustine had in winning Hansel over. What was a pirate really doing with these allegedly righteous souls? What was in it for him? A chance to fulfill his violent tendencies? Was Violet paying the Order for their help?

If Hook made Hansel hesitant to accept the Order's offer, Merlin quelled most of those fears. He seemed like a nice guy, and one with plenty of experience in dealing with magic. He was just the kind of man who could help Hansel disenchant a mirror or break a complex curse. *They can really help me. They can do everything I've been meaning to do without harm.*

Hansel was almost ready to give in and ask for their help, and then he looked at Hua Mulan and the darkness crashed over him again. He had already grown too familiar with the voice that spoke to him when the shadows invaded. *She doesn't want to help your sister. She wants revenge for Liam. Don't trust the Order, huntsman. Stick to my plan, and I shall grant you everything you dream of and more.*

Hansel squeezed his eyes shut and tried to block out her voice. He tried to focus on beautiful things: horses thundering through a meadow, the smoke of a campfire carrying stories up to the stars, crystal waterfalls purifying the earth . . . Snow and her flawless soul.

The voice broke through his thoughts. *Reap their souls, huntsman.*

Get out of my head!

I'm not in your head, dear. You should know that by now. I will soon be everywhere. Reap their souls. Now, or I will kill your sister right here and show it to you every day.

Hansel! Help me! Please don't let her kill me!

At the sound of his sister's scream, Hansel gritted his teeth. *Okay, okay, okay! Tell me what I must do.*

Concentrate, huntsman. Let your anger extract everything you hate about the Order. Do not let their number or their credentials intimidate you. You are so much more powerful than they. You don't want them to foil our plan, do you? Do it now.

Jacob finished his tea. "So, Hansel? Have we appealed to your better nature?"

Beads of sweat gathered on Hansel's neck. If he eliminated the Order just to find that the Ivory Queen was tinkering with his mind, he would never be able to forgive himself. On the other hand, if he didn't act fast and the queen did something to his sister . . . .

Hansel, please!

Hansel narrowed his eyes, feeling the darkness possess his soul again. "*No.*"

He raised his hand, pointed at the beastly man, and a stream of darkness poured from his fingertips, like rippling shadows. Jacob didn't have time to react. The dark ripples swirled around his body, closed in on him, and compressed him into a smaller form. It all happened in less than a second. Before Hansel raised his fingertips, Jacob Isaac Holmes was a living being. In the time it took Hansel to lower his hands, Jacob became something else: a stone, a dark gem like midnight imprisoned in a diamond. The gem fell to the ground with his cup of tea and landed among the sea of soul husks that fell ages ago in the Cavern of Ombra.

Without a word, the four remaining members of the Order of the

Bell sprang to their feet and spread out, tromping over hundreds of other stones in the process. Hansel stood slowly, and then he did something he'd never done before. He levitated. It came to him as naturally as walking. He ascended to the height of the ruby prisons, blinked, and when he opened his eyes again, his vision was sharper.

Hook withdrew a cutlass with his good hand while Hua Mulan produced a blade of her own. From somewhere toward the cavern's mouth, Augustine Rose raised her blunderbuss and took aim.

But it was Merlin who posed the greatest threat when Hansel was in the air, because the mage also knew how to levitate. He soared high above the stone table until he was eye level with Hansel, sneering at him with his palms turned up to the sky. His irises glowed a deep orange, and his goatee twitched with rage. "You don't know what you've done, boy."

Merlin clapped his hands, pushed his arms outward, and a wide column of emerald-green fire erupted from his palms. Its heat warped the air around him, gathering momentum as it approached Hansel. Meanwhile, there was another tremendous bang as Augustine fired her gun again. Hansel merely smirked as the flames and the bullet approached, letting the warmth lick his face before he vanished and reappeared behind Augustine in a mist of shadows.

"I can't have you firing that again, granny."

Hansel clamped his hand on Augustine's shoulder, fully prepared to envelope her in darkness and turn her into a gem, but he heard a *whoosh* behind him and vanished before Hook's cutlass could take his head. Hook cringed when his blade narrowly missed the peak of the silver bun on the back of Augustine's head.

Augustine whirled around and slapped Hook across the face. "Watch where you're swinging that thing!"

"And you watch where you're pointing your artillery, love." Using the curve of his hook, the pirate tilted Augustine's blunderbuss to the ground.

"Focus!" Mulan snapped.

Hansel reappeared in the air and put Merlin in a chokehold from behind, pressing the crook of his elbow against the mage's throat. Hansel sneered at the three members of the Order on the ground as Merlin clutched at his Adam's apple, desperately trying to pry Hansel's arm away as the color drained from his face. "It would be humiliating for a magician to die of asphyxiation, would it not? Take your shot at me, old woman! Save his life!"

Augustine cocked her gun again and narrowed her eyes. "You don't want to test me, dear. I can hit a mosquito in the dark if it tries my nerves long enough!"

"Then hit me!"

Augustine fired. In the time it took for the bullet to leave the gun, Hansel turned Merlin into a black gemstone. It fell to the ground with a soft thud, and Hansel vanished again, exploding into dark smoke and reappearing next to Carla DiLegno's prison.

"*Merlin*!" Hook cleaved the air. "I'll peel the flesh off your bones, lad! Come down here and face me like a—"

Hook became a gemstone.

Hansel descended back to the ground and stepped on what used to be the pirate. On either side of him, Augustine pointed her blunderbuss and Mulan held her sword in front of her.

"Well, well. So the two women are all that's left. Some powerful order Violet came up with. It seems she'll never learn that I've always been one step ahead of her."

Augustine's hand trembled. "You're not Hansel."

"Not entirely. You think Hansel alone could've taken down your men? Jacob Isaac Holmes, Merlin of Camelot, and James Hook were some of the bravest warriors I've *ever* known. Their souls make beautiful repasts. As will yours."

Hansel's head swiveled. With a snap of his fingers, Augustine Rose dropped to the ground as a dark gemstone.

"As for you, Hua Mulan—"

"She'll never love you."

Hansel gritted his teeth. "What did you say to me?"

"Snow White. She'll never love you, even if Prince Liam never returns. She'd be better off alone than with you."

Her remarks caught Hansel off guard. While he boiled under the surface, Mulan broke into a dash quicker than lightning, snatched something out of Hansel's vest pocket, and stopped to finish the last of her tea, a cocky gleam in her eye as she smacked her lips.

"I hope you'll finish yours. That's good tea." She used her blade to deflect a stream of shadows that Hansel shot out of his fingertips, and she gripped the item she had stolen from his pocket: a long black dart. "I'll be back to finish this, Hansel. I'd use this time to restore my honor if I were you, because I won't be coming back alone."

Hua Mulan smirked, tilted her head, and plunged the tip of Hansel's dart into her own neck, leaving Hansel seething in a cavern of broken souls as the woman warrior escaped into a new realm.

CHAPTER TWENTY-SIX

TODAY—THE NEW WORLD: MARYLAND RENAISSANCE FAIRE

Enzo felt like he was in a zoo. Renaissance jail was no joke, at least to those who had ever been inside of it. It was a horse-drawn wagon, caged and sealed with a large padlock for all the faire's spectators to see and laugh at until somebody else paid ten dollars to bail them out, or their jailor decided to let them out in an act of mercy.

As happy as he was to be out of that hot suit of armor, sitting on a moving bale of hay wasn't that much of an improvement to his day. At least Rosana was there, and Pietro, well, Enzo would just have to deal with him being there, too. Pietro was the only one who looked happy, stretching both legs in front of him on a long hay bale.

"You look comfortable," Enzo said.

"About as comfortable as I can be, considering you pretty much broke my ankle."

"Oh, chill out, Pietro. I didn't even know that was you." Enzo paused and gathered his thoughts. "And did you really have to go all Iron Man on me and tackle me to the ground, *after* you'd already thrown your stick at me? How did you do that? More importantly, why?"

"What can I say? I'm a sore loser. You knocked me off my horse, and I got mad."

"Well, it's probably your fault we're sitting in a moving cage," Rosana pointed out. "But I still don't understand what *I'm* doing in here. I did nothing wrong."

"It wouldn't have mattered what *any* of us did," Pietro said. "That little jerk meant to put us here all along."

"You mean the king?"

"No, I'm talking about *this* guy." Pietro pulled the knife-thrower figurine out of his pocket and tossed it to Enzo.

Enzo caught it, studied it, and smiled. "You got my figurines back!"

"Yep. You're welcome, kid. Anyway, this guy talked to me before he threw us all in jail. He came from my world, and apparently he's been looking for us, too."

"Your world?" Enzo said sarcastically. "You mean Fairytale Land?"

"Exactly."

Rosana elbowed Enzo in the ribs, and his whole body hurt. "Seriously? Do you still not believe everything that's been going on? Pietro's story, Madame Esme, these figurines?"

Enzo blew a raspberry and put his head in his hands. "I don't know what I believe anymore, Rosana."

Pietro's eyes lit up, and he beamed at Rosana. "Wait, *you* believe me?"

"Yup. I have a question, though. If you're Peter Pan, how come you grew up?"

"He's *not* Peter Pan. And he didn't grow up. He's like twelve."

"First of all, um, *rude*, and second of all, being a kid gets hard. Grown-ups are always bossing you around, telling you what to do, and nobody believes you. I knew this one kid who got eaten by a chameleon wolf because nobody took him seriously. Every time he told his parents he saw the wolf, it changed colors and blended in with trees and stuff, and when his parents stopped believing him, it ate him."

Enzo rolled his eyes. "That's not how the story goes. The boy who cried wolf was a liar."

Pietro threw his hands up. "See? Even still, the kid gets no respect."

"Enzo, what proof do you still need that something strange is going on? Is it still not enough that you saw your dad vanish? Pietro flew, and apparently I was invisible for a while!"

"You what?" Pietro asked. "Cool! I think your mom used to be able to do that too."

"I said I don't know what I believe right now, okay?" Enzo said. "Just let me process everything. Until I'm sure I'm not in a coma or something."

The wagon stopped moving, and the man in green approached the cage with a plate full of funnel cake fries. "You are *not* sleeping, chum."

Enzo sprang to his feet and grabbed the cage, putting his face between the bars. "You! Let us out already! We have things to do!"

Rosana followed suit and approached the cage. "Pleeease? I don't understand why I'm in here."

The man shoved a funnel cake fry into his mouth and spoke with his mouth full. "I'm sorry, lads and fair lady, but I bear good reason."

"Let us out, man," Pietro pleaded. "We can talk about your situation."

"I've a condition for the boy." The man leaned in and locked eyes with Enzo. "Sir Enzo, Madame Esme said you are to take me home. Should you agree, I will liberate you from your prison."

"Hey now," Pietro said, "I'm trying to get back to the other place, too, buddy. I have a wife and a son there. I'm not opposed to you joining us. We just don't know how to get there."

Enzo rolled his eyes. "Pietro, will you pay him the ten dollars so we can get out of here?"

"I would gladly do that if I *had* ten dollars, kid. But conveniently, jail is the one place where they don't take MasterCard or Lady Visa, and there's no ATM in sight."

"I'll settle for your good word," the man said.

"Dude, you can have all the words you want. I promise, I swear, I oblige, I consent, whatever. We good?"

The man aimed a palm at Pietro. "I wish to hear them from Enzo."

Enzo pointed to himself. "*Me*? Why me?"

"Because you're the lad who has been charged with taking me home."

Enzo scratched his head. "Do you not have a car? You need a ride or something? I literally have no idea what you're talking about."

"Madame Esme told me you'd come someday. Did she not tell you to find me?"

"She's a phony. If she knows the future, why hasn't she won the lottery?"

Rosana rolled her eyes and gripped the cage bars. "Look, mister, what was your name?"

"Prince Liam."

"Please ignore the boy on my right, Mister Liam," Rosana said. "Enzo's having trouble believing everything that's been going on lately, but yes, Madame Esme did tell him to find you. His dad carved a figurine that looks like you, and she told me that we're supposed to follow the signs. Enzo, do you have the figurine?"

"Yeah, but—"

"Give it."

Enzo sighed, removed the figurine from his pocket, and then jammed it into Rosana's palm.

"Look, this is you. There's one of me, too, and there are others! A gloved woman, an Asian woman, an old man, and the guy who took my mom. Come with us and help us look for them. I'm pretty sure if we all come together, we'll find a way to get you back home."

Liam took the figurine and smiled. "Stars, that's uncanny."

"That's *Pinocchio*," Pietro said. "Most gifted Carver in two worlds."

Enzo held out his hand. "Give it back to me, and let us out."

"And you'll do me the honor of returning me to my world?"

"I'm not doing you any honors. You forced me and Pietro into a jousting tournament, and now you have us stuffed in a cage."

"You know, the kid has a point, dude," Pietro said. "Was all of this really necessary?"

Liam shrugged. "You've my deepest apologies. Madame Esme

informed me that a dark man was here looking for you. I had to disguise you and put you in the king's show. It was the best way to hide you until he gave up and left."

"But jail, though?" Pietro whined.

"Please forgive me. I only wished to gather you in one place to request your consent."

"I don't consent," Enzo said. "You're a jerk."

"I think the people of the Old World would contest that theory, chum. I was known as the most charming, virtuous, and noble lad in all the land."

Pietro winked. "Yeah, well, in *this* world things change, bro."

"Let us go," Enzo demanded.

"Please consent in taking me home."

"No."

And then a new voice joined the conversation, that of a stern sounding middle-aged woman. "Liam, I order you to release your prisoners immediately."

Liam laughed without turning to identify the voice. "Release my prisoners? By the authority of whom?"

"By the authority of your old master."

A small, important-looking Asian woman strode up behind Liam and tapped him on the shoulder. In her grey business suit, high-heeled pumps, and with the Bluetooth in her ear, she stuck out like a sore thumb. She crossed her arms and tapped her foot as Liam spun around, eyes wide with something like fear.

"Mulan! How are you here right now?"

The woman held up a finger and shushed the man. "Let's get one thing straight. We may not be home right now, but everything I've ever taught you still applies. You will *never* call me by that name again, understood?"

"Yes."

"Yes, what?"

"Yes, Master."

"Wonderful." The woman tilted her head and smiled warmly at Enzo, Rosana, and Pietro. "Ah, the saviors! How wonderful to see you three are well. Give me just one second with this so-called *knife thrower,* and we'll get you on your way in no time." She tugged on Prince Liam's elbow and dragged him off to the side.

Enzo blinked, shook his head, and tapped Rosana on the shoulder. "That lady's one of my figures! Did Liam just call her Mulan?"

Rosana smirked. "Yep. And she called us the saviors."

Enzo collapsed onto the bale of hay, and Pietro gave him a light kick with his good foot. "Now do you believe me, kid?"

Before Enzo could think about Pietro's question, Mulan was briskly walking back to them. She took a large key from Liam and unlocked the cage. "There you go, soldiers. You're free men and woman again."

"Yes!" Enzo exclaimed. "Thanks, Miss! Pietro, get us out of here!"

"Hold on. No need to hurry off without Liam," the woman said.

"Um, he's not coming with us."

"Of course he isn't going with you. There's hardly any room for more in that dingy little pick-up truck. *I* have a jet. You're all coming with *me*."

CHAPTER TWENTY-SEVEN

TODAY—THE NEW WORLD: MULAN'S PLANE

Enzo had never been on a plane before, and he couldn't believe that his first experience came so abruptly. Then again, he wasn't quite sure what to believe anymore.

It had been a strange trip with Pietro already, from Richmond to New York City; from flying off of the Empire State Building, to chasing a shadow; having his future told by a woman who referred to herself in the third person, to fighting Pietro in a jousting tournament orchestrated by some weirdo who thought he used to be a prince in another life.

Now, Enzo was on Hua Mulan's private jet. He didn't bother to ask questions before they left; he was just happy to leave the Renaissance Faire. He, Pietro, and Rosana collected their belongings from Pietro's pick-up while Liam collected his own things from the faire. Pietro's only question was, "What do I do with my truck?" and Mulan assured him that it would be fine where it was.

As soon as they stepped on the plane, Enzo decided that the woman had it all: flat screen televisions, beige leather seats with cup holders and foot rests, pearly-bright lighting, and mini fridges stocked with soda and chocolate milk. There was even a game console, which Pietro had turned on right away. Instead of windows, screens projected digital images of everything from outer space to the Great Wall of China.

Enzo and Rosana settled in a pair of recliners while Liam turned his sights on an acoustic guitar that hung from one of the plane's walls. He strummed his own tune, slow and sad, and mouthed the words to himself. He was tentative and thoughtful about every word, as if he were still trying to come up with them. Enzo studied him and tried to guess what his real story was.

Rosana raised a footrest and turned to Enzo. "Where do you think we're going?"

"I have no idea. I'm actually a little tripped out over the fact that we just got on a stranger's plane."

"Why? We're obviously still on the right track. We were supposed to find these two, right?" Rosana aimed an elbow at Mulan. "Liam and Mulan. We have to stick with them."

"Why do we need them, though? I don't get that."

"Because we're looking for your figurines, remember? Madame Esme told us to follow the signs."

"Right. The signs."

Mulan emerged from the front of the plane twenty minutes after takeoff, handing Rosana and Enzo a pair of cold sodas. "Would either of you like a sandwich or anything? I'm assuming we'll be up in the air for a while."

Enzo cracked open his soda and took a grateful sip. "Thank you, ma'am. I'm good, though. Um, where are we going, exactly?"

Mulan took a seat across from them, slowly crossed her legs, and leaned forward. "Well, I was kind of hoping you'd tell me, Enzo. You're the key to unscrambling this whole mess."

Enzo wanted to trust her. There was kindness in her eyes and sincerity in her face, and she had been upfront with him so far. "What kind of mess are you talking about?"

"I'm sure you already know about the mess I'm referring to, Enzo.

There's a terrible evil rising. It's throwing the kingdoms out of whack, which is precisely why you haven't seen your mother in three years."

Enzo narrowed his eyes. Here was another person who was going to start babbling about separate worlds. He elected to ignore the part about the kingdoms and focus on his mother. "How do you know about my mom?"

"Because I've seen her."

Enzo's jaw unhinged. "You . . . know her? Is she okay?"

Mulan nodded. "She's fine, Enzo. When I saw her, she was asleep. If I may tell you, Enzo, it's the strangest thing to finally meet you. You look just like her."

Enzo got that all the time. He would go to the store with his parents, and they would encounter a family friend who would be stricken by the resemblance between Enzo and his mother. *But you have your dad's nose,* they'd add.

Enzo thought of Madame Esme's vision, the one with his parents imprisoned in rubies. "And my dad?"

Pietro turned off the videogame and brought his seat closer. Liam also lowered his guitar and joined the others.

"And my mom?" Rosana chimed in.

"Where are they? Is that where you're taking us?"

Mulan calmly raised a hand to stop the questions. "I'm sorry, but I only saw Enzo's mom. She was in the Cavern of Ombra back home."

Enzo furrowed his brows.

"As for going there right now," Mulan continued, "we can't do that quite yet. I do know that's where we need to go, but I have to confess that I don't know how to get there. I was told that's where you come in, Enzo."

"Well, it's not like *I* know anything. I've wanted to find my mom for a long time now. If I knew how to get to where she is, I would be there by now. Who's been telling you guys that I'm supposed to take you back home?"

"Madame Esme?" Rosana guessed.

"Precisely," Mulan said. "But you see, I left on my own free will. My home was in danger. I came here to seek aid and warn Hansel's potential victims."

"Hansel? *Victims*?" Pietro said.

"Surely, Esmeralda informed you all?"

"Pietro wasn't with us for that part," Rosana said.

"Then let me give you the short version. Hansel is under the control of a dark queen who should have disappeared years ago. She's trying to come back and using Hansel's body as a vessel. But to come back in her true form, she needs to gather seven pure souls in the Cavern of Ombra. I think most of them come from this world, but when I escaped three years ago, he only had one: Enzo's mother."

Enzo's head started spinning. "So this Hansel guy took my parents to another world, and this is because he wants their souls?"

Pietro fidgeted with his armrest, the light in his eyes distant and dull. "Hansel was my friend," he whispered.

"He is not the man you know any longer," Mulan said simply. "And mark my words: He'll be back for you. You're with me because I intend to protect you, and apparently, you all are supposed to make the final stand against the Ivory Queen."

Enzo held up a palm. "Hold up. This is the second time I've heard this Ivory Queen mentioned. Who exactly is she?"

Mulan took a deep breath. "She's Queen Avoria of Florindale. She governed most of the Old World for ages, except for a few provinces. Neverland, for example."

Pietro winked at Enzo from behind Mulan.

"She didn't have control over all the Old World, but before she disappeared, she meant to seize that control," Mulan continued.

"And that would've been a bad thing, lads," Liam said, "especially because she killed more than half of her own population."

"That's not very queen-like," Rosana said. "How did she do it?"

"By force. Fear and control. She took people's souls in her quest for power. One terrible day, a thousand and one men, women, and other beings went to battle with Avoria, determined to stop her tyranny once and for all. I am the only living survivor on the side of good from the short Battle of the Thousand. Queen Avoria took the souls of the rest in a single burst of dark energy."

Rosana's eyes widened. "The queen took a thousand souls? How in the world did you survive that?"

"I'm not sure, but I think it was because of my sword, *Guāng zhī jiàn*. When the blast hit, a cocoon of light surrounded me. I was protected from Avoria's darkness. When it fell away, I was alone, and my sword had transformed. It was *Qiān ling jiàn*—and much heavier. I think the blade absorbed a part of my comrades' souls, something Avoria couldn't use."

Pietro's and Rosana's faces faded to white. The pieces clicked. Hansel and this queen were looking for souls again, and their families were among them.

"I recognize that this can't be easy. But you should know that I feel *very* confident about this. The fact that I found the three of you together means the realms are still safe—and so are your loved ones. If I'm correct, they're all sleeping right now. If he gets one of us, then we have cause to worry, but we're going to look out for each other. You should also know that I served the Order of the Bell. That means one of the most powerful fairies who ever existed appointed me to guard the kingdoms, no matter what the cost."

"Fairies," Enzo said slowly. "So, there really are, like, other worlds out there?"

"As sure as I live."

Liam stared at his feet, unresponsive, and Mulan beat him on the back of the head. "Have you stopped listening?"

"I apologize. What were we talking about?"

"Home."

"Oh, right! Master, I need to know about my wife. Is Snow safe?"

Enzo and Rosana exchanged an incredulous look. *Snow?*

"I know nothing of Snow at the moment, Liam. I'm sorry."

"Wait a minute," Enzo said. "Are you talking about Snow as in . . . ?"

"Snow White. That is correct."

Liam put his head in his hands while Enzo sat in a mild stupor. The more he'd come to understand, the more he couldn't believe.

"Anyway, we're together now, and the next step is to figure out where we're going . Enzo, where would you like to go?"

"Why aren't we going *home* yet?" Liam interrupted.

"Because we don't have everyone we need. First we have to gather the rest of our people, our new Order of the Bell, and hope that that gives us a way back into the realm."

"The Order of the Bell?" Pietro said. "How come I'm just hearing about that for the first time?"

"Because we did our work in secret. It was me, the kind but beastly Jacob Isaac Holmes, the powerful sorcerer Merlin, Augustine Rose, and pirate Captain Hook."

"*Hook*?" Pietro bolted up from his chair. "You used to work with that codfish?"

"If we can focus on the matter at hand—"

"I hate that stupid pirate! You mean to tell me that lying, cheating, conniving son of a witch was also a guardian of the realm?"

"That is correct. You should know that he was also one of the bravest men I ever met, and anyway, he's no longer alive."

Pietro crossed his arms and chewed on his lip.

"In fact, none of them are. I am the last surviving member of the Order, and I need you all to help me defend us now. You do know, Liam, that this means you will have to fight too."

An awkward silence pervaded as Liam rubbed his elbows. "You know I hate fighting."

"The greater good requires your action, Liam. I told you this day would come."

Rosana nudged Enzo. "Show her the figurines."

Enzo inched his hand into his pocket, silent as he thought about everything. It was all too much to believe, but given everything that had occurred in the past two days, he could no longer discount these stories as fiction. At least, not completely.

He withdrew the figures and passed them to Mulan. "My dad made these for me. We already found you, Rosana, and Liam, but there are three more."

"That man kidnapped my mom." Rosana poked the carving of the man in the orange hat.

"And Hansel kidnapped my dad. I saw him," Enzo added.

Mulan combed through the small collection of figurines in her palm. Enzo noticed that she seemed to fixate on one in particular. She held it up to the light and studied it from all sorts of angles, and Pietro tapped her on the shoulder with childlike curiosity. "Hey, Mulan, isn't that—?"

"I think it is. She does look very different in this form, but if I'm not mistaken—"

"That's Heather McClavender," Liam finished.

Enzo and the others exchanged confused looks.

"Annnd that's *not* who I was thinking of," Pietro said. "Who's Heather McClavender?"

"You obviously don't keep up with your pop culture. Heather McClavender is a grand name in Hollywood right now. Fairly new name, I guess, but she rose to fame pretty quickly. She played an inspirational teacher from the ghetto last year, she was in a musical about going to college, and she did this rom-com with Chris Campbell or whichever one of the Chris's. Oh, and she's also Tinker Bell in the new Peter Pan movie that's about to come out."

"Are you *serious* right now?" Pietro thrusted his arms up. "Why is everyone making movies and Broadway shows about my life right now? I don't remember giving anybody permission to do this!"

Mulan grabbed a silver laptop and flipped it open, her fingers flittering across the keyboard. "We have to find her. Do any of you recognize the old man?"

Nobody said a word.

"Heather McClavender. Age twenty-five, born in Los Angeles, California, credited with eight critically-acclaimed movies over the past three years." Mulan brightened her screen and turned it so everyone could see the Wikipedia page. Sure enough, the woman in the photo was the same one Enzo's father had carved. Her hair was shorter and darker in the photo, cropped into a tight bob, but the face was unmistakable.

"*Really*?" Pietro said. "She looks so much like—"

"Tomorrow night she'll be at the red carpet premiere for *Peter Pan: The First Lost Boy*," Liam said, leaning over Mulan's shoulder.

"Okay, now I'm mad," Pietro fumed. "I signed *no* releases for this and—"

"Then I suggest we be there, too," Mulan said. "Unless, of course, you have other ideas in mind, Enzo. After all, we're all converging around you. Know that the Ivory Queen will eventually need to be dealt with permanently, but my primary mission is the same as yours: to rescue your families and thwart Hansel's plan."

Enzo hated that everyone stared at him, waiting for answers he wasn't sure he had yet. He couldn't figure out why Mulan had so much faith in him, but he liked her, and she was the kind of woman he would hate to disappoint.

Liam's eyes showed something like desperation. Here was a man who would do anything to get back home and see his wife again. Was he really married to *Snow White*? If so, he couldn't be so terrible.

Pietro leaned forward with his hands clasped together, probably deeper in thought and more shaken than Enzo had ever seen him. Enzo suddenly felt bad for the man. All this time, Pietro had only tried to be a friend. He had only wanted to help. In fact, that's how it always was. Enzo couldn't possibly count all the times Pietro had been there over the years, dropping him and Zack off at school, teaching them to spar, helping them make blanket forts, among countless other things. Pietro might as well have been his uncle, and Enzo never thanked him for being around and racing him across the states to help him find his family without a second thought. He always discounted Pietro as the goof, somebody who only cared about fun at the expense of responsibility. He was a kid in a grown-up's body, living in his own world. Perhaps some of that was true, but he had always been a good friend. Pietro looked at Enzo now with a sort of sadness in his eyes and then nodded once as if to say, *I believe in you.* Maybe it was time to be there for Pietro as much as he had been there for Enzo.

Finally, Enzo looked at Rosana, and her face showed hope. He was still getting to know her, but from what he'd come to know so far, Rosana was a girl who dreamed big. She was the first to believe Pietro when he started talking about his identity. She believed Madame Esme at her fortune booth. Enzo didn't think Rosana was naïve and gullible; she was intuitive. She knew things naturally, somewhere deep within. She believed what couldn't be seen or understood. It came naturally to her. Enzo noticed the way her whole face smiled when she moved her lips. She was with him one hundred percent.

Enzo looked back at everybody and nodded. "Let's go to Hollywood, then."

Mulan smiled proudly and disappeared to give her pilot instructions. They would land first at Mulan's private estate in Los Angeles, California, and there they would rest and make a plan. In the meantime, they were to enjoy the flight and consume all the soda and chocolate milk their hearts desired.

Liam changed into a button-down shirt and some jeans, and he isolated himself in a corner with Mulan's guitar. Rosana curled up in her recliner, balled her sweater into a pillow, and went to sleep. Mulan stayed up front with her pilot, a small man named Ricky, and that left

Enzo with Pietro and an open carton of chocolate milk.

"Hey, kid, I'm sorry about, you know, being a sore loser at the Renaissance faire."

"You were being a sore loser. But hey, I probably broke your ankle, so I'm sorry too."

"Nah, it's not broken." Pietro wiggled his foot. "I was just being a baby."

Enzo reclined his chair and stared up at the ceiling. Pietro followed suit. "Pietro?"

"Mhm?"

"Are you really actually . . . ?"

"Am I really Peter Pan? Well, what do *you* think?"

Enzo didn't answer. He crossed his arms behind his head. "And my dad's really—"

"Yep. Your dad's really Pinocchio. We used to play together when he wasn't even a real person yet. And now, well, he's probably one of the most genuine people I've ever known. And he had a good son too. You're just like him in some ways. Your mom, too."

Enzo smiled. "Pietro? You really think they've been sleeping all this time? Mom and Dad? Zack and Wendy?" *Wait a minute. Wendy. Wow.*

"Well, I hope so, buddy. I'd like to think that when we finally find them, they'll be having some peaceful dream and feel like they've only been gone a day."

Enzo nodded, hoping the same thing. "You think they've been dreaming about us?"

"Maybe. Let's be real, Zack's probably dreaming about sports or a girl. Wendy? She's either thinking about me or some *book*. Your parents? No question. I bet they're dreaming of a normal day for the DiLegnos. All three of you together, maybe a cherry cobbler going in the oven, your dad working on some amazing project? Yeah, kid, I bet they're even dreaming of us right this second . . . dreaming about being together. Just like old times."

CHAPTER TWENTY-EIGHT

TWENTY-FIVE YEARS AGO—
ROUTE TO DARK CASTLE

Pinocchio had no idea how long he and Alice had been walking together. It seemed that the further they traveled, the longer the road became, pushing the Dark Castle further away.

All he knew was that dread welled up in his stomach when he saw that it wasn't getting any closer. The incoming rainclouds sealed the moon away from him, compounding his fear. He thought of the day he'd tried to catch a rainbow. He'd wanted nothing more than to touch it and see if it stained his fingers. Instead, he rambled about for hours, watching it recede as he trudged through woods and small villages where houses of sticks and straw had fallen to the ground. When Pinocchio had returned home, his legs were encrusted with dry mud, and flecks of paint chipped off his eyes and left his vision incomplete, like looking through a keyhole. His father was furious and refused to repaint Pinocchio's eyes for a week. From that day on, Pinocchio hated rain, and he never tried to catch a rainbow again. Trying to get to the Dark Castle, however, felt strangely similar.

They walked for what seemed like an eternity before Alice pulled on Pinocchio's sleeve. "Pinocchio! Look!" She pointed to a cluster of thorny shrubs beside the road. "It's a rosebush! Remember, that's how

Violet put the queen to sleep!"

Indeed, the shrubs were adorned with blood-red roses that bloomed before Pinocchio's eyes. They seemed to be caught in an endless cycle of death and rebirth. The buds bloomed, growing into roses bigger than apples. Then, as quickly as they sprang into existence, they wilted and crumbled to ashen dust, only to regrow once more.

"Don't touch it!" Alice snapped, and Pinocchio was surprised to feel her slap his wrist away. He didn't realize he'd been reaching for the flowers. "Please don't touch it. I only wanted to show you because that must mean we're finally getting closer. Right?"

And then, Peter's voice called out from behind them, accompanied by the rich tones of Wendy Darling's laughter. Pinocchio and Alice spun around to see their friends running toward them, hands interlocked.

"Wendy!" Alice said. "What are you doing here?"

"We're having *fun!* We're on a grand adventure together!"

Peter blew a raspberry as he approached Alice and Pinocchio. "Race ya to the door! Last one there is a smelly codfish pirate!"

Peter spread his arms and prepared to soar off the ground.

Wendy shook her finger. "Hey! You can't fly the rest of the way! That's cheating! You wanna be a grown-up, don't you?"

"Okay, fine, we'll run until we get there!"

"Oh but that's so *far!*" Alice complained.

"Hardly!" Peter jammed his finger in the air and pointed over Alice's shoulder. "We're right at the gates!"

Pinocchio turned around, expecting to confront the overwhelming stretch of winding road, but, instead, he was astounded to behold a colossal iron gateway. The spiky tops grasped at the sky, caked in rust like dried blood and laced with grey vines that looked like they might burst into ashes on contact. As soon as he looked at it, it inched open and beckoned the group forward with a sickening creak. Pinocchio swallowed and felt as though he'd forced a block of ice down his throat. *Why couldn't it be locked*?

"That's impossible," Alice breathed. "It was so far away a minute ago!"

"Perhaps you're getting tired?" Wendy said. "It must have been a trick of your imagination. We're here now."

And indeed they were. Peter smirked, unleashed a guttural battle cry, and charged though the gate. Wendy, Alice, and Pinocchio proceeded more slowly. Pinocchio gulped and wiped some sweat from the back of his neck before he crossed the iron threshold.

Everything beyond the gates was even more terrible. Rosebushes continued to cycle endlessly through life and death. Pockets of earth boiled up from the ground and erupted into flames. The ground was dotted with gemstones blacker than ebony and slightly bigger than the palm of Pinocchio's hand. He had never seen any stones like them before. But the castle was by far the most terrible. Jagged, dark, pointed, and asymmetrical, it looked like it was stabbing the sky. Whenever a column of fire burst from the ground, it illuminated the edifice and Pinocchio could faintly make out his reflection in the blackness of the castle's surface. It was like the opposite of a shadow puppet, and his reflection looked like a ghost.

"This is awful," Wendy said. She called out to Peter, who had raced up a set of marble steps and turned to taunt his friends from the castle's polished-ivory door. "Peter, come back here! I don't want to go inside."

As soon as she spoke the words, the castle gate creaked again and sealed the children inside the courtyard.

"I don't think we have a choice anymore," Pinocchio whispered.

"Come on!" Peter called. "We're already here. Let's go get our mirror."

The rest of the kids approached the door together, which was almost painful to behold the way it contrasted with the darkness of everything else around them.

"So, do we knock?"

"*No*, idiot, we're here to steal something!" Alice said. "We can't knock."

"Maybe it's open?" Pinocchio forced himself to touch the door. It was cool and smooth to his fingers. He gulped, held his breath, and turned the metal knob.

The door swung open without a sound, and the children stared at the scene before them.

For a place with such a jagged, dark exterior, the inside was alarmingly radiant and symmetrical. Light filled the room with the warmth of a gold chandelier that hung still from the ceiling. A purple carpet stretched from the door to a grand staircase, which funneled up to creamy-white walls before branching into two more staircases. The two paths interlaced with each other and wound around the room, hugging the walls until each ended with a single red door. The tiled floor bore the peachy color of flesh, and its shiny surface formed a perfect mirror of the rest of the room, making the staircase look like an enormous hourglass.

The castle interior would've actually been quite beautiful, had the walls not been fixed with strange paintings of a woman in a white dress. Her cheekbones were like knives, and her hair fell past her shoulders in a fiery cascade. In every painting, she wore a crown that matched her dress: bone white and adorned with seven red rubies.

Pinocchio tugged on Alice's sleeve and pointed to the largest painting in the room, directly in the center of the wall. It featured the same woman, but it was the only one large enough to display her piercing brown gaze. "The lady in the painting, is she the I—?"

Peter clapped a damp hand around Pinocchio's mouth, smearing his lips with sweat. "I don't think you should say her name in here, Pin."

Pinocchio wanted to say, *Are you finally scared?* but he couldn't force his tongue to move. Judging by the thick silence, nobody else could, either. They knew Peter was right. There was no need to invoke the name of evil when they were already at its doorstep.

Huddled together while Pinocchio's heart hammered against his ribcage, the four kids stepped inside. The door closed on its own with a long creak and a loud *boom*!

"Oh, that was so loud!" Alice gasped. "She's gonna wake up!"

"She's probably already awake," Peter said.

"Violet said she only wakes up when somebody tries to take her mirror away."

"But we don't know what that means, Pin. That could mean she'll wake up when somebody touches it, grabs it, goes into her bedroom wanting to take it, goes into her castle—"

"*Shhh*!" Wendy hissed. "Let's just get in and get out! Where's the mirror?"

"East tower," Pinocchio recalled.

"Which way is east?"

Nobody knew.

Wendy pointed to the staircase. "The stairs go off in two ways. We have a half chance either way we go, right? One of those has to go east."

"So do we—?"

"Split up and make it faster?"

"Please, no," Pinocchio said, "I want us all to be together if she wakes up."

"Pin, we need to do this as fast as we can. I want to get out of here," Peter said. "How 'bout me and Wendy go left and you and Alice go right? Five minutes, and then we meet in the middle? We'll meet right back here, under the chandelier."

As soon as Peter spoke the words, Pinocchio heard the distant ring of snapping metal, and he looked up to see the light fixture hurtling toward Peter. Pinocchio seized his friend by the elbow and tugged forcefully until he stumbled out of the chandelier's path. Peter landed on his knee and winced before the chandelier made contact with the ground.

Crash!

Fire erupted instantaneously, creeping out of the rubble and turning the purple carpet to dark ash and thick smoke.

Peter rubbed his knee, eyes wide with shock. "Thanks, Pin..."

"We have to put the fire out!" Wendy said.

"There's no time!" Alice protested. "We need to go!"

Alice grabbed Pinocchio's hand and raced up the steps with Peter and Wendy hot on their trail. With every step, Pinocchio's lungs convulsed from exhaustion and fear, and the oozing smoke. As they approached the split in the staircase, the painting of the woman in white loomed closer and she glared at the children, piercing holes through their souls. Pinocchio hated the painting, and yet he couldn't peel his eyes away. He knew that the Ivory Queen was watching him. She'd been watching them since they left Violet's den. She'd sent the serpent after them. She'd opened the castle gates for them, sealed them inside, and dropped the chandelier. She would destroy her own castle to protect her mirror.

Above the painting, lightning flashed behind a stained glass window depicting a rose in full bloom, throwing an eerie red light across the room. When the lightning struck, Peter's shadow stretched across the floor and tore away from his heels, dancing along the walls before zipping up the left branch of the staircase.

First Peter looked angry, balling his hands into fists and flaring his nostrils, but then his eyes took on a determined, defiant gaze. His shadow spiraled up the steps and disappeared.

"Follow it, plebeians!" Peter thrust his finger in the air. "It knows where the mirror is!"

"Roger!" Pinocchio said, feeling much braver.

"My name is *not* Roger!"

Winding around the hall with the spiral staircase, Pinocchio was reminded of a cyclone, ascending higher and higher into some unknown danger. The steps seemed to narrow as they climbed hand in hand, trying to race the rapidly dissipating smoke that pushed its way up to the ceiling. Pinocchio willed himself not to look down after what seemed like thousands of stairs. He kept his eyes forward and up, glued to the red door.

And then there it was. Rounded and barely tall enough to fit an average-sized grown-up, the door was probably the castle's least threatening feature.

Peter turned to face his friends, his face solemn and determined. "My shadow went through this door," he said. "The mirror's there, too. Can you feel it?"

Peter was right. Pinocchio was beginning to understand what his father meant when he would say he felt something in his bones. "*It's about to rain, Pinocchio. I feel it in my old bones.*" "*Today's going to be a lucky day at the market; I feel it in my bones!*" And now Pinocchio knew, the magic mirror was behind that red door. He felt it in his bones. But if that mirror was there, that must have meant—

"*She's* in there, too," Alice whispered. "What are we gonna do? If she wakes up, she could eat our souls!"

"We have to move as fast as we can," Peter stressed. "As soon as we see the mirror, we grab it and go."

"But how do we escape?" Wendy asked. "The fire is almost to the stairs!"

"We have to intro bize."

"Improvise?"

"Yeah, that too. Are you all ready? Hold hands, and don't let go."

Pinocchio gulped and the group formed a train, Peter at the front and Pinocchio at the back. He couldn't decide whether to close his eyes or keep them wide open when Peter grasped the doorknob and turned. Ultimately, he found himself incapable of peeling his eyes away from what was inside.

A sleeping woman lay face-up in a large canopy bed, her hands folded across a withered rose on her chest. She wore a clean white dress and a crown of ivory and rubies perched atop her fiery red hair, which flowed neatly and undisturbed past her shoulders. She probably hadn't budged an inch since she first lay down. Pinocchio hadn't expected her to look so *peaceful*. The subtle smile that breached her lips actually made her look quite beautiful, though his father had told him many times that what was beautiful was not always good.

Though the queen's eyes were closed, Pinocchio could've drawn a line to where she would have been looking. Perched neatly against a stained glass window, overlooking her horrible courtyard of fire and darkness, sat a gleaming ivory pedestal. Only two objects adorned the pedestal.

The first was a crystal pumpkin-shaped jar filled to the brim with black orbs, shiny and spongy, like the ones Pinocchio had seen outside.

The second was the mirror.

Flat, clean, oval-shaped, and fixed within an ivory frame, the mirror certainly looked like it belonged in a creepy castle. It didn't look terribly different from Violet's mirror, but it had a different pull to it.

Sweat coated Pinocchio's hand as well as Alice's, and for a short while, the kids stood in the doorway, looking at the scene in front of them.

"Okay," Peter whispered, "we're going to grab it, and we're going to fly out of here. I'll carry you all."

"You'll carry all of us plus the mirror?" Wendy said. "You can't hold all of us."

"We just need to make it out of the castle gates, and then we can run the rest of the way home."

"Let's just do it already." Alice squirmed out of Pinocchio's grip and scurried ahead of Peter, taking care not to look at the sleeping woman. She seized the mirror.

Pinocchio, Wendy, and Peter huddled together and watched Alice yank on the ivory frame, pulling, wiggling, and leaning back with all her might, trying to free the enchanted object from the pedestal. They looked back and forth between her and the sleeping queen, watching for any signs that the wicked woman was about to stir.

"It's stuck," Alice whispered. Her face glistened with sweat, and her eyes welled up with tears. "It doesn't want to move."

"All of us together," Peter said. "Hurry, the fire is spreading!"

Dark wisps of smoke invaded the room. Against his better judgment, Pinocchio sealed the door, well aware that he was trapping his friends and himself in the room with a mad woman. Smoke continued to ooze through the crack under the door. He ran to Alice, following Peter and Wendy. Each of them seized the mirror with two hands.

"Pull!" Alice yelled, not bothering to keep her voice down any longer.

"Harder!" Peter cried.

"I'm pulling as hard as I can!" Pinocchio's fingers protested in pain.

"Why won't it move?" Wendy whimpered.

Pinocchio leaned back and felt something press against his thigh. He released his grip. He reached into his pocket and then pulled out the ivory knife that Violet gifted him.

"I have an idea," he said.

"That's not going to work," Wendy said.

"Stand back," Pinocchio said. He brandished the knife, applied the blade to the base of the mirror where it met the pedestal, and made a sawing motion. To his surprise, the blade cut through the base like butter. He grinned and continued to saw, carving a clean line between the dresser and the ivory frame. "Thank you, Miss Violet."

A face appeared in the mirror, startling Pinocchio out of his procedure. It was a man with grey hair and a hooked nose, his eyes weary with exhaustion. The man blinked a few times, studying Pinocchio's face.

A wide smile spread across the man's cheeks, and he spoke with a voice that filled the room, "Have you come to set me free, boy? I can hardly believe my fortune!"

"Shhh!" Peter pleaded. "Yes, we will get you out soon. Just hush for a minute!"

"You've no idea how long I've been trapped in the World Between! I thought I would never see the moonlight again. I owe your company my sincerest gratitude! Oh, how wonderful it is to see friendly faces after all this time." The old man's face drew closer, and his lips flattened against the surface, as if kissing a window. "Mmmwah!"

Pinocchio carved faster, sawing cleanly through the border. "Sir, you need to keep it down. We're trying not to wake up the I—"

This time it was Alice to clap her hand over Pinocchio's mouth.

The man in the mirror turned grave. "Mm. Don't speak her name, boy, lest you suffer the same fate as the poor souls in that crystal jar."

Pinocchio's eyes flickered back to the pumpkin-shaped urn.

"Those are *souls*," Alice whispered.

"Soul husks, fair lady. Avoria extracted souls from strong-willed beings to draw power for herself."

Pinocchio paused, his fingers going cold with fear. "Sir! You told us not to speak her name! Why did *you* say it?"

Alice, Wendy, and Peter's mouths hung agape and their eyes widened like dinner plates, confirming that they had the same fear.

"Dawdle no longer, lest she wake and reap your souls as well." With that, and with no acknowledgment of Pinocchio's question, the man faded from the mirror's image.

Crack!

Pinocchio finished sawing with a final, hurried swipe, and the mirror separated cleanly from the pedestal. He pocketed his knife and grabbed the mirror by the edges, but what he saw in his reflection made his heart stop.

Pinocchio looked over his shoulders, and his eyes confirmed that the mirror hadn't lied.

The sleeping woman was gone.

"She's awake!" Alice screamed. "It's the old man's fault! He said her name!"

Peter's shadow raced out from underneath the canopy bed and hovered next to Pinocchio, who hugged the mirror close to his chest.

"We've gotta get out of here!" Peter said.

On instinct, Wendy grabbed the jar full of gems and hurled it through the stained glass window. A sea of red, green, and yellow shards rained from the frame.

"Hang on." Peter grabbed Wendy's hand and floated in the air.

Wendy extended her hand to Alice. “Grab on!”

“Pin,” Peter said, “hold that mirror tight, and don’t be afraid, okay? My shadow will carry you down.” He hovered higher off the ground, Wendy and Alice firmly attached, and then he soared out the window.

Pinocchio hugged the mirror and squeezed his eyes shut as a firm pair of arms wrapped around his waist from behind. Peter’s shadow lifted him effortlessly off the ground. As Pinocchio sailed out the window, rain splattered his face. Columns of fire continued to erupt from the courtyard, their warmth licking his legs, but he didn’t dare open his eyes until his feet touched the ground again.

Pinocchio was far from home, probably with a horrible witch after him now, and he had no idea what she was capable of. But when Peter’s shadow put him down and his friends put their arms around him, his heart warmed up again, and he had to smile. They’d accomplished what they’d set out to do. Pinocchio freed the mirror from its horrible master, and he escaped in one piece with his best friends. He’d found the dark rainbow.

He knew he would get the mirror safely to Violet and be on his way to the New World soon. But something was still about to go *terribly* wrong.

He could feel it in his bones.

CHAPTER TWENTY-NINE

TWENTY-FIVE YEARS AGO

The Dark Castle was empty.

Two winding staircases dissolved from bottom to top, the fire crisscrossing and winding its way up through the hall, engulfing every painting and tapestry in a wall of flame.

The floor no longer had reflections, nor was there anything left to reflect. It opened into a fiery pit, swallowing bits of rubble and turning everything to ash.

Canvas.

Gold.

Stone.

Wax.

Souls.

One of the last things to fall into the pit was a large canopy bed, empty except for one small object, a heavy crown of ivory and shining rubies.

The bed toppled into the infernal fires, reduced to smoke and ashes before it could touch anything else, and the crown followed, spinning, tumbling, and glistening in the flames. It took on an eerie glow, plunging for time untold until it landed in a bed of rock. It glistened within the embers, and then the ground absorbed it. The earth churned, as if chewing on the headpiece, until a cavern began to form. A hollow, rotund chamber bubbled in the center of the earth, where seven red gems pushed their way out of the walls.

One hundred feet above, the castle stood no more.

The fires died away. In the night's stillness, the ground repaired itself, and a fresh coat of dirt, grass, and shrubbery appeared where the castle used to stand, leaving no trace of the horrible structure it once supported.

But in the center of the land, a figure stood, adorned in white with her hair billowing in the wind. Though the surface was still, she could feel the earth rumble from deep within, and a thin smile spread across her lips.

She had awakened, and so had her cavern.

CHAPTER THIRTY

THREE YEARS AGO—THE OLD WORLD

Violet dreamed of her final months at the Dark Castle, as she often did.

The dream was always the same. It started in the castle foyer, where Violet faced a single open door, wooden and bordered by a stone arch, a faint blue light whispering through the crack. The door belonged to Victor Frankenstein.

Dr. Frankenstein was a man shrouded in profound secrecy, never roaming from his lab unless summoned by Avoria. He only ventured from his study with a black coat that swept the floor when he walked. The way the hood shrouded him, Violet was sure nobody had seen his face before. She would've been surprised if anybody knew his eye color. Whether or not he was inside his lab, he aggressively forbade *everybody* from entering, even the queen.

So when Violet saw that Dr. Frankenstein's door was open for the first time, she had to know what was behind it. Just one little peek inside his lab couldn't hurt, right?

She put her face up to the door and whispered his name.

The silence was her invitation. Glancing over her shoulder, she pulled the door open and descended into the lab. For the most part, she wasn't impressed. Tubes curled around the room, bottles glowed on the tables, and electric blue sparks fizzed from a metal contraption. *Boring.*

But a simple leather book beckoned Violet to the table.

The book must've been close to a thousand pages long, its spine loose with pages fraying along the edges. Beside it, an oily quill rose dutifully from an inkwell. Unable to quell her curiosity, Violet opened the cover. The first page was simple enough: *Research Notes* printed in elegant handwriting.

Violet cast her gaze on the tattered tabs protruding from the book's edges, on which Dr. Frankenstein had scrawled dozens of various topics ranging from *Properties of the Soul* to *Interrealm Travel* and *Corporeal Resurrection.*

Bewildered, intrigued, and a little afraid, Violet turned to the first tab, where she observed a detailed drawing of a sword, notes and measurements scrawled along the edges. *Guāng zhī jiàn—Sword of Light. Material: Soulsteel. Length: 1.3 yards. Weight: Varies.*

Dr. Frankenstein labeled the next page *Model of the Human Soul,* on which he drew what looked like a gingerbread cookie, a body without gender. In the center, Violet beheld a shape like a cracked sunflower seed, opening outward like a book and revealing a small sphere, which had been drawn with a dotted line. Arrows pointed to the seed's different parts. The outside was labeled: *Shell. Durable. Semi-corporeal. Binds man to physical body. Useless to foreign hosts. Not recommended for consumption.*

The inside, the perforated sphere, was labeled: *Nucleus. Fragile. Incorporeal. Binds man to personality, strength, and ability. Transferrable to foreign hosts. Safe for consumption? Hypothesis: Special nuclei absorb properties of enchanted artifacts over time. Merits further research.*

Violet turned the page again and found a strange math problem. She mouthed the symbols to herself. *Gingerbread cookie minus sunflower seed equals . . . rock?* The drawing after the equal sign appeared to be a diamond, but it was labeled *Soul Husk. Gelatinous. Colorless. Resilient. Merits further study.*

Toward the end of the first tab, Violet froze on a page where Dr. Frankenstein had drawn an enormous serpent, wide-mouthed and glassy-eyed. He wrote measurements for the teeth and body, and he labeled the page: *Project Kaa. See: Corporeal Resurrection.* She gasped.

"Violet!" A stern voice sounded behind her.

Violet slammed the book shut and spun around to face her father, her heart slamming against her chest. "I'm not touching anything, I'm just—"

"You should not be in here! If the doctor catches you snooping, there's no telling what he'll do! You'd do well to stay out of his way."

"I'm sorry, Father, I just—"

Clanggg! Clanggg! Clanggg! Clanggg!

Violet had never heard the bells of Florindale in her dream before, but for the first time, the dream was different. The bells rattled the room four times. Violet's father acquired a faraway look in his eye, staring through the wall.

Violet gulped. "Father?"

His voice came out slow and fuzzy, as if through water. "The Order of the Bell is broken. Jacob Isaac Holmes has fallen."

Clanggg!

Violet clapped her hand to her mouth. "No!"

"Merlin of Camelot has fallen."

Clanggg!

"That's impossible! They can't—"

"James Hook has fallen."

Clanggg!

"Augustine Rose has fallen."

Clanggg!

Each clang, each fallen warrior, was a jolt to her bones, shocking Violet's senses.

"Hua Mulan has disappeared."

Violet willed herself out of the dream, and her eyes snapped open. She was back in present day, sprawled out on the large cushion in her den.

She blinked, chewing her lips and rubbing her hands together. It wasn't just a dream. It was never just a dream. It was an omen of terrible caliber.

She looked at the wall, and a sword appeared next to Hua Mulan's image on the mural. *Qiān ling jiàn.* The Sword of a Thousand Souls, and the most beautiful blade Violet had ever seen.

Mulan was gone but alive. Did Hansel send her to the New World? Violet wasn't too sure. If the Order had confronted him and revealed their intentions, surely he would've spared nobody. It would have been too great a risk to let any of them live, even if they fled the Old World. Mulan must've escaped. She meant to leave the realm. She was looking for help.

Violet had been confident that the Order could talk sense into Hansel. She had faith that he would do the right thing. Instead, he reaped her friends' souls.

No. It was the queen. It was always the queen. Hansel was a noble man, just as his sister was a brave girl.

Violet fought back a tear. She mustn't think of Gretel.

Violet looked at the sword in the wall, summoning her resolve. Thinking about the past wasn't going to solve anything. Hiding in her den would do much less. She had to act. She had to confront Hansel herself and demand that he release his prisoners. Avoria must never return.

With her resolve and her anger, Violet braced herself, and she vanished from her den.

She popped up outside of Hansel's cottage, surprised by its new atmosphere. Not a bird in sight. The breath of a thick chill in the air. Certainly not the former home of Snow White.

Violet marched up to the front door, flung it open without knocking, and she found Hansel sitting alone at his table with pie and milk.

"Miss Violet! I wasn't expecting you today." He raised his plate. "Dessert?"

Violet scrunched her nose. She wasn't going to fall for that innocent charm. "Hansel, I'm taking a stand right now! I gave you a chance in the mine. I let the Order give you a chance, too, and now I'm telling you that you need to release your prisoners and call off your plans, or you will regret it for the rest of your life!"

Hansel frowned. "I don't understand. Why are you speaking to me this way?"

"You know why. You're taking hostages in the mines for the Ivory Queen. And I think *you're* the reason my father's missing. Even before the queen took hold of you, you were going to take any measure to get your sister back, even if that meant endangering another human life!"

Hansel stood and paced around the room, wringing his hands and avoiding eye contact. "Yes, ma'am, you are correct. I banished Lord Bellamy from the realm out of my own volition. I sent him away because I couldn't get him to agree with me on the future of the mines. I always had a feeling Gretel was down there, Violet. My sister saved my life when we were little. It's my given right to do anything I can to return the favor and get her back."

"At what cost? Can't you see what you've already done, in addition to banishing my father? Where's Mulan? Where are her friends? Where's Prince Liam?" Violet found herself back on her feet, her face growing hotter and her voice growing louder with every word. "You bring my people back to me this instant, and you let that woman go!"

"There's nothing I can do. Hua Mulan? She left on her own. As for Prince Liam, well, he had it coming for a *long* time, and so does anybody else who stands in my way. The Carver's wife? She's collateral. There're no hard feelings."

That did it. Violet was furious.

"*Hmph!* Take *this*!" Her wand appeared in her hands, long and slender, and she scrunched up her face really small. She flicked. A thin stream of red sparks shot from the tip and arced directly into Hansel's eye.

"*Ow!*" Hansel pressed the heel of his hand up to his eye, the other one watering with pain. "I can't see anymore! Oh, stars, it burns!"

Violet raised her chin triumphantly. "That'll teach you. Now I'll ask you again, give up your work with the Ivory Queen, *now*."

"You're a witch, you know that?" Hansel growled. "You're manipulating the people of the realm to get what you want. You manipulated the Order. They'd still be alive if it weren't for you. How does that make you feel, Violet?"

"*Gahhh!*"

Another flick. Another stream of sparks. Another direct hit in the other eye.

Hansel had found her weak spot. Her guilt. Her breaths came out in heavy puffs through her nose, her chest caving in and out with her lungs. Meanwhile, Hansel was wailing with both hands covering his eyes.

"You've blinded me! You she-demon!"

"Oh, *shut up*, you big baby! The effects are only temporary. Now you sit down and you listen to me, or I'll hit you some place far more sensitive!"

Hansel tumbled back onto the floor and pouted. "I can't see anymore," he growled. "I can't see."

Violet tapped her foot and stared down at Hansel. She let out a long sigh. She had to admit she felt sort of bad for the man. She wasn't planning on having children any time soon, but she imagined this is how it would feel to spank a child. Violet knelt and spoke in a soft tone, "No, Hansel. You can't see right now, and do you know why? It's because you've been *blinded*. You've been *blinded* by the queen. Now listen to me. If you keep doing her work, I know you think you're going to get your sister back, but what I want you to understand is that she will not help you. She's using you for her own selfish gain, and when she has what she wants, I'm pretty sure she'll destroy you. I can't let that happen. Not to you, and not to those people you're kidnapping."

When Hansel pulled his hands away from his face, his eyes were red and moist, and he wasn't looking at anything in particular. "That's very admirable, Miss Violet, but I don't think there's anything you can do. There's nothing any of us can do except finish the job. She keeps getting in my head, showing me all these awful things and making me feel so powerful and strong and then ripping it all away." He sniffled. "You don't know what this is like, Miss Violet."

Oh, my poor heart strings! Violet stroked Hansel's cheek, thumbing his scar. "There, there. I can't begin to understand what you're going through. I can only hope that we'll find a way to stop it. For that to happen, though, you must agree to help me."

"Do what you must do, then."

Violet straightened her back and shook her head. "It is not my intention to destroy you. I didn't come here expecting to stop the queen's rampage. If the Order of the Bell couldn't do it, how could I expect to?"

Hansel tilted his head, his eyes seemingly staring through the fairy. "Why did you come here, then?"

"To slow her down."

Violet snapped her fingers and a lavender flame appeared at the tip of her thumb, a small wisp dancing like a candle. She cupped her hand, flicked her wrist, and the flame expanded into a sphere, whispering its warmth to her skin. Its heat warped Hansel's face in a thin haze. Violet's wings fanned out behind her and her flapping accelerated, fueling the flame and nurturing the ball of fire.

Hansel flashed a wicked grin, and that's when Violet knew the queen had taken over again. He opened his mouth, and an icy voice came out instead of his own, "Stupid girl. You really think you can harm me with fire?"

"Avoria." Violet smirked. "It's been a long time, *Stepmother*."

"But it has."

The flame rotated in Violet's palm. "I don't suppose you're going to let Hansel out of this deal now, are you?"

"My dear, you make it sound as though I'm holding him prisoner. As though I forced his hand. He sought me, love, and he chose to be my huntsman."

Violet shook her head. "It's never that simple. Not after your rampage in Florindale. Not after what you did to my father!"

"Oh, you break my heart. We both know your father was a troubled man. I just wanted to put him somewhere safe, for his own good. Now, why don't you put out that flame? You can't hurt me with it anyway."

Violet laughed. "Good thing it isn't for you, then."

Hansel narrowed his eyes. "Then why play with fire?"

"To buy everyone some time."

With that, Violet thrust her arm in front of her and launched the ball of fire over Hansel's head. It soared around the corner and into Hansel's bedroom, from which the sound of running liquid filled the air before Avoria screamed. It was a long, terrible bellow of sheer agony, piercing Violet's eardrums, rattling the windows, and buzzing the door.

And then it stopped, and Hansel slumped forward on the ground, drowsy and weak.

A small pool of silver liquid flowed into the living room and seeped into the floor.

Violet smiled triumphantly.

She had managed to melt a small part of the mirror.

She could not truly destroy it herself–it would be foolish to think otherwise–but if she focused all of her magic into one good burst of flame, she could do just enough damage to weaken the link between Avoria and Hansel. She would still have a tight grip on his mind, but she wouldn't be able to communicate with him through the mirror quite so often.

Wherever Mulan was, whatever she was doing, she may have more time to do it this way. Until then, Violet feared she would have to play the waiting game.

"*Hmph.* That'll show her," Violet said to herself.

And that's when she felt a sharp pinch in the back of her neck—a deep sting—and she watched the world melt away.

She woke up some time later on a warm, damp surface with the sun beating down on her face. A light breeze tickled her hair, and she listened to the sound of wind on water, churning waves that licked the land. The light breeze grew louder and louder until a rush of liquid crashed over her bare feet and sprayed her in the face with miniscule droplets of ocean mist.

Startled, Violet jumped to her feet. She was on a beach, staring out at an ocean she'd never seen before. The beach close to Florindale possessed waters clearer than crystal. This water was dark blue. She doubted she could see her toes if she walked into it.

She looked down at her body and clamped her hand over her mouth. Instead of wearing the long purple gown she was used to, she sported some sort of stretchy fabric outfit that left her legs, arms, and belly uncovered. She wouldn't have dreamed of wearing such an outfit.

Additionally, her whole body felt awkward. She could still stand, but her balance felt off. It was something about her back, like she had suddenly lost weight between her shoulder blades. *How is this possible?*

Violet looked over her shoulder, and that's when she realized why she felt so funny; she no longer had wings. *No! No. Nonono.*

Another rush of water surrounded her ankles. In her surprise and her lack of balance, she toppled onto her side and swallowed a disgusting mouthful of ocean. She coughed, sputtered, and spat, trying to purge the salty taste from her tongue. When the wave retreated, Violet crawled along the sand, trying to find a dry patch. The ground felt good on her legs, soft and gentle, and she liked the way it sparkled. Her knees left small indentations along the beach as she crawled and tried to process the rest of her surroundings.

Violet's heart smiled when she saw that there were tons of people along the beach, and they were all so happy! Kids constructed mini-castles with tiny pails and plastic shovels. Some slathered wet sand all over their arms and legs. A group of teenagers blasted music unlike anything Violet had ever heard, using some strange magical contraption. They also ran back and forth tossing a white disc, while another group buried a friend and turned him into a sandy mermaid. Older people strolled with hands interlocked, some walking their dogs, and some pondering the ocean.

Ahead, Violet saw lights everywhere. A luminous wheel as tall as her den turned endlessly. She watched the suspended carts rock back and forth in the breeze, and she also noticed that there were *people* sitting in the wheel. And that wasn't the most magnificent part. The most exciting thing was the strange machine racing around at the speed of light on a long, mountainous and serpentine metal road. Screams trilled from the machine, but they weren't screams of terror. They were made of something else. She tried to remember if she'd ever heard a happy scream before.

Violet scratched her head and started walking toward the machines. "What a strange new world."

CHAPTER THIRTY-ONE

TODAY—THE NEW WORLD: HOLLYWOOD

After spending every day for the past three years throwing knives in a plastic fairytale town, this strange kingdom called Hollywood was something new for Liam.

For one thing, how did people manage to dress this way? Back at Mulan's estate, she gave him several garments he didn't understand—apparently they were called *soots*—and told him to put them on. When he managed to figure out how everything went and put it all on—with some help from Enzo, who pointed out that "Dude, you have the jacket on *completely* backward"—he felt like a court jester. The worst part was the pair of black boots Mulan made him wear. He squeezed into them, took a few practice steps to adjust to the heel, and then stared down at them in shame. "Are these made from *dragon skin*?"

Pietro raised an eyebrow, his mouth twisted in an amused grin. "Oh, you should probably know, bro, dragons don't exist here. I tried to ask for one at this pet store, and they looked at me funny."

"Won't *we* get funny looks wearing this obscene apparel?"

When they arrived on the red carpet, Liam was glad to know he had been wrong. All the gentlemen were wearing something similar.

Mulan looked like she was wearing a mirror. Her white dress

glittered violently in the sun, throwing daggers of light into Liam's eyes as they walked together. The plan was simple. Mulan and Liam would stick together. Rosana, Enzo, and Pietro would be another group. They were to find Heather McClavender, gently persuade her of their cause, and leave.

Liam noted the cameras and reporters and whispered into Mulan's ear, beginning to wonder how they were going to steal an actress from a red carpet premiere, "I have a question. What if people, you know, wanna talk to us?"

Mulan sighed, maintaining a forced smile. "On television? They won't, Liam. Reporters don't recognize our faces. People don't want to talk to movie stars they don't recognize. They want to talk to Bradley Cooper."

"Who?"

"The point is, *not you*."

Liam scratched his head. "But, you know, Rosana tells me I'm called Prince Charming in this land, and people can probably see your dress from Florindale. What if they talk to us anyway?"

"Then you smile and nod, and you tell them what they want to hear. Now, will you stop worrying and help me look for our friend?" Mulan raised her eyebrows at Liam and shook her head. "And here, let me fix your tie. You look ridiculous, Liam. Have I taught you nothing about how a proper prince should present himself?" She gripped his choking device between polished fingernails and gave it a sharp twist.

Liam cringed, narrowed his eyes at Mulan, and went on talking. He still had a million questions, the first of which was, "So what exactly have you been *doing* here in the New World? How did you come to own a flying machine and a private estate?"

"I'm an *actress*, remember? We are both *actors*, and we make *movies*." Mulan elbowed him swiftly in the gut. She forced the words through her teeth, holding a cheesy smile between her lips. Her eyes clearly said, *This is not the right time, you idiot!*

Liam nodded obediently. "And one more question: What do we do when we actually find Heather McClavender?"

"Hope she recognizes us."

"Why would she recognize us?"

"Because she came from our world, Liam. And let's get one thing clear: Her name is *not* Heather McClavender."

⌘⌘⌘

Since he hated dressing formally, Enzo couldn't blame Liam for complaining about his suit. However, he couldn't deny that Rosana looked amazing. She had chosen a red-satin gown that hung below her knees. She also curled her hair and did something sparkly with her eyelashes. In the limo, he sat next to her and tried not to stare at her face.

It didn't help that Pietro made things incredibly awkward. Throughout the whole ride to the theater, Pietro leaned back and smirked at Enzo, occasionally doing a side eye at Rosana as if to say, *I know what* you're *thinking about!*

Enzo could've dealt with the knowing gazes, but Pietro didn't stay silent for long.

Shortly after they got out of the limo and separated from Mulan and Liam, he threw his arms around Rosana and Enzo's shoulders and dragged them in a "buddy hug." With a big grin, Pietro said, "Don't you two look wonderful today? Rosana, I barely know you, but look at you. You come here in a classy dress and your classy shoes, with your hair done all classy, while other women in this world walk around in garbage bags and animal fur. Look at Cruella over there, wearing a zoo, and look at you, with all your class. You, Rosana, are just so classy!"

Rosana giggled and rolled her eyes. "Um, thanks, Pietro."

"And *you*, Enzo, can I just say that seeing you in a suit and tie makes me feel like a proud uncle right now? I remember you when you were a teeny tiny little baby"—he pinched the air with two fingers—"and now look where we are! Look where *you* are, buddy! You are a grown man in your suit and tie. You are spry. You are swanky. And you are one smart guy, too. The son of Pinocchio! What a catch, am I not right, ladies of planet Earth? Oh, it seems Rosana's the only one listening to me!"

"Oh my God, Pietro." *Can I crawl under a rock and die now?*

"You're welcome, kid. Now where do I find that little codfish who's pretending to be me in this movie that I never authorized?"

Enzo shrugged. *How are we supposed to find* anybody *at an event like this?* He felt like he was about to play the world's most frustrating real life version of Where's Waldo? Everybody was either holding a camera or facing one, and there was barely any room to breathe. He wondered how he was going to find Mulan and Liam again, let alone an actress he'd never met before.

One thing Enzo had to admit to himself: Walking amongst the stars was a cool experience. He saw several actors he recognized. He wasn't necessarily excited to see any of them because he didn't watch a lot of their movies, but he thought about how much his mother would love to be there. It was sort of a routine for her and his father to sit down and watch a movie together most nights before bed. Once a week, she would make popcorn and mix a bag of chocolate covered raisins into it. She would do the same for Enzo, though he'd stopped watching movies with them when he started junior high.

His mom loved movies more than anybody he knew. Zack was a close second. He even convinced Enzo to movie hop one Saturday at the mall. They managed to see a superhero movie about a man with dog-like powers, a space opera about Abraham Lincoln—starring an actor named Link Abrams—and some gory-vampire-war movie before an usher caught them and called Pietro to pick them up.

The first words out of Pietro's mouth were, "So what'd ya see, boys? I really wanna go see *Four Score and Seven Lightyears Ago*."

So Pietro bought three tickets to the Lincoln movie, and they all watched it again. Enzo thought it was kind of stupid, and Pietro thought it was boring, but it was Zack's favorite. Zack would never believe that Enzo was standing ten feet away from Link Abrams at a red carpet premiere. Red-haired and clean-shaven, Link looked *nothing* like a galactic president in person.

Enzo tapped Rosana's shoulder. "Hey, would you mind taking a picture of me and Link Abrams? I want to prove to my friend that I saw him."

"Are you sure that's a good idea? What if he wants to know what movies you've done, what you're working on, *who you are*?"

A female voice overflowing with raspy enthusiasm spoke behind Enzo, and he wheeled around to see a brunette woman tottering up to him in bright-green, pointed heels that must've been seven feet tall.

To his great horror, a cameraman followed.

"Why, *hello*, dawlings! If it isn't one of our young Hollywood couples, live and in the flesh! And don't you two look absolutely *ravishing* today! Are you ready for your interview?"

Enzo's mouth hung open in a stupor. *Young Hollywood couple?* Oh gosh. "Well, uh . . . ."

The woman attempted a smile, but all she managed was a stiff upturn at the corners of her lips. "Aw, the young stars are nervous! How positively *endearing*! Is this your first time on the red carpet, dawlings?"

"First time," Rosana spoke. "We're pretty excited. It's a humbling experience, you know? Very surreal."

Pietro poked his head between Rosana and Enzo's shoulders. "Exactly! And I just wanna thank—"

"The young lady speaks with such *poise*!" the woman cried. "It's adorable. Tell me, now, who are you most excited to see on the red carpet?"

"Heather McClavender, of course." Rosana rocked forward on her toes. "She's been my idol since, like, birth."

The woman threw her head back and laughed a strobe-like cackle. "Let's not exaggerate, dear! Ms. McClavender has only been making movies for two years! Anyway, look no further, darlings! She's just over a hundred feet behind you! May all your other red carpet wishes come true tonight!"

⌘⌘⌘

When Pietro wheeled around and saw her, his jaw anchored him to the ground.

It was she indeed, purple gloves and all, and reporters, movie stars, and cameras surrounded her. Seeing the woman as a wooden figurine was strange enough for Pietro, but seeing her in person was entirely surreal. Sure, the New World had altered her appearance a bit—he didn't see how it wouldn't have—but there was no mistaking that familiar face . . . her berry-blue eyes, pointed nose, and bow-shaped lips.

The only thing that was missing was her wings.

"Violet!" he called excitedly. "Miss Violet!"

Pietro felt like he was on a string and somebody was pulling it toward the woman responsible for bringing him to the New World. He broke into a run, stumbling over his own ankles and finding that it was quite hard to run in formal shoes.

Someone tugged on the back of his coat, and he heard Enzo yelling for him. "Pietro, where are you going? Who's Miss Violet?"

But Pietro's feet carried him away while he yelled, "Violet, Violet!"

Suddenly the dirtiest man in the world, a short, stocky security guard, stepped out in Pietro's path. The two men collided, and the impact stopped Pietro like a brick wall, especially because the man sneezed directly on Pietro's suit.

Hatchooo! A thunderous, throat-shattering nasal eruption. Sneeze spray went everywhere.

Pietro held his arms up and narrowed his eyes in disgust. "Gross, dude! *So* rude."

The stocky man wiped his nose with a dusty sleeve. "Bless me. Sir, I'm afraid you have to be VIP to move beyond this point."

Pietro smirked and put on his best charm voice. "What if I told you I'm Peter Pan?"

"Yeah, even Peter Pan's not special. VIP only if you want to speak to Ms. McClavender."

Pietro backed away from the guard. "Aw, *come on!* This is important, man." He took a deep breath, stood on his toes, and waved his arms. "Violet! Miss Violet, look at me!"

People stared from all directions, but the actress in the purple gloves kept her eyes on her cameras.

"I'm afraid I'm going to have to escort you out of here, Mr. Pan. You're disturbing the peace."

"But, no! I need to see her; you don't understand! Wait a minute. You believe me?"

"Sure I do. You're Peter Pan, and I'm one of the seven dwarves." The man seized Pietro's elbow with an iron grip and started dragging him away. "Let's go, lost boy."

⌘⌘⌘

The second Rosana saw the security guard, she knew she had to act.

Pietro's outburst was not ideal for their mission. She wouldn't be surprised if he ended up on TMZ. "Violet! Miss Violet!" She could see the headline already: *Crazy Fan Loves Heather McClavender Too Much, Ruins 'Peter Pan' Premiere.* And the video would go viral for everyone to see. By morning, there would probably be a fan-made remix of Pietro on auto-tune. They would never be able to go anywhere without someone recognizing him.

When that stocky security guard stepped out in front of him, though, she knew there was deeper trouble.

They all look the same, she thought. *The man who took my mom. The men on the Empire State Building.*

She hit Enzo's shoulder and grabbed him with both hands. "Enzo! That man works for Hansel!"

Enzo narrowed his eyes and rubbed his shoulder. "First of all, ow, and second of all, what do you mean? That's a security guard, and he's about to throw Pietro out of here for acting like a total idiot and embarrassing himself."

Rosana sighed. "Will you trust me on this? We need to help Pietro. We really, really need to help Pietro."

"And draw more attention to ourselves? Rosana, this is *not* a good idea. Let the guard throw him out, and we'll go get Mulan. We'll talk to Heather ourselves, bring her with us somehow, and we'll meet up with Pietro when this is all over."

"*Ugh!* Enzo, you can be so infuriatingly stubborn sometimes! If you're not with me on this, *fine*. I'm gonna go help Pietro myself."

"Rosana—"

She whipped around and raced down the carpet, shoving past Link Abrams and several reporters, all of whom spun their cameras and aimed them at her as she ran.

"Violet! Miss Violet, look at me!"

Pietro struggled, trying to pry the man's fingers open before pounding on the guard's hairy knuckles.

"Pietro!" Rosana called. "*Hey*! Let him go, you big stupid oaf!" She made a running dive for the guard and caught him on the ankle, closing her hands around a thick leather boot.

An elderly woman in a peacock dress covered her mouth and aimed a long nail at Rosana. "That girl attacked the security guard! Is anyone filming this?"

The man was strong. Even with Rosana's fingers clamped tightly around his leg, he kept walking, dragging her along the ground as she tried to yank him down. "Let him go! Let him go! Fall *down!*" *Oh gosh this is actually humiliating...*

"Somebody get her off the ground! She's ruining a fabulous dress!" another woman exclaimed.

"Who is she?" a bald man asked. "Is she in this Peter Pan movie? I don't recognize her."

"Who *cares*?" Several cell phones came out. "This is a great story!"

Rosana was sure her dive was going to save the day, but as the large man's ankle dragged her around, she was becoming pretty sure she had doomed everybody.

⌘⌘⌘

Mulan heard the rumor before she heard the commotion. A crazy man near the entrance was being escorted off the premises for disturbing the peace.

Whatever. That actually seemed to be a common occurrence in the New World. People weren't as tranquil in California as they were back in, say, Florindale, for instance. In three years, she'd seen people throw fits everywhere from a Starbucks line to a yoga class. Sometimes this resulted in nothing but funny looks; sometimes people got escorted away. Mulan didn't care.

And then she heard another rumor: "A girl tried to tackle the security guard!"

"Well, what did the first guy do?"

"Basically ran around screaming like a chicken. Trying to get Heather McClavender's attention. And like, nobody even knows who he *is*."

Great.

Mulan grabbed Liam's sleeve and made a beeline for the entrance, walking coolly and quickly.

Liam stumbled behind her as he spoke, "What's going on? Did you see her?"

"No. But she's certainly about to see us."

AUDIO TRANSCRIPT:

STARGLE MAGAZINE

RED CARPET INTERVIEW WITH HEATHER MCCLAVENDER

STARGLE MAGAZINE: So, Ms. McClavender, in this movie, you play the very important role of Tinker Bell, the magical fairy who helps Peter Pan in all of his misadventures through Neverland. Can you tell us a little bit about what it was like for you to play a fairy?

HEATHER MCCLAVENDER: It was definitely an interesting

experience and one that I sometimes struggled with, to be honest with you.

S.M.: Juicy! Can you elaborate on that for us?

H.M.: *—laughter—* It all comes down to the vision. I wanted to take some artistic liberties and really portray Tinker Bell the way I've always seen her, but directors sometimes have their own ideas and there isn't a whole lot of wiggle room there. I kept insisting that the proportions of Tinker Bell's wings were way off, for example. In real life, she could never fly with those itty-bitty stubs! But the director moved to keep them how they were. So that can be exhausting.

S.M.: *—laughter—* Well that's showbiz, darling! Anyway, I got the chance to review the film the other day, and you were *fantastic*.

H.M.: Oh, gosh, thank you! That's very sweet.

S.M.: But, you know, I have to tell the readers that I found myself very surprised by the rather dark aspect of this retelling.

H.M.: Like what do you mean?

S.M.: I mean, Peter Pan, a classic fairy tale that many people know and love and grow up with. This film actually defies conventions by putting a very tragic twist on the boy who never grew up. How did you first react when you read the script and realized that this retelling wasn't going to give Peter Pan a happy ending?

H.M.: You know, we have a lot of fun as a cast and I listen to my friends talk about how much fun they had reading the stories or watching cartoons and escaping to that so-called dream land, and so, for them, I think it was a big shock when they got to the big twists, but, in the end, you have to realize that these fairytales were also influenced very heavily by reality, and unfortunately reality sometimes includes tragedy. Even for the heroes.

S.M.: Without giving too much away for our readers, can you shed some light on how that comes about in *Peter Pan: The First Lost Boy?*

H.M.: Hmmm, my mind immediately goes to one scene in particular where my character has to make a tough call to save her island, and she makes a decision that she thinks will be best for everyone but she doesn't foresee how these choices might affect young Peter in the long haul. You see her sort of grappling with that at the end. She has this chance to save the boy from certain doom, and when he can't escape his fate, she realizes that it's really been her fault from the beginning. So there's that dual tragedy there: the hero's dilemma, and the one we all face at one point or another.

S.M.: Those are marvelously profound words, Ms. McClavender! Can you relate to your character in this way?

H.M.: Oh if only you knew *—laughter—* I can relate to Tinker Bell in many ways.

S.M.: Give us more, Ms. McClavender.

H.M.: Well, for one thing, I knew Peter Pan.

S.M.: Come again?

H.M.: I helped Peter Pan grow up. He was just a little boy and he wanted to grow up, so I helped him.

S.M.: *—laughter—* I see you're still in character after all this time! What an inspiring testament to your dedication as an actress, and one that I think Hollywood's uprising actors and actresses can learn from. Do you have any other advice for tomorrow's stars?

H.M.: Don't be afraid to dream! Drink lots of orange juice. Burn bright and fly, and don't let anybody take those dreams away from you!

S.M.: Yes! Such passion! We are all so very proud of you, Ms. McClavender. You have gone from a virtually unknown name to a force to be reckoned with, and once everyone sees this wonderful movie, the whole world will know the name of—

UNIDENTIFIED VOICE #1: Violet, we've come to collect you!

H.M.: *—gasping—* Hua Mulan? Is that really you? In all the realm, I cannot believe my eyes right now!

S.M.: If we may continue the interview, I just have some questions about—

VOICE #1: Violet, I believe Peter Pan's in trouble. I've also come with the daughter of Alice and the son of Pinocchio, as well as—

H.M.: Liam.

UNIDENTIFIED VOICE #2: Stars! You know my name?

H.M.: Dearest prince, I know all my people. Have I heard you correctly? The daughter of Alice and the son of Pinocchio?

S.M.: Ms. McClavender, if we can refocus—

VOICE #1: And Peter Pan.

S.M.: *—muffled—* Lester, are you still recording all this?

H.M.: *—shouting—* Take me to them at once! Thank you, Stargle Magazine, for this wonderful interview, but we must conclude. *—quick footsteps—* May the light be with you, okay?

CHAPTER THIRTY-TWO

TODAY—THE NEW WORLD: HOLLYWOOD

Enzo couldn't believe how fast the situation unfolded.

He was still recovering from Pietro's unwanted wingmanship toward Rosana—and his embarrassing screaming to get Heather McClavender's attention. Then, Rosana did a straight-up *dive bomb* onto the security guard's ankle, and apparently the man was the Incredible Hulk or something because he kept dragging her right behind him with Pietro's elbow in his hand. Cameras were everywhere.

What do I do? Enzo thought. *I can't get myself thrown out, too. We have to get that actress.*

And tell her what? Hi, lady, I'm Pinocchio's son, and I need you to help me stop a soul-eating witch?

No way.

It became a real circus as everyone from magazine reporters to Link Abrams pulled out their phones and started photographing the incident. Enzo had never been more embarrassed in his life. The point of sneaking into a red carpet premiere was to keep this discreet, wasn't it?

Then he heard Mulan's voice from somewhere in the crowd, and the rest of the buzz went dead quiet. "Violet, we've come to collect you!"

Violet? There was that name again. Pietro had used it, too.

"*Hua Mulan,* is that really you?"

"Violet, I believe Peter Pan's in trouble! I've also come with the daughter of Alice and the son of Pinocchio!"

Well, so much for a discreet operation.

Enzo considered the possibility that Rosana could be right. The security guard *did* look a lot like the strange man on top of the Empire State Building, as well as the funny looking figurine his father had carved for him.

And then he saw Heather McClavender bolt from her interview, lifting her purple gown an inch so she wouldn't trip on the lace. Cameras switched angles and aimed for the runaway actress. Violent flashes of light popped everywhere and clicked among the stars. The crowd shifted and reconfigured to get a better view of Heather, and suddenly Enzo was very aware that his friends were no longer in sight. They weren't the center of attention anymore.

Mulan and Liam emerged from the crowd, and Enzo felt a handful of fingernails dig into his shoulder.

"Enzo." Mulan's almond eyes sparked with an accusatory gleam. "Where are Rosana and Pietro?"

"I don't know. Security has them."

"You were supposed to stay together."

Enzo's face turned hot. "And get kicked out with them? Is that what you expected me to do? Because I can get myself kicked out of a red carpet premiere, no problem."

"I expected you to defend your friends. We're supposed to be in this together, but evidently, we're going to have to split up. You're going with Violet. Liam, you're going that way."

Enzo's mind reeled. "Who's Violet?"

Heather McClavender clicked through the crowd, elbowing and nudging through reporters and movie stars with some assistance from Liam. She stopped next to Enzo, took a long look at him, and bowed.

"Miss Violet, I present to you the son of Pinocchio." Mulan put a hand on Enzo's back. "We can do more intros and catch up later. Enzo, get your friends back." Mulan pushed into the crowd again, and Enzo immediately lost sight of her ebony sheet of hair.

Enzo couldn't believe what happened next. The woman formerly referred to as Heather McClavender kissed Enzo lightly on the cheek, ignoring the sea of reporters. "I'm Violet, fairy guardian of the Old World. You look just like your father."

Enzo thought his heart might stop. "You knew my father?"

"Yes, but there's no time to explain. What do you call yourself, son of Pinocchio?"

"Enzo. Short for Crescenzo."

"Please take me to your friends, Enzo. Whatever you do, do not stop moving. May the light be with us."

Enzo raised an eyebrow. "The light. Exactly. Come on, then. I think they might've gone that way."

Violet followed Enzo, heels made soft pocking noises on the carpet, and suddenly all the lights were flashing on him, the boy who got a kiss on the cheek from Tinker Bell and now had her following him around after she ditched an interview with Stargle Magazine. Enzo found microphones in his face, reporters asking, "Who *are* you?" and a few girls a little younger than him even shoved hats and t-shirts under his nose, demanding autographs. He ignored them, craning his neck for signs of Rosana or Pietro.

Violet kept a firm but gentle palm on his shoulder. "Just keep moving, Enzo," she said softly. "Ignore these people."

A horse-faced woman in a ball gown threw her hands up. "*Ignore these people?* Heather McClavender said she wants to ignore her fans! I don't want to watch this movie anymore."

"No, no, no. That's not what I meant."

Up ahead, a thin cloud of dust drifted in the air. "Just a little farther!" he told Violet. "Look for the dust cloud!"

"How funny. I also knew a man with a dusty cloud over his head."

"Yeah, well, some people haven't heard of showers."

"Oh, I can't *wait* to have one of those tonight!"

Enzo's mom had a go-to movie whenever anybody in the family got sick: *The Wizard of Oz.* He must've seen it four thousand times, not including Kindergarten when his teacher had him be a Munchkin for the musical. More specifically, he was a member of the Lollipop Guild, whom he actually found terrifying. Listening to Violet talk, Enzo flashed back on all four thousand times he'd seen *The Wizard of Oz.* She had a kind of dreamy, musical quality to her voice that reminded him of Glinda the Good Witch.

And then some people reminded him of flying monkeys.

"There!"

Enzo pointed into the distance, where Rosana stood up and dusted off her knees. The security guard held Pietro tightly by the elbow, and a second, much cleaner man of equal stature had taken Pietro's other arm. Pietro had given up calling for help and resorted to biting the guards' hairy fingers. They approached a velvet rope, where the red carpet ended and the rest of civilization began.

Enzo accelerated to a run, battering through the crowd and trying to create a path for Violet. "Rosana!"

As he approached her, Rosana bent down, removed a high-heeled shoe, and launched it ahead of her. It arced over the stars and reporters, and when it came down, it conked the cleaner guard in the back of the head. He dropped instantly and went to sleep.

Enzo sped past her, brushing her sleeve and briefly catching her eye in his path.

"Hey *you!*" he called out. "Let him go!" He left Violet and Rosana far behind, gaining on Pietro and the guard.

He made it past the rope and turned the corner, where the man was about to drag Pietro into a dark alley smelling of garbage. For a fleeting moment, Enzo imagined himself doing a flying leap, tackling the man, and bringing him to the ground. But did he really want to touch the unhygienic guard?

Well . . . for Pietro.

Enzo pushed off with the balls of his feet and let his momentum carry him, spreading his arms and landing cleanly on the guard's back.

It was as if the man didn't even feel it. He trudged forward, not acknowledging the extra hundred-and-thirty-five pounds on his back. Enzo wrapped his legs around the man like a monkey and started pounding on his thick shoulders. Pietro looked at him and grinned.

"Hey, kid."

"Sup, Pietro." Another bash, this time on the big man's head, spilling a load of dirt from his hair. "Let him go, you jerk! He didn't do anything wrong!"

"Enzo, I blew it. I ruined this quest. I'm a big stupid."

"Shut up, Pietro. We'll talk about it *later*!"

"No, kid. There might not be a later. This guy works for Hansel. He's taking me away."

"No he's *not*. I said shut up."

"Yes, I am." The man's throat rattled with phlegm and irritation. "Peter Pan is the sixth sacrifice, and the queen wants him tonight. If I were you, I'd give him a chance to talk and say your goodbyes."

Enzo clamped his hands over the guard's eyes and dug his heels into his chest. "*You* shut up! You're not taking him anywhere!"

"He's not," a thick, masculine voice said, "but I am."

A dark figure in leather and cloth appeared at the end of the alley, almost as a shadow.

Enzo would know him anywhere. He climbed off the security guard and stared the new man in the eye. "Hansel."

"Hello, Carver's son. And, Peter Pan, how long has it been? Feels like ages."

The dirty man marched Pietro to his boss. Then, to Enzo's great horror, he turned around and pulled a small pistol on Enzo. "Don't move another muscle, boy."

All the words faded from Enzo's mind. Terror washed over him as he stared at the barrel of the gun. *Oh, man. This is it. This is really it.* He squeezed his eyes shut and lowered his head. "Please."

Pietro thrashed and squirmed in the short man's grip. "No! Get that thing out of Enzo's face! Drop it *now!* What is all this, Hansel?"

Hansel raised his arms to the sky. "This is me cleaning up the bread crumbs, Pan. Your new life in this filthy world left an unpleasant stain on our own. Did you never stop and consider the consequences of your desire to grow up? What that would do to our realm? Did you really think you, Pinocchio, and Alice could simply take off without affecting somebody else? Without affecting an innocent soul?"

"Uh, yeah, we kinda did." Pietro scratched his head. "Look, can you *please* tell your stinky man to drop the gun, and I'll go with you in peace? I can't let you hurt the kid." Pietro's eyes filled with tears.

"Well, you were *wrong!*" The way Hansel's face seemed to stretch when he yelled the word would haunt Enzo for the rest of his life. It seemed the man had become even more evil since Enzo saw him a few days ago. "You were dead wrong about leaving without consequences, Pan."

"No, I was wrong." Violet's voice sounded from behind. She followed the alley with Rosana, Mulan, and Liam. "Hello, Peter. How handsomely you've grown."

Pietro's face lit up through his tears. "Violet!"

The four approached side by side with their arms up in the air as a sign that they weren't armed. Violet walked until she was shoulder-to-shoulder with Enzo. Enzo had to admit, her presence steadied his nerves a bit.

Hansel snickered, his eyes gleaming with arrogance. "Wow. You've assembled quite the party here, Enzo. The daughter of Alice. And *you* two, the passive prince and the woman warrior who trained him to be so perfect . . . so perfectly *infuriating*! Your wife's doing quite well, by the way, Sir Prince. I'm sure she thinks you abandoned her, but hey, maybe she'll get over you."

Liam's hands shook as they crept to his belt. Enzo wondered if

Liam was looking for his knife. “Stars, Hansel, if you didn’t have a blunderbuss on that boy right now—”

“What would you do? Fight me? You don’t know how to fight.”

“Jinn, please lower the weapon,” Violet cooed. “I know you to be a gentle man with a heart of gold. Do you really want to harm a young boy?”

Hansel clucked his tongue. “Violet, you started this. Does it ever concern you that you sent three innocent children to retrieve something from an evil queen, with *no knowledge* of the full extent of the mirror’s enchantments? Do you sleep soundly at night knowing this is all your fault? And while I spent the last three years collecting families one by one, you’ve been living a life of fame and riches?”

Enzo tilted his head at the woman. Hansel’s biting words to her made the least sense of all.

Violet’s face remained calm. For a while, she said nothing. Her gaze flittered to the ground as she pondered. “Every day, Hansel. I regret it every day. But I stand for good, and good people choose to do something about their mistakes!”

The guard shook his head, a rivulet of mucus running onto his lip. Enzo worried that the man might sneeze, lose control of his reflexes, and squeeze the trigger involuntarily. “I have enough ammo for all of them, boss. Just say the word.”

“*No!*” Pietro spat.

“That’s enough out of you,” Hansel barked. He made a zipping motion with his hand, and Pietro’s lips shut tight at the same time.

That’s just freaky, Enzo thought.

Liam spoke up, “You’re a good man, Jinn. Snow trusted you all. You’re good people, and I hope you’ll listen to the love in your heart instead of the darkness in Hansel’s.”

Jinn lowered his head.

Hansel sighed. “Jinn, you’re not going to shoot any one of them because we don’t know which one we’re going to need as our seventh sacrifice. When the queen gives us the okay to complete the ritual, we can come back and you can do whatever you want with the rest of them. Anyway, I grow bored, the queen grows impatient, and your presence makes me vomit barrels of hate. I'm sure I'll see you all again very soon."

Hansel produced two darts, and Jinn pulled out a third. Hansel seized Pietro and smirked at the rest of the party. Pietro, whose lips were still sealed, eyed Enzo with a look of sorrow. It was a look Enzo had never seen from his upbeat, goofy neighbor.

"No! Pietro!" Enzo broke into a sprint with Liam close behind. But darkness swallowed Pietro, Hansel, and Jinn, while Enzo ran into a brick wall.

Liam, having attempted a diving tackle, ran headfirst into a dumpster wall.

"Pietro!" Enzo sank to his knees, letting all the emotion of the past couple of days finally pour out. "Pietro!"

Violet knelt and looked at him the way a mother looks at an injured child. "Enzo, I'm sorry. I'm so sorry for all of this."

Enzo rubbed his face, pulled on his hair, and took a deep breath. He swallowed his tears, stood, and glowered at the woman in front of him.

"You," he seethed, "Hansel said this is all your fault."

Mulan raised a hand in protest. "Enzo, please be gentle. This is the guardian of the Old World here."

"I don't care! I just lost my dad and one of my *best friends* in less than three days. I've finally lost everything, and I want to know why. I want answers! I want to know everything she knows!" He leaned closer to Violet's face, his breath rippling with hot anger. "What did you do?"

CHAPTER THIRTY-THREE

TWENTY-FIVE YEARS AGO–VIOLET'S DEN

Only the clicking of heels filled Violet's den as she paced back and forth, wringing her hands and taking deep breaths. Her steps were slow and unevenly timed, especially when she got to the end of each back-and-forth round. When she got to the window, she'd stop and stare. *Where are they? Shouldn't they be back by now?* Every speck of movement piqued her attention. A flash of red. A shadow on the ground. A rustling tree.

They're okay. They're going to be fine.

More time would pass. Violet would shuffle to the other side of the room, where the mirror hung on the wall. She'd gaze at herself and hang her head in shame.

Am I using these children? Deep down, her heart told her she was.

No, her mind argued. *They asked for a way to go to the New World. They want to grow up, and I'm offering them a way.*

Wrong. You're being selfish. You lied to the kids. You told them the mirror was the only way to travel between worlds. You're only thinking of your father.

At least she would be helping everybody in the end, right? Pinocchio and his friends would get their wish, and if everything worked correctly, her father would be freed. She was trying to do what was best for the greatest number of people possible.

But there was also Merlin's warning.

When Violet discovered the mirror shortly after she put her stepmother to sleep, she consulted the most gifted mage she knew to learn its secrets. Merlin spent an entire day in Violet's den, conducting countless tests and struggling to pry the mirror off the wall until he had determined that it was never going to budge by means of human—or fairy—strength. Ultimately, he packed his things, straightened his back, and stared into his reflection, stroking his goatee.

"I'm embarrassed, Miss Violet. For the first time, I must admit defeat. The rules and intentions of this object are not as clear as its reflections. I've no idea from where or whence it came—only that there is at least one copy. Together, these mirrors brim with human life and wish-granting properties. As as you've done me the honor of consulting me for professional advice, permit me to make one suggestion." Merlin let go of his peppered goatee, his lips in a flat line. "Destroy this mirror. I cannot ascertain as to how you should, but I must recommend that you keep trying. It's for your own good."

While Violet had verbally agreed, she couldn't shake the sense of duty to her father. What harm could she possibly do, especially if she was helping children as well?

Shortly after Pinocchio and his friends left, Gretel fell asleep on Violet's cushion, and the fairy had tucked her in. The poor girl had been so distressed and frightened, and Violet spent the first hour soothing her and telling her stories.

"Do you believe in happy endings, little one?"

Gretel clutched a blanket to her chin and stared up at the bejeweled ceiling. Her eyes were red from crying, but they acquired a subtle gleam. "I guess so."

Violet rubbed the girl's forehead. "You must believe a little harder.

Happy endings exist. Remember when you saved your brother from that candy witch? That was a happy ending, right?"

"I guess so."

"You don't seem so sure."

"I pushed a lady into the oven. It was mean."

Violet frowned. "What would've happened if you didn't push the witch into the oven?"

Gretel shrugged, and her blanket shifted a few inches. "I don't know. Maybe Hansel would've gotten hurt."

"And how would you feel today if that had happened?"

"Sad."

"How are you feeling right now?"

"Sad still."

"There are different kinds of sad, Gretel. Sometimes sad makes you hurt right *here*." Violet reached out and tapped Gretel's belly. "That's when you've done something that makes you feel icky. We know we're not supposed to hurt other people, right?"

Gretel nodded.

"But if you hadn't defended yourself, you would be hurting right *here*." Violet tapped Gretel's chest, right about where her heart rested. "And Hansel might not be here, and the witch would've kept hurting sweet children like you two. I know you feel icky about hurting the bad woman, but you would've been hurting *more* people if you didn't stop her. Does that make sense?"

"I guess so."

⌘⌘⌘

Violet felt she had been staring out at the world for days, wringing her hands and watching for any sign of her questers, before a small parade appeared in the horizon. There were four of them marching in a line.

Violet clutched her chest. Who was the fourth? Was it the queen?

She heaved a sigh of relief when she realized the fourth was a young girl. It was Peter Pan's crush, and she walked beside the brave boy leader with her hand wrapped around his. Pinocchio marched at Peter's other side, and the two boys shared the burden of the ivory mirror. The mirror's surface gleamed, casting glints of emerald green and cardinal red about the land. The boys didn't appear to struggle with it, holding the frame up high between the two of them. And finally on the end, Alice walked with her red cloak tied around her waist.

Violet thought her heart might soar clear out of her chest. Happiness tickled her fingers. "Children! Oh, children, you've succeeded! You've completed your task!"

When they entered with their faces and clothes coated in thin films of dirt, Violet embraced each of them with a hug that could melt a bar of chocolate. She wiped their faces with a wave of her hand, took the mirror, and leaned it against her wall.

"Please sit down and rest, my dears." She conjured four cups of water and handed them to the children.

Gretel stirred to life, sat up, and rubbed her face. "You came back!"

The other kids smiled wanly.

"Please, tell me what happened." Violet wove her petite fingers together at her waist.

"My shadow got away—"

"There was a *huge* scary snake—"

"We saw these funny little miners and—"

"The queen's castle caught on fire—"

Violet managed to process all four voices at the same time, and she didn't like what she was hearing.

"Was it scary?" Gretel asked.

Pinocchio cringed. "I don't want to go back there ever again!"

Violet touched her fingers together. "Did she wake up?"

A collective nod this time.

Alice's face turned ghost-white. "She vanished from her bed! We never saw her again."

Violet chewed her cheek. She was now responsible for the

awakening of the same woman she put to sleep in order to protect the realm. Would it all be worth it in the end? Where was she now? "We must hurry then, children. She could be on her way *here* for all we know. I must get you all to safety."

Pinocchio's eyes lit up. "To the New World?"

"Are you ready to face it, children?"

The kids looked at each other tentatively, perhaps wondering if one would object, but nobody did.

"Even you, Wendy?"

Wendy stared back at Violet, and the fairy could see the little gears churning within her brilliant mind. She hadn't expected the girl to join them. In the end, she just nodded.

Alice stood. "Gretel, are you coming with us?"

Gretel slowly wrapped a small section of her dress around her finger as she cast her eyes down and avoided her friends' gaze. She barely shook her head.

Alice scurried to Gretel and hugged her. "But I'm gonna miss you!"

"I'll miss you, too," Gretel said, her eyes misting up.

"Aw, that's okay, gals!" Peter said. "We'll come back and visit whenever we want! Right, gang?"

The other kids affirmed, and Violet smiled weakly.

"Come and hug me goodbye, children."

With every hug, the murky nature of the unknown anchored Violet's heart to the ground. What would happen now? Or in the children's lives? She was on the verge of changing her mind . . . of telling the kids she was sorry, but they would have to find another way to go about their wish.

Nonsense. Nothing could happen.

"Be happy and healthy in the New World, kids, and there's only one rule: You can't tell anyone who you are or where you've come from."

"Why not?" Pinocchio asked.

"Because people already know your stories, but they don't believe them. They won't understand you, and people are funny. They fear the things they don't understand."

Alice nodded.

"Sometimes, children, cruelty is born out of fear. In some places, there may even be worse things than the Ivory Queen. You must be strong."

Violet picked up the new mirror. It seemed to have grown heavier since it arrived, but only marginally. She gripped it firmly and walked it to its twin on the wall. Both mirrors tingled with color, like they'd been washed with a rainbow.

"My dears, all four of you, please join hands."

The children looked at each other, and then at Gretel, who had begun to cry.

"We'll miss you, Gretel," Pinocchio said.

Gretel covered her face with her elbow, choking out the next words, "I'll miss you, too."

Peter smiled at Violet. "Thank you, Miss Violet, for everything."

"Thank you for touching my life, children. May the light always be with you. Close your eyes and repeat after me, now. A place to love, a place to grow; a brand new world I wish to know."

The kids squeezed their eyes shut and repeated, "A place to love, a place to grow; a brand new world I wish to know."

They repeated it three times, opened their eyes, and looked at each other, still gripping the mirror's edges.

A minute passed in silence.

Was Merlin wrong? Violet wondered.

Wendy blinked. "I should've known this was all a game," she said. "Nothing's hap—"

An ugly cracking sound whipped the air, and the children disappeared.

⌘⌘⌘

Violet sat with Gretel for another short while, though it seemed to her like an eternity.

She stared at the mirrors, chewing her nails and rocking from side to side with Gretel. Why hadn't her father appeared yet? Did she endanger the children's lives for nothing? Did the children even make it to the New World? She saw them leave, but she had no way of knowing where they had actually gone.

I should have listened to Merlin.

"Miss Violet?" Gretel asked. "Do you think Peter meant it when he said they would come back and visit us?"

Violet frowned and shook her head. "I don't know, little one. I do not know if they'll ever have the power to do that. This may be forever, Gretel."

And then Violet heard *her* voice, like poisoned honey on ice. "Forever? Come, now, Stepdaughter. Forever is relative."

Violet wheeled around and clapped one hand over her mouth, pulling Gretel close with the other. A woman in a white gown towered in front of Violet, fiery red hair flowing past her shoulders.

The Ivory Queen had returned.

"Avoria."

"Greetings, greetings," the Ivory Queen droned. She advanced a few steps, yawning and stretching her arms to the sides as she walked. "I've come to thank you, Violet, for letting me catch up on some much needed beauty rest over the last ten years. I've just woken up, and I must say I feel *quite* rested." She bent down and placed her hands on her knees. "And hello to you, little girl. You must be new to the realm. I'm Queen Avoria, ruler of the land, but most have come to refer to me as the Ivory Queen. I think it's my color choice." She reached out and ran a bone-white fingernail along Gretel's cheek.

Gretel spun around and buried her face in Violet's dress.

"What do you want?" Violet demanded.

Avoria smirked. "I merely seek to reclaim what you've taken from me. My mirror. My reign." She sighed. "The moment your child army set foot into my castle, I smelled them in my dreams. I wanted them. Children's souls taste the sweetest."

Gretel whimpered in Violet's arms.

"Do you know why I spared them, Stepdaughter? Why I gave them time to leave?"

A chill ran down Violet's spine.

Without waiting for Violet to pry, the Ivory Queen answered, "Because I'm a merciful queen. Mercy is my policy, unlike some of the other wicked souls you'll find in our realm. *You*, putting me to sleep for ten years! I suppose the apple doesn't fall far from the tree, does it, dearie? Your father is quite ruthless, too. What a deliciously dysfunctional family we are."

"You imprisoned my father in the mirror!" Violet snapped. "After he tried to reason with you! Is that your definition of *mercy?*"

A blue vein appeared in Avoria's face as she yelled, "Your *father* tried to take my power away! The power that I needed to defend myself when Frankenstein's *thing* turned on everyone! Everyone thought Kaa was *my* serpent! My plan!"

"Isn't that what you told everyone? That Kaa was your weapon?"

"Yes, but only against the giants! Not against the people! How was I supposed to know he would feed on their souls? That day I let him bite me in Florindale Square . . . Couldn't you see what I really meant to do? I wasn't *trying* to gain his powers; I was *trying* to let him kill me so that the people would know I didn't set them all up for death!"

"This would all sound so noble if you didn't grow so hungry for power after your bite," Violet said, her face hot with rage. "The people didn't want you dead because of the serpent. The people wanted you dead because you started taking their souls to keep your power."

The Ivory Queen clucked her tongue. "People always fear that which they don't understand. Just like your child army, slaying my darling serpent. Or your father. He found out that I was reaping souls and demanded that I stop. Did he never understand that once I stop, I die? In fact"—she advanced closer to Violet and Gretel—"I'm quite hungry right now. It's about time for my breakfast, and as I said, children's souls taste the sweetest."

"*Be gone!*" Violet waved her hands and thrust her arms out in a push of magical energy. "Don't you *touch* the girl!"

The invisible force knocked the Ivory Queen on her back, and she slid ten feet along the floor, scattering her hair in a mess behind her head. She sat, caught her breath, and laughed. "Is that really as much as your powers have grown, Violet? I'm disappointed. I wonder how your father would—?"

Shoop!

A sucking noise emanated from the mirror, and Avoria screamed as an invisible force pulled her off the ground. The mirror turned into a sort of vortex, swirling with energy and funneling inward like a cyclone, and it was pulling Avoria into her own prison.

Avoria kicked her legs somewhere on the other side of the vortex, and she clutched the mirror's frame. The upper half of her body clawed at the floor as Avoria screamed, "Curse you, wretched girl! You horrible, venomous girl!"

Violet spread her wings and swept the tearful Gretel into her arms. "Close your eyes, my dear. You don't need to watch this."

The vortex took hold of the Ivory Queen's fiery mane. It was a gruesome sight. Avoria's hair fanned out behind her, pulling her scalp and stretching her face so that her nose appeared longer and the insides of her eyelids were exposed.

"Little girl!" she shrieked.

Gretel pried her face away from Violet's waist and peeked at the wailing woman.

"Help me! Don't let me die like this!"

Violet hugged Gretel tighter. "Gretel, don't you listen to her! She means to trick you!"

"You can be a hero, girl! You'll be forgiven for killing the witch of the wood!"

"You've no right to speak to her, Avoria! Your damnation is your own fault! She doesn't have to save you from it!"

"Come, little girl. Take my hand. Take just one step over and pull me out of here."

Gretel squirmed, and Violet held her tighter. "Gretel, don't do this!"

"I can help, Miss Violet! Maybe she'll be nice if we help her!"

"No, she won't, Gretel. You don't understand her like I do! Don't listen!"

And to Violet's great horror, the little girl kicked her in the shin and pushed herself free from the fairy's arms. "I'll help you!"

Gretel took three small steps before the vortex caught her too. *Shoop!* She caught herself against the frame and grabbed Avoria's hand, leaving Violet screaming behind her. "*Gretel, why are you doing this*?"

"That's it, little girl. What a brave soul you are." With a jerk, the queen ripped Gretel off of the mirror's frame and thrust the girl behind her.

Violet fell to her knees and sobbed, watching Gretel sink farther and farther away into the spinning portal, her terrible screams growing fainter, not fully fading out until much later.

"You're a witch!" Violet screamed. "You'll be stuck in that mirror for all eternity! I'll make sure of it if it's the last thing I do!"

"Don't you worry, dear. It won't be the last thing you do. You, your wretched people, and their future generations will live for a *very* long time, suffering as I have and tenfold. Until then, I suggest you prepare for my return. I'll be back."

The Ivory Queen released the frame, sneering as she soared into the mirror's dark depths. The portal closed with a hollow metallic ring.

All was deathly silent.

CHAPTER THIRTY-FOUR

THE OLD WORLD

Violet cried for hours, feeling lost, alone, and ashamed. She must have spilled an ocean of tears before the portal opened up again.

This time, the mirror didn't take anybody with it. Instead, it spat out the man known as Lord Bellamy, Violet's father.

He hit the ground with a sickening crack. For a long moment, he lay sideways, wheezing, his hair longer than Violet remembered, completely silver and ragged, and his robe caked in dirt.

The mirror closed and Violet drew a breath. She clutched her chest and dashed to her father's side. She rolled him on his back and threw her head on his chest, sobbing into his robe.

The old man coughed, his chest rocking violently with every sputter. "Violet! What's happened to me? What's happened to *you*?"

Violet pulled her father into a sitting position and hugged him as tightly as she could, determined never to let him go again.

She didn't even know what to say.

⌘⌘⌘

After she told young Hansel the news, she summoned five of the bravest people she knew to the Clocher de Pierre. The bells sparkled with the light of new day.

Far below, people danced in Florindale Square for the first time in ages.

"Look at them," Violet said. "They celebrate and rejoice in her disappearance, but I believe you all know that Avoria will use *any* means necessary to come back. When that happens, I need you all to stand with me, and I need you all to keep silent in order to keep the peace among the realm."

"I am always with you in a fight against the queen," Jacob Isaac Holmes said. "My Belladonna would be, too, if she were here. If Avoria means to come back, I will have my vengeance."

Augustine brushed Violet's shoulder. "I'm with you, too, dear. That woman deserves what's coming to her, and this old lady still has *plenty* of fight left in her."

Mulan nodded, folding her hands behind her back and gazing upon Florindale Square. "I'm at your service, Violet. My father was the leader of the army that fell to Avoria and her monster. For him—and for the Thousand—I'll make sure she pays."

Hook sat on the ledge, carving his initials into a stone. "You cannot win a fight without a pirate, and I'm the best there is."

Violet's heart soared to see such determination and resolve from the people of her realm, the people she cared about. "Wonderful. Go about your lives and be happy we have this period of peace. When I need you, Quasimodo shall ring the bells of Florindale, and as always, that will be the cue to come together and defend your people. At any cost."

"The Second Order of the Bell!" Jacob declared.

"Shall we sign our names in blood as a testament of our loyalty?" Hook asked.

Violet cringed. "Spill no blood, James. Your word is enough."

The members of the Order departed one by one, with Merlin being the last to leave. Violet found it hard to meet his gaze.

"Miss Violet, you haven't told us everything," Merlin said.

Violet mindlessly traced Hook's rough initials on the ledge. "The mirror took a little girl with it."

Merlin pressed his lips into a flat line. "I did warn you."

"You did, and I'm ashamed and horrified by my own actions. That's why I trust you above all to do one thing for me."

"What's that?"

"Hide the mirror. Please. Use your magic, and seal it away in a secret place where nobody would think to look for it. Not even me."

CHAPTER THIRTY-FIVE

TODAY—THE OLD WORLD

The Flying Man was still conscious when Hansel brought him back. He knew because Jinn, still clad in his New World security outfit, had been spraying him with a water gun.

"Stop! Stop! Stop!" Peter protested. "I'm not even thirsty!"

Hansel sighed, weary and irritated at all the horrible people he'd been forced to see in the New World. "Dispose of the aquatic blunderbuss, Jinn. Go tend to your mining." He slapped Peter on the shoulder, and the man fell to his knees. It was funny how the darts affected people. Most went straight to sleep, but some like Peter Pan just got weak. "Welcome home, Flying Man. Feeling nostalgic at all?"

Peter shifted some weight onto his palms, attempting to stand up but apparently finding it too difficult. It certainly wasn't easy for one to find a sense of balance on the black stones. Peter's gaze whirled around the Cavern of Ombra, studying the people in the walls. "This . . . What is this?"

"Think of it as a homecoming celebration. See how many people have been waiting for you? Look!" Hansel gestured to a giant ruby. "There's your old buddy Pinocchio. Poor, poor man. I believe you remember his wife, Carla? How 'bout Alice? Remember her?"

Peter's eyes watered.

"How 'bout your wife? Your boy?"

Peter covered his face with his sleeve, his breathing growing heavy and uneven. His voice broke as he attempted to yell, "*No*! Zack! Wendy! Wake up!" He scrambled to his feet, bursting with nervous energy. He waved his arms as he screamed. "Zack, wake up! Wendy! Wake up, wake up, *wake up!*" He lowered his head and broke into violent sobs.

"It's shocking, is it not? Seeing them like this after all this time?" Hansel approached him in slow strides, stark malice in his harshly angled brows. "And now you know how I felt when you and your friends took Gretel away from *me*. When I learned she'd been trapped in a mirror all these years, while you knaves grew up and played house in the New World."

Peter said nothing. Only broken breaths escaped from his throat.

Hansel sneered. "Look what's become of your life in the New World. Was it worth it, Peter? Casting your childhood aside, raising a son and getting attached to him, just to have him ripped away from you? To know he'll suffer at the mercy of the queen?"

In a sudden movement, Peter leapt to his feet, gritted his teeth, and seized Hansel's collar.

"Get them out of there!" he roared. "Wake them up!"

"Sorry, Peter. No can do."

Hansel snapped his fingers, and Peter appeared inside a gem of his own, upright and unconscious like the rest of them.

Hansel took a step back to admire his collection. His lips parted in an impish grin, and he counted the rubies:

One

Two

Three

Four

Five

Six.

The Carver, his wife, and the girl who found the rabbit hole; The

Flying Man, his lifelong sweetheart, and their teenage son.

Six.

"You are nearly done, huntsman. You've done well." The voice came from everywhere. Hansel didn't bother looking for her anymore. She was always within his mind. "Come to the mirror, and I will show you the seventh sacrifice."

Hansel appeared at his home and approached the mirror.

"Mirror and Illustrious Queen, I have accomplished all tasks you have bestowed upon me thus far. I have been asked to gather seven for you, and six have been presented."

"That is correct. You have done well."

"Now, if you may, please reveal to me the seventh sacrifice."

Silence.

"Well?"

Silence. Hansel's heart thudded in his fingers as he anticipated the mirror's image. Who would it be? The girl with the red cloak? The passive prince? No, Hansel knew. Surely, it would be The Carver's son.

"As you wish."

A ghostly image faded into the mirror, and Hansel's heart stopped cold. He shook his head.

How could this be?

"Surely there must be some mistake. Are you sure it isn't The Carver's son? Or the young girl? Not even Hua Mulan?"

"There is no mistake, handsome. Bring me the one I seek, and you shall reap the fruit of your labors."

Nauseous and dizzy, Hansel stumbled away from the mirror.

It was at that moment that Wayde entered the room. The red-faced man looked at the mirror, and his eyes rounded in horror.

"Mister Hansel?"

Hansel reached into his vest.

"You're fired, Wayde."

And with the swift poke of the dart, Hansel sent Wayde far, far away. He covered the mirror and collapsed into bed, pulling his covers tight over his ears.

I can't do this anymore. I can't go through with this.

CHAPTER THIRTY-SIX

TODAY—THE NEW WORLD

The sun straddled the line where the water meets the sky, and Rosana stood on Violet's balcony, watching the changing colors bounce off the Pacific Ocean. Though Rosana could hardly call the day a peaceful one, she finally let a moment of tranquility wash over her. For the past hour, Enzo had been inside telling Violet stories about Pietro and his son. Mulan and Liam sparred on the beach, and Rosana watched them with a smile as they battled with each other and the rolling tide. Sipping a soda, she settled into a beach chair and rested her eyes, letting the breeze sift through her hair. When she heard the sound of lazy footsteps on wood, she sighed.

Enzo stood over her in his newly washed Muse shirt and a pair of khakis. He stared at the water, silent and brooding, before looking down at Rosana and rubbing the back of his neck. "Hey. Mind if I sit?"

"Nope."

Enzo plopped down on the deck and tucked his knees into his chest, resting his arms on top of them. "Pretty cool view, huh?"

"Yep."

He nodded. "I've never really had the chance to see anything like this before."

Silence.

"You?"

Rosana rolled her eyes. "Me, what?"

"Have you ever seen a sunset like this? By the beach?"

"Nope." Rosana wanted him to go away. She was still mad about his arrogant passiveness on Hollywood Boulevard.

Enzo grabbed the back of his neck again. "So uh, that was a really impressive throw back there. On the red carpet, I mean, when you threw your shoe at that dude?"

"Yeah?"

"Yeah."

"Well, thanks."

"Yep."

Another minute passed before Enzo spoke again. "So, how 'bout Heather's story? Or, uh, Violet. About our parents, magic mirrors, Hansel's sister disappearing . . . Some pretty crazy stuff, huh?"

Rosana put a palm on her forehead. "Oh my *God*, Crescenzo. Really?"

Enzo's nose crinkled. "You used my full name! Are you mad at me or something?"

"You and your infuriating refusal to see anything that's right in front of your face!" Rosana leaned into Enzo's face. "Yes, I'm mad at you. Are you happy now?"

"Well, uh, no, not really."

"Of course not! You wouldn't be happy if a thousand puppies slid down a rainbow with ice cream cones and told you you'd never have to do homework again."

Enzo scratched his head. "I mean, I'm kind of allergic to dogs, so—"

"*Ugh!*" Rosana stood up, determined to do a classic storm-off, but Enzo shot up and stood in her way.

"Wait a minute. Aren't you gonna tell me what I did wrong before you storm off on me? Why are you so mad? You were fine when we got here, you were fine when Violet told her story, and suddenly you're just so, I don't know, *mad*."

The sun dipped lower, washing Enzo with a cool pink glow as Rosana spoke, "I'll tell you why I'm mad at you. The world keeps throwing you bones, Enzo, carving signs for you about all of this. Your parents went missing and you had someone like Pietro to take you across the country and help you find them. Then, when he tried to tell you the truth, you threw it back in his face. I tried to warn you about the security guard in Hollywood, and you literally *stood there* and let him drag us away. I mean, do you realize that if you would have done something sooner, Pietro might still be here with us?"

Enzo turned away, his arms wilting at his sides. "Wow. That really hurts."

Hearing the pain in his voice almost made her regret saying it. She expected him to be angry, not hurt. Apparently, he agreed with her. "Well, it's very true, and it's about time somebody finally told you to stop being so passive and cynical and *moody*. I'm happy you're finally starting to buy into all of this, but believing is only part of the deal. You have to *act*. People are counting on you, Enzo. A lot of people."

Enzo crossed his arms. "Anything else while you're at it?"

"Yes. Stop calling everything 'crazy.' Please."

"What about when one of the seven dwarves pulled a gun on me? I'd say that was pretty crazy."

"Hansel and the dwarves are *mad*."

"I'll say."

Rosana glowered at Enzo, her hands on her hips. When he finally made eye contact, some of the anger melted off her face, and she sat down again. After a deep breath, she said, "I have this strange feeling that we're all gonna get there somehow, to their world, I mean, and we're going to be too late. We won't all be coming back together."

Taking his own seat again, Enzo's expression flattened. "Why would you think that? That's depressing."

"It's just a feeling. Call it intuition, I guess."

"I don't believe you." Enzo turned his head away in mock defiance. There was even a hint of a smile on his face. "We're rescuing them *all*, and we're coming back with them."

"That's the most positive thing I've heard you say, *ever*."

"Guess I'm learning a little something from you."

Rosana grinned, her mood softening. "Did you already show Violet your figurines? We only have two left, right?"

Enzo dug the carvings out of his pocket. "Yep. The old man and the dwarf. I still have to show them to her. The only thing I keep wondering now is, after we find everyone, then what? We all join hands and wish upon a mirror or something?"

Rosana giggled. "I definitely wouldn't doubt it, Enzo. Oh, and by the way, I *like* your full name."

⌘⌘⌘

An hour later, the group convened around a cozy bonfire outside Violet's beach house. They toasted marshmallows, drank tea, and told stories, which, for Enzo, took on a whole new level of interest knowing many of them were real. Enzo had heard the story of Snow White many times as a kid, but hearing Liam tell it from his side was a different experience. The man was hopelessly in love with her, and his passion bled through every syllable of his tale. Rosana kept her chin on her fist, leaning in the whole time and looking at Liam like he was her favorite pop singer.

"And now I would do anything and everything for Snow. I would fight a hundred dragons, cross a thousand bridges, die a million deaths for her . . . ."

Rosana blew her nose. "That is literally *the* sweetest thing I've ever heard. All the stories said you're charming, but like, wow."

Enzo guessed that in the Old World, Liam was probably like a medieval Ryan Gosling. He probably had all the ladies swooning over him and all the guys wanting to be best friends with him. Even Mulan teared up at his story. Enzo thought he'd appreciate it more if he'd ever been in love. But there was so much he didn't know, and so little he understood, it was hard to know where to begin asking questions. So he started with Mulan.

"In all the stories, you come from China," he said. "Is there an alternate reality China in the other world or what?"

"Not necessarily. The stories are correct. I was born in China in the 1300's. I dressed like a man, went to war in my father's place, and saved my homeland from invaders. All of that is true. After that, we went to the Old World, and my father, Hua Jiahao, became a commander of the Florindale army. I had been there ever since."

"Wait, so you're seven hundred years old? And how did you get to the Old World? If you can come and go as you please, why are we still here?"

"Time is funny between the realms, Enzo," Violet said. "So are the passages. We still don't understand all the barriers, and we've always felt it was best to keep it that way. Few people in the Old World even know this one exists, as many of you don't know about ours."

"In my case, my ancestors granted us passage to the Old World, but that was an extremely rare case. It was a sort of karmic favor to my father, intended as a one-way trip."

Enzo shook a flame off of his marshmallow. "So my big question is how do *we* all get to the Old World? Have you earned any karmic favors?"

"It could take me another seven hundred years to build up enough karma to ask my ancestors for another trip back." Mulan smirked. "I'm kind of a Powerball winner."

Liam scratched his head. "A Powerball? Sounds rather dark. Should any one person have that much—"

"No, no, Liam. I'll explain it to you later," Mulan said with a laugh. "I won the lottery and bought a jet, a limo, and a house. I also have a ship. My technology led me to Madame Esme about a week ago, and she told me about Liam. She also told me that you might save us all."

"Was Madame Esme from your world?" Rosana asked.

Mulan nodded. "She has a story for the ages."

"Stars!" Liam said. "She was from our world the whole time?"

"Wow. This is all so cra"—Enzo caught a glimpse ofRosana's raised eyebrows—"absurd."

Rosana flashed Enzo a cheesy grin.

"Hey," he continued. "I think I may know who else is here from your world."

"And who might that be, young Enzo?" Violet asked.

He passed her the remaining figurines.

"It worked," she breathed. "Your father became a Carver. He carves the things you need to see. It is such strange fortune that he also carved you the miner named Wayde—and my father."

Enzo's jaw dropped, along with everyone else's. *No way.*

"Your *father* is one of the figurines? He's here?"

Violet nodded. "Oh, he's here alright. In fact, we can go see him tomorrow if you'd like. He works at a little diner less than a mile from here, and I should say that he owes your parents a tremendous favor. After all, they were the ones to rescue him from Avoria's mirror."

CHAPTER THIRTY-SEVEN

TODAY—THE OLD WORLD

Every time Hansel put somebody new into the Cavern of Ombra, the realm darkened. After he imprisoned Peter Pan, the sky turned the color of a plum. When Hansel peeled his eyes open the next morning, he was certain it was still night. Not a single ray of light streamed into his room. Not a single bluebird sang him good morning.

Instead, he awoke in a film of sweat with a heavy sensation in his stomach. He remembered the time he ate the candy that coated the witch's house in the Woodlands. The sugary window, the light chocolaty bricks, the graham cracker roof tiles paved with fluffy icing . . . It was divine, until it wasn't anymore. If the witch weren't about to kill him that day, the punching sensation inside his belly would've done the trick.

On this particular day, he woke up with that same feeling.

With all the strength he could summon, he pushed himself out of bed and opened his window to let some air into his stuffy room.

Clouds like graphite, charcoal, and ash funneled above him in a dreary haze. Lightning filled the cracks between, illuminating the sky in blinding momentary bursts only to cut to black once more. Thunder grumbled all around, and Hansel thought of giants dragging their feet along a ragged mountain, of bridges crumbling to dust, of the ground opening up and swallowing the sky. Swallowing *him*. The darkness, the lightning, and the thunder rippled beyond Hansel's line of sight. He imagined it must have blanketed the entire realm.

Fear prickled his heart and ruffled the skin on the back of his neck.

I caused this, he thought. *I plunged our world into a dark place.*

Unable to contain his stomach any longer, Hansel hung his head out the window and vomited onto a patch of dry, uprooted moonflowers.

He couldn't be a part of this anymore. Where was his strength?

Gretel, I don't know what to do. I don't know how to fix this anymore.

He thought about the image in the mirror and lurched again.

He couldn't spend another moment by himself.

He couldn't keep the secrets to himself anymore.

He needed a friend untouched by darkness. He needed light.

With this revelation, Hansel dragged himself to the first place he could think of: Snow White's home. With every step, his limbs and his heart grew heavier, like cement ran in his veins. Over time, trees had shed their leaves and shriveled into crispy husks. Birds stopped singing and perusing the skies. There were no more deer, no more squirrels. There was no more life.

The only remaining bit of light in the land radiated from Snow's castle, which stood white and gleaming, but only marginally. Once blinding, it faded to a dull twinkle . . . the eye of a white tiger in a black jungle. It was just enough to give Hansel a morsel of hope that Snow might understand what he had done. That she could save him.

Snow emerged from the castle with stark malice on her face and a silver crossbow in her hands, leveled directly between Hansel's brows.

"Snow!" Hansel raised his hands. "It's just me! It's Hansel."

The crossbow didn't move. "Do you come alone?"

"I come alone."

Slowly, Snow lowered the crossbow. It seemed that the recent years had taken a small toll on her. Her face, while still full of youth and beauty, showed signs of restlessness. It was mostly her eyes, pinker than usual, and thin lines had formed around her mouth.

"I'm sorry, Hansel. It wasn't my intention to threaten you. I just feel the need to stay on guard. Liam's still missing and . . . ." Snow pointed her nose to the sky, indicating the dismal state of their surroundings.

Hansel took a step forward. "I understand. Can I join you for a short spell?"

Snow ran a hand through her hair and sighed. "Of course. Please, join me. I'll make us some breakfast."

She beat a soft rhythm on her lap as she turned around.

Hansel's heart soared to be in the presence of a friend. At rock bottom, that's all one needed. He could settle for friendship. Yes, that's all he needed.

He followed her inside the castle, determined to come clean.

CHAPTER THIRTY-EIGHT

TODAY—THE NEW WORLD: CALIFORNIA

Every time he closed his eyes, Enzo saw either Pietro or his father. He relived those moments of helplessness dozens of times, tossing and turning on one of Violet's couches. Earlier, Violet had given him some cheese and crackers with a steaming mug of chamomile tea, but despite his drowsiness, sleep wouldn't come.

On a couch across the room, Liam called out in the middle of the night, "You're going to be okay, my friend."

Enzo rolled onto his elbow. Liam lay flat on his back with his arms bent neatly across his chest, staring up at the popcorn-speckled ceiling. His posture reminded Enzo of a vampire, but the man probably slept like that so he could be up in a hurry if he ever needed to defend himself. Defensive sleeping strategies probably came with the territory of being a prince in a land of dragons and soul-sucking evil queens.

"Sorry?" Enzo said.

"You're going to be alright. They won't take you as long as I'm close by."

Enzo flopped back onto his pillow. "Oh. You think I'm worried about Hansel." He smiled. "Thanks, Liam. That's really cool of you, but that's not why—"

"No, no, chum. You're not afraid Hansel will take you; I suppose you *want* him to take you. I'm talking about the nightmares. That's why you're really awake. You'll feel much better in the morning if you let sleep come to you, Enzo. Our hour of action arrives."

Enzo lay still. He hated to admit it, but Liam was right. Enzo wanted Hansel to come back and take him away. At least whatever fate awaited, Enzo wouldn't suffer it alone. He'd be with his parents. He'd see Zack, Wendy, and Pietro again. If they were all going to lose their souls to some horrible witch, then Enzo didn't see why he should keep his soul, either.

Liam wasn't lying, however. When Enzo managed to fade into sleep, he rested peacefully. There were no nightmares, no visions of Pietro or his parents. No dreams whatsoever.

Daylight snuggled in when Violet tapped him on the shoulder and stirred him to life.

"Good morning, sleeping beauty. Brunch in half an hour, 'kay?"

Enzo nodded, a little embarrassed to see that everybody else was already awake, but he felt well rested. He yawned and stretched his limbs, crackling his toes. His shoulders felt loose and limber. After one of the best showers he'd ever had—seriously, how many people had soap dispensers built into the shower walls?—he felt ready for anything.

"Enzo," Violet said, "I've told my father you're coming. We feel it's best if not all of us go, so Liam will accompany you. After all, I'm the laughing stock of *Perez Hilton* right now. If all five of us walk out the door together, it's gonna be like *bam*, paparazzi everywhere."

"Solid. Guess this one's a mission for the guys, then?" Enzo turned to give Liam a fist bump.

Liam leapt back, leaving Enzo bewildered. "Whoa, whoa, my friend! There's no need to threaten me with your knuckles. Kindly lower your hand, please."

Rosana giggled. "No, Liam, you have to hit your knuckles against

Enzo's. It's like a handshake in this world. Guys do it to 'bro out' with each other."

Liam scratched his head. "Bro out? With such a violent gesture?"

"Will you just hit my fist already?"

Liam sighed, curled his hand into a ball, and swung his knuckles into Enzo's with a loud pop.

Enzo winced and shook the pain out of his wrist. "Ow, man!"

The others in the room laughed, especially Liam. "You did ask me to hit you, chum. *Bro-ing out* is alarmingly gratifying if I do say so myself."

Violet smiled. "Okay, boys, go speak with my father and try not to kill each other. We're going to have girl time here."

Enzo rubbed his knuckles and brought them to his lips. "Okay. So, uh, where exactly are we going?"

"Sirenetta's Diner. Out the door, one block to your right, crisscross the intersection and you'll be there. Look for a big mermaid statue. It's unmissable. I guess I don't have to tell you what my father looks like."

"How 'bout a name?"

"Dominick. Dominick Bellamy."

⌘⌘⌘

After a short walk and a rather interesting conversation about dragons, a ten-foot brunette mermaid statue beckoned Enzo and Liam into Sirenetta's Diner. When Liam pushed the door open, the smell of coffee assaulted Enzo's nostrils, reminding him of Pietro's caffeine addiction. Sunlight illuminated the smoke on the grills, the black and white checkered floor, and cardinal sparkles on faux leather seats. The sizzling of bacon cut through the sweet vibrato of Zooey Deschanel's voice on the jukebox. The only thing that really set Sirenetta's apart from the diners Enzo saw on TV was the abundance of clamshells and seaweed on the walls. There was also a shoebox-sized shelf filled with forks of assorted sizes and colors, where somebody had painted a sign labeled *Dinglehoppers*.

Enzo and Liam spotted the old man right away; he was stirring a dash of chocolate syrup into a glass of milk behind the counter. Beneath his white paper diner hat, his eyes were a bit red and his nose was crooked. He was also one of the tallest people in the room. Liam and Enzo approached the counter, took a seat, and then awaited the man's attention.

"Welcome to Sirenetta's Diner, gentlemen. You boys ever dined here before?"

Liam cut right to the chase. "Are you Mr. Bellamy?"

The man's face fell into a tight frown, but Enzo assumed by the figurine that the frown was just his natural expression. "I am he. The Lord of the Diner."

"Violet sent us," Enzo said.

"Mm. You mean *Heather*, yes?"

"Sure?" Enzo was still trying to figure out the rule on what he should be calling the Old World people. He supposed Pietro would forever be Pietro to him and he understood why he needed the new name, but he didn't feel that somebody like Violet, who wasn't a part of any story Enzo had heard before, needed an alias.

Mr. Bellamy plopped two brunch menus in front of Liam and Enzo and poured them each a cup of coffee, to Enzo's dismay. Then the old man leaned over the counter and furrowed his eyebrows. In a tense whisper, he said, "Your presence brings *ruin* to my happy New World life! Where you go, trouble will surely follow. Now, what can I serve you this morning?"

Without missing a beat, Liam said, "Stars! The biscuits and gravy plate sounds terrific!"

Enzo elbowed Liam in the side and cleared his throat. "Uh, sir, I'm not sure how much Heather told you, but we were wondering if you might come with us. We're on an important quest right now, and we need you." He pulled mini-Mr. Bellamy out of his pocket and stood the figure on top of the menu.

Mr. Bellamy took a fleeting glance at the carving and scribbled onto a notepad. "Great. Two biscuits and gravy plates. How do you like your eggs?"

"Very much!" Liam cheered.

"Scrambled?" Enzo said. "But sir—"

"They'll be up shortly." Mr. Bellamy snatched up the menus and stalked away.

Liam drummed his fingers on the table, seemingly unfazed. "Stars, I'm hungry."

"What the hell, man? Aren't you annoyed at all? Mr. Bellamy made it very clear that he doesn't want to come with us. He's gonna be a pain and all you can say is 'Stars, I'm hungry?'"

"What? I *am* hungry. Besides, we've nothing to fear. I'll get him to come with us. What is it that you people call me in this world's stories? Charming? Be patient and eat your meal, chum. Remember that we're in a public place and must converse with him carefully."

Brunch arrived on a black fish-shaped plate, and Enzo had to admit, the food was divine. The golden biscuits melted in his mouth; the brown crisp of the bacon and the lightly salted potatoes complimented the fluffy scrambled eggs. It almost approached the caliber of breakfast Enzo's mom used to make in the mornings. His dad wasn't bad in the kitchen, but they both knew it was his mother's sacred domain. They ate quickly, Liam shoveling food into his mouth like sand from a dump truck. Enzo gave him his coffee and drank a glass of water instead.

Mr. Bellamy didn't acknowledge them while they ate. Instead, a blonde waitress checked up on them and refilled their drinks. When they finished, Mr. Bellamy dropped off the check and walked away. Underneath the check, which read, *On the house*, Enzo found a note scribbled in red ink:

I know why you're here. Meet in parking lot in five.

⌘⌘⌘

"Simply put, gentlemen, I'm not coming with you. Neither is my daughter."

"But, sir, we need you both. There's a queen trying to go back to your world, and she's gonna consume a bunch of peoples' souls through a magic mirror and—"

"Precisely," Bellamy said. "That's why we're not going with you. That witch is my wife, and I'll have you know that she put me in a magic mirror for many years. Oh, the horror of that place! Her imprisonment serves her right, and if she's trying to get out, I'll have no part of her reign of terror. The Old World is no sandbox. You know not the power of which she's capable, but *I* do. I will not have my daughter and I exposed to this witch any longer. We're safe here. Do you know what I do at night, boy? I watch Netflix. I read books. I fish and play poker with my neighbors. You would have me give all this up to put myself in my wife's crosshairs again?"

Enzo sighed, unable to expel the annoyance through his lungs. How could one person be so infuriatingly stubborn?

Oh, Enzo thought shamefully. *I suppose this is how I've been acting myself.* He thought of Rosana's lecture to him on the beach. He thought of Pietro's adamant refusal to fail his family. He thought of Mulan's no-nonsense attitude and Liam's fundamental Boy Scout-kindness and Violet's enchanting story. *I should say that he owes your parents a tremendous favor*, she said. It had taken a lot of tough love to get through to Enzo, from a lot of people he didn't even know he *could* love, but they'd broken the dam, and a wall of determination burst forth. *This old man's about to get that same treatment, and I'm not going to wait for backup.*

"Mr. Bellamy, people are in actual danger, and you're going to bring up these selfish reasons to do nothing about it? I'm ashamed, man. Your daughter seems so brave, and you're going to run from your problems. If there's anything I've learned just by looking for you these past four days, it's that when things go wrong, you can't stand there and blame other people and still expect good things to happen to you. If you don't act against the queen, Mr. Bellamy, you deserve whatever consequences come to you."

Mr. Bellamy clenched a fist. "I will *not* be spoken to in this—"

"Furthermore, you should know that my father and one of my *best* friends are two people in danger right now. And you know what? They're also the people who put themselves directly in the queen's path to free you from the mirror. Peter Pan, Wendy, Alice, and Pinocchio are half the reason you're even here right now, and they deserve your help. So do their wives, children, and friends. They're some of the best people I know, and I know now that if we want them back, we need to do something about it. We're running out of time, sir. If you're not gonna help us, I really hope you know how to help yourself, because you can't hide from her forever. I'm getting my family back, Mr. Bellamy, with or without you!"

Enzo drew a deep breath, feeling both proud and winded. *Man that felt good!* Liam and Mr. Bellamy said nothing, evidently dumbfounded.

"Mm." Mr. Bellamy rubbed his pointed chin, and Enzo decided the old man reminded him of a vulture. He didn't see how Violet could possibly be related to Mr. Bellamy, but maybe genetics worked differently in the other realm. "Crescenzo, son of Pinocchio, you're a cheeky one, but you possess gumption. You may be the one to lead us against Avoria after all."

Contemplative silence hovered between the men. *Did I hear that correctly?*

Mr. Bellamy removed his paper hat. "I'll join you in your stand against the Ivory Queen, boy, but I hope you understand what this is. Rescuing your family is just the beginning. Once we start this, we're committing ourselves to a much grander battle. I hope you're ready." Mr. Bellamy leaned in, lowering his voice, "One further warning to you, boy: Should any harm come to my daughter in our trials, you shall be the first to blame."

Enzo gulped. "Understood, sir."

"I shall meet you at her house in precisely one hour. I suggest you prepare."

Mr. Bellamy returned his cap to his head and reentered the diner, ready to scribble orders and stir chocolate milk again.

Enzo jabbed Liam's shoulder. "Guess we didn't need your charm after all!"

"I suppose we didn't! I'm quite proud of you, I must confess." Liam made a tight fist and held it in front of him. "Shall we clash fingers, my friend?"

CHAPTER THIRTY-NINE

TODAY—THE OLD WORLD

"Coffee?"

Hansel took a seat and shook his head at Snow's offer. "I'm quite fine, thank you. Perhaps you'd like me to prepare some for you?"

Snow was already busying herself with fires, kettles, and coffee beans. "Nope. I have it, Hansel."

Ignoring the fact that Snow's speech had been shorter and harsher than he'd ever heard it, Hansel asked, "Don't you usually have people to do this for you? Maids and cooks? Butlers?" He looked around. They were all alone in the vast castle. "Where is everybody?"

"Gone," Snow said simply. "I sent them away to search for Liam."

Hansel suppressed a pang of guilt in his gut. "In all this darkness?"

"Yes."

"And still no sign of him?"

"No. But I *mustn't* give up hope. I know he's still alive somewhere. The day I give up hope is the day I . . . ." She swallowed, shook it off, and returned to her coffee.

Hansel stood and brushed a gentle hand on Snow's shoulder. "But do you ever worry that he may not return? That he may be . . . you know?"

"Do you recall what you told me about Gretel a few years ago, when

I asked you to take over the cottage? And I asked you if it was a good idea to keep looking? Do you remember what you said?"

Hansel stared somewhere beyond the wall, remembering the occasion. It seemed like so long ago, yet it remained vibrantly fresh in his mind.

"*When somebody that close to you dies, you feel it.*"

Hansel nodded. "Of course I remember."

"Good."

Silence passed between the old friends. Only the bubbling of the kettle and the soft crackle of fire could be heard before Snow continued, "You know, I've always been inspired by your determination to find her. The hope you maintain . . . that hero mentality. I admire it, Hansel. It's because I know you that I won't give up hope on Liam."

Hansel thought he might melt like butter. Snow's words tapped him softly in his heart, but they also jabbed him in the gut. He sat and willed his mind to calm down.

Snow smiled. "Now, surely you're here for a reason, yes? It's been a long time. What have you been up to?"

Deep breath, Hansel. You know she can help you. You know she would want to. "Snow. What would you say if I told you I know where Gretel is?"

"I would say that's wonderful news, but I also have to ask how that's possible after all these years. Are you speaking in fact?"

"Yes."

Snow creased the corners of her eyes. "Then where is she?"

"Remember the mirror in my room? Well, she's inside it."

Hansel watched Snow's confusion melt away. "Oh my goodness. It all makes sense. A mirror, where nobody would think to look for anybody but herself."

Hansel nodded, weaving his hands together.

"We have to get her out for you! How do we do that?"

"That's just it. I need your help. It's dreadfully complicated, but I need you to help me kill a queen."

Snow's jaw fell open. "Kill? Hansel, I couldn't!" She shook her head. "Wait a minute, this isn't the same queen that—?"

"That poisoned you? No, Snow. It's not the same queen. It's Avoria."

"But Avoria's been missing for—"

"No. She means to come back. I've done a terrible thing. In my quest to find Gretel, I awakened the mirror. Avoria and Gretel are *both* in there, and Avoria asked me to find seven people to let her out." The heaviness in Hansel's voice caught him off guard. He clutched his forehead, using all of his strength to keep tears from flowing. "And I couldn't resist her. I started doing her bidding, but I couldn't finish. I've kidnapped, I've killed, I've . . . Oh, God, what am I?"

Snow covered her mouth. "Hansel!"

At the sound of her sweet voice, Hansel broke. He fell into Snow's lap and wept, barely able to speak. "I don't know who I am anymore. I-I don't know what the future holds, what to do to save her. Please, just tell me what to do."

Snow put her hands in her hair. "I don't know what to say."

His sobs were so violent that they jittered every inch of his body. Finally, Snow touched the center of his back and tried to steady him. "I really don't know what to say, Hansel. I don't know what to do. Just calm down, and we'll try to come up with something."

"What can we do?" Hansel moaned. "I've doomed us all."

Snow shook her head, suddenly determined. "No. You've given me hope. If your sister's been in the mirror all these years, then perhaps Liam's in one of the mirrors, too. We can get them both back somehow. I know we can."

Hansel wiped his face and squeezed Snow's soft fingers. "Listen, I know where Liam is too. He's not in the mirror; he's somewhere else."

"Somewhere else, like *where*?" Her voice acquired a cautious edge.

"Promise to let me explain and—"

"*Where* is he? Is he one of the queen's seven?"

"No, no. He's not one of the seven; he's—"

Snow jerked her hand away and took a step back, her voice growing heavy and loud. "What did you do?"

"I had to send him somewhere where he couldn't interfere, but I can get him back for you. Let me explain—"

Snow spun away from Hansel and buried her head in her hands. "No, no, no. No!"

"I'm so sorry—"

"*No!* All these years I've trusted you! I trusted you to be my friend, and you've done the unforgiveable. You're the reason I've been so alone for so long! All this time, you've been everything that's wrong with this realm. You've been the source of all my pain!"

Hansel's tears streamed haphazardly from his eyes.

Snow's lips fell into a flat line, her eyes cold with anger. "I can't believe I've been so stupid. My blind trust in you and my naïve determination to see the good in everybody has been my biggest shortcoming. My husband, the love of my life, missing all these years because of you."

"Snow, all I need is your understanding. Don't you see? Together, we can make things right! I'll get Liam back!"

"You'll say anything to save your sister." Snow picked up her crossbow again and fixed its gaze on Hansel's heart. Snow gritted her teeth. "Get out."

Hansel dropped to his knees, palms on the ground, and lowered his head. "I'm *begging* you. *Please.*"

"Get out of my home, you monster!"

In an acknowledgment of defeat, Hansel pulled himself up and nodded. The threat of the crossbow wasn't as heavy as Snow's icy gaze, and even that wasn't as painful as knowing he deserved it. He had knowingly harmed many others for his own selfish gains. For his desire to be a hero and to have his sister home for good. For that, he allowed a terrible queen to use him to destroy everything.

With Snow's rejection of his friendship, nothing mattered anymore.

With his eyes on the ground, he started for the door, and he could feel Snow tracing his path with the tip of her crossbow.

Before he made it outside, Hansel paused. "If you're not going to help me undo this"—he swallowed a knot in his throat, churning his pain into anger—"then you might as well serve your part in it . . . your destiny as the seventh sacrifice. I'm sorry, Snow."

Feeling the darkness take him over again, Hansel raised a hand, fingers stretched long and tight, brimming with the power of the mirrors.

In that same instance, Snow fired her crossbow.

CHAPTER FORTY

TODAY—THE NEW WORLD

Rosana adored Violet, but the woman was a terrible cook and she knew it. She scurried about her kitchen in a blur, refusing Rosana's help. Four broken egg yolks and a burnt batch of hashbrowns later, she threw up her hands and admitted defeat. "Two years in this stupid world and I still haven't gotten the hang of electric stoves! I'm calling for delivery!"

"No, it's fine," Rosana insisted. "Do you just have, like, cereal or something?"

Violet scoffed. "Please. Cereal's a joke. Your modern day artists paint these dopey talking bears and goofy, happy pirates on the boxes and make a mockery of us all. Cereal is an insult to my realm."

"I agree," Mulan said. "Have any kindergarten class spend a day with Hook. They'll never look at this Captain Crunch the same way again."

Rosana looked away. Captain Crunch was her favorite cereal.

Violet pulled some bagels from a pantry. "Oh, Hook. And Merlin and Mrs. Rose and Mr. Holmes." She set the bagels down without opening them. "Gosh, I feel awful."

"Don't," Mulan said. "Do you trouble yourself over the Thousand Souls as well?"

"I didn't order the Thousand into battle."

"But you still feel responsible for them," Mulan guessed.

Violet acquired a faraway gaze. "Every day. So many people lost their lives that day . . . Belladonna, Cinderella, Jack Frost, Rapunzel, that poor baker of Drury."

Rosana's ears perked up. "The muffin man?"

"Oh, his muffins were dazzling, Rosana, but he was known for so much more. He made cakes and turnovers, quiches and crepes." Violet cleaved a bagel in two. "I miss home," she sniffed.

"We'll get there," Mulan assured.

Rosana ruminated on the whereabouts of her mother and the bizarre scenarios that unfolded since she met Enzo and Pietro. *Poor Pietro*, she thought. *I promise you, Mom and Pietro, I'll bring you both back.*

A new and disturbing thought crossed her mind. *What if they won't want to come back?* She hoped they would. If Violet's story was correct, their wish to grow up and see the New World had set everything into motion. They popped up somewhere in the United States, and the power of the mirrors sucked the Ivory Queen into a shimmering prison before spitting out Violet's father. From what Rosana had deduced, the mirrors probably functioned on a sort of trade system. If one brought them together to grant a wish, they would spit out their captive, but they would always draw another in.

If I'm right about that and the queen means to get out of the mirrors, who would end up in her *place?* Would it be the seven people she had asked Hansel to gather? The idea of her mother being trapped in a mirror for all eternity terrified her. Then again, if the stories were true, her mom had been inside of a mirror before. She spent nearly a week in a world beyond a mirror. Rosana couldn't wait to ask her mom about that.

The more she pondered, the more one thing became abundantly clear: They would have to destroy the mirrors.

Violet handed Rosana a bagel with strawberry cream cheese. Rosana took a hearty bite, chewing thoughtfully and staring out the window. The ocean rolled back and forth outside, a giant shimmering mirror of its own, pulling fragile castles into its depths and spitting up broken shells and crystalline glints of sand.

At one point, the ocean spat out something bright orange . . . a warm shade of pumpkin, and just a little smaller, as well. It was enough to catch Rosana's attention, but in the time it took her to blink, the object was gone again. She supposed she was getting used to that trend in her life. People and things vanished and appeared seemingly at random. Even she did.

"How about some TV while we wait for the boys to come back?" Violet clicked on a large flat screen, and Rosana was horrified to see a freeze frame of her face on the pop gossip program called *Grant!* hosted by an obnoxious middle-aged man of the same name. The words "Red Carpet Catastrophe!" had been imposed onto the image of her clinging to a security guard's ankle, her mouth open mid-scream.

Rosana was now a meme.

Grant zipped around in front of the image, his crazy highlighted hair bobbing around his head. "When we come back, we need to have a serious talk about this red carpet catastrophe! Who are these fascinating unknowns who attracted so much attention at the Peter Pan premiere yesterday?" A quick montage flashed on the screen, featuring Enzo in a full sprint, Mulan screaming among a crowd of stars, and Pietro looking defeated as the dirty dwarf dragged him away. "And, like, what's the deal with Heather McClavender? We sit down with a reporter from Stargle Magazine, who offers an exclusive eyewitness account of this juicy story! Don't you touch that dial, mkay?"

Rosana sighed. "So embarrassing."

"It'll fade away, hon," Violet promised. "People care about celebrity news for two minutes and then something else distracts them."

Mulan's lips remained in an irritated curve.

"But I'm a *meme* now," Rosana complained. "I hate being the center of attention. I mean, a lot of the time I don't want to be noticed. Lots of people dream of getting famous. I'd rather not be seen."

Violet fluttered her lips. "Your mother was very much the same. People thought she was looking for attention after her trips to Wonderland. She would've preferred to disappear. I must confess that it's the strangest thing, encountering the offspring of those dear children I once knew. You remind me so much of them, and yet you're so fascinatingly unique." She turned and smiled, but Rosana noticed that she seemed to be staring through her. Violet whipped her head around as if searching for lost keys, and Mulan did the same.

"Where'd she go?" Mulan said. "She was sitting right here!"

Well, this is awkward, Rosana thought. *Apparently, I've vanished again.* "I'm, uh, sitting right here, still."

Mulan jumped. "We cannot see you!"

"But I'm right here." Rosana stood up and tapped Mulan on the shoulder. The woman's eyes widened in fear.

"Sorcery!"

"Magical," Violet breathed, "just like your mother."

Rosana wrinkled her nose. "Wait a second, like my mother? What about—?"

"Violet! Miss Violet!" A tap on the window and a nervous, muffled voice interrupted her.

All three women jerked their gaze to the sliding glass door, where a short, red-faced man tapped a pudgy finger against the window.

Violet jumped up and scurried to the door. The man appeared to be making bouts of intense eye contact with her, but his gaze was fleeting and he would sometimes tuck his chin into his chest. Violet slid the door open and the man stumbled inside, sandy-footed with his beard in a wet clump. He promptly hugged the woman, soaking her dress with what Rosana could only assume was seawater.

Ignoring the fact that this man had just tracked sand and ocean into her home, Violet reciprocated the hug with bewilderment written on her face.

"Wayde!"

"Miss Violet! Boy, am I ever glad to see you!"

Violet and Wayde separated, and the next thing Rosana knew, she was on her feet, twenty feet away from the couch, and securing a chokehold on the man she had formerly been introduced to as Wayland. Anger rippled through her veins and she brought Wayde to the ground, her knee pressed firmly into his chest.

"You took my mother away, you creep!" Rosana screamed. "Give her back to me! Give her back!"

Wayde's arms flailed at his sides, and his rosy cheeks darkened. "Can't . . . breathe."

"Rosana!" Violet gasped. "Release him at once!"

Rosana softened her grip on Wayde's throat, but she dug her knee further into his torso, soaking her jeans in salt water. She was guessing she was still invisible, but it was hard to tell because Wayde didn't seem like the type of man to make eye contact anyway. Violet and Mulan implored her to let Wayde go, but neither of them made the effort to pry her off.

"Rosana, what's gotten into you?" Violet asked.

Rosana ignored Violet and interrogated Wayde through clenched teeth. "Six months ago you abducted a woman from a subway in New York City. Alicia Trujillo. Alice. Ring any bells?"

"Please," Wayde sputtered. "Let me go?"

"Look at me!" Rosana growled. In that instant, two pairs of hands seized her under her arms and pried her off the dwarf. Rosana squirmed and wrestled, but Mulan and Violet were a strong team together. When Rosana was back on her feet, she noticed that Wayde was finally looking at her, jittering with fear.

Mulan placed a firm hand on Rosana's back. "Sit back down, okay?"

"He took my mother away! I wanna talk to him."

"We'll talk about everything, dear. I'm most interested in your special *ability*, but let me speak to Wayde first." Violet patted Rosana on the shoulder and helped Wayde to his feet. "Want some water? Bagels? A towel?"

Wayde took a second to recover his breath, panting and heaving while the color returned to his face. "Whew. Thank you, Miss Violet. Daughter of Alice, I want to apologize. It wasn't my intention to take a girl's mother away from her, and I haven't lived comfortably with my actions."

Rosana scowled. "Yeah? Well, how 'bout you look me in the eyes and tell me that again, hm? Then maybe I'll care."

"Rosana, please," Violet pleaded.

Rosana crossed her arms and sank into the couch.

"Now, Wayde, I understand Rosana's suspicions and anger toward you. Yesterday, a man named Peter Pan was taken hostage by two of your friends."

Wayde pouted at the ground. "I know, Finn and Jinn. We've all done terrible things to serve our boss."

"You mean Hansel," Mulan said. She extended her palm and shook the man's hand. "Wayde, I'm Hua Mulan. I'm from your world."

"Oh! I've heard s-such grand stories. It's an honor, ma'am."

"Let's refocus. I escaped from our home to gather forces against Hansel. More appropriately, against Queen Avoria. Are you still working with Hansel?"

Wayde shook his head. "I don't think any of them will want to anymore."

"Why's that?"

"I have a question," Rosana interrupted. "How did you get here?"

"Hansel sent me back. He's gone m—"

"So you didn't come here with the intention to help us or anything, did you? Are you here to take one of us away? Cart us off to this Ivory Queen?"

"N-n-no, you must listen to me! He's—"

"Can't we tie him up or something?" Rosana threw her arms up. "Why are we trusting him?"

Mulan gave Rosana a stern look. "If you can't control your temper, Rosana, we'll tie *you* up. We must listen to what he has to say."

Violet nodded at Wayde, inviting him to continue.

"We must go back, Miss Violet." Wayde's face pleaded as hard as his voice. For once, his eye contact didn't waver. "The land is dark. Strange. Not the same. I think it's because of what the mirrors are doing, and the people Mr. Hansel's been bringing back. And he only needs *one more* before he fills all the seven crystals!"

"Did he send *you* to find the last person?" Mulan asked. "Be honest."

"That's just it! We n-need to hurry and get back to the Old World because Hansel's already on his way to find his last sacrifice all by himself, and once he does, we're out of time! He didn't want my help; he sent me back because I learned who he was looking for!"

"Wait," Violet said, "he's on his way already? Is it one of us?"

"That's just it," Wayde repeated. "It's not any of you at all. The queen's seeking the fairest in the land, and she doesn't live far from Mister Hansel! I saw her face in the mirror, and . . . Oh, we *must* rescue Snow White!"

A door clicked shut behind Rosana, and Liam's shaking voice startled her out of Wayde's story.

"No . . . Not Snow."

CHAPTER FORTY-ONE

TODAY—THE NEW WORLD

Enzo was still in shock when Mr. Bellamy arrived at Violet's house. It wasn't hard to see that Liam was in shock as well, distressed even, and reasonably so. Enzo watched the prince share a brief reunion with Wayde, who apparently had been an old friend in the other world. He had also been one of the seven miners conspiring with Hansel. When Enzo learned this, he shot Rosana a meaningful look. *Can we trust this guy?* Rosana returned a dismissive shrug, but Mulan nodded as if to confirm her approval. The miner shook Enzo's hand, his grip noncommittal and gaze falling somewhere beyond Enzo's nose.

What bewildered Enzo the most was the idea that Hansel wasn't coming for any of them, and that's what Enzo had been counting on. He would never forget Hansel's words when they first met. *You'll see your father again soon. I'm sure I'll be back for you and The Flying Man any day now.* In a bizarre defiance of expectations, Wayde revealed that Hansel was going after Snow White instead, and there wasn't much time to spare.

Upon Mr. Bellamy's arrival, Wayde recounted the story again, and the old man sat on the couch and drank iced tea and mumbled ambiguous *hm*'s. At the end of Wayde's story, Mr. Bellamy drummed his fingers on his glass, smearing cool tea-sweat along his fingertips. The corner of his lip turned up in a hard grimace. "*Hansel.*" Mr. Bellamy's tone was venom in Enzo's ears. "He came to me, looking to buy the mines. Said he was looking for his sister."

Violet lowered her head.

"Threw a royal fit when I denied him, and that's why I'm here." Bellamy cast a pointed gaze on his daughter. "Violet, has it not occurred to you how dangerous it will be to return? Avoria, she's—"

"Terrible, Father, I know. But I have a responsibility to our people. And what if the darkness spills into *this* world? Then what? We've got to stop her."

"Mm." Mr. Bellamy lowered his glass and pressed his fingertips together. Enzo was still rather proud of himself for convincing the old man to come along, even if he was still voicing the ghost of doubt. "Then what do you suppose we do?"

"We must rescue my wife," Liam said. "*I* have to save my wife. My friends, it's been *agony* not knowing what's become of her, but I've kept faith that she'll be okay. Knowing she's alive gives me strength to go on, but if something happens—"

Mulan held up a hand. "Nothing is going to happen, Liam. Yet something *must* happen on our part."

Enzo suddenly felt six pairs of eyes fall on him. Well, five. Wayde was always looking *through* him.

"Um, why's everyone looking at me?"

"Because you brought us all together, Enzo," Violet said. "Through your father's work, you gathered us to stand against the dark. Your heart led us here."

Enzo surveyed the room, now able to put real faces and personalities to wooden facades his father had been carving for years.

Enzo chuckled and rubbed the back of his neck. "Um, guys, my heart didn't bring us together. That was all Pietro. Mulan. Luck, even.

All I've done is stand around and—"

"Let me stop you right there, dude," Rosana said, "because we do *not* have the time to sit here and listen to you bash yourself. If it weren't for you, I would still be sleeping in the subway. I would be pickpocketing people who look like tourists. I would be cussing at the police because they haven't done a thing to find my mom. If you and Pietro hadn't barged into my life, I'd—"

"Pep talk later," Mulan said. "What are we doing, Enzo? As much as you don't believe it, you got us here. What's the next step?"

Enzo rose and paced around the room. "I just don't know! I mean, I'm sorry. I wanna bring everyone home more than anything, but I don't know how to get us there. My dad left me these figurines, and that was it. I didn't even know he was Pinocchio until, like, two days ago. I know nothing."

Wayde wove his hands together. "If I may, everyone, I-I wasn't aware that all of you were intent on helping me save Snow White, but if you're all going to join me, well, I know how to get us back."

"And how are you going to do that?" Rosana piped up.

"It's actually quite simple, and I'm rather surprised that you didn't stumble upon the entrance yourself, Miss." Wayde paused, and Rosana gave him a pointed look.

Liam leapt off the couch, puffing his chest in knightly determination. "An entrance to the Old World? Where, chum, where?"

Wayde smiled nervously. "It's in the underground of the land you call New York City. There's a hidden tunnel that leads straight into our mines."

"*What?* All this time!" Rosana crossed her arms. "No, I don't believe you."

Enzo's mind reeled. A gateway to another world, right in the Big Apple's underbelly. Whatever it was, it was probably covered in gum older than he was and fossilized pizza grease, sealed by the glue of dry soda stains. He, Rosana, and Pietro could've stumbled upon it mere days ago and ended this whole thing. *No*, Enzo thought, *that's stupid*. He couldn't win this fight alone. He needed these people, just as much as they needed him to unite them.

"Can you take us there?"

"Of course, Mister Enzo! I had rather hoped you would all come back with me. I can take you there as soon as you're all ready."

Violet made a decisive fist. "Well, then, *are* you all ready?"

"Let's go," Rosana said. "I'm ready."

"I can call Ricky to ready the jet." Mulan whipped out her phone.

"Wait a minute," Liam asserted, holding up a palm. "Should we not have a plan?"

"We'll plan on the plane," Enzo said. "We're all together—that's the important part. Let's go back to New York, and on the way, Violet, Mr. Bellamy, Liam—*all* of you—tell me your stories again. In detail."

CHAPTER FORTY-TWO

TODAY—THE OLD WORLD

He didn't want it to happen. He *really* didn't want it to happen. More than anything, Hansel didn't want any harm to come to Snow White, or to anybody else for that matter.

When Snow fired her silver crossbow, though, his impulses spilled from his body. The next minute, Hansel found himself with his arm secured around her from behind, a shining bolt pressed into the tender crook of her neck.

Perspiration gleamed from his forehead and his arms. Words poured from his mouth in a voice that was half his, half ice, "This isn't how I envisioned our conversation going, *fair lady*."

Snow winced. "Sorry to disappoint."

"Drop the crossbow."

Snow stood defiantly still.

"Now."

"If you do this, Hansel, I promise you will regret it. Let me go, and I won't hurt you. We can go our separate ways, like we should have done a long time ago."

"Don't flatter yourself, sweetheart. You can't do a thing to hurt me." That wasn't entirely true. Snow hurt Hansel several times, inflicting pain deeper and fuller than anybody else had ever been capable of in his life, starting with the day she invited him to her wedding. He pushed the thought from his mind, refusing to give her control. "And we've been on separate paths for a long time already."

"No secret there."

"Lose the weapon. It isn't my intention to harm you, but I shall not ask again."

"I won't. I don't care what you do to me. There's no greater pain than living without my husband. If I'm to be a part of your scheme for the queen, then I'm not going quietly."

Hansel cringed and snapped his fingers. The woman wilted in his arm. Her midnight hair fell into a mop in front of her face. She dangled over the crook of Hansel's elbow, her fingers uncurling like flowers in bloom. The crossbow clattered to the ground.

The evil presence within Hansel wanted to smirk, but the human part of him fought it. He turned to the side and covered his mouth with his free hand, forcing down the bile that crept up his throat. He had put her to sleep with the snap of his fingers, quicker than she could bite into an apple, and he could probably wake her just as easily. He had absolute power, the kind he never meant to use on her. He wanted to wake her and apologize profusely, but as he told Lord Bellamy ages ago, nothing could stand in his way of retrieving his sister, not even Snow. Not when he was *this close*.

He turned Snow over, cradled her on her back, and fought back tears while brushing the hair out of her pale, sleeping face. "My friend. My companion," he breathed. "I never wanted you to become a part of this. I'm sorry. So sorry." With his ankle, he scooted the crossbow out of his way, swallowed his emotion, and shifted the girl so that she hung over his shoulder. Taking one last look around her empty castle, he started for the front door. "This will be over very soon, Your Majesty. I promise."

Hansel shut the door with his elbow and took a hard look at the winding road home. One way or another, it *would* be over soon. He had in his arms the last piece of the puzzle. The last of Queen Avoria's requests. Until Snow's face appeared in the mirror, it had been relatively easy. Sometimes it weighed upon his conscience, but never upon his heart. Kidnapping strangers was easy. Stealing old friends wasn't so hard either. After all, they had all gone on to new things without giving a thought to the world they left behind. They'd also aged enough that they didn't seem to be the same people Hansel used to play with long ago.

Kidnapping Snow White, the fairest in the land . . . he'd never forget that.

He stepped somberly into the courtyard, where water cascaded from a marble fountain and stone columns shot up around him, paving the way to the road. Thunder pierced his thoughts while lightning danced in and out of his peripheral vision, fleeting phantoms in the dark.

A jagged horizontal line appeared along the horizon.

Six figures, none particularly tall, walked side by side, their heads bobbing up and down with every step. Flashes of lightning illuminated their husky silhouettes. Hansel would've known them anywhere, well before their faces came into view.

The dwarves moved silently. Solemnly. There was a time when they wouldn't go anywhere together without humming, drumming, or singing songs to pass the time. Tonight, the thunder was their song, an irregular drumbeat. The hollow heart of the land.

Hansel shifted Snow in his arms and lowered her onto the marble fountain. Her fingertips dipped into the water. He dried them before folding her arms across her chest. She reminded him of the way she looked when she was poisoned: serene and divine. He stood in front of her, making a vain attempt to obscure her from the dwarves' view as they approached, their boots scraping the courtyard ground.

The men halted. Garon lowered his pickaxe. Worry lines were

written on his forehead, anger in his eyes. He approached Snow and gazed upon her face.

"Mister Hansel, what has occurred?"

Thunder rumbled as the dwarves waited for an answer. Hansel's expression remained unchanged. He looked around and noticed the other men had brought various objects: pickaxes, bows, knives, Bo with his basket of apples.

Hansel's mouth dried up. "Please stand aside, Garon."

Garon lowered his head and pressed his ear against Snow's stomach, checking for respiration. After a long minute, his eyes acquired an accusatory angle. "What have you done?"

"And where's Wayde?" Zid grunted.

"Why is she sleeping like that? Has she been poisoned again?"

"Does she breathe?"

Garon curled his fingers into unsteady fists. "You've harmed her."

"She merely rests in a gentle slumber," Hansel said.

"We saw her face in the mirror, Mister Hansel. She also signaled for us today. She beat our rhythm for the first time ever."

Hansel shook his head. "She's in no danger. I've been with her the whole time."

Zid took a bold step forward, his face scrunched with suspicion. "*Exactly*."

Chann aimed a finger at Hansel. "Wake her up, Mister Hansel."

Hansel remained stiff.

Finn plucked the string of his polished bow, raising an eyebrow. "Well?"

Simply put, Hansel didn't know what to say. He usually found his wits at their sharpest when he was threatened. But he'd never been threatened by this many friends before. Not by a group of people who looked so determined to protect a woman he cared for. Watching Zid sling his axe over his shoulders, Finn pluck at his bow, and Bo swing his basket, Hansel suddenly felt powerless. They were supposed to answer to him, but it seemed as though their love for Snow had negated their susceptibility to darkness. He couldn't influence them anymore, nor could he control his own emotions.

Hansel made a T with his body, putting his arms out at his sides to shield the woman behind him. These would likely be his last moments with her; he wanted every minute of her to himself.

Reflexively, the dwarfs popped into a line again and sprang into defensive stances, their feet spread and their elbows loose.

"You've gone too far, Mister Hansel," Garon said. "You shall not harm Snow White!"

Hansel waited for the power to come to him, but there was only human rage. Rage at the destiny that had befallen him. Rage toward the dwarves for their intervention. Rage against himself.

"This is bigger than you. Bigger than me, or *her*. You cannot prevent this."

Garon drew a breath and faced his friends. "Gentlemen."

With a single nod, the courtyard exploded into battle.

An arrow grazed Hansel's earlobe. He ducked in time to dodge one of Bo's apples soaring over his head, from which tiny seeds and fruity pulp burst forth when Garon's pickaxe struck the core. Adrenaline became Hansel's vehicle, guiding him around the flying projectiles and under the dwarves' massive hunks of iron. He ducked, arched, and leapt, astonished by his own agility. The best he could do was defend himself, as he had no weapons on him. He worried that if he ran back inside to retrieve Snow's crossbow, the men would carry her away and she'd slip from his grasp once again.

A sharp twist of Hansel's torso and an upward palm thrust produced a sickening cracking sound in Chann's nose. While Chann registered the injury, Hansel wrestled a knife from the dwarf's fingers, spun around, and slashed through Finn's bow, breaking the cord into a dark frayed mess. Chann, weaponless and roaring with resolve, seized the bridge of his nose and shoved a boot into Hansel's rib cage.

Crack!

Hansel didn't know if it was the sound or the sensation of cracking bones that brought him closer to blacking out, but in the time it took for him to hesitate, a plump, red apple conked him in the back of the head, and for a brief moment, stars exploded in front of him. He cleaved the air with Chann's knife, gaining some distance between the angry men. With a haphazard slash, a streak of blood spilled onto the ground, and Jinn howled in agony. Hansel had cut a deep slit in the man's shoulder.

Blood.

Hansel couldn't remember a time he'd ever spilled another's blood.

Chann dropped his pickaxe and resorted to swinging his good arm, while Zid charged Hansel with a handful of wood and metal ready to swing at him. Zid bared his teeth, his irises on fire, and let out a loud cry. "*Aaahhh*!"

Hansel danced out of the way just in time, continuously dodging the barrage of weaponry. His eyes wanted to wander back to the blood on the ground, but he couldn't afford the lapse in attention. Evading another blow from Zid's axe, Hansel reached into his vest...

Nothing.

He had used his final dart on Wayde. There was no choice but to finish the fight.

Summoning his lower body strength, Hansel leapt onto the marble fountain across from where Snow lay, beckoning his attackers to continue assaulting him. When Garon aimed his axe at him, Hansel hooked his ankle into the crook of the iron and jerked his knee with tremendous upward force. The angle, coupled with the momentum, brought Garon cleanly off his feet and sent him careening over the marble. He crashed face first into the fountain with a thunderous splash accentuated by the rumbling of the land.

Hansel hadn't yet lowered his foot when Zid swung again, aiming for his lower leg. Hansel brought his foot down on the miner's face and pushed his body weight from the other leg, bringing Zid and his weapon to the ground with a face full of blood.

When Hansel looked forward, he was surprised to see the silver crossbow glinting in the distance, his sprinting heart falling in perfect aim.

Bo was holding the weapon. Sometime during the fight, the sneaky little dwarf had abandoned his apples and snuck into the castle to retrieve it.

Finn, Jinn, and Chann froze, not daring to compromise Bo's aim.

"Think about what you're doing, Bo," Hansel spoke. "It was not my intention to harm any of you tonight. I'm the only one who can wake the fair lady from her new slumber. If you shoot me, Snow White will *never* wake up."

"Liam will come back!" Bo protested. "Liam and Violet and all the good people who have gone missing! Somebody will wake her up, just like they did before!"

"You would count on that? You would shoot an old friend? Have I not provided for you? Given you a home, a job, a friend?"

"You used us! You corrupted us to serve your selfish needs! We should've listened to Lord Bellamy. You're a *monster*, Mister Hansel. You'll never be worthy of your sister's gratitude, or of Snow White's affection!"

Something fiery and wrathful stirred inside Hansel, suppressed only gently by the woman beside him.

He'd gone so far to get to this point. He corrupted the incorruptible. He kidnapped the pure and innocent. He spilled blood in a royal courtyard. He conspired with the dark. All of his actions brought him to this point: a man who stood in front of Snow White, who had been powerless to save herself from her fate as one of the seven.

They were *all* powerless in the grand scheme. The dwarves. Lord Bellamy. Miss Violet. The Order of the Bell. The Carver and his wife, and the people who had grown up in the New World. Gretel. Nobody could defy the destiny that Queen Avoria had chosen to activate.

Except for Hansel.

He could end it all. He could end the reign of terror for which he'd become a mere puppet. He could defy the Ivory Queen.

It's what Gretel really would've wanted. We didn't burn a wicked witch just to let evil triumph. To let Snow White die. Neither of them stood for that.

Hansel gazed at Snow, peaceful and solemn, and he looked back at Bo. "Then end it," he coaxed. "Please."

Finn, Jinn, and Chann exchanged glances.

The silence was maddening.

Hansel gritted his teeth. "*Do it!* Put me down! Nobody's safe as long as I'm alive."

Chann nodded at Bo, and that's when the youngest dwarf took a deep breath, closed his eyes, and fired. "Goodbye, Mister Hansel."

The bolt seemed to ripple through the air in slow motion. Hansel used that time to bid the world goodbye.

I get to die a hero. I get to die proud.

Snow, Gretel, I'm sorry for all the troubles I've caused these realms.

I'm sorry for all the harm I've done. No more harm shall come. Goodbye.

The bolt was inches away from Hansel's chest when something splashed in the fountain behind him and a bulky hand curled around his ankle. Hansel looked down and met Garon's gaze, his beard soaked and his eyes filled with fire. Garon tugged on Hansel's ankle with a swift jerk, and Hansel's skull struck the ground before the bolt could pierce him.

But the silver bolt didn't stop there, of course. It merely lost momentum, yielding to a downward trajectory. It splashed through the fountain's crystalline cascades, finished its curve, and plummeted . . . down, down, down, and directly into the chest of Snow White.

Not even the thunder reacted.

A dark red rivulet of blood trickled through Snow's dress, staining the marble and churning with the fountain's waters.

The dwarves froze.

Hansel's blood ran cold.

"No!" he spat. "*No!*"

Scrambling to his knees, Hansel trampled through the fountain and darted to Snow's side. He laid his head on her chest. Had she been breathing to begin with?

Give me a heartbeat, he begged. *One beat.*

He heard nothing.

The white-hot rage bubbled in his stomach again, but this time, he couldn't quell it. It spread through his veins, burning his toes and consuming his senses. His vision blackened. He could *hear* the darkness, a sickening churning and bubbling sound in the surface of his ears. All he could *taste* was evil, a bitter, stale burn at the tip of his tongue. His fingers tingled, and his calves burned. He couldn't bear it anymore.

Hansel turned his head up to the sky and screamed, his voice fusing with something like ice.

And then a pulse, something purple, elusive, and hazy, rippled from Hansel's body and soared through the courtyard like a bounding panther. The dwarves gasped, still in shock from what had occurred. A second later, they were all gone. The pulse evaporated, and in its path, very little remained.

The courtyard's columns exploded into dust.

Snow remained lifeless and bleeding on the marble fountain.

Hansel lay wheezing and wilted beside her.

And six oily black gems speckled the courtyard.

CHAPTER FORTY-THREE

TODAY—NEW YORK CITY TUNNELS

Enzo never would've believed it if it hadn't happened to him.

After a long day of travel on Mulan's jet, the group followed Wayde's lead in New York City. Enzo could tell by Rosana's posture that unlike Mr. Bellamy, Liam, and Mulan, she wasn't buying Wayde's assertion that there was a portal to the Old World in New York City's underground. She kept her arms crossed and her lips pursed, silent until the skepticism finally burst from her lips.

"Okay, can you please explain to me how you really believe there's a door to another world hiding down here? I mean, millions of people have been down there every day for a couple hundred years. I used to sleep there."

Violet gasped. "You slept here?"

"Yes. I had nowhere to go when my mom went missing. We had an apartment together, but it's not like *I* paid the bills. I left before they could make me leave."

"You poor thing! And you had no friends or family to take you in?"

Rosana shook her head. "Nope. I was homeschooled so I didn't make a lot of friends, and as you can guess by me being the daughter of Alice, I don't know my family. We were each other's only comforts."

Violet looked like she was about to cry. "But why stay here? How did you keep safe?"

Rosana shrugged. "I felt productive here. I thought I'd find a clue about my mom's disappearance here. And I don't know, nobody ever really bothered me. It's like nobody saw me. I'm pretty good at blending in."

Enzo watched in awe as Rosana vanished before his eyes again. *Poof.* "Well, you're doing a pretty good job of it now. We can't see you. *Again.*"

Violet's eyes lit up. "Rosana, where did you get your jacket from?"

Rosana faded back into the light and shrugged again, the shoulders of her hoodie hugging her neck. She made a face. "Really? You wanna talk about fashion at a time like this?" She sighed and gently pulled on one of the drawstrings. "It was a hand-me-down from my mom."

Violet grinned. "As I suspected. Rosana, this was my gift to her. It once belonged to yet another. It's curious that it chose to take such a form in this world, but it seems nobody wears cloaks and capes here. I believe your jacket has the power to render you invisible, so long as you wish not to be seen."

Rosana didn't look impressed. "Well, that's cool, I guess. Too bad it can't *find* people who vanish into thin air."

"But that's what we're about to do. We're about to get our families back." Enzo shot Wayde a knowing gaze. "Right?"

"Correct, Mister Enzo."

"I just don't believe him," Rosana admitted. "I looked forever for any sort of clue about where she went, and there's nothing down there. The police couldn't even find the stupid apple, and now you're telling me there's a whole entrance to the Old World. Either way, I'm mad. If it's not there, you lied to us. If it's there, I'm still mad because I can't believe I missed it! I can't believe you literally walked out of New York with my mom."

Wayde turned even redder, sweating profusely.

Liam swept a hand on Rosana's shoulder. "Take it easy, lass. Anger is not our ally. If we're to face Hansel, we need to keep a level head." He turned to Enzo. "Am I not correct, chum?"

Enzo made a thumbs-up. Liam was starting to grow on him. Everyone was. Enzo didn't care much for the old man, and he barely knew Wayde, but he was grateful to have them all together.

Mr. Bellamy wrinkled his nose when the group set foot in the subway. He tapped Wayde on the shoulder. "How far along is this portal, boy?"

Wayde scanned the subway station. "Why it's not far at all, sir. A short way down; I'm quite sure."

"Has this portal always existed?" Violet asked. "I've heard of various methods of travel between the worlds, but I was always so certain that there were no direct pathways."

"Um, that's our fault, Miss Violet. Me, Garon, Zid, and all the others . . . well, we knew about the paths. There were several that led from our mines into this realm, but we kept them secret. We didn't draw them on our maps. One mineshaft led to a strange place called the Grand Canyon. Another connected to a Phoenician canal, or was it Venetian? And one led to the pyramids of Giza. There were others, but we destroyed them all. This is the only remaining direct portal." Wayde looked ashamed in his confession.

Violet bit the inside of her cheek. "That was a dangerous secret to keep."

"Is it more dangerous than two evil mirrors that take hostages when you make wishes with them?" Enzo challenged, although he immediately regretted his remark when Violet's expression sank.

Liam arched an eyebrow. "The lad has a point."

Violet changed the subject, pulling her purple gloves on. "So, how much farther now?"

"Just a few—"

"*Hey!* Oh my God, that's Heather McClavender!"

"May the light be with us," Violet muttered.

A group of teenagers had pointed at her and broken into a run, pulling out their cell phones and pushing past the slower-walking subway folk.

Violet reached into her purse, procuring a thick pair of sunglasses and a flowery purple hat, making Enzo wonder why she hadn't been wearing them before and what difference they really could've made. Violet lowered her head and kept walking.

Random passersby directed more attention to them as the teenagers approached. A short girl with horn-rimmed glasses raised her phone to take a selfie with Enzo. "Like, I don't actually know who you *are*, but I saw you on TV, and I have to know you!"

"Uh, no you don't." Enzo never thought he was claustrophobic or had any sort of social anxieties, but when more people started swarming him and his friends, something kicked in. His heartbeat skyrocketed.

"Ms. McClavender! Sign my shoe!"

"Hey, didn't you say your name was Mulan or something? That's a wicked name!"

"Who's the hot guy?"

"Who's the old guy?"

"HeatherohmyGodyouhavetofollowmebackonTwitter!"

"It's Tinker Bell! Joey, take a picture of me and Tinker Bell!"

"Heather McClavender's a *fake*!"

"Can I be in your movies?"

"Hey, where'd the chick in the hoodie go?"

"Do you have a dog?"

The more Enzo thought about it, the more people reminded him of bugs when there were too many of them in one place. Ants fighting over crumbs. Bees swarming over a hive. What stressed him out the most was that if there really was a door to the other world close by, how were they supposed to get through it with so many people watching them?

When a copy of *Stargle Magazine* flew off the newspaper stand and knocked a blue-haired skater's phone out of his hands, Enzo figured out the answer.

The skater boy turned around. "Hey! Who threw that magazine?"

Three more magazines soared off the rack and into the crowd, the spine of a *Vogue* skimming a fez off a tall man's head.

"Did you see that? Those magazines just jumped off that rack over there!"

The crowd's attention turned to the magazine stand, where a small Asian woman stood behind the counter, rounding her lips in confusion.

All the *Men's Journals* glided away simultaneously with the *Men's Healths*. The *Entertainment Weekly*s followed, spreading their pages like the wings of a bird before they landed on people's heads. Soon, the magazines and newspapers were jumping off simultaneously, each deliberately aimed at the obsessive Heather McClavender fans.

When there were no more magazines, trash started flying out of a nearby garbage can, like a foul, gum-covered volcano spewing soda bottles and ketchup packets.

Enzo grinned. *Oh, that Rosana.*

For a short while, it was all a spectacle to the swarming crowd, but when a levitating pair of chopsticks flung warm drops of soy sauce into the crowd and a bottle of soda exploded into their faces, they started running.

The boy with the blue hair cupped his hands and shouted into the crowd, "The subway's haunted, bro! Everybody run! Run for your lives!"

That's when Enzo realized that crazy fans weren't bugs at all. They were bulls, and the blue-haired boy had started a stampede. Trash continued to soar while the crowd fled, and Enzo pushed through them in the opposite direction. Violet, Mr. Bellamy, Mulan, Liam, and Wayde followed close behind.

It wasn't long before they were the only ones in the subway station, and Rosana appeared again, covered in everything from barbecue sauce to pizza grease.

"*Ewww*," she whined, her expression crinkled with disgust.

Enzo doubled over in belly laughter, howling harder than he had in days, weeks, or even months. He laughed until he was red in the face, forcing his words out between breaths. "And *that's* how you clear a subway!"

Rosana aimed a finger at Enzo's nose. "Enzo? Shut it!"

Mulan patted the girl on the back, Violet and Liam beaming proudly at her side. "You're a soldier, Rosana."

Mr. Bellamy said nothing. His face indicated that he wasn't happy with the way Rosana smelled, but then again, Mr. Bellamy's face was always like that.

Liam rubbed his elbows. "Miss Violet, you have some intensely terrifying fans."

Violet sighed. "I know it."

Wayde cleared his throat. "If I may, I know we're quite proud, but we should really hurry. This place could fill up again any minute, and we must save Snow!"

Liam nodded solemnly. "Indeed. Please lead us to the door, chum."

Wayde gestured to the walls, white-tiled and painted with gold stars on one line. "We're here."

Enzo scratched his head. "Ummm, all I see is a wall."

"Well, that's a good start. After all, this isn't supposed to be easy to find, but surely you've got to see a little more than that?"

Enzo squinted. Rosana rubbed her hands along the walls, presumably looking for cracks or keyholes. Mulan rubbed her chin, studying the tiles.

"I've got nothin'."

Wayde wrung his thick hands. "Mister Enzo, has your eyesight gone bad?"

"I don't see anything, either," Rosana said. "I knew we couldn't trust you!"

Wayde's jaw dropped. "Does nobody see the stars?"

Enzo threw his hands up in frustration. "Well, I saw those!"

"Then this is simple, Mister Enzo! Your way to the New World is right in front of you."

"I don't get it."

By the looks on everyone else's faces, they didn't, either.

"Count the stars, Mister Enzo."

Enzo sighed, tracing the line of stars with his gaze.

"Count them out loud."

Are you kidding me right now? Enzo rolled his eyes. "One, two, th—"

"Stop." Wayde aimed a sweaty palm at Enzo. "Now you need to *wish* it open."

"We're wishing on a star?" Rosana asked. "Really?"

"The second star to the right," Wayde confirmed. "It's been here the whole time."

Rosana shook her head. "That's ridiculous."

"Mister Enzo, I don't mean to rush you, but we should make haste."

"Yes!" Liam agreed. "Wayde, shall we all assist in the wishing?"

Wayde returned a single nod. "If you all insist that you're ready to leave this world, then wish upon the star."

Enzo imagined Wayde's words as a vine, slithering into his ears and planting roots deep into the part of his heart that experienced fear, doubt, and skepticism. Wayde had just invited the group to witness the truth, a truth he and Rosana weren't prepared for. Sure, the past few days had been incredibly strange, from learning that his neighbor could fly to learning that his own father used to be a marionette, but if these truths could exist in the world Enzo had grown up in, what existed beyond its borders? How could either of them hope to save their parents? And even if they *could* save their parents, how could they ever confront them again? Enzo didn't think he could look his mom and dad in the eye ever again. Violet's story about the mirrors had confirmed that his father's past was full of secrets, and they'd started bubbling up in his life like mosquito bites. To go and confront those was to leave the land of the familiar and the last traces of normalcy behind him. Finally, how long would it be before he could pick up where he left off?

"I'm ready," he forced himself to say. He gave his friends a knowing look, and they each returned their own nods and determined gazes. "Let's get out of here."

Wayde flashed a half smile. "Focus on the star, Mister Enzo. All of you. Focus on the points and the center, on the whole thing. Now join hands, close your eyes, and make a wish. Wish for your family's safe return. Wish for Snow. Wish for safe passage into the realm of old."

Enzo closed his eyes. Rosana's warm fingers closed around his palm, almost electrifying his arm. He squeezed back, and Mulan wrapped her iron grip around Enzo's other hand. Taking a deep breath, he focused on his mother's face. *I'm on my way, Mom. I wish I were there with you right now.*

And then he heard a voice: *You've always been with me, my son.*

Huh?

He knew he wasn't imagining it. Her voice was clearer than water. It was almost as if she was standing right in front of him. She kept talking, and Enzo almost lost his balance when the floor moved beneath him. It was like a conveyor belt had started, gradually picking up speed. He didn't dare open his eyes.

I've been dreaming of you and that firefly in your eyes. You were never too far away.

Mom?

We're right here. Pino, put down your artwork for one second and greet your son.

Enzo, my boy, you've done it! I told you they weren't just toys.

No way, man, is that Enzo? *What took you so long to find us, buddy?* Zack's voice sounded exactly the same as Enzo remembered it.

Enzo was so absorbed in the voices that he couldn't pinpoint the moment when he stopped feeling Rosana's hand on his, or Mulan's grip. He knew he was still squeezing, but he felt like only his family and the Volos were with him.

A woman: *Zack, behave. You should be thanking him right now. He's about to get us out of here. Thank you, Enzo. You're such a nice young man.*

'Ey, Enzo! You kissed the girl, yet?

His mother again: *We'll see you soon, my son. Much sooner than you know.*

A bright light washed over Enzo's eyelids, and he let them snap open.

He wasn't in New York City anymore.

CHAPTER FORTY-FOUR

THE OLD WORLD

The Old World smelled musty. Enzo quickly realized he was in a mine glistening with metals and strewn with colorful gems.

Rosana and the others were still right beside him, but almost all of them had changed. Liam looked, well, more princely, with fine white ruffles on his shirt and gloved hands ready to pluck out the black dagger that had appeared in his thick leather belt. Rosana wasn't wearing a red hooded jacked anymore, but a heavy hooded cape tied over her shoulders and flowing all the way down to her ankles. Wayde seemed to have shrunk about a foot, and a pickaxe rested over his shoulder.

Mr. Bellamy still looked terrifying, but now he was almost royally terrifying. It was probably the long black robe that made him look like a judge. Enzo imagined the old man pointing a bony finger at him and sentencing him to jail, or at least detention.

Mulan no longer wore a business suit but a suit of armor, with red plates on her chest, shoulders, and legs, all decorated with golden swirls. An exquisite blade had also appeared in her hands, branded with Chinese characters.

The most dramatic was the change to Heather McClavender, who suddenly looked a lot more like a Violet. Her skin took on a faint periwinkle hue, her dress sparkled even in the darkness, and strangest of all, she had grown *wings*. Actual wings.

Yet Enzo himself didn't feel any different. Only one change had occurred: his pocket grew heavier. He reached within and closed his fist around something cool, slender, and smooth. He withdrew his father's carving knife.

Everyone else marveled at their own changes for a minute, Rosana fluttering her cloak and Mulan studying her magnificent blade.

Violet flapped her wings and grinned. "We're *home*."

The next voice Enzo heard was Wayde's, "Follow me, please! We must make haste to the Cavern of Ombra!"

So they ran, following Wayde and adhering to his commands, "Watch your wings, Miss Violet!"

Enzo found himself distracted by the colorful walls and strange layout of the mine, but he kept up, thinking of his family. Nobody seemed to tire, but he couldn't tell if they'd ran for hours, minutes, or days when Wayde led them through an opening in the wall.

They'd entered a dim, frigid cave strewn with spongy black rocks. Enzo first saw the pedestal in the center that read, *PROPERTY OF THE IVORY QUEEN.*

Rosana clapped a hand over her mouth and aimed a finger at the sky.

Enzo followed her finger. His heart dropped into the pit in his stomach.

No. Nonononono!

CHAPTER FORTY-FIVE

TODAY—THE CAVERN OF OMBRA

When Enzo saw his parents, all the words evaporated from his mind.

It was just like Madame Esme's vision. His mom. His dad. Pietro, Zack, and Wendy. There was a woman he'd never met before, but he knew she was Rosana's mom, Alice. All of them encased in massive crystals far beyond anyone's reach. Most terrifying was their posture, upright and stiff, almost completely straight, with only a slight bow of the head as they slumbered.

Enzo's knees hit the ground, and silent sobs convulsed in his throat.

Rosana screamed, "*Mom!*"

Violet and Liam rushed to their sides. "Take it easy, friends," Liam whispered. "You must compose yourselves. I understand your despair, but if Hansel's com—"

"I'll kill him! I swear, I'll do it! That's my . . ." Enzo wiped a tear from his face. "That's my family! My best friends! Rosana's ma. Hansel had no right—"

"Hansel had no will," Mulan said. "He's a puppet. If we want to free these people, we need to destroy the root of this venomous tree."

Liam straightened his back, put a fist over his heart, and concentrated. "Snow is very close by. She's not alone."

"What do we do?" Rosana asked. "How do we fight if Hansel or, uh, that queen shows up?"

Nobody said anything.

Then Enzo perceived a dark shape—a slender hole in the light—whipping around the cavern as if trying to get his attention. It was the one strange thing he recognized from the other world.

Enzo tugged on Rosana's sleeve. "That's Pietro's shadow!"

A second shadow stepped out of one of the enormous gems, lean, lanky, and spiky-haired. It danced around with the first, doing a sort of Irish jig all the way to the cavern's mouth. The two shadows almost looked alike, but Enzo could easily tell the silhouettes apart. He just couldn't believe where they came from.

"*Zack*?"

The second shadow made a thumbs up, pumped its fists like it was cheering, and pounded its chest. Both Pietro's shadow and Zack's shadow curled their palms inward, beckoning Enzo forward.

"We gotta follow them."

Rosana shook her head. "But shouldn't we be here to stop Hansel?"

"Hansel's not the real bad guy," Mulan said. "I see now why everybody has been failing to win. We can't confront Hansel face to face. Not yet, at least." She brandished her sword and gave it a quick swipe through the air. "It's the *mirrors* we want."

Enzo chewed on his lip. The stories added up. The trouble didn't start with Hansel. It started with the queen. It started with the mirrors. As long as the mirrors existed, the danger would always continue. They could free Gretel, but who was to say the mirrors wouldn't pull someone else inside once they did so? Who was to say somebody else wouldn't find them and use them for evil if they stopped the Ivory Queen? The cycle would continue unless somebody deliberately interrupted it.

"I believe you are correct," Violet said. "We must destroy the mirrors, once and for all, but we mustn't leave this cavern unguarded. Hansel will come here, and when he does, we need to be ready. We must do everything we can possibly do."

"I'm staying here," Liam said. "I wanna be here when my wife arrives. Even if I can't stop Hansel, I can slow him down."

Mulan squeezed Liam's shoulder. "I'm proud of you."

"If we succeed in destroying the mirrors, Hansel should be more vulnerable." Violet rolled up her sleeves and stood next to Liam. "But you're not staying here alone. If Hansel succeeds and puts Snow in that ruby, Avoria will come back. I want to be here if she does."

"You will do no such thing," Lord Bellamy said. "As your father, I—"

"Run if you want to, Father; I don't care. I'm staying here."

Lord Bellamy frowned, fidgeting as though he might flee. Then his face softened, and he stroked his chin. "There's a lot I've been meaning to say to that woman. I hope I *never* get the chance, but if I do . . . ."

Wayde straightened his back and raised his chin, looking bold. He looked each person in the eye before saying in a clear tone, "I want to help destroy the mirrors."

Enzo smiled.

He, Rosana, Mulan, and Wayde would go together. As for the other three . . . a sad thought crossed his mind.

"Look, if we don't all see each other again—"

"No time for that," Mulan declared. "The shadows are moving. We must follow."

Enzo looked up at his parents. At Pietro, Zack, Wendy, and Rosana's mother. *I'll get you guys out of there. Promise.* "Well then, I guess good luck, everyone."

"Good luck to *you*, son of Pinocchio! Daughter of Alice! Mulan, the Woman Warrior! And Wayde, the Fearless!" Violet said. "May the light be with you."

Enzo gave Rosana a firm nod, and they sped off on their way, chasing shadows through the mines and into the darkness of an unknown world.

⌘⌘⌘

The cavern fell eerily silent after the crowd followed the shadows.

Liam paced back and forth, treading lightly on the gems beneath him. He kept his hand near his dagger, flexing his fingers and trying to recall Mulan's lessons.

"Why do you resist me, Liam? When I tell you to attack, you attack!"

"I don't want to fight, Master. Violence is never the answer."

"There may come a day when it will be. Will you be ready? I'll make a man out of you yet."

Liam clenched his fists. *I'll make you proud, Master. I'll show you what a man I've become. I'll be brave for these people.* He looked around the cavern and saw Violet chewing her nails, occasionally eyeing gems and concentrating really hard. Lord Bellamy sat with his hands folded and his face in its perpetual state of disgust.

"You don't seem nervous," Liam pointed out.

"I'm not," Lord Bellamy said. "I'm angry. This was *not* the way. I see that snot-nosed boy again, I'll strangle him for convincing me to come back here."

Violet glared at her dad. "Not appropriate, Father. That boy has our best interests in mind."

"That boy has his own interests in mind. I don't care for him."

"You don't care for anybody."

"I came back, did I not?"

"Begrudgingly."

"Your simple-minded conclusions bewilder me."

"And your stupid-headed arrogance makes me sick!"

"Cool it, you two," Liam hissed.

Lord Bellamy and Violet crossed their arms and turned their backs to each other, noses in the air, but they ceased their argument as Liam kept watch on the cavern tunnels, fingers close to his dagger.

When the dark figure emerged with the girl on his shoulder, Liam froze.

Snow's sleeping face left a pit in Liam's stomach, but the shining wound on her chest ground his knees into sand. It took all his strength to keep standing. *Be brave. Be brave for her.*

Hansel. Liam imagined he'd come in snickering, dancing around the cavern like an imp, but in fact, Liam had never seen anyone look so miserable. Hansel's face was shiny and damp with tears, his hair matted with sweat, and his posture loose like a broken blade of grass. He stalked into the cavern without a word, making eye contact with nobody. Then he stopped, shifted the woman off his shoulder, and cradled her, looking at her as a child might gaze upon a treasured broken toy. That's when it all clicked; Hansel was in love with Snow White. A sharp fire ignited in Liam's stomach, and he reached for his dagger.

"Hansel!" he bellowed. "Your time has come! Release my wife this instant!"

Hansel looked up at Liam, misty-eyed and tight-lipped, and shook his head. "I'm sorry, Liam. I can't do that. If I don't finish this, she'll kill Gretel. She'll kill us all somehow."

"Put her down or the queen will be the least of your troubles!"

Lord Bellamy held up a bony hand. "*Silence*, boy, lest you get us all killed!" He advanced forward with both his palms up. "Hansel, do you recall our last conversation?"

Violet wrung her hands. "Father!"

Lord Bellamy paid Violet no attention. Hansel merely nodded.

"And what did you tell me before your betrayal? Before you sent me to the other world?"

Rivulets of tears cascaded into Hansel's dimples. "I told you nothing was going to stop me from getting my sister back."

"Mm. So you did." For the first time, something like a smile crept into the corners of the old man's mouth, but it must've felt wrong on his lips because it quickly melted away. "Has it occurred to you that the queen doesn't wish to help you? That all this time, it is *she* who truly stands in your way?"

"That's a lie," Hansel breathed. "She's only tried to help me. She has yet to lie to me." He thrust a finger in Violet's face. "But you hid this from me! You lied since the night Gretel went missing. You both tried to cover what happened to her." Finally Hansel turned to Liam, his eyes red with rage. "And you snuck into my house like some venomous miscreant and tried to destroy the mirror! The one portal of communication between my sister and me! You've all done nothing but try to hurt me. Queen Avoria wants to help."

Violet frowned. "I'm so sorry for keeping secrets from you, Hansel. It's the worst thing I've ever done. I regret it every day. But there's a reason I never told you, and this is precisely it! If you finish this ritual, Avoria will come back, and she will hurt everyone, including you. And I wouldn't be surprised if Gretel didn't come back with her."

"More lies!" Hansel bellowed. "Every time you open your mouth, you spill your myths upon this ground. You would have me give up everything and assume that my kin is dead. It would serve you right if you—and if *they*"—Hansel waved a hand at the seven grand rubies—"lost all the things you loved the most and had the whole world against you while you did everything in your power to bring them back." He flashed Liam a sad smile, the tears congealing into sticky films on his face. "Yes, that would be justice of the most divine caliber."

"Enough!" Teeth bared and quick-footed, Liam lunged forward with his knife bound to his grip, ready to slash. The dagger came down right about where Hansel's shoulder should've been, but several things happened in slow motion between the peak of the dagger's path and the moment it met a solid surface.

First, Hansel took one last sad gaze at the woman on his other shoulder. He whispered something to her, but all Liam made out was a silent flutter of his lips.

Hansel snapped his fingers. It was the loudest sound in the cavern, a deliberate click compounded by the adrenaline in Liam's heart and the dark echoes of the chamber walls. On cue, the love of Liam's life vanished from Hansel's shoulder.

No!

The ground lurched beneath Liam's feet, rippling his calves and jittering his bones. He brought the knife down in a feral rage, but the ground was rumbling far too heavily for Liam to account for the shift in balance. His knees and ankles betrayed him and he hugged the ground, his dagger plummeting into the gems. The dark gems jiggled and stirred, cushioning his fall yet throwing him severely off balance as he struggled to get back to his feet. His mind swirled. *Snow! Where did she go! What has Hansel done to you?*

Violet screamed and Hansel collapsed on the ground, Lord Bellamy's mouth pried open in terror, and Liam knew he had his answer. He clawed a sweaty palm at the ground until he could face up again. All of his fears were confirmed.

Red.

The cavern turned bright red. Luminous. Terrible. And Liam knew why.

He looked up, and there wasn't a single empty ruby in the wall. Seven enormous jewels—seven giant prisons containing seven pure souls.

And at center stage, in the largest and brightest ruby, the body of Snow White stood dormant and stiff. Liam flew into frenzy, clawing the air and swiping at nothing.

"Snooow!" he yelled until his throat felt raw with pain and broken with anger. He screamed so loud that he drowned out the sobs of both Violet and Lord Bellamy together, who almost certainly had to be screaming out of fear that the witch was about to return.

Liam tore the air until he was back on his feet, screaming in vain and crying because he knew there was no way to get her out. No way to get her back.

The red light began to fade.

The gems were darkening.

The red drained, all the color and luminosity gently washed away and yielded to the dark hues of ashes, then midnight, and, finally, nothingness.

Snow's face was the last he saw of her before she disappeared . . . a pale shadow of death encased in pain.

When the stones turned fully black, they shrunk, like air escaping a balloon. What used to be bigger than Liam's entire body became the size of his head, and then his finger.

There was a soft pop, and the seven stones dropped to the ground.

That was how Liam would remember the last time he saw Snow White before she went away.

Before they all went away.

And before a humanoid lump rose from the ground, the stones peeling away to reveal a head of fiery red hair, a stoic, pale face with beautiful iron-clad features, slender shoulders, a lean torso, and smooth legs thinly masked by an ivory white dress.

Snow White and the other sacrifices were gone.

The queen had returned.

CHAPTER FORTY-SIX

TODAY—THE OLD WORLD

Nobody said a word. Nobody wanted to believe she was really there. And nobody wanted to believe the seven had vanished. Snow. Pietro and his family. Pino and his wife. Alicia. All gone, and here was the name of evil, live and in the flesh.

She stood tall, youthful in an unnatural sort of way, pale like milk, and the first thing that Hansel noticed was that she came alone.

In the stillness of the cavern, Liam became hyperaware of the hammering of his heart, the rushing of blood through his veins, and the stillness of his lungs as the Ivory Queen mechanically scanned her surroundings. She moved her head as if on a swivel, and then she flashed a wicked grin that raised her pointed cheekbones.

"Hello, my dears." Her voice was deep and throaty, laced with a hiss as though she'd swallowed a snake.

Liam scrambled to his feet, retreating to Violet's side. Violet gripped her father's arm.

Avoria yawned theatrically, and then she turned her gaze to Hansel. She approached him with slow, calculated steps, the dark gems churning beneath her. He wanted to turn around and run when she reached out and took his palm in her icy fingers. She brought his hand up to her lips, and Hansel was sure she was going to bite him. Instead, she kissed his hand, and his blood ran cold.

"Thank you, my huntsman," she purred. "Your services are no longer required."

Hansel stared back at the woman, deer-eyed with his mouth agape. "But what about my sister?"

Avoria scratched her chin, staring into space like she was trying to remember something.

Hansel swallowed a lump in his throat. "Please, ma'am, what about Gretel? Does she get to come back?"

The Ivory Queen snapped her fingers as if a lightbulb went off in her head. "Oh, Gretel! That dear precious little girl, bless her heart." Avoria tilted her head to the side. "*No*."

The word might as well have been a sword, simultaneously sawing through all the delicate strings of hope that had held Hansel together for years. He blinked for a moment, staring dumbly at the Ivory Queen, and then he crumbled like a marionette, a heap of sobs and tears on a bed of broken souls.

Avoria shot a look at Lord Bellamy, a twisted smile hanging on her lips. "Hello, handsome. It's been ages."

Lord Bellamy's voice shook as he replied, "Avoria."

Violet stepped forward, appearing braver than either of the men in the room despite the glistening film of sweat on her forehead. "You don't deserve to be here! What about that poor girl, and all those people you had Hansel steal away for you!"

Avoria rounded on the fairy, cupping her chin in her milky white hands. "Violet, I've been excited to see you again. After all, my captivity was entirely your fault, as was that little girl's. You shouldn't meddle with magic you don't understand." For a brief moment, her face contorted into something ugly. "For all of that and more, I hate you!"

Violet made a fist. "Then why don't you do something about that?"

"Oh, I would say that is a most excellent idea."

Liam gasped as the handle of a bronze sword appeared in his palm, hefty and beautifully forged. He looked at Violet and Lord Bellamy. They each had one too, as did the Ivory Queen. Hansel remained crumpled on the ground, a broken shell of his former self. Liam almost felt sorry for the guy, but he was too preoccupied by his own heartache radiating in his fingers and toes as he thought about Snow. He decided that he didn't want to live anymore. He didn't even want to fight, but Mulan warned him that this day would come. He would vanquish the queen in the name of his wife, and then he would turn the blade on himself.

Avoria brandished her sword, flicking the tip at nothing in particular. "A fair fight to the death, yes? No soul sucking, no magic, because I'm most merciful and I've been somewhere dreadful for ages. Hansel, you can sit there and cry. As for me, I should very much like to stretch my arms and legs a bit, and perhaps exact some revenge?"

Lord Bellamy arched a brow. "I know exactly how you feel, *my queen*."

The three companions and their opponent raised their weapons, and before anyone could blink, the battle had begun, a dance of swords and flying blades in a cavern of darkness, made all the darker by Liam's rage and Hansel's sobs for the sister he had lost forever.

⌘⌘⌘

It wasn't long after the shadows took off that they split into two different directions.

The run through the mines was exhausting, and Mulan was starting to think she had made a mistake in coming back to this terrible realm. In the New World, she would never have had to run miles and miles with a thirty-pound sword in her hands.

When she and her companions emerged at ground level, the land soaked in darkness and kissed by too many lightning strikes, the shadows split up. The slenderer, spiky-haired shadow zipped off to the north, while Pietro's went south.

"What now?" Rosana asked.

Mulan leaned her sword against a rock and stopped to catch her breath. "We have to split. It's the only way. They're leading us to two different mirrors."

Enzo gazed around wildly, processing the world around him. "I'm going after Zack's shadow."

Rosana nodded. "I'll follow."

Mulan chewed her lip. "You two don't know this land."

Enzo had already broken into a sprint. "I don't care. See you when this is all over."

"Wait! Enzo, wait!" Rosana sped off after Enzo, and the two teens faded into the horizon.

Mulan shook her head. She put her hands on her hips and looked at Wayde. "Guess we're going after Pietro." She scanned her surroundings, seeking the dancing silhouette, but it had already fled. Mulan cursed. "Where did he go? He's supposed to wait for us!"

Wayde wove his fingertips together. "Well, if I may, ma'am, I know where Pietro wants to go."

"Where?"

"My house, where Mister Hansel resides."

Mulan grabbed her sword. "Take us there."

Wayde led her through the forest, past the house where Lord Bellamy used to live, and into the clearing where the dwarves had built their cottage years ago. Mulan doubted the cottage always looked this black, crumbly, and musty. Spider webs stretched across the windows and the door. And the grass had withered away around it.

Mulan cleaved the webs with her sword, and Wayde heaved the door open. As soon as they entered, Mulan stumbled. The sword grew substantially heavier in her grip, as if somebody had sat on the handles while she was holding it.

She took a deep breath and wiped her forehead. "Something doesn't feel right."

Wayde led her into Hansel's bedroom, where the mirror remained flat on the wall. It looked slightly warped, and a hard shining puddle melted away from it. "Please, madam! We must hurry!"

Mulan took a seat on the ground, clutching her chest. "We're too late."

Wayde's eyes watered. "W-why do you say that? We're not too late."

"We've lost, Wayde. I had this sword when I went to battle against the queen the first time. I remember it grew heavier and heavier each time she took somebody's soul away. It must weigh a hundred pounds now. The seven are gone."

"Stop it!" Wayde demanded. "Smash the mirror! Please! Have faith, Miss!"

She shook her head sadly, and then her lips parted in both fear and wonder when she saw Pietro's shadow on Hansel's bed. Wonder over having found it again. Fear over having realized that it had gone limp. If a shadow could die . . . it was an image that would haunt her for life. A hole in the light that could never be filled.

Mulan bared her teeth. *If I can't save any of you, I can at least do this in your name.*

She approached the mirror, avoiding her own reflection as she studied the frame instead.

"That's it!" Wayde said. "Come now, smash it to bits!"

Mulan firmed her grip on the burdensome blade, imagining that her palms were bound to the handle. Heaving the metal with all her strength, she took the first strike.

Thwack!

Nothing. An electric twang surged through her elbow.

Wayde raised a fist in the air. "You can do it!"

Mulan winced. "Help me."

Wayde dabbed at a film of sweat on his forehead and rubbed his hands together. He reached for his pickaxe. "Right."

Mulan swung again.

Smack!

Clang!

Thwack!

Smack!

Clang!

"Come on," Mulan growled through clenched teeth. She repeated this with more intensity each time her blade impacted the mirror, Wayde thrusting his entire weight into his own swings. "Come on! Come on! *Come* on! *Come onnn*!"

Crashhh!

Mulan could barely believe her eyes when the crack spidered across the surface, breaking her reflection into a hundred tiny pieces. Her face lit up in triumph. With a final jab, she thrust her blade into the mirror, feeling the sword grow lighter, and then—

Whoosh! There was a heavy sound like eardrums popping after an ascent on her jet.

Shards of glass fanned across the room in an explosive burst, accompanied by a hefty wind, muggy and warm like the breath of a giant.

"*Get down*!" Mulan thrust her forearms over her brows and tackled Wayde to the ground, aiming her back to the sky as the mirror showered her with metallic dust. She was lucky to have her armor. Larger shards rocketed out of the frame, impaling the walls. She listened to the glitter rain upon them for a minute, chipped glass tinkling and pinging all around her, and then she heard two new sounds.

First, there was the clatter of metal on wood. Something awkwardly balanced had fallen; Mulan knew it because she heard it hit in three different points. She turned around and confirmed that it was her sword, laying to rest behind her. Not only flat on the floor, but broken, cleanly in three pieces. She looked above the ruins of her old weapon, and the mirror frame fell dumbly to the ground.

Then, Mulan heard coughing and sputtering from slightly above her. Mulan knew the cough, a male throat, laden with youth yet infused with enough depth to be that of a grown man.

Mulan lifted her head. Glitter had showered Hansel's room and left an outline of her body on top of Wayde, who lay dumbfounded and winded on his back. She craned her head and identified the source of the coughing.

There on top of Hansel's bed, pale yet sprightlier than ever, was The Flying Man, stuck to his shadow once more. Mulan thought her heart might rocket from her chest.

Pietro shook a cloud of silver dust from his hair and rubbed his face. When he saw Mulan, he gave her a flashy wink.

"Miss me, kids?"

CHAPTER FORTY-SEVEN

TODAY—CAVERN OF OMBRA

Liam was exhausted.

How was it possible that one woman could take three people in a sword fight, and none of them could land a single blow? He, Violet, and Lord Bellamy had been attacking the Ivory Queen from all angles. Liam thought he had learned every offensive maneuver known to man, and woman, as Mulan proved to him, and Violet managed to impress him as well. Lord Bellamy was slower and sloppier with a blade, but he defended himself well.

With their combined efforts, the fight should have been simple. It was anything but. Liam had no idea who trained Avoria to defend herself, but she was not human. The queen was showy and arrogant, even leaping far away and pausing for a yawn at one point. She talked quite a bit, taunting and teasing and cackling all the way. That used to be a weaknesses that Mulan stamped out of Liam. "*Close your mouth and open your reflexes. Your brain should be one hundred and fifty percent here. Use your words later.*"

Liam did exactly as he was trained to do, and yet the unscathed Avoria had managed to spill his blood. She nicked him in the right side of his neck, breaking enough skin to let a crimson rivulet run into his shirt. He winced, rolled his shoulders, and kept fighting. He was losing strength fast, like somebody had pressed a boulder on his lungs.

Avoria spun her sword like a windmill, her sinister smile flashing between the blades. "I shall offer you a deal, handsome . . . a way for all of us to walk away with what we want."

Don't talk, Liam thought to himself. He broke the queen's windmill motion. Avoria whirled around just in time to block an uppercut from Lord Bellamy.

Meanwhile, Hansel had been lying against the walls for quite some time, lapsing into fits of sobs every now and then before completely shutting down.

"Eliminate the huntsman, Liam," Avoria said. "Kill the man who made your wife disappear. I'll give you several reasons why you should." She slashed at the air, narrowly missing one of Violet's wings. "Number one: Hansel was my puppet, as you all so keenly observed. He did my bidding, and my bidding never bode well for any of you. And see, when you cut the puppet off its strings, the show stops. There's nothing to see anymore. Do that for Hansel, and I'll leave you all alone as a gesture of good faith. Number two: Can you not see that the man is in dire agony? Finally coming to terms with the idea that his dear sister is *never coming back?* It's broken him after all these years, and do you know why he's so upset? It's because he never avenged her. He had *hope*. Years of misplaced hope that he'd see her again, and when you cut the hope off of its strings, the puppet breaks again. You face a similar situation, handsome. Your wife is gone for good, and you have the chance to avenge her. If you kill Hansel, you save your friends by appeasing me, save yourself from becoming a broken shell like he is, and commit a beautiful, noble act of mercy, because the hunter clearly doesn't want to live."

Avoria snapped her fingers, and all the swords disappeared. Thin light broke through the cavern from a crack in the ceiling and cast a dim glow on the weeping Hansel, oblivious to what was going on around him.

"What will it be, my dear?" Avoria said. "Kill him, or fight me until I break you all?"

Liam sank to his knees, uncomfortably burdened by the offer. He would never think to take another life, but for a chance to silence the queen? He rubbed his face and pondered.

Violet scurried over and put her hand on Liam's shoulder. "Liam, don't listen to her."

Lord Bellamy glared at him. "Do it, boy. 'Tis the lesser of two evils."

"Shut it, Father! You know very well that if he kills Hansel, she won't stop! She's just trying to make another puppet out of somebody! Liam, you can be *king* someday. You can rule all of the Old World. The realm should be yours. Don't let Avoria corrupt you!"

Liam balled his hands into fists. "I . . . What about the greater good?"

"What would Snow tell you to do?"

Smack! A thunderous noise shook the cavern, bringing a layer of dust to the ground.

Clang! Avoria's expression fell.

Thwack! The gems on the ground began to jitter.

Smack!

Clang!

Thwack!

Boom!

Light.

A large hole in the ceiling had opened, casting pale moonlight into the cavern. For a moment, the light was glaring. Liam covered his eyes to readjust to the change in luminosity. He stood and dusted off his knees, and he was surprised to find that his footing was incredibly solid. There was no more sensation of walking on rubber or sponges.

Liam opened his eyes. There were no more dark gems on the ground.

Instead, there was—

"*Snow*!"

Bandaged, healthy, and beautiful. There she was, standing right in front of him, and he had to blink several times before he was convinced she was real. She wrapped her arms around him, face streaked in tears, and he pulled her into an embrace not even an ant could squeeze through. "Liam!"

"We're never getting away from each other again, Snow."

Behind her, Pino and Carla DiLegno, Wendy Darling-Volo, and Alicia Trujillo stood in the moonlight as well, each looking awake and happy to be alive, yet confused.

For a minute, everyone forgot about Avoria. Pino flexed his fingers and threw his arms around his wife, kissing her tears away. Alicia approached Violet in a state of disbelief before they shared a friendly embrace. Wendy hugged her neighbors, and for a short moment, all seemed well, but where was Pietro? What about his son?

Avoria laughed, a deep laugh that sounded from both her nose and her throat, cutting off the happy reunions.

Pino's eyes widened. "It's the Ivory Queen!"

Liam pulled Snow close to him, troubled and confused. If the sacrifices had returned alive and well, why was Avoria still fine? "What's so funny? You've lost!"

"You all think you've *won*? You think you're so righteous and that your so-called ideals of goodness will always let you prevail. Let me ask you, Violet, what was the point of all this? Your return to a world you've all but forgotten?"

Violet clenched her fists, standing beside Pino and Carla. "All we wanted was to free these innocent people, and we've done it. That's why we've won!"

"Be that as it may, *my* ultimate goal was always to come back, to reclaim my rule, and escape that dreadful wasteland in the looking glass. So really, it is *I* who has won."

Liam scoffed. "You'll never rule this place again! The people hate you!"

"My dear, naïve little prince, I don't need this realm anymore. All the while, you lovelies have been warming up a better one for me. A place even larger, stranger, and far more wondrous than our dear homeland and its boring caverns and mountains and crumbling bell towers. You've shown me a world covered with rippling oceans and lush forests and extravagant buildings that scratch the clouds . . . a land where people even worship thespians." Avoria glowered at Violet. "How very easy it will be to get them all to follow somebody with *real* power. I'll take the New World, thank you very much."

Alicia narrowed her eyes. "Dream on, witch. You get nothing! We'll stop you *wherever* you go!"

Lord Bellamy flinched. "Hush, girl! She'll suck the souls right out of us!"

Avoria cackled and palmed Lord Bellamy's stubbly chin. "Your soul has no value to me. As for the others, I already took everything I needed. You have your worthless shells back, but I have the precious nucleus. All I needed for my escape were your precious gifts. Watch this."

The Ivory Queen aimed a palm at the sky and ascended. She spread her hands apart and five shadows appeared across the cavern, each more frightening than the last. They were all humanoid and resembled Avoria in some way, but they each had a terrifying distortion, be it a hole in the stomach, four arms instead of two, or a serpent-like head. The shadows swirled around the room, making Liam dizzy.

"No," Violet whispered.

"Yes, my dear. I've always wanted to do that Peter Pan thing. But the fun doesn't stop there!" With a snap of her fingers, Avoria and her shadows disappeared. *Poof.*

The cavern fell eerily silent.

"Stars," Liam breathed. He pulled Snow close to him. "Stand close. She's not *really* gone."

A deep whisper sounded in Liam's ear. "*Boo.*"

And she was back, hovering in the air with her shadows. Avoria grinned and pointed a long finger at Alicia, who fell ghost-white with fear. "I learned that one from you, Alice. You feel like you've gone mad, yet? Don't worry, you will."

Avoria soared and cackled, blinking in and out of sight, happy to show off her new abilities while her audience remained helpless. She came back to the ground, took a seat on her pedestal, and crossed her legs. "As for your punishments, I have something far more suitable for you. I'm going to leave you all here to suffer tenfold for my captivity. I promise you'll be far too distraught to care about your New World once you discover what's happened to your darlings." Avoria clapped her hands to her cheeks in mock terror. "Oh, those poor souls!"

Liam's heart dropped.

Wendy balled up her fists in front of her. "What have you done with our kids?" She turned to Violet and whispered, "Where's my husband? My son?"

Avoria feigned confusion, aiming a polished nail back at herself. "*Me*? Why, I've been here the whole time, talking to you silly plebeians! Ask not what I've done to your children. Ask what they're about to do to themselves. Was it not your grand plan to keep me talking? To keep me, *ahem*, distracted while your little ones run off and attempt to destroy the mirrors?" Avoria smiled knowingly. "A most admirable plan. But as Violet never learned, I'm always one step ahead."

Wendy's lip twitched. "You miserable crone. Shut up or get to your point!"

"The point is, while you've been trying to distract me, I've been distracting *you* while one of my faithful shadows has been hard at work carving me a door into your precious New World. The gift of The Carver." She winked at Pino, and his knees buckled. "A door only I can get to . . . A door fit for a queen!"

"There are other ways back," Violet said. "We'll follow and stop you."

"I think not," Avoria taunted. "My darlings sealed every other entrance as well."

In a surge of anger, Violet conjured a ball of purple flame and hurled it at Avoria. Avoria caught it like a baseball, twirled it around in her fingers, and then flung it at Lord Bellamy. "Catch!"

Lord Bellamy dove out of the way just in time, moaning and wheezing. Violet stooped to his side and helped him up, her lips pulled into a worried frown.

"Be smart, stupid girl," Avoria snarled. "You never had a chance to destroy me. You're lucky I'm merciful."

Carla gripped Wendy's arm. "I'm gonna go find our kids. Come with me."

"Oh, you're free to leave of course," Avoria announced. "You'll be too late, anyway. Before I leave you all forever, I want to leave you one souvenir. Something to remember me by."

Nobody's expression bore more fear than Lord Bellamy's. Avoria stared at her husband, smirking and laughing, and then she veered on her heel and approached Hansel instead. She took his chin in her fingers.

It seemed as though nobody had noticed Hansel until that moment. Snow's lips flattened into a thin, hard line, and Carla grabbed her husband's shoulder. "That's the man who brought me here!"

Avoria smirked. "My dear huntsman, I'm so sorry about your sister. She's a wonderful person who deserves a fulfilling life outside the mirror, but sometimes life doesn't give you what you want. For all your hard work and unwavering dedication to the cause of freeing me, I choose to spare you from the agonies that are yet to come."

Hansel gulped.

"Oh, you poor man! You're so nervous! Don't worry, handsome, this trick doesn't hurt a bit. I learned it from Merlin."

Something like a spring activated inside Liam. He dashed across the cavern and slashed Avoria on the shoulder with his dagger. A thin streak of blood soaked through her dress, but the wound closed immediately. "Leave him alone."

Avoria whirled around and seized Liam's wrist. "Such bravery, such heroism for a passive man who was pondering murder not so long ago. I should reward you instead."

Liam swallowed a lump of fear in his throat. "You don't scare me."

"I doubt that, handsome. You want to pretend you have nerves of steel and a heart of gold? *Fine*, I'll make it easier on you!"

Avoria placed an icy palm on Liam's forehead, and his blood flushed cold. It started in his cheeks, filling his head like ice in a bucket, and he noticed that he couldn't blink anymore. He couldn't open or close his mouth. The sound of Snow's blood-curdling screams echoed until his hearing faded, sand filling the ears. The cold spread to his shoulders. He couldn't roll them anymore. Liam reached out and slashed at the queen one more time, gently scratching her arm before the skin healed again. His elbow locked in place mid-slash as the cold rippled through him, binding his fingers to his dagger. His chest, legs, and feet followed within less than a nanosecond, and full paralysis locked Liam in place.

He watched helplessly as the queen stepped back, admired him, and produced a group of shadows. They all ascended in the air together, the queen solid and stoic while her shadows danced around her with stark, calculated movements.

The last thing he heard before he went completely deaf was her icy voice, "Goodbye, my loves!"

Within seconds, she and her shadows were gone for good.

Avoria was free, or at least headed for her alleged door, and Liam was bound to the ground, slowly fading from consciousness as his body went numb and his vision shut down. His heartbeat slowed to a stop.

It was almost as though he'd been turned to metal.

CHAPTER FORTY-EIGHT

TODAY—VIOLET'S DEN

Zack Volo awoke to the sound of wind over water, sea salt spraying on rock somewhere below him. At least, that's what he thought it was. He'd never actually seen the ocean before.

What a nap, man. He felt like he'd gone to bed hours ago, but he also felt like he'd slept for years. His joints felt loose and limber, his mind crisp and fresh. There was only thing that that didn't make sense. *Where am I?*

Zack hoisted himself up to his elbow and rubbed the heel of his palm over his face, trying to take in his surroundings. The room seemed to be made of rock, the ceiling luminous and bejeweled. There was a huge cushion, a mural on the wall featuring five faces and a bell, and—

"*Zack*!" Tackled by one-hundred-and-thirty-five pounds of his best friend, Enzo DiLegno. "Zack, I can't believe it's really you!" Enzo stuck the tips of his pointer fingers in the corners of Zack's mouth and tugged. "Wait, *is* it really you?"

Zack pulled back and gave Enzo a gentle shove. "Hey, Enzo, what's gotten into you, buddy? Who else would I be?"

Enzo stood up. He looked taller than Zack remembered. "Zack! Boy, am I glad to see you!"

Zack scratched his head. Enzo was acting like a total dork. "Okay? It's not like we don't see each other every single day already but, uh, glad to see you, too, I guess. By the way, where are we, and how'd we get here?"

Enzo stepped back and for the first time, Zack noticed that there was a pretty girl with them, dark-haired, lightly tanned, and wearing a long red tablecloth-looking thing on her back. She looked him in the eye and tilted her head before exchanging a look with Enzo.

"Um, this is Rosana. She's kind of a new friend. Rosana, Zack."

Zack nodded. "Hey."

"Hello."

Enzo blew a raspberry and rubbed his face. "Uh, would you believe we're in a fairy's den right now? And that you sort of, um, flew us here?"

"Like in a plane?"

"Like, your shadow. We all *just* made it up here and then your shadow went all stiff and dead and—"

Now it was Zack's turn to tilt his head. He and Enzo liked to play pranks on each other sometimes, and they worked best when one of them could get his dad involved. They could play along for days, and their faces would never betray them. Usually, the jokes were a lot cleverer than this. "Dude, you're slacking. I mean, nice touch with the rock room being a thousand feet in the air and the chick with the Red Riding Hood cape, but come on. You can do better. Where's my pops?"

Enzo shook his head. "We have a lot to explain, bro. We can do that soon, but right now there's something we have to do, and I don't think we have a lot of time." He pulled Zack to his feet and walked him to a large mirror on the wall, where Rosana stared into the gleaming surface with her arms folded. "You gotta help us break this thing."

Zack studied his reflection. He didn't remember looking so tall. He also saw the first signs of scruff and rubbed his chin. The stubble was like gentle sandpaper against his fingers. "Okay, that's a little weird. How long have I been asleep?"

Enzo's eyes crinkled. "Two, three years?"

"Ha! You're silly, Enzo. I guess I'll play along for a bit. But hey, this is a nice mirror. Why do you wanna break it?"

Rosana held up a hand. "Zack, your friend is telling the truth about all of this, but the most important thing you need to know right now is that this mirror is dangerous. Really bad things have happened because of it."

Zack scratched his head. "Either you got a good actress, Enzo, or you did a good job lying to her. Even *she* seems to believe everything you're saying." He turned back to his reflection. "I don't wanna break this. It probably costs a freaking fortune! This is probably, like, eighty years of bad luck if we smash it."

"Lot more than that if we don't," Enzo warned.

Enzo thrust a foot onto the glass, and Rosana did the same. For the first time, Zack became aware of Enzo's frantic demeanor. Sweat glistened off his forehead. He bared his teeth. He grunted as he drove his heel into the glass, only to bounce back without leaving so much as a footprint. Even Rosana, whom Zack had known for all of about two minutes, couldn't fake it like this.

"Jesus, guys, you really wanna bust this mirror down, don't you?"

"Yes," Enzo growled. "Now help us, dude. Please."

"It's not that hard to break a mirror. 'Member when you broke my window with your toy sword and your mom made you write my mom an apology letter?"

"Zack, this is *not* the time." Enzo grunted.

"Alright, I'm concerned. This really shouldn't be that hard for you. Let me give it a shot."

Rosana leaned against the wall to catch her breath.

Enzo stepped aside, sweat dripping from his nose. "Be my guest, then."

"Watch how it's done." Zack rolled his shoulders, popped his neck, and took a deep breath. *In through the nose*. His foot shot out. "Hya—*ah!*" It was like kicking a sensitive trampoline. It jolted his toes, knee, and ankle and threw him to his back. When he looked up, the mirror tingled with a strange blue light.

"Zack!" Enzo pulled him back to his feet. "Are you okay?"

Zack ran a sleeve across his forehead. "What the hell is that thing? Enzo, what's going on?"

Enzo said nothing.

"Maybe we don't need to break it anymore?" Rosana said. "I mean, if Zack's back, then that means maybe the queen isn't a—"

"We're breaking it. I don't care. It's evil, Rosana, and you know it."

"Why don't you just stab it?" Zack said, half-sarcastically.

"Stab the mirror? With what, Zack, a fork?"

Zack pointed to a small shining blade in Enzo's jeans, the blade with the ivory handle he had seen so many times when he went to the DiLegnos' house. "Isn't that your dad's knife? I was only joking anyway. Let's leave it alone and go home."

Enzo's eyes twinkled with excitement and wonder as he took the knife from his pocket, running his finger along the handle and staring into the metal.

"Is that the knife that made our carvings?" Rosana asked. "Is that—?"

"The gift of The Carver. You two! This is what we need!" Enzo spun the handle through his fingers.

Zack had gone from amused to confused, and from confused to scared in a matter of a few minutes. He didn't say a word when Enzo approached the mirror again, its surface still shimmering with an eerie blue pulse that was completely unnatural for a mirror. Zack even thought he could hear it *whispering*.

"It took me all this time to believe," Enzo said, "but you were right, Rosana. Believing doesn't count for anything unless you're willing to act. It's time to end this." He bit his lip. "But I'm a little nervous. I mean, what if something goes wrong? We don't really know what's gonna happen. If this works and The Carver's knife breaks this mirror, then what?"

"Well, everything should go back to normal, right? Isn't that how magic works?"

"How should we know?" Enzo studied Rosana's face, and Zack almost had to fight back a cheer. Enzo clearly liked this girl. "I guess I just wanna tell you that if something goes wrong, I want you to know how I've started to feel about—"

Rosana vanished into thin air, and Zack couldn't stifle his gasp. "Dude!"

Enzo shrugged, rubbing his neck. "It's okay, man. She does that sometimes."

No way.

Rosana appeared again, quick as a blink and red as a cherry. "I'm sorry. Why don't you focus on breaking the mirror?"

Enzo nodded. "Okay. Well, then, here goes nothing, I guess. Ready?"

"Aye, aye, captain."

"Smash it, bro! Smash the weird demon mirror!"

"Okay." Enzo raised the knife over his head, easing it like a pool stick with each count. "One."

The mirror pulsed even brighter.

"Two."

Did the mirror just *scream*? Rosana covered her ears.

"*Three!*"

Crashhh!

A thunderous shattering sound filled the room.

A bright white light flashed as though the world had been dipped in milk.

A gust of wind tore Zack cleanly off his feet and high into the air, carrying him like a tornado, but all he could see was white, and then dark. Pitch black. Rosana and Enzo's screams tangled somewhere with his own cries and the screeches of the wind.

Gotta hand it to you, Enzo. Most twisted prank ever.

He accelerated. Flying through nothingness.

And then he lost consciousness.

CHAPTER FORTY-NINE

TODAY—SNOW WHITE'S CASTLE

Seven men sat at the table.

When they woke up in the courtyard, everybody had questions, ranging from, "What happened to us?" "How did we come back?" "Where's the Ivory Queen?" "Where's Mister Hansel?" But these questions were suppressed by a deep, intense sadness for the woman kneeling on the floor beside them, crying at the foot of a gold statue. Nobody could believe it when Wayde had appeared in the distance, carrying the treasure on his back. At first they were awestruck by the belief that there was an artist capable of rendering such emotion in a face of gold. The way the eyes captured the moonlight, one could see both determination and fear. The clenched teeth might as well have come out of a pirate's mouth, so perfectly were they shaped and grooved. From the veins in his neck to the creases in his gloves and the ridges of his dagger, somebody had rendered Prince Liam *perfectly*. But why choose such a horrifying pose for such a tranquil man?

When Snow White appeared behind them, sobbing like never before, the dwarves understood, and the relief of waking up wilted away. There was no happy reunion, no exchange of nostalgia, no tears of joy.

"The queen is b-back," Wayde said. "I watched Hua Mulan break the mirror with her own sword, and when we found Snow, we found Mister Liam, just like this. The queen did it, and then she disappeared."

"Preposterous!" Zid pounded a fist on the table. "I'll teach her a thing or two! Where did she go?"

"To take the New World," Wayde said.

"Well, we certainly can't let that happen," Garon said. "How are we to stop her?"

Wayde shook his head sadly. "I-it's no use. I checked the mines. Violet tried everything. All the pathways to the New World are sealed, but Avoria made a door somewhere. One door that we'll never find. Nobody's getting in or out of this realm unless she wants them to."

Snow stood and mopped a stream of tears from her face. "I refuse to believe that! I'm going to kill that witch myself for all the pain she's caused my husband and me." Her gaze went frigid as she studied the statue. She threw her head back and screamed, "*Do you hear me, Avoria? I'll kill you!*"

The dwarves exchanged uneasy looks. They hardly recognized the woman before them. "Um, Your Majesty, do you think that maybe there's a way to turn Mister Liam back to normal? Back to the way he was?"

Snow ran a fingertip over a gold cheek. "I don't know. I've never seen this before. But if there's a way to reverse it, you can bet I'm going to find it. I'm going to get him back, and I'm going to kill Avoria if it's the last thing I ever do."

The words hung in the air for a while, and Garon stroked his peppered beard. "Wayde, what else has occurred with the queen's return? What of Mister Hansel?"

"Mister Hansel's fine. I think he's himself again, and he's with Violet, but he's a broken man. His sister didn't come back. Additionally"—Wayde wrung his hands, eyes glistening with tears—"two young ones may have gone missing. Possibly three."

VIOLET'S DEN

The mirror lay on her floor in glittered ruins and pungent silence when she arrived. Mulan, Hansel, and Lord Bellamy accompanied her.

"Miss Violet," Mulan said, "where could the children have gone?"

"I'm afraid I don't have a single clue." A tear glistened in her eye. "This isn't how it was supposed to happen."

"That's what you get for meddling, my dear," Lord Bellamy said. "We should have stayed put. You've made things worse, and now I have no choice but to—"

"No!" Violet snapped. "This is not the time to assign blame, Father! If we hadn't come back, Hansel's—I mean, the Ivory Queen's—captives would be gone. Soulless. If it weren't for Mulan's work and the children's bravery destroying the mirrors, everybody would be gone and Avoria still would have gone to terrorize the New World. Mulan, thank you for your bravery."

Mulan bowed gratefully. "One thing bothers me, though. If the seven returned, then that must mean—"

"That they *all* returned, yes. I can feel them. The Order. The Thousand. Maybe even General Jiahao."

A smile flickered on Mulan's lips at the mention of her father. "Then how is Avoria alive and strong? She took those souls for strength, and the souls went back to their bodies."

Violet's mind flashed to her recurring dream, to the day Dr. Frankenstein left the door to his lab open. She shook her head. "All she needs for power is a soul's nucleus. All a body needs is the soul's shell. I think your sword linked all those shells to Avoria's body somehow, and when you stabbed that mirror, you returned the shells to their rightful bodies. She kept its essence, the part that binds you to your abilities."

Mulan tilted her head. "I'm sorry, but I'm not sure I follow."

Violet essentially had the tabs of Dr. Frankenstein's book memorized.

Properties of the Soul. Light and Darkness. Corporeal Resurrection.

Interrealm Travel.

A smile crossed her lips. "Then we need to find the man who can explain it to us, and we need to find Avoria's door."

Mulan faced the water beneath Violet's den. "So what's our next move? We're not truly going to stand here and accept Avoria's reign over the New World, are we?"

Lord Bellamy nodded. "Yes, we are, girl. Let the past be our lesson, or you will not like what's coming next. We're much safer here."

"No, we are not," Violet insisted. "We need to gather the Order once more. We need to *expand* it, unite the entire realm! Neverland, Oz, Florindale, the Woodlands, every creature of the sea . . . we'll need them all on our side. Mulan, are you up to the task of helping me recruit and train a new army?"

Mulan bowed again. "I'm at your service, Miss Violet."

"Wonderful." Violet turned to Hansel, who was red-eyed and broken. "As for you, Hansel, I'm going to give you a chance to redeem yourself for all the trouble you've caused. I know there's much more good in you than bad. Without the influence of the queen, you can prove your worth to everybody."

Hansel nodded glumly.

"I'd like you to seek Avoria's door. The queen spent much time inside your head. You can use that to your advantage. You know her better than anybody. Today, that may be our greatest gift. Will you accept my opportunity?"

Another tearful nod.

"Please don't cry, Hansel. I believe there is hope for you yet. Sometimes bad things happen to good people, but sometimes, magical things occur. Remember this as you remember your sister"—she picked up a shard of glass on the ground, and in the reflection, her father stormed away with fire in his eyes—"and as I will always remember the brave acts of the son of Pinocchio and the daughter of

Alice. May the light be with them."

PINO'S CHILDHOOD HOME

Carla DiLegno paced back and forth. "So let me get this straight. All this time I've been married to . . . Pinocchio? And you're Peter Pan, and you're Wendy, and you're Alice, and we were all kidnapped and sent to this fairy tale world, and we have no idea where our kids are. Am I forgetting anything?"

"Just that an evil witch will probably destroy our homes," Pietro added. "Our real homes."

Carla sank into a wooden chair. It creaked and whined beneath her. "Everyone always told me I had a loony imagination. I read too many books."

Alicia raised her eyebrows. "Join the club."

Pino scrambled around the room, pleased to have his limbs in working condition again. He was back where he belonged, but he still looked distressed as he pored over carpentry, fabric, and colored paints. "I don't know where my father is. I don't know where my son is. This is our fault. We were never supposed to leave this world in the first place."

Alicia shook her head. "That's an awful thing to say. There isn't a minute of my life that I regret our decision to grow up and see new worlds. The best thing of my life came out of that. I got my daughter. You have a son! That's a gift!"

Wendy sipped some coffee, pursing her lips after every tiny swig. "And yet something's wrong. Did you hear that witch? She made it very clear that our kids are in danger. How are we supposed to help them? Where do we look? We're *stupid*, Alice. We left this place for selfish reasons, and now everyone's paying the price. What if our kids are—?"

"Having the time of their lives somewhere?" Pietro offered.

"How can you be so impossibly and infuriatingly calm, Peter? Ever since you came back to us in the cavern, all you've done is make jokes and find things to laugh at and discount everyone's worries! Why can't you take anything seriously for once in your—?"

"Because that's how I am, Wendy! That's how I deal with things, okay? After all this time, I thought you would be the first to understand that. Don't point your finger at me and try to make it look like I'm not afraid or like I can't handle responsibility." Pietro smiled. "Besides, I traveled across the country with those kids. They're fierce. Wherever they are, they'll be fine."

Pino gripped Pietro's shoulder, smiling warmly. "Thank you, my friend, for taking such good care of my boy and bringing everyone together."

Wendy grimaced. "Pino, I'd appreciate it immensely if you wouldn't defend him right now. This isn't a time for talking. This is a time for acting. I'm going to look for our children! Is anyone coming with me?"

Alicia shook her head. "I hate to say this, but I don't think there's much use. Not right now, at least."

Pino wrinkled his nose. "Come again? Why would you say that?"

"Our kids. I have an impossible feeling. I'm pretty sure I know where they are."

Carla crossed her arms, giving Alicia a critical look. "How could you know such a thing?"

"Because it's a place I've been to before," she said, "and it's stayed with me all these years. I kept trying to forget it, but it's a part of me now."

Pietro scratched his head. "Wait a minute. You don't actually think they're in—?"

"Yes."

"*Where?*" Carla said. "At this point, I doubt you can surprise me any further."

They waited for Alicia to answer, but she didn't say anything. She simply stared out the window, her gaze following a bone-white rabbit hobbling around a patch of dry garden.

LOCATION UNKNOWN

When Enzo came to, he was laying on a black flower petal the size of a king bed. An orange crescent moon shined down on him, and he could have sworn a cat was growling in his ear.

"Whoa!" Enzo rolled off the flower in a panic, fell ten feet, and his head landed on something soft.

"Hey, get off me, Enzo!" Rosana complained.

"How 'bout both of you get off me?" Zack panted. "I can't breathe, and you woke me up!"

Enzo pushed himself up to his feet and dusted off his knees and elbows. *What is this place?* It seemed he had woken up from a dream and found himself in a nightmare. The last thing he remembered was stabbing a mirror with his father's knife. Now, his surroundings were murky, grim, and highly unnatural. Flowers towered higher than trees he'd seen in Virginia, clouds the color of graphite threatened to burst overhead, and—Enzo's heart almost stopped—a bee the size of a horse hovered around. Thankfully, it was only interested in the giant flowers.

Did it work? Zack had come back. Did that mean his parents were safe? Pietro, Wendy, and Rosana's mom? Where were they?

A new voice sounded in the distance. A young girl. "Look! New people!"

An old man's voice echoed, "*Caspita*! I'll be darned . . ."

The little girl scurried up to the group, where Rosana and Zack rubbed their temples and stared wide-eyed at their surroundings. The old man, gray-haired yet nimble, followed close behind. They looked normal. Not like the kind of people he would expect in such a creepy environment.

Before Enzo could stop her, the little girl reached out and touched his face. "Hi," she said. "Are you here to rescue us?"

"Well, uh—"

The old man shook his head. "Let's not get our hopes up, little one. They fell from the sky! Unless they have a way back up there, I'd say they're as trapped as we are."

"But *she's* gone, so now we can try to get out of here."

"Yes indeed." Under his breath, he added, "Before the king changes his mind."

Enzo massaged a kink out of his neck. "Um, hi guys. My name is Crescenzo DiLegno. These are my friends, Zack and Rosana. We don't really know where we are, but maybe we can all help each other out? What is this place, and how long have you been here?"

"Crescenzo," the old man repeated, a flawless Italian accent rolling off his tongue. "Zack and Rosana. What a grand twist of fortune! My name is Geppetto, renowned Carver and merchant of the Old World. I've lost track of how long ago I fell down that mineshaft, trying to find my boy. They say there's more than one way to get here. Some people fall down rabbit holes. Some people go through mirrors. You must tell me your own story. Getting out is the tricky part. You'd never believe me by the looks of this place, but it appears we're in a place called Wonderland." He shrugged. "At least, that's what young Gretel here believes."

TO BE CONTINUED

Acknowledgments

The Carver himself may have been able to do everything with two hands, but it takes many more to carve a book! Shout out to the real MVPs of this tale!

Hi Mom! You're basically Superwoman. Thank you for always believing in me with all your heart, whether I was doing homework, trying to write an actual novel, or spewing nonsense X-Men fan fiction in the third grade. For delivering grilled cheese sandwiches and hugs and Dr. Pepper at all the right times. For being the Carla to my Enzo. All my love and gratitude forever.

Mrs. C, thank you for believing not only in this story, but also in my whole love of writing since the elementary days. For your spot-on book recommendations and guidance all these years.

To my "dream team" of beta readers: Maira, Josh, Avon, Silvia, Lauren, and Sue. You each carved something invaluable into this project, whether you binged and raved, went chapter- by-chapter and wrote pages of notes, or did some combination of the two. Thank you for your time, encouragement, and honesty.

Alicia: I want the world to know that you were the first believer. You guided Enzo and Pietro out the front door. You believed in Hansel. You dared Liam to be bolder and Violet to be deeper. And through your support, you inspired me to be better.

Krystal and Kay: You are the fairy godmothers of this story. Thank you for giving me the tools to live the life of a storyteller and for being the first to bring Enzo to life. Extra hugs to Janelle and Mara, to Eliza and her beautiful formatting work, and of course to Kim G for these beautiful new covers!

I have so many other thank yous to say to an assortment of inspirers and cheerleaders. Ciara. Fred. Sarah Annunziato and Enrico Cesaretti. All the musicians on my writing playlist and the loyal ear buds that make them sound so sweet. Uncle Ed and Aunt Denise. Whoever made the first cup of coffee in life. We'll be here for fourteen thousand years if I keep going, but seriously, my heart thunders with gratitude for all of you and many others. Thank you!!!

What a thrill ride this has already been, and it's full speed ahead! Let's meet again in Wonderland. Bring a friend, because this next chapter just might drive you mad . . . .

About the Author

When Jacob Devlin was four years old, he would lounge around in Batman pajamas and make semi-autobiographical picture books about an adventurous python named Jake the Snake. Eventually, he traded his favorite blue crayon for a black pen, and he never put it down. When not reading or writing, Jacob loves practicing his Italian, watching stand-up comedy, going deaf at rock concerts, and geeking out at comic book conventions. He does most of these things in southern Arizona.

https://authorjakedevlin.com/

Made in the USA
Lexington, KY
29 September 2018